The
BLESSED

ALSO BY ANN H. GABHART

The Outsider
The Believer
The Seeker
The Blessed

Angel Sister

The Scent of Lilacs
Orchard of Hope
Summer of Joy

The
BLESSED

A NOVEL

ANN H. GABHART

Revell

a division of Baker Publishing Group
Grand Rapids, Michigan

© 2011 by Ann H. Gabhart

Published by Revell
a division of Baker Publishing Group
P.O. Box 6287, Grand Rapids, MI 49516-6287
www.revellbooks.com

Printed in the United States of America

Library of Congress Cataloging-in-Publication Data
Gabhart, Ann H., 1947–
      The blessed : a novel / Ann H. Gabhart.
          p.   cm.
      ISBN 978-0-8007-3454-1 (pbk.)
      1. Shakers—Fiction. I. Title.
PS3607.A23B57 2011
813'.6—dc22   2011007577

Scripture used in this book, whether quoted or paraphrased by the characters, is taken from the King James Version of the Bible.

11   12   13   14   15   16   17   7   6   5   4   3   2   1

Dedicated to everyone
who has ever felt the urge to dance
to welcome spring.

A Note about the Shakers

American Shakerism originated in England in the eighteenth century. Their leader, a charismatic woman named Ann Lee, was believed by her followers to be the second coming of Christ in female form. After being persecuted for those beliefs in England, she and a small band of followers came to America in 1774 to settle in Watervliet, New York, and there established the first community of the United Society of Believers in Christ's Second Appearing, more commonly known as Shakers. By the middle of the nineteenth century, the Shakers had nineteen communities spread throughout the New England states and Kentucky, Ohio, and Indiana.

The Shaker doctrines of celibacy, communal living, and the belief that perfection could be attained in this life were all based on revelations that Mother Ann claimed to have divinely received. The name *Shakers* came from the way they worshiped. At times when a member received the "spirit," he or she would begin shaking all over. These "gifts of the spirit," along with other spiritual manifestations, were considered by the Shakers to be confirmation of the same direct communication with God they believed their Mother Ann had experienced.

In the late 1830s at the height of the Shaker population, three young girls in the Watervliet village in New York claimed to be visited by angels. A tide of mysticism quickly swept through all the villages and reached its most fanatic extremes in the mid-1840s. During this Era of Manifestations—or as the Shakers commonly called it, the Era of Mother's Work— the Believers' worship services were closed to those of the "world" and many gift-songs and inspirational drawings were received by society members. Also, some among the Believers became chosen instruments who received hundreds of spiritual messages from Mother Ann and other early Shaker leaders, angels with melodic names, biblical saints, and figures famous in history. In 1842 each Society of Believers was instructed by the Ministry to select a hill or mountaintop as a sacred feast ground. Here spiritual feasts were held twice a year where the Shakers carried out elaborate pantomimes of various activities, such as dressing in fine garments, eating fruits from heaven, and washing themselves clean of sins in imaginary fountains.

Some Shaker historians consider this era damaging to the Shaker societies, because many of those receiving visions and messages from above were younger members, and this resulted in a breakdown of the order of discipline established by the Ministries. The visions died out after a little more than a decade. The sacred feast grounds were deserted and many of the spirit drawings were hidden away for years as the leaders once again concentrated on disciplined work and free worship.

In Kentucky, the Shaker villages of Pleasant Hill and South Union have been restored and attract many visitors curious about the Shaker lifestyle. These historical sites provide a unique look at the austere beauty of the Shakers' craftsmanship. The sect's songs and strange worship echo in the impressive architecture of their buildings. Visitors also learn about the Shakers' innovative ideas in agriculture and industry that improved life not only in their own communities but also in the "world" they were so determined to shut away.

1

Autumn 1843

Isaac Kingston didn't think his Ella would really die. Not actually stop breathing and die. She'd told him she would, but he didn't believe her. At least not soon enough.

A person didn't die because her mother wasn't there to stroke her head. If that could happen, he would have died when he was thirteen, but here he was still breathing while he watched them lower his beautiful Ella down into the ground. Every breath seemed a betrayal of his love.

He'd brought her home. He had to. The Fort Smith doctor who bled Ella advised Isaac to wait for her fever to abate before making the trip back to Louisville, but the doctor didn't understand. He wasn't the one being haunted by the memory of Ella looking him right in the eye the day before the fever hit and telling him she'd die if he didn't take her home. It was Isaac who had to live with that memory seared into his soul.

She'd been telling him the same thing every day since they'd left Louisville weeks before, until the words had meant no more than someone mentioning the sun shining or the rain falling outside. Not that he didn't feel bad that she was unhappy. He did. He loved her. So some of the time he tried to kiss away her sadness. Other times he would grab her in his arms and dance her around their tiny boardinghouse room until she laughed. But there was no laughing once the fever struck, and he began to feel her words might be prophetic.

So he'd given up his westward dream, sold his horse and gun to hire a wagon to take her overland to the Mississippi River and then for the ticket up the river to Louisville. He'd carried her up the steamboat's gangplank before daylight so nobody would know how sick she was and try to stop him from bringing the fever on board. He had been so sure being on the way home would pull her back from the fever. Bring the light back to her eyes. But when he whispered their progress up the river toward Louisville into her ear, her fever-glazed eyes stared at him with no recognition, and it was her mother she called out for.

He told her over and over that he was taking her to her mother. Patiently at first and then angrily. She had to understand how he was giving up everything to do what she wanted, but the words *too late* whispered through his mind and turned his anger into sorrow. She died before they reached the Ohio River.

Now the preacher Ella's father had gotten to say words over her grave was talking about Ella going home to a better place. The home awaiting all who reached for the Lord with faith and sincerity.

A chill wind blew across the open hole that was swallowing Ella and ruffled the pages of the worn Bible the old man held. His hands trembled as he smoothed down the tissue-thin page and continued to speak the Bible words without looking down to read them. No doubt he had spoken the same verses over hundreds of newly departed souls.

"Yea, though I walk through the valley of the shadow of death, I will fear no evil." The preacher's voice quavered and sounded properly mournful.

Why couldn't it have been the old preacher who had walked through death's shadow instead of Ella? Isaac's eyes shifted from the preacher to Ella's ancient grandmother. The old woman had to be pushed in a chair everywhere she went and now sat huddled in a black shawl with tears gathering in the deep wrinkles on her cheeks as she stared at the grave of her youngest grandchild. Why couldn't it have been her?

Isaac looked down at the coffin. Why couldn't it have been him? It should have been him. This was the second time in his life he'd stood in a graveyard with those thoughts. But everybody told him that was wrong when they buried his father.

Nobody told him he was wrong this time. Ella's parents would have gladly pushed him into the grave and covered him over if that would have brought their Ella back to them. Judge Carver had his arm around his wife, holding her up. Isaac was able to bear the judge's accusing eyes on him, but the despairing look in the eyes of Ella's mother smote him. Ella looked like her mother. Delicate with beautiful pale skin and often the hint of a tremble in her fingers. Ella had needed a man like her father to hold her up and shelter her.

Instead Isaac had ripped her away from her family and headed west where he planned for them to start a new life. The kind of life he wanted. One full of adventure and challenge. Ella had no desire for adventure. She wept when he said they were going west. He held her gently while she cried, but he didn't change his mind. Instead he assured her he was strong enough for both of them. He talked of the land they'd work, the children they would have, and because she loved him, she had gone with him. He'd never considered the possibility that she might refuse to go. She was his wife.

The judge offered to buy them a house if he would stay in Louisville. When Isaac told him he didn't need a house, only opportunity, the judge ordered him to leave Ella behind. To go west and establish his claim, if that was what he had to do. When he was settled, he could come back for Ella. Isaac should have listened. Then he wouldn't be standing beside Ella's grave, mashing down the desire to knock the Bible out of the old preacher's hands if he spoke one more word about the Lord calling Ella home.

The Lord hadn't called anybody home. Not that Isaac was on good enough terms with the Lord to ever hear the first thing he might call out. He'd sat in some churches. First with his mother. Then with the old farmer who gave Isaac bed and board in exchange for his labor after his father's death tore their family asunder.

The McElroys believed in church, but they lived a far piece from any church house, so they didn't make the trip more than four or five Sundays a year. Even so, the old couple hadn't neglected spiritual matters. Mrs. McElroy made him read the Bible out loud to her by candlelight nearly every night after the supper meal. She claimed the Scripture could be a powerful comfort and help if a person let the Lord's message speak to his heart, but Isaac had let the words slide off his tongue without paying them much mind. Bible words were for the old and the fearful.

And the dead.

The preacher's mournful words kept spilling out of his mouth. He read through the funeral psalm, but he didn't close up his Bible the way Isaac hoped he would. Instead he thumbed through it searching for more Scripture. The rustle of the pages was loud in the silence. Once he found the proper spot, his preacher voice grew stronger and lost its quaver.

"God is our refuge and strength, a very present help in trouble."

The preacher looked up at the sky and then across the grave at them and spoke the Bible words again as if he feared they hadn't heard him the first time. Then the quiver was back in his voice as he went on. "Sorrow comes to us all. May you lean on the good Lord's strength and call upon his help to carry you through."

Isaac let his hands curl into fists against his side, crushing the stem of the yellow flower someone had handed him. What good did it do to call for help now? Ella had needed help a week ago. When the fever was burning through her. He stared across the grave at the preacher who met his eyes without turning away. He was the first person to do so since Isaac had brought Ella home dead. Everybody else couldn't seem to bear letting their eyes light on him. Isaac understood. He couldn't bear the sight of his own face in a mirror when he was combing his hair.

But the old preacher's eyes settled right on him as he kept going in his preacher voice. "The Lord giveth and the Lord taketh away. As for man, his days are as grass: as a flower of the field, so he flourisheth. For the wind passeth over it, and it is gone. But the mercy of the Lord is everlasting to everlasting upon them that fear him. Amen and amen."

Amen. That was a Bible word Isaac was glad to hear fall out of the preacher's mouth. Isaac stared at the grave that held Ella. They were all waiting for him to drop the flower he held down on her. He kept his eyes on the ground. He couldn't do it. His feet wouldn't move forward. His hand wouldn't turn loose of the flower.

The silence pounded against his ears and he almost wished the old preacher would start up with some more Scripture. Anything to push the silence back. The seconds stretched into minutes. A bird began to sing in a tree not far away, and while only seconds before, Isaac wanted some noise to break the silence, now he wished for a rock to silence the bird. With a keening wail that sliced through Isaac, Ella's mother gave way to her grief. The undertaker, a man so slim and gray in his black suit that he seemed part of the shadows, produced a chair from those shadows to push under her before she could fall. A woman Isaac didn't know and the preacher knelt beside her to offer comfort.

The judge stepped up beside Isaac and whispered fiercely in his ear. "For the love of God, Kingston, do what has to be done so we can leave this place."

But what Ella's father didn't understand was that Isaac didn't think he could leave this place. Not and surrender Ella to the earth. An even more piercing wail rose from Ella's mother behind them.

When Isaac didn't move, the judge gave him a little shove toward the grave. "You killed her. Now be man enough to bury her."

Do what had to be done. That was what his mother told him after the boilers of the steamboat *Lucy Gray* had blown up and stolen his father from them. They did what had to be done. He had to go to live with the McElroys. Marian had to go live with the Shakers. And she, his mother, had to marry the dour old banker, Mr. Ludlow. Nobody was promised happiness. But if everybody kept going—kept moving forward and doing what had to be done—then maybe around some corner happiness might be waiting. At least for some of them.

He had thought to round that corner with Ella. Out west where opportunity awaited those brave enough to chase it. That's where happiness could be found. And now it was all dust. Dust to dust.

Isaac stepped forward at last and dropped the aster he held into the grave. Ella's father followed after him and then the others. It was done. What had to be done was done.

None of his family had shown up for the funeral. Too many miles separated them. And too many years. He hadn't seen his mother since he was eighteen and left the McElroys. That visit hadn't gone well with Old Man Ludlow hovering in the shadows behind Isaac's mother, anxious to see him away from his door. What choice did she have but to send him off to make his way as best he could? She and the sour banker had no children, but there were Isaac's young brother and sister to consider.

She had kissed Isaac and then held his face in her hands for a long moment before she said, "You're like him. Like your father. Live like him."

Isaac knew what she meant. His father had carried enthusiasm for life in his pocket and shared it with everyone he met. Everything was an adventure to him, and an opportunity. The steamboat explosion had ended that and plunged them all into new lives. And now another death had plunged Isaac into despair.

Isaac hadn't gone back to see his mother since that day. The only one he kept in contact with was Marian at the Shaker town. He'd gone to see her there a couple of times. She claimed to be content. Claimed to want to be shed of the world. So perhaps she had turned the corner to happiness, even though she hadn't used that word. Peace and perfection seemed to fit better on the Shakers' tongues and on Marian's. And there in that village with those solemn people, it could be she would never have that happiness or peace ripped from her.

He'd sent Marian word of Ella's death but not with any expectation she would make the journey to Louisville. While she didn't deny he was her natural brother in the worldly way, she claimed no part of that world now. Her life was there in the village at Harmony Hill with her Shaker brothers and sisters. So there was no one to put an arm around Isaac, to offer a word of sympathy.

In every face as they moved away from the grave toward

the carriages waiting to carry them back to Ella's house, Isaac saw the reflection of the judge's condemnation. *You killed her.* It was almost a relief when the judge stepped in front of him as they were leaving the cemetery to block his way to the carriage that had carried Isaac from the house to the burial ground.

While Ella's father was several inches shorter than Isaac and stooped a bit by age, what he lacked in size, he more than made up in authority. He was a judge. When he spoke, people did as he said.

He tipped back his head and glared at Isaac from under the black rim of his hat. "You took our child from her home and stole her from us."

"She went with me of her own free will." Isaac was surprised to hear his voice speaking up in his own defense.

"She went with you in tears." The judge's voice grew even harsher. "You are not to darken our door ever again."

"I didn't kill her. The fever did." His words sounded lame even to his own ears.

"A fever you took her to find. She would still be alive if you had stayed in Louisville. If you had let me build her a house where you could have lived." The judge's voice cracked and his eyes flooded with sorrow. "She would have never wanted for anything. And now all I can build her is a monument over her grave."

"Your sorrow is no deeper than mine. She was my wife." The hard knot of pain inside Isaac's chest made it hard for him to breathe.

"A wife can be replaced. A daughter cannot." With his mouth tightened into a grim line and his hat pulled down low on his forehead to hide eyes awash with tears, the judge turned and stalked away from Isaac toward his waiting carriage.

Silently Isaac watched him go. He had nothing left to say.

He was empty of words. Empty of feelings. He'd dropped it all in the grave with Ella along with the flower. His spirit was crushed by her death. As crushed as the autumn leaves underfoot on the pathway. The man who had wanted adventure and love, the man Ella had fallen in love with, that man was gone.

The carriages left the graveyard in a slow, somber black line. Even after they had disappeared from sight, Isaac imagined he could hear Ella's mother's anguished keening.

He didn't turn back to look at the grave. He could hear the gravediggers putting the dirt in on top of Ella, but he couldn't bear to look at them. Instead, he began walking back toward town. The old preacher offered him a ride with a goodly amount of kindness in his voice, but Isaac claimed he'd rather walk. He told him he needed to be alone. He couldn't have borne the old man praying over him all the way back to the city.

He didn't deserve prayer. He didn't deserve to still be breathing in and out. But he was. His beautiful, fragile Ella was not. Because of him.

2

Spring 1844

Lacey Bishop swept the kitchen floor as though the little bits of dirt she'd tracked in from the back garden were going to sprout legs and crawl up her skirt like field mice gone mad. If skunks could go mad with foaming mouths, why not mice?

Her pa's words warning her about rabid skunks echoed in her head all these years later. *Be careful out in the woods, Lacey girl. You never know what you might run up on. Could be something rabid. Something mean.*

She'd take her chances out in the woods. It was in kitchens and sitting rooms that folks came to grief. She might only be nineteen, but she'd lived plenty long enough to know that.

She swept the dirt up in a pile and then gave it a push with her broom toward the door, open to the early spring air. It was a good broom. A Shaker broom brought in by Preacher Palmer a couple of weeks before Miss Mona took a turn for the worse last fall.

He'd brought it into the kitchen and handed it to Miss Mona before he went off to do his preacher visiting. Miss Mona acted like she'd gotten some kind of prize as she ran her fingers over the broom straws with something akin to admiration.

"Those Shakers," she'd said in her high, fine voice. "They might have some odd ideas on worshiping, but they do have a way of making the least things better. Things nobody else would bother with improving. Just look at this broom. It's made for sweeping a wide swath. Ten times better than those old round brooms that weren't good for much but sweeping ashes back into a fireplace. I've heard tell that they war against dirt over there in their Harmony Hill village. That they're always sweeping and cleaning something." She looked up at Lacey and then back down at the broom. "One thing sure, a body has to admire their brooms."

Miss Mona had a way of admiring everything, even Lacey. Maybe especially Lacey.

Lacey had lifted the broom away from Miss Mona and took a spin with it around the room. "Is it true those Shakers dance to the Lord the way they say?"

"I've heard it is, but I can't say from seeing it myself. Elwood never thought it would be proper for us to go curious seeking to any of their services, what with him being a sanctified Baptist minister and all. Sadie Rose told me she went once though. Years ago with her father. They took a picnic and ate it out on the Shaker grounds with those strange worship songs of the Shaker people filling the air around them."

"Did she see them dancing?" Lacey stopped her twirling and looked at Miss Mona.

"That she did. She and her sister went and peeked in the door at them. She claimed it was a sight to behold. All those Shaker men and women as alike as peas in a pod, dancing up and back in some kind of strange dos-à-dos. And then all of a sudden she said they started stomping the floor as to how they were killing snakes. Started the whole building to shaking. From the way she tells it, I think it like to scared Sadie Rose to death."

"I didn't think anything could scare Miss Sadie Rose." Sadie Rose was the head deacon's wife at Ebenezer Church, and she had a way of getting things done.

"She's not one to get the trembles over easy," Miss Mona agreed with a laugh. "But Sadie Rose was some younger than even you at the time. And stomping in a church house wasn't exactly something she had ever seen before."

"I can't imagine anybody stomping and dancing in church."

"It is hard to think on and I don't know if they do such anymore. I don't suppose anyone outside their village can know that now, since they've closed down their meetings to outsiders, or so Elwood heard. Somebody told him they were claiming some kind of spiritual revival sent down from their Mother Ann, the one they think was the daughter of God or something akin to that. It all sounds too strange for the likes of me." Miss Mona shook her head at the thought of such an outlandish way to believe. "But you can ask Sadie Rose about that meeting she saw. She'll tell you it made her eyes go wide."

Sadie Rose was Miss Mona's best friend in all the world. Or at least that's what Miss Mona had thought. Lacey took another swipe at the floor, even though there wasn't a speck of dirt left to sweep anywhere. It was Sadie Rose's words she was wanting to sweep out the door and scatter to the wind. The woman had just left. Sadie Rose claimed the church ladies were only trying to help, but it sounded like gossip words to Lacey. The very idea that they could think anything indecent might be going on in the preacher's house!

Lacey had the urge to throw a plate down on the floor to break into a hundred pieces just so she'd have something to sweep again. But that might wake up little Rachel. Plus

Preacher Palmer would notice if they were a plate short. For a minute Lacey thought about going ahead and breaking two of the plates, but then she sighed. It didn't do any good to take out her spite on the dishes.

She propped the broom up in the corner by the back door. She'd take it out later and sweep off the porch to keep things neat the way Miss Mona had taught her. Miss Mona was like the Shakers in that way. She couldn't abide dirt. And now the poor woman was covered over with it. Lacey mashed her mouth together in a tight line to keep the tears from springing up in her eyes. A body couldn't cry forever, but she did miss Miss Mona. Maybe after Rachel woke up from her nap, they could think on what flowers to plant on the grave once the worry of frost was past.

Dear little Rachel. A ray of sunshine in a dark house. Lacey went to the doorway between the kitchen and the sitting room and leaned against the door casing to watch Rachel's chest rise and fall. The child liked to climb up on the daybed and sleep where Miss Mona had spent most of her days the last three years before the Lord had called her home. Sudden like, or so it seemed to Lacey, even though Miss Mona had been afflicted for years with a kind of wasting sickness that made her prone to trembles and weakness.

Miss Mona said they'd tried to find a way to rid her of the weakness when it first came on her, but nothing any of the doctors did ever helped. Finally Preacher Palmer said it must be the Lord testing them to see if they were faithful and they'd have to try to pray down a cure.

Even though Miss Mona was a mighty praying woman, no cure ever came down. She claimed not to be put off by that. She said the Lord answered prayers in lots of different ways, and maybe Lacey coming to be with her was the Lord's way of blessing her instead of removing the affliction. When Lacey didn't understand how Miss Mona could not be perturbed by the Lord's indifference to her suffering, Miss Mona opened up her Bible. She helped Lacey find the Scripture where Paul wrote about his own affliction, and how, although the Lord didn't remove it from him the way Paul asked, he did give him the strength to bear up under it.

"The Lord sent me you, Lacey dear. Without the trembles I'm afflicted with, there'd have been no reason for Elwood to fetch you home to help me. The Lord blesses us in many wondrous ways," Miss Mona had said.

Lacey looked up straight at Miss Mona that day. "So you're saying your trembles is a blessing." She didn't bother to hide the doubt in her voice even with her finger still on the Bible page Miss Mona had asked her to read.

"In a way. You're a gift for sure." Miss Mona smiled at her. "So though I might be hard-pressed to look favorably on my weak spells, I do look very favorably on you."

"Following that trail of thinking, I'd have to think my pa marrying up with the Widow Jackson and bringing her home after my ma died was a blessing, seeing as how it led to me being here." Lacey stared at Miss Mona without smiling back.

"It did lead to you coming here."

"The Widow Jackson wasn't never any kind of blessing." Lacey shut the Bible with a firm snap as if she needed to be sure Paul's affliction stayed inside and didn't leak out on them. They didn't have need of more of those kinds of blessing gifts.

"Reverence the Lord's Word," Miss Mona said mildly. That was one of the many good things about Miss Mona. She never got too bothered by anything Lacey said or did.

"Sorry," Lacey stroked the Bible's black cover as though to make amends. "But I've told you how the widow treated me and Junie. She nigh on killed Junie that day she hit her with a skillet. Poor Junie had a knot on her head big as a hen's egg, and two black eyes. That woman was no blessing."

"But the Lord made good come of it." Miss Mona raised her eyes up to the ceiling and spoke in her prayer voice. Without even taking the first peek at the Bible page, Miss Mona could quote Scripture and not get one word out of place. "And we know that all things work together for good to them that love God."

She brought her eyes back down to Lacey as she went on. "That goose egg opened your father's eyes and made him take note of what was happening. That's why he took Junie back to Virginia to live with your mother's sister, and you know how good your little sister's been doing there from the letters you get from time to time."

"But he didn't take me." Lacey hated the way her voice got all whiny when she said that. She hadn't even wanted to go to Virginia. Not really. And her father had done what he could to protect her from the widow after that. Something Miss Mona gently prodded her to remember.

"Now you know it took some soul searching for your father to give you both up. And you've told me how you were better at keeping out of the way of your stepmother."

Miss Mona always referred to the Widow Jackson as Lacey's stepmother, but Lacey never put any word about "mother" toward her. She supposed the woman had stopped being a widow or a Jackson the day Lacey's pa married her and she was a mother now too. She'd been in the family way when she talked Lacey's pa into farming Lacey out with the preacher. The last Lacey heard, they'd had three boys. Her brothers, but she'd never laid eyes on them. Her pa and the widow had moved to the western part of the state before the last boy was born.

When they decided on moving, her pa came to the preacher's

house to tell Lacey goodbye, but he hadn't brought even the oldest boy along. Too young for church or visiting, he said. He'd have taken Lacey home with him then. Claimed the widow had had a change of heart. Lacey saw through that easy enough. The only change in the widow's thinking was in how much work there was to do. She needed somebody to chase after those boys.

Even if she'd wanted to give the widow another chance, she wouldn't have left Miss Mona—she'd been with her for nigh on two years by then. Miss Mona treated her like a treasured daughter, teaching her to read and to sew and to sing. Lacey had chores to do, right enough. She had to make sure there was food on the table for the preacher, but Preacher Palmer wasn't particular about what he ate. More than particular about a lot of things, but food never seemed to interest him much. Miss Mona said he was too involved thinking on spiritual matters to worry with how the potatoes were cooked. Lacey thought it wasn't just holiness he was thinking on then, and she was knowing it now that Miss Mona wasn't there to be between his eyes and Lacey. Something that busybody Sadie Rose had surely noticed too.

The woman claimed to have nothing but Lacey's best interests at heart. And the church's too, of course. A deacon's wife had to think about what was best for the church.

Sadie Rose had sat at the kitchen table with Lacey and fingered the handle of her teacup while they talked about Rachel and the rag doll Sadie Rose had made her. The doll was a cute thing with eyes and mouth in neat dark blue stitches on the cloth face and hair of black yarn.

"Like yours," Sadie Rose told the child as she brushed back Rachel's dark curls that were hanging down so low on the little girl's forehead that they were nearly in her eyes.

Lacey even noted disapproval in that gesture. That she

hadn't trimmed the child's bangs the way she should have. But while Rachel had always sat still as a tree stump for Miss Mona to cut her hair, she took the wiggles every time Lacey came at her with the scissors. Lacey wasn't wanting to poke out one of the child's eyes, and she had no desire to ask Preacher Palmer to hold the little girl steady. She had no desire to ask Preacher Palmer anything. Which made what Sadie Rose came to say even more ridiculous.

It took the woman a while to come to the point. First she had to catch Lacey up on all the sick in the church and then ask a dozen things about how Rachel was doing. Miss Sadie Rose talked over the top of Rachel's head like she didn't think the words would sink down to the child's ears. Lacey knew better than that. It hadn't been that many years since she was a little child herself with people talking over the top of her head after her own mother died.

Of course Miss Mona wasn't actually Rachel's mother. Sadie Rose knew that. Could be that was why she took it upon herself to be sure the little girl was properly seen to. The truth was nobody knew who Rachel's mother was. At least not her natural-born mother. But Lacey knew who mothered her. The child had called Miss Mona mama, but Lacey did the mama things. Kept her fed and clean and held her when she cried. And loved her so powerful it hurt sometimes. Rachel couldn't have the first memory of the mother who'd left her on the preacher's backdoor steps when the poor little child wasn't more than a few days old. Tiny and helpless and precious.

As Sadie Rose rambled on about how Lacey needed to do this or that to be sure Rachel stayed healthy, Lacey fastened her eyes on the child playing with her new doll. Her mind wandered back to that first day when Preacher Palmer had talked of carrying the baby over to the city of Lexington. Miss Mona squashed that idea before it much more than got out of the preacher's mouth. While what Preacher Palmer said pretty much went as law for everybody else in their corner of the woods, in the house it was Miss Mona's words that mattered most. She never said them loud or anything, but when she spoke up to the preacher, he paid her mind.

Lacey could remember as well as if it had been yesterday the feel of baby Rachel in her lap as she tried to spoon tiny bits of warm milk mixed with honey into her mouth. Of course they hadn't been calling her Rachel yet. It was a week before they settled on Rachel as the baby's name. After Lacey's own mother. A good Bible name, Miss Mona said. But that day with the preacher's words clanging in the air overtop the baby's pitiful mewling cries, the milk had dribbled out of the baby's mouth. So Lacey had dipped a cotton handkerchief into the milk mixture and let the child suck it off the rag.

Miss Mona had looked right straight at Preacher Palmer and said, "The Lord set that baby down on our doorstep, Elwood. He was surely intending on us keeping her until her mother got able to come back for her."

"You can't take care of a baby, Mona. You can't even take care of yourself."

The preacher sounded agitated, but Lacey hadn't looked at him. She didn't let her eyes light on him very often. It wasn't exactly that she was afraid of him, but he did have a way of making her uneasy.

Miss Mona's voice was soft and patient. "But Lacey can. Maybe that's why the Lord sent her to us first. Because he knew what was coming."

That was a little over four years ago now. Miss Mona would have said the Lord knew this day was coming too. This day with Sadie Rose sliding her eyes all around the room while she figured out the best way to say what the women of the church had sent her to say. Lacey guessed she should have given

Miss Sadie Rose some slack instead of turning her contrary ear toward her, but it was Miss Mona who knew all the right answers. The answers the Lord handed down to her straight from heaven or put on the pages of Miss Mona's Bible plain as the morning daylight coming in the east windows. Lacey wasn't privy to those answers. Any answers she was looking for seemed to be as hard to see as the bottom of the well out back.

"How old are you, Lacey?" Sadie Rose asked. She didn't need Lacey to answer. She knew already. She just wanted the number to come out of Lacey's own mouth.

"I'll be twenty in May." Lacey got up and filled their cups with the tea left in the pot. She needed to be moving. She put her hand on Rachel's head. When the little girl smiled up at her, Lacey asked, "What are you going to name your new baby doll?" Maybe if she could turn the woman's attention back to Rachel, she'd forget her other questions.

"Maddie," the little girl said at once. "Like in the stories."

Miss Sadie Rose smiled at Rachel. "What stories are those?"

"I can't tell you. They're secret," Rachel said without looking up.

"Oh." Color rose up in the woman's cheeks. She wasn't accustomed to anybody keeping secrets from her.

Lacey busied herself setting out the cookies Sadie Rose had brought on Miss Mona's prettiest plate and hoped the woman wouldn't demand more from the child. The stories weren't anything important. A bad feeling was growing inside Lacey about whatever words Sadie Rose was going to finally spit out at her, and confessing to making up silly stories about talking animals and fairies and such whenever Preacher Palmer wasn't in earshot didn't seem to be something that Lacey should do right then.

"You make a fine sugar cookie, Miss Sadie Rose." Again

Lacey tried to ease the conversation in another direction. "I'm the worst at baking. Miss Mona tried to teach me, but my biscuits are always hard as rocks and my cakes flat as cornpones. It's a good thing you ladies are always baking cakes and pies for the Reverend or he'd never get anything sweet."

But Sadie Rose didn't take a cookie off the plate. She wasn't about to be distracted again. The sun would be sinking soon and she had to get home in time to stir up her cookstove fire and get her family supper. "And how long has it been since your father brought you here to see to Miss Mona's needs?"

Again the answer wasn't a mystery, but Lacey didn't see any need in trying to slip out of the noose now. "I was a few months past my thirteenth birthday."

"Already a near grown woman. Plenty of girls start looking for a husband along about that age," Sadie Rose said.

"Miss Mona always told me there wasn't any need being in no hurry." Lacey bit into a cookie. Its sweet taste didn't make the moment any sweeter.

"She was right enough about that. But you're more than near grown now, Lacey. You're every bit a woman, and there's some that think it's not exactly proper you living here with the preacher, seeing as how our dear Mona has passed on."

Lacey put the cookie down. It was time to look whatever was coming square in the face. "Then what are they thinking I should do? It's not like any fellows are coming around to knock on my door."

"I never noted you giving any of the fellows the first bit of encouragement." She spoke the words as if pointing out some lack on Lacey's part, while any pretense at a smile disappeared from the woman's face.

"True enough," Lacey admitted. She'd never met the first man she wanted to give the kind of encouragement Miss Sadie Rose was meaning. Lacey had hopes that man might be out there somewhere, but so far he hadn't shown up in the Ebenezer community.

Rachel must have heard the sharp edge that had come into their voices. She put her new doll under her arm and climbed up into Lacey's lap to run her finger and thumb up and down the edge of Lacey's apron. She'd been doing that since she was a little baby.

Lacey tightened her arms around the child as she looked across the table at Sadie Rose. "And there's Rachel."

"She's not your child, Lacey. She wasn't even Mona's child, though the child called her mother. Strange as it seems in a community small as ours, nobody knows whose child she is. It's always been my guess that somebody carried her in here from some other town. That there must have been some sort of shame about it all. No proper marriage or such."

Lacey wanted to put her hands over Rachel's ears and stop the words from going in. Preacher Palmer had told her often enough not to talk back to the churchwomen. To remember her place. Most of the time, Lacey did. But this time she stared straight at Miss Sadie Rose's face and spoke her words with force, like testifying to some basic truth of the spirit. "Whatever the reason for her being here, I know whose child she is now. She's mine."

Thank goodness, Rachel hadn't been bothered by their words. With Lacey's arms strong around her, she'd snuggled down in Lacey's lap and gone to sleep. And more goodness thanked, Sadie Rose had given up talking sense to Lacey and gone on home to tend to her own family.

Now Lacey sighed as she turned away from letting her eyes dwell on little Rachel and went to stir up the embers in the cookstove to start the preacher's supper. Preacher Palmer would know Miss Sadie Rose had come to call. The cookies on the table gave evidence to her being there. If he knew the purpose of the woman's visit, it could be he might send Lacey away. Lacey would just have to pray that if that happened, he'd let Rachel go with her. He had never shown all that much interest in the child. More times than not, the very sight of her seemed to be a hurt to his eyes.

Miss Mona said that was because he'd wanted babies of his own and looking on Rachel reminded him of that loss. A loss Miss Mona always took complete blame for. She cried sometimes when Lacey was reading about Hannah in the Bible. Said she supposed the Lord never answered her prayers for babies because she couldn't have ever willingly surrendered her baby completely to the Lord the way Hannah had done Samuel.

But then she'd mop up her tears with her handkerchief and smile as she said, "But the Lord, he answers prayers in all sorts of ways. Now I've got both you and Rachel. Some blessings pop up like mushrooms around a dead tree stump and surprise you when you least expect it."

Lacey needed a few of those mushroom blessings right now.

3

It wasn't right. Lacey knew that as she stood beside Preacher Palmer in front of his preacher friend. It was worse than not right. She felt the wrongness of it down through the core of her being, all the way out to her toes. But nobody with the first lick of sense expected everything to go right all the time. At least nobody who had piled up a few years of living. Sometimes a body had to do what had to be done, right or wrong, to make something more important right. That's how this was. She didn't have any other choice. Not if she wanted to keep mothering Rachel.

Rachel stood beside her, her face pressed up against Lacey's leg so hard her nose was bound to be mashed sideways. The little girl didn't like strangers. Lacey figured that was because of how she'd once been left lonesome on the preacher's doorstep, even though there was no way the child could actually remember that. All she had ever known was Miss Mona and Lacey taking care of her. Lacey put her hand on Rachel's back and held it steady there. She wasn't sure which of them was drawing the most courage from the other's touch.

"We come here today to join this man and this woman in lawful matrimony."

The Reverend Williams had a deep voice, somber and cold.

Lacey imagined him preaching on hell and shuddered. Or maybe it wasn't his woeful sounding voice so much as the matrimony words he was intoning that made her shudder. In her fanciful dreams, the idea of marrying had joy, like July sunshine warming a meadow full of daisies with butterflies all aflutter and meadowlarks trilling their songs. But here in this man's parlor, Lacey couldn't imagine the first bit of joy—only condemnation.

Condemnation was what Preacher Palmer claimed to be trying to keep away from his door, but Lacey had doubts this ceremony would stop the church ladies from talking. None of them had come along to the town to witness what their gossipy imagining had brought about. The only people in the small parlor besides Lacey, Preacher Palmer, and Rachel were the Reverend Williams with his resonating voice of doom and his thin, sharp-featured wife who stared at Lacey as though she were some kind of Jezebel. Lacey supposed churchwomen were churchwomen wherever, and she was just as glad none of the Ebenezer churchwomen were there to add their frowns to the load of misery Lacey was already feeling.

Preacher Palmer said there wasn't any need in a crowd gathering. Especially since Miss Mona hadn't been in the ground overly long. That's why the church ladies weren't going to be all that happy with Preacher Palmer's solution to their worries about the propriety of Lacey continuing to sleep under the preacher's roof.

In a separate bed yet for a while. There wouldn't be any way the women could know that, but at least Lacey had managed to finagle that promise out of Preacher Palmer. How long she could hold him to it, she didn't know. Folks thought preachers were something special with spiritual fortitude that overcame normal lusts, but Lacey had been in the preacher's house long enough to know he was a man like any other. Maybe worse

34

than some, because of the way folks thought the Lord spoke through him like that gave him extra privileges.

While Miss Mona lived, Lacey had been able to scoot away from that bothersome look that came in his eyes at times. Early on she'd learned to hide behind Miss Mona, who understood the temptations that could beleaguer a man, even a man of God. Miss Mona was as good a person as Lacey was ever likely to meet this side of heaven, and she did admit to loving Preacher Palmer beyond reason, but she didn't close her eyes to the fact that he wasn't as saintly as some imagined him to be. No man other than Jesus Christ was ever perfect, she told Lacey.

"Look at King David," she'd said once. "That man wrote psalms that so overflow with love for the Lord that we're still reading and storing his words in our hearts today. And the Bible says David was a man after the Lord's own heart. Imagine that. And yet he was brought low by lust."

The word "lust" seemed to sit uncomfortable on Miss Mona's tongue. Her cheeks burned red, but she didn't change the word. And while she never once mentioned Preacher Palmer when she was talking about King David's falling to temptation, she did make sure Lacey knew to take a bath where no wrong eyes could see.

Now wrong eyes were poking clear through her, and Lacey felt like she was tiptoeing along the edge of a crevice that might spring open wider and swallow her whole. But she'd always had good balance. Never once tumbled off the stepping-stones in the creek back in the woods where she and Junie used to play before their mama died. And what had she been doing but balancing ever since? Keeping out of Widow Jackson's way. Protecting Junie. Staying away from Preacher Palmer's eyes while seeing to Miss Mona.

There was always some kind of balancing to do in life.

Standing there with the matrimony words pounding into her ears was no different. Preacher Palmer was on one side with a frown that could summon up storm clouds, and Rachel was on the other side with enough sunshine to make whatever storm Lacey had to run through worth getting soaked down with trials of the spirit.

And though Miss Mona had moved on up to heaven, she had still somehow come through to help Lacey balance things out. At least that was how it had seemed to Lacey the night she and Preacher Palmer sat at the kitchen table to come to their agreement while Rachel settled into sleep in the upstairs room.

"Deacon Crutcher has brought to my attention that there's some talk in the church," Preacher Palmer pronounced after he told Lacey to sit down across from him.

No more than two days had passed since Sadie Rose had shown up on their doorstep with her sugar cookies, rag doll, and busybody advice. It appeared the woman was not willing to leave the issue of the decency of the preacher's living arrangements solely in Lacey's hands.

The preacher's eyes narrowed on Lacey as he waited for her to say something, but she made out like she didn't have the first idea of what he was talking about as she looked down and began rubbing a spot of flour off her apron.

When the silence dragged on too long, she finally murmured, "There's always talk in the church."

That was God's own truth. Three people got together under the Lord's roof, and two of them would be talking about the other one not doing something proper. Before Miss Mona died, Lacey hadn't been to church services for a good while. Miss Mona had lacked the strength for the walk to the church building, but they observed the Sabbath with their own worship hour by reading out of the Bible and singing a hymn or two.

Miss Mona knew how to bring the Lord down and make him real for Lacey. She experienced more worship in one Sunday with Miss Mona than she had in the two dozen Sundays since sitting on the hard pews listening to Preacher Palmer. The fault was in her. She knew that. Since Miss Mona passed on, Lacey seemed resistant to the word of the Lord. As if he'd done her a wrong turn and she didn't see the need of offering herself up for another round of sorrow.

As she waited for Preacher Palmer's next words, she kept her eyes on her apron and swallowed down the sigh that wanted to heave out of her. It appeared that such bouts of trouble came along to seek a body out even when that person was trying to stay small and hidden from the notice of the Lord. And the preacher.

"True enough," Preacher Palmer agreed in his pastor voice. "But a church can't long stand united when that talk is about their leader."

She didn't know what to say to that, because she couldn't deny the truth in his words. In her mind she was already wondering what she could use to carry off the books Miss Mona had given her over the years and hoping the preacher had another house in mind that might need a hired girl. One that would take her and Rachel, but even as she thought it, she knew there wouldn't be any such house as that. He'd simply be shed of them both. Soon as he found Lacey a place, he'd carry Rachel down to the city to turn her over to whoever would take the child off his hands.

Lacey folded the edge of her apron over and then over again. Just the thought of that, of Rachel being given over to strangers, loaded down her heart with so much pain that it seemed to be sinking down into her stomach. How could the Lord take Miss Mona and leave them in such a predicament? Miss Mona had always prayed and done what was right. Maybe that was the problem. Maybe now that Miss Mona was gone, Lacey hadn't prayed enough. If so, she was willing to make some changes.

She pushed out her words. "Miss Mona would tell us we need to pray over those who see problems where there aren't any."

"You can rest assured I pray over my people every day. Not an hour goes by that I don't reach up for the Lord's hand in guidance. I walk in prayer." Preacher Palmer's voice didn't sound a bit prayerful. Instead he sounded almost angry. "I never had need of Mona telling me to pray."

"I wasn't aiming to say you did," Lacey said softly. "But I do miss her prayers for me."

Preacher Palmer shifted uneasily in the chair across from Lacey, as if her mention of Miss Mona's prayers smote him. Lacey guessed the grief was even heavier on his heart than it was on Lacey's after the years the two of them had been together. Longer than Lacey had lived, Miss Mona had told her once.

Lacey sneaked a look up at him. His face was hard as stone as he stared out toward the door. His nose was long and sharp, and his eyes more gray than blue and just as sharp in a different way. His long legs twitched a little, and she thought he was wishing he could just get up and go do some walking and praying right then. But he stayed in the chair as silence fell over them. The fire popped in the cookstove and the teakettle sang as the water in it began to steam. Lacey hadn't washed the dishes from their supper yet, and she wished she could get up, pour the water in the pan, and make the dishes rattle as she washed them clean. The silence overtop them was too loud. Especially after she'd invited in Miss Mona's shadow to sit down with them.

She stared back down at her apron and waited. Preacher

Palmer opened and closed his hands on the table as if his rheumatism might be paining his fingers. She thought of offering to fetch him a hot rag to bring him some comfort, but she didn't move. Instead as the silence between them deepened, she allowed her mind to slide away from the worrisome feeling growing in the kitchen to the story she'd been making up for Rachel that morning.

Now that Rachel had the new rag doll, she wanted a Maddie story every time, and Lacey had put Maddie in a heap of trouble in the story that morning. Had her scrambling up a tree to get away from a wildcat. They'd left her stuck up in the tree, too scared to climb down, because as Lacey explained to Rachel, what a person could do in a panic, the same person might not be able to do when the panic leaked out of them. Lacey was thinking she might have to bring fairies into the story to sprinkle some courage dust on Maddie. Lacey liked putting fairies into her stories even though Miss Mona had warned her that the Bible didn't make the first mention of fairies. She had suggested Lacey put angels in her stories instead, but it didn't seem right to be making up foolish little stories about angels. Fairies, yes, but not angels. Angels came down from the Lord, but fairies were nothing but a flight of imagination.

Courage dust. That was what she needed right at that moment, but the fairy thoughts deserted her when the preacher started talking again.

"There's just one thing to do. We'll have to get married."

"Married?" Lacey's voice came out in a squeak. Her eyes flew up to Preacher Palmer's face and stayed there even after she saw that look in his eyes that brought uneasiness down on her. He couldn't have said what she thought he said. He couldn't be suggesting she marry him.

"It's the answer the Lord gave me." His words came out

like he was revealing a truth in one of his sermons. The Lord saith. "The only answer."

She stared at him and wanted to laugh. He was older than her own father. A man with deep wrinkles around his eyes and gray in his beard and bony hands with bent and knobby fingers that she couldn't imagine ever touching her in any kind of caress. But he kept looking at her, waiting for her to say something, and she forgot about wanting to laugh. Instead she wanted to run out the door and go throw herself on Miss Mona's grave. Maybe crawl in there with her. Marrying Preacher Palmer would be about the same thing.

Her eyes popped open even wider at the thought. "I couldn't—"

The preacher held up a hand to stop her before she could get out the necessary words. "You have to."

As though to make sure she didn't escape, he reached across the table to grab her. His fingers dug hard into her upper arms, even though she sat perfectly still and didn't try to pull away from him the way she wanted to. His eyes burned into hers as he said, "It's the only way you can stay here with Rachel."

He knew the thing to say to get her attention. He was a preacher, after all. He knew about people's weaknesses and the power of love. When she just kept staring at him with her mouth hanging open, he began talking in a calm voice the way she'd heard him talk to those in his church flock who'd been knocked low by some trouble.

"It may seem a strange thing to you, Lacey, but I'm not as old as you're thinking I am. And while I loved Mona, she's gone now. On to a better place in heaven where she's happy. You can be assured of that."

"Is she looking down on us?" Lacey asked. She scrunched her shoulders together and tried to shrink away from his touch.

He loosened his hold on her arms but didn't let go. "If she is, she'd understand this is the Lord's answer to our dilemma."

He spoke the words strong, but it was easy enough to tell that he wasn't all that sure they were true. His eyes shifted away from Lacey to the side for a moment, as if almost expecting to see Miss Mona sitting there beside them. Lacey would have prayed her down if she could have. A ghost wouldn't be a bit scarier than staring at Preacher Palmer and hearing what he was proposing. She tried to think of the right words to say, but nothing—absolutely nothing—came to mind as she kept staring at him, seeing him differently than she ever had before.

His eyes came back to land on her, but now the sure preacher eyes were gone as doubt crept over his face. He must not have planned on her looking at him with such dismay. He let his hands slide off her arms but kept his eyes tight on her as he moistened his lips before he started talking again.

"I can see this isn't something you've given consideration to. And I suppose that is understandable, but marriage between an older man and a young woman in need is not uncommon. I've performed several ceremonies joining two such myself. Those unions turned out to be beneficial for all involved."

Lacey found her voice. "I always thought marrying was something a person did after falling in love. You can't be thinking on that kind of love, can you?"

Again the preacher shifted in his chair uneasily and a bit of color climbed up into his cheeks. Lacey hadn't ever seen that happen except when he'd been out in the cold too long.

"I am a man, Lacey. And not too old for such thinking. I loved Mona as you well know, but due to her condition we hadn't shared any kind of intimate marital relationship for many years." His eyes bored into Lacey. "But I am a man."

Lacey thought it was good she was sitting down, because

41

her head was spinning. She put her hand flat against her forehead in hopes that would help her think of a clear answer. But there was no answer. No right answer. The clock kept ticking. The water kept whistling in the teakettle. Lacey kept breathing in and out, even though she was feeling more and more like somebody had punched her in the stomach.

Finally she pushed out the words that had to be said. "You aren't saying you want to love me like that. Like a man for his wife?"

"Not exactly like I loved Mona. But I do feel desire for you, Lacey. Any man might. You're a very pretty young woman. And I will promise to take care of you." His voice changed, softened into a pleading tone instead of a demanding one. "It's an exchange that will favor both our needs."

Lacey had never spent much time thinking on how she looked. When she came to live with Miss Mona, she was beanpole skinny, with brown eyes too big for her face and mouse-brown hair chopped off short. Pretty was not a word she'd ever heard spoken in regard to how she looked. Not even by Miss Mona, who had loved brushing Lacey's hair and catching it up in ponytails or braids after it grew out long and wavy. But now with the preacher's words ringing in her ears, Lacey supposed her face had filled out some and that she'd plumped up in other ways as to how a woman should. Even so, she had no desire to be pretty to the preacher's eyes.

"With words spoken or not, I couldn't lay down with you." Lacey looked straight at him. "I couldn't."

"Not even for Rachel?" Some of the pleading tone faded from his voice. Now it sounded more wheedling.

"I can't see what Rachel has to do with the two of us laying down together."

"To keep our little family intact. To see that nothing

42

changes here in our home." He kept his eyes steady on her. "Not just my home. Your home too. If we can do it proper."

"What do you think Miss Mona would think proper?"

"For the sake of all that's holy, Mona is dead." He slammed his fist down with the words, bouncing the dishes stacked on the end of the table.

Lacey scrunched as far back in her chair as she could, but she didn't turn her eyes away from his face. "That doesn't change what she'd think proper."

Preacher Palmer shut his eyes and blew out a slow breath. He didn't say anything for such a long time that Lacey thought about sliding off her chair and running out the back door to find some dark place to hide awhile. But then there was Rachel in the little room upstairs. So she stayed where she was and counted the ticks of the clock in the next room while trying to keep her heart from sinking down to her toes.

"All right, Lacey," he said finally. "I'm not going to force you into anything you don't want to do. But I think the Lord and Mona would agree that something has to be done. I can see you need time. Time I'm willing to give you. We can get married and keep things as they are. Rachel will have a home. You will have a home. And I'll have someone to cook my supper."

"And the other?" Lacey thought it best to be straight and clear on what he expected of her.

"I've promised you time. Not forever, but long enough. You're a woman the same as I'm a man. Both of us have needs to be met." He reached across the table and stroked the top of her hand with his bony fingers. "Will you agree to that? For Rachel? For me?"

What choice did she have? She needed a roof over her head. She needed Rachel in her lap.

That was how come she was standing there between the

two of them—Rachel and Preacher Palmer—hearing the question she didn't want to answer.

"Do you, Lacey Bishop, take this man, Elwood Palmer, to be your lawfully wedded husband to love and obey in sickness and in health till death do you part?"

The silence in the preacher's parlor grew deeper and deeper. The preacher's wife stared at Lacey. Lacey could feel Preacher Palmer shifting uneasily on his feet beside her. And still the expected words wouldn't come out of her mouth. The preacher in front of them read the question again. Lacey opened her mouth but had no voice.

Finally Preacher Palmer answered for her. "She does," he said as he grabbed her right hand and squeezed it so hard Lacey thought her knuckles might pop out of her skin.

The other preacher kept staring at her and she managed a nod. That seemed good enough and the deed was done. Till death do them part. A tear slipped out of the corner of her left eye and traced a path down her cheek. She didn't try to pull her hand free of the preacher's or move her other hand off Rachel's back to wipe away the tear. Instead she blinked her eyes to keep any more tears from slipping out. She was a grown woman who had made a choice. There wasn't the least bit of need crying over it now that it was too late to change.

4

Fog rising from the Ohio River swirled about Isaac as he leaned against a post and peered down at the river. The cold, dark water beckoned him. He could take one step forward and let the river swallow him. Have done with it. He'd heard it said drowning wasn't such a bad way to die. That a person floated down into the watery depths and oft as not didn't even fight against the water filling up his lungs. At least not after the first shock of not being able to breathe. For a certainty it had to be easier or at least quicker than starving. Or dying of sorrow.

People said that last didn't happen. That nobody ever died of sorrow. But then Ella had. Sorrowed herself into a fever and turned loose of life as easily as dropping a pebble into a pool of water. The pebble she'd tossed—the life she'd given up—was still making rings in its wake these months later.

Her father was not about to let the surface of Isaac's life settle into any kind of calmness. The judge wanted vengeance. An eye for an eye. A life for a life. No mercy in his court. Nor was there any in Isaac's. His life was no longer worth the food he needed to put in his mouth to keep him alive. Even if he had a way to get that food.

Food. His empty stomach made it hard to think about anything else. Except Ella. Food and Ella. Ella and food.

Those first few weeks after Ella was put in the ground, he had wandered the streets with no purpose to his steps and often as not ended up at her grave, wishing he could trade places with her. Some nights he slept there, stretched out on the mound of dirt as if he might reach down in it and still embrace her. Other nights he made his bed wherever dark overtook him.

Somehow he made it through the cold months. He wasn't sure exactly how. It was all as foggy in his brain as the air enveloping him on this day. He squeezed his eyes shut, and Burton Hayes was there frowning in his head. The old store-keeper never smiled. Not even at his customers. But he'd let Isaac sleep in the store's back room with a sack of beans for a pillow as long as Isaac kept the snow off the walkways around the store. There'd been other odd jobs now and again to make a few coins to buy food. Jobs he couldn't remember now, even when he tried, while other things he couldn't forget. Like how cold it was up in the cemetery and how his footprints had spoiled the pristine snow piled on top of Ella. The snow melted. Mud took its place. Others gave him handouts, but charity had a way of running out. Especially when the judge let it be known kindness to Isaac could mean trouble from him.

Isaac stared down at the murky water and was glad it wasn't clear enough to bounce any kind of reflection back up to him. He knew how sorry he looked. Just the day before, he'd come face-to-face with that truth when he'd turned a corner and almost stumbled over a cracked mirror somebody had tossed out behind a building. For a few seconds he hadn't believed the reflection could be his. The stranger staring out of the mirror held little resemblance to the man who had left for the West in such high spirits last year to seek his fortune. That man with hopes and dreams had been buried with his Ella.

He had leaned toward the mirror as if to peer deep into it and somehow find the image of the man he used to be. But up close the mirror's crack ran right through the middle of his face and skewed his reflection. That was as it should be. He was cracked and broken, little more than a shell of a man going through the motions of living. His hair straggled down over the dirt-encrusted collar of his shirt. His cheeks looked hollow and his eyes haunted. He slammed his fist into the mirror and watched the glass splinter and fall to the ground.

It was a minute before he noticed the blood dripping off his fingers. He lifted up his hand and watched the blood pulsing up out of the cuts on his knuckles before he finally pulled out his handkerchief, soiled though it was, and wrapped it around his hand. The cuts didn't matter. It wouldn't have mattered if he'd cut off his whole hand. Nothing about him mattered. He was a man without hope or a future. A man who had descended so low that he wasn't above picking through trash to find a crust of bread to eat. A man who would never find work in this town but with no will to leave it. A man getting what he deserved as he teetered on the edge of despair. A man the judge was determined to push over the edge.

A man ready to surrender to the push but not able to make the jump himself. What was it in a man that kept him clinging to life even when that life was naught but misery? Isaac shut his eyes to the pull of the water as he leaned his head against the rough post and trembled until his teeth chattered.

The chime of church bells echoed through the fog, and Isaac counted off the bongs of the hours. Seven. He wondered if the sun was shining up above the fog or if clouds were heavy all the way to the heavens. He was so cold. The damp river fog had the bite of ice in it. Not normal for April. But winter

47

hadn't given up its hold on the city this year. Or maybe it was only the winter Isaac carried in his soul that kept spring from him. Perhaps others around him were welcoming the spring while he had been condemned to never see the sun again. Just as Ella would not.

Isaac looked up in hopes a shaft of sunlight might break through the fog just for him. A last wish granted before he gave up living.

Nobody would miss him. Nobody would even know he had died unless his body washed up on the riverbank somewhere. Maybe whoever found him would bury him and say words over his grave. That was as much as he could hope for. His mother would never know what became of him. Nor would Marian. He would pass with no more notice than a bird falling from the sky.

A bit of Scripture came unbidden to his mind, a legacy of his years of Bible reading with Mrs. McElroy. He couldn't recall the exact words of the verses, but the gist of them tickled his memory. Something about not a sparrow falling but that the Lord knew and how a person, any person, was surely of more value than many sparrows. But as he kept looking up at the fog thick over his head, he didn't feel as valuable as a single sparrow feather. He wished he'd paid Mrs. McElroy's Bible teaching more mind. Then maybe he'd know how to pray some sunshine down on his face, some forgiveness down on his soul.

"It might be best to step back a bit, my brother." The man's voice carried an echo of cheer as he took hold of Isaac's arm. "There's the feel of ice in the fog this morn, and you wouldn't want to be slipping into the deep with no one about to pull you out. I would give it a try, but it's a fact that I'm not much of a swimmer and not half as big as you. So the end result might be that we'd both be off to meet our Maker. And to be truthful, that wasn't a journey I had plans to make on this day."

The man's grasp was firm and Isaac let him pull him back from the edge of the dock.

"Come. You look to be in need of some morning sustenance. The same as I am." The man kept talking as if not even noting Isaac's gloom. "I came down here to see what steamboats had come in, but that appears to be a job better done without so much fog about."

Isaac went with him. His stomach had been empty too long to allow him to turn down the offer of food. No matter what the eventual cost. But it wasn't right not to give the man fair warning. Isaac stopped halfway up the wooden steps from the river. The fog was lifting and he took a good look at the little man beside him. He'd been right when he'd said he wasn't much more than half as big as Isaac. The top of his hat barely came up to Isaac's shoulders. It was a broad-brimmed affair that struck a memory in Isaac's mind. He'd seen such a hat before, but he couldn't quite recall where.

The man tipped his head back to look up at Isaac. "You needn't be worried about any harm coming to you from me. As if you could even imagine such from a man as small in stature as me." His bushy black eyebrows almost came together in a line over dark eyes that might have looked fierce if they hadn't been softened by the sparkle of kindness. At that very moment, a ray of sunshine burned down through the fog to touch them both.

"The harm I thought might come was not to me but to you."

The man eyed him for a long moment. "A man intent on evil would give his victim no warning. You do not appear to be a dangerous man."

"Not harm from me, but because of me. I've made an

enemy of a powerful man in this town. A judge who has found reason to throw others in jail for giving me a few coins to buy food."

"The judges of the world are of no concern to me. I answer to a higher judge." The man put his hand on Isaac's arm again and started back up the steps. "But it could be I should have introduced myself. I'm Brother Asa Jefferson."

"A preacher?"

"Nay. Not so much. But yea, a brother to any in need, and I get the sense that might be you. Our Mother Ann instructs us never to neglect doing good to those we meet."

"Mother Ann?" Again there was that echo of a memory that Isaac couldn't quite capture in his head. Perhaps the cold and lack of food was stealing his power to remember.

"Yea. The leader of our group of Believers. I am sure you have knowledge of the Christ who preachers tell you died for your sins."

"I've not spent much time in church lately, but I seem to be good at making people die," Isaac said. "At least as far as other people go. Don't seem so good at it for myself." He looked back down toward the riverfront with some regret.

Brother Asa's smile faded but not his look of kindness as he said, "Why don't we rest here in this spot of sun a moment before we continue on? The dampness of the morn is making my rheumatism act up and the gift of the sun's warmth is the best healing power I know." He sat down on the steps, and Isaac dropped down beside him as the riverfront began to stir to life and workers tromped past them on the steps with barely a glance.

Isaac raised his face up toward the sun. If only the sun had broken through the fog a few moments earlier to give him his last wish, he might even now be floating in the river facedown. And if this little man hadn't come along. Isaac tried to ignore his stomach's anxious growling as he waited for the man to speak. To say what he might want from Isaac. There was always a price to pay for charity doled out. A chance to work would be best, but Isaac was guessing the man had in mind to do some preaching at him. If so, he could give ear to his sermon in exchange for the promise of food. It had been two days since he'd found anything to eat. Hunger was perching on his shoulder like a vulture patiently biding its time.

The little man briskly rubbed his knees and elbows, so perhaps he'd spoken the truth of needing a rest. Then he took off his hat and balanced it on his lap as he peered straight into Isaac's face. "Have you killed someone, my brother?" The man's voice held no condemnation.

Isaac didn't turn from the man's eyes as he answered the question with truth. "Not with gun or force, but there are some who lay the blame of a death on me." Ella's face floated before him and he dropped his eyes down to stare at his hands. The handkerchief still wrapped around his hand was stained with blood, but none looked to be fresh.

"And do you put that blame there as well?" The man took hold of his hat and slid down to the step below Isaac so he could keep peering up into his face.

"She's dead and I live."

"And so you think you should stop living too? Take the heavenly Father's will for your life into your own hands and cut your days short of those he has laid out for you?" The man glanced over his shoulder toward the river and then back at Isaac. His eyebrows glistened with the moisture of the morning mist.

"I was hearing the invitation of the water," Isaac admitted. "But I was too much a coward to answer it."

"Nay, my brother. It is living that oft takes courage. A

cowardly man looks for what he imagines will be an easy escape from his troubles, but that man dooms himself to eternal punishment since how can he beg our Father's forgiveness for such a sin once he is dead? Such a decision should be one that we wrestle with, as Jacob wrestled with the angel of the Lord when he was running from his sin. Dying is not meant to be easy. Not if it isn't the Lord's will."

Isaac turned his eyes away from the man back toward the river where the fog was nothing more than wisps of mist now as the sun won the morning battle. After a minute he said, "The thought of it seemed easy. Just jump in the river and don't come up for air."

"Have you ever been witness to a man drowning?"

The man's voice wormed into his ears, bringing to mind things he had no wish to think on. He thought about standing up and walking away, but his empty stomach demanded he see the man's words through.

"I was on a riverboat once when the boilers blew. Men and women and children drowned that night. Those that weren't killed in the explosion." Isaac looked out past the little man toward the middle of the river. The water had been murky that day too. The day his father had died.

"You must have been blown clear of the boat and had knowledge of staying afloat. Was that the way of it?" Brother Asa pushed on with his questions.

"I was on deck. Everybody said I was lucky. That my father loaned me his luck and that's why he was below deck where he didn't have the chance to make the shore. Of course the boat caught fire."

"An inferno on water." The man shook his head at the thought. "I've seen it but once, but care not to see it again. Providence had me ashore at the time. Providence perhaps kept you on deck in the same way. It is a good thing to embrace

Providence at times and to thank the Lord for such. Instead of feeling guilt for what you cannot change."

"Many told me the same."

"And you gave no credence to their words?" Brother Asa lifted his thick dark eyebrows. "Or do you have other reasons for despair?"

"There are always reasons for despair," Isaac said.

"You speak truth especially for those of the world," the man said with that echo of cheerful acceptance in his voice as he stood and placed his hat on his head. "And hunger is one of them. Come. I've kept you talking too long when it is your stomach I hear talking back to me."

Isaac echoed his words. "Those of the world." He'd heard that said before, and suddenly he knew where he'd seen men dressed like the man in front of him. "You're a Shaker."

The man smiled. "That is what those of the world call us, and while we are comfortable with the moniker, our true name is the Society of Believers in the Second Coming of Christ."

"I know."

Isaac's knowledge seemed to surprise the man. "Do you?" The man studied Isaac. "Were you perhaps raised by the Shakers then and are one of those lured away from our villages by the temptations of worldly living?"

"No. My sister went to the Shakers when our father died. She's still there. In a village not far from here called Harmony Hill."

"The very village I call home. And what might your sister's name be?"

"Marian. Marian Kingston."

"Then you must be Isaac." The man's smile got wider as he put his hand on Isaac's shoulder.

Isaac frowned and wanted to shrug the man's hand off his shoulder. It seemed too odd, the man knowing his name.

53

The man laughed. "Have no fear, my brother. I didn't divine your name." Brother Asa's smile disappeared. "Sister Marian mentioned her concerns for you during one of our union meetings. She said you were suffering much sorrow as do many who depend on the relationships of the world for happiness. But be assured, peace can still be possible for you."

"I don't see how. My wife died." Isaac hesitated and then went on. "Because of me." The words tore a new wound through the middle of his heart to match many others until he thought it must surely be near collapse.

"Yea, I see your sorrow. But Providence has put us on the same path this day. Come, my brother. Let us go fill your hungry body with proper sustenance. Only then can the sorrows of the soul be tended to." He reached a thick, blocky hand down toward Isaac.

Isaac stared at the man for a long moment before he reached to take the man's hand. He remembered Marian once telling Isaac that the Shakers were dead to the world. And wasn't that what he wanted? To be dead.

Isaac stood up and followed the little man. Perhaps Providence had played a part in their meeting this day, and he would find a way to die without surrendering the very necessary need to breathe.

5

It was good to have a full stomach again. But even better to have the cheerful Brother Asa walking along beside him with no worry dragging down his step. Nothing seemed to bother the little man. Not the chance of trouble coming his way because of his kindness to Isaac. Not the ridicule that some they passed on the street shot his way because of his short stature.

"Look there. That Shaker feller's done danced his legs off to his knees," one of the men they passed said right before he stuck a foot out to trip Brother Asa.

Isaac grabbed the little man to keep him from falling. Then he doubled up his fists ready to show the other man bent over with laughter something not so funny.

Brother Asa caught Isaac's arm and pulled him on down the street. "The man has a noble idea. Of a truth it would be a fine thing if I had worn off my legs laboring our worship songs. That would surely make my lack of height a gift, rather than a burden." Brother Asa smiled over his shoulder at the man with no animosity at all, but his smile faded when he turned back to Isaac. "It is not our way to resort to fisticuffs, my brother. The Believer's path is peaceful."

"I'm not a Believer," Isaac said, his hands still clenched in fists. The man's laughter trailed after them.

"True enough. And I fear just as true that you have no peace."

"Peace." Isaac's shoulders drooped as the anger drained out of him. "It's a fine-sounding word, but nothing I think to ever know again."

"Peace of the spirit can be difficult to obtain in the world, but at Harmony Hill doors to peace will open up to you that you cannot begin to imagine now." Brother Asa threw out his hands as if pushing open those doors. "A gift from Mother Ann to those who seek the truth of right living and live the Shaker way."

Doors to peace. Isaac had no right to go through those doors. Nor did he have the right to make Brother Asa think he could be converted to a Shaker. The man had been kind to him. The least Isaac could do was be honest in return.

Isaac glanced over at Brother Asa and then stared down at the walkway as he said, "If I went with you to your village, it would be only for the food. Not as one with any idea of converting to your beliefs."

Isaac expected his admission to upset Brother Asa, but it seemed nothing could do that. He didn't look a bit put off. "Many before you have done the same. Winter Shakers some. Those who come for a season and leave. Others stay and become true and faithful to the Shaker way. But I daresay none were ever disappointed with the fruits of our table. Our food is plentiful and our sisters very fine cooks." Brother Asa's smile spread across his face again. "Plus all who come must work for their place at our table."

"I want to work. No one will hire me here."

"Yet you stay." Brother Asa's words weren't a question, but his voice carried a query.

"I had no way to go," Isaac said, but knew as he uttered the words they weren't true. In the five months since Ella had died, he could have walked away from Louisville or maybe even finagled a passage on one of the steamboats. It was Ella who kept him there. Ella in that cold grave on the hill outside the town. He couldn't simply desert her there and go on about his life as if nothing was different.

Brother Asa was eyeing him. "Do you have children from your union with this wife you lost?"

"No. We were only wed a short time before she took the fever."

"You are a mystery, my brother. But Mother Ann warns us that worldly love can cause much upheaval in a man's life." Brother Asa turned his eyes away from Isaac and began walking again. His good humor returned as he kept talking. "The sort of upheaval I have never experienced. I doubt any woman ever looked on me with a lascivious eye. Praises be! Mother Ann has surely guarded me from such temptations."

"What about before you went to the Shakers?"

"I was but a young lad when my natural mother brought me to the Shaker village. She may have known the worldly motherly love for me. I cannot say of a certainty. I have only the vaguest recollection of a gentle face under a black cap telling me goodbye. I don't remember tears on her face or mine."

"She left you there?"

"Children are well cared for among the Shakers. A fine place to grow up. I can vouch for that." Brother Asa smiled over at him. "Of course except for that dancing one's legs off to the knee." The man laughed out loud. "I will have to share that one with Brother Henry. While joviality is not a common thing as it is our duty to tend with serious minds to our appointed tasks, Brother Henry and I enjoy a laugh now and again."

"You seem to be always smiling," Isaac said.

"In the world, a smile can oft turn away trouble. Especially for one such as myself. One who wishes to live in peace with all."

"Trouble is not always so easily shed," Isaac said.

"Perhaps not in the world, but if you can leave your grief behind and return to Harmony Hill with me, your troubles will become less burdensome. And there are our bountiful tables to consider." Brother Asa raised his eyebrows at Isaac.

"How long would I have to stay?"

"There is no requirement for a period of time. All who come among us are free to stay or leave at any time. We hold none in bondage as some of the world do. The desire for true salvation is all that binds us."

Isaac looked at the man in front of him and bit back his words of unbelief. There was no salvation. No God who cared what happened to Isaac. That was more than evident, else he and Ella would be happily building a new life out in the western territories.

Brother Asa must have read his mind. "Worry not, young brother. You are only required to listen. Your heart will be free to make its own decisions of the path you choose to follow, but I pray for a decision of joy for you and not one of worldly sorrow."

"She's only been gone a few months. Don't you think I'm supposed to be sorrowful?"

"Indeed. In the world that may be so. But at Harmony Hill you will become a different person. The worldly Isaac will fade away and Brother Isaac who embraces peace will come forth. The sorrows of the world will be dead to you."

"There are many ways to die."

"And it seems you have pondered some of them. But the death of which I speak, the death to the world a Believer embraces, delivers one into a new life of abounding love from our Mother Ann and the Eternal Father as we give our hands to work and our hearts to God. That is the Believer's way." Brother Asa slowed his step and peered up at Isaac.

"Marian has told me it is a good way. At least for her."

"Then it is settled. You will go with me when my business is concluded at the waterfront later today."

Isaac hadn't actually said he'd go with Brother Asa, but neither did he contradict the little man now and say he wouldn't.

Brother Asa stopped in front of a shop and pulled money out of his pocket to buy a new set of clothes for Isaac. When the shopkeeper narrowed his eyes and stared long at Isaac's face before turning them away, Brother Asa stuffed his money back in his pocket as he cheerfully claimed that Mother Ann must be guarding the Shaker coin.

"The clothes made by our sisters at Harmony Hill will serve you better than anything we might buy here." He glanced back over his shoulder toward where the shopkeeper stood in the door staring after them. "He looks to be regretting turning away good coin."

"Or only waiting until a policeman comes by to send a message to the judge."

Isaac moderated his step to match the little man's shorter stride even as he kept his eyes on the street ahead. The last few weeks he'd slipped back into the shadows whenever he spotted any of the watch. It just seemed the better part of wisdom to stay away from the law. A man with no place to lay his head was a vagrant, and other bums on the street warned him that vagrancy was oft considered a crime. A one-way ticket to the inside of a prison cell, especially in the judge's courtroom.

He glanced over at the man beside him. The food so recently in his stomach sat uneasily as he thought about how it was surely only a matter of time before the judge found out about Brother Asa showing him kindness. When he did, he'd find some reason to have the strange little Shaker brought before his bench.

"Who is this judge? The one so determined to keep you hungry." Asa peered up at him with a good bit of curiosity.

"My father-in-law," Isaac said. "Although I don't suppose he would admit to that relationship now."

"Ah, the father of the young wife whose death has spread a mantle of guilt over you."

"She would still be alive if I hadn't talked her into going west with me. She didn't want to leave her mother."

"So you forced her to go with you?"

"I didn't bind her to me with ropes or chains, if that's what you mean. She was only bound by our wedding vows."

"It is a truth that the vows of matrimony oft cause much stress and sorrow for those of the world. In our village we shut such personal worries from us."

"But what about love?" Isaac asked. "Don't you shut out the chance for it as well?"

"Those of the world think that, but we at Harmony Hill are abundantly gifted with love. Of that you can be certain. There is much more peace from loving all as brother or sister as the good Lord revealed was the proper way to Mother Ann. The intended way."

Brother Asa must have seen the doubt on Isaac's face. He smiled as he went on. "I must beg your forbearance, my brother. I shouldn't try to load you down with too much preaching. That is one of my faults that I often have need to confess. Filling the air with an excess of words and giving the one listening no time to understand. A person should not hurry his tasks nor should he load down a young brother's ears beyond what he can hear."

"That's all right. Listening is the least I can do after you bought me food."

"No payment was exacted for that. A Believer is bound by the charity of his heart to help those in need. You were hungry. I had the means to change that, and now you have the means to help me by coming along to the waterfront to be an aid in loading my wagon with the building supplies I have been sent to carry back to the village."

At the waterfront the steamboat had come in with the building material for the Shaker village. Not lumber, since Brother Asa said the Shakers used timber off their land for planks and beams but ordered some iron supports shaped to suit their needs to save building time. The boat had also brought sheets of glass they loaded in the wagon with great care.

They were stuffing padding around the glass for the journey back to the Shaker village when Isaac spotted Officer Neal some distance down the dock. "Trouble's coming," Isaac told Brother Asa as he slipped out of sight behind the wagon.

He grabbed the little man's arm to pull him back behind the wagon with him, but the Shaker man shook off Isaac's hand. "What need do we have to hide? We are doing no wrong."

Isaac hesitated. He didn't want to desert his new friend, but wrong was open to interpretation. That same spark that had kept his feet from sliding off the dock and plunging into the river that morning now sent him scurrying for a place in the shadows behind some barrels before the police officer came any closer. He wanted to run farther away, to disappear down some alleyway, but instead he made himself as small as possible as he peeked out of a crack between the barrels. Brother Asa kept packing padding against the glass without even glancing down the dock toward Officer Neal, who was coming toward the Shaker man with purpose in his steps.

Purpose that Isaac feared. Not only for himself now, but for Brother Asa too. What would he do if Officer Neal tried to haul the little Shaker away? Isaac pulled in a deep breath to quell the panic rising in him and then was afraid to let it out for fear the noise would give him away. At least it was Officer Neal and not Cox. Cox kept his bludgeon at the ready and didn't care how many innocent heads he might break. Once he hit a poor bloke, the man was always found guilty of something.

But Neal would give a man a chance to talk before he hauled him away. Mostly to line his own pockets. He had the tendency to look the other way if a man dropped a few coins and forgot to lean down to pick them up. For sure Isaac had no coins to drop, but Brother Asa had coin jingling in his pocket. If he would pull it out and offer it to the officer.

Isaac thought about leaning out of his shadows to give Brother Asa that advice, but he feared attracting the officer's eye. So instead he sat silent and wondered when he'd become such a mouse of a man. Too fearful to do harm to himself. Too fearful to attempt to prevent harm to another.

"Good day, Officer," Brother Asa said with that same note of cheer in his voice that had been with him all the time Isaac had walked beside him. "It's good to see the sun out so bright. Time enough in the year for a man to work up a bit of sweat in his labor, wouldn't you say?"

"I would, I would. Winter has lingered long past its welcome this year, but the sun's got the promise of summer in it today." Officer Neal pulled out a dingy handkerchief and wiped off his brow. After he stuffed it back away, he peered at the little man and said, "It's been awhile since I've seen you here in these parts, Brother Asa."

In his hiding place, Isaac felt a whisper of relief. At least the Shaker man wasn't a stranger to Officer Neal.

"Yea, that it has," Brother Asa said. "But we're building a new barn and had need of supplies."

"For dancing?" The officer's voice carried the hint of laughter.

"Nay, our meetinghouse serves us well enough there. Our brothers built it fine enough to stand for many years." Brother Asa tied down a rope he threw over the back of the wagon.

"I been hearing about some strange doings happening down there in your village."

"We've had a season of spiritual rainfall on our village for a truth. The kind the world struggles to understand."

"You fellers have odd cornered. Nobody's doubting that. Me, I sing a hymn in the church house on Easter morning and Christmas Day. That serves me well enough. A man on the watch has little time for churchgoing at any rate, seeing as how there's no stop to the mischief that goes on."

"So are you out looking for mischief makers this day?" Brother Asa walked around the wagon to pull the rope tight down on the other side.

"Fact of the matter, I am. A mischief maker they tell me you was seen with this very morn."

Isaac wanted to shrink down smaller in his hiding place, but he kept his eye to the crack as he strained to hear every word.

"Oh?" Brother Asa didn't sound the least concerned even as Isaac's heart began a slow thumping in his chest. "I did buy a man down on his luck breakfast this morning. Isaac he said was his name. Don't think he gave a last moniker." Brother Asa had the rope tied down. He leaned back against the side of the wagon and looked up at Officer Neal. "Would that be the man you seek?"

"It would. Isaac Kingston."

"And what wrong has he done? He seemed harmless enough

when I met him. Although a hungry man can be driven to desperation at times."

"Maybe desperate enough to stab a man and rob him of his pay, you think?" The officer fingered the top of his bludgeon that was sticking up out of his belt.

"Did that happen?" Brother Asa didn't seem to notice the officer's hands.

"That it did. On this very dock late last night. The wounded man gave a fair description of his attacker. It put me in mind of Kingston."

"I doubt the man I fed breakfast had a knife, and if he'd had any money, he wouldn't have had reason to be hungry, now would he?"

"Knives can be pitched in the river easy enough, and perhaps you ran up on him before the taverns came open."

Brother Asa seemed to ponder the officer's statements a moment before he spoke. "That could be, I suppose."

Isaac's leg muscles tightened, ready to run if Brother Asa turned his eyes toward his hiding place behind the barrels. It would be years before Isaac would see the light of day again if Officer Neal collared him. It wouldn't matter that he was innocent. He'd been on the dock. Others had seen him there. While he hadn't stabbed anyone—would never even consider stabbing anyone for money—nobody would believe him. Nobody. Perhaps not even Brother Asa. Isaac held his breath and waited.

The two men out by the wagon seemed to be waiting too as they eyed one another. Finally the officer said, "You weren't down on the docks in the midnight hours, were you, Brother Asa?"

"You're not thinking on me as a suspect, now are you, Officer? You know a Shaker man owns no weapons of violence. It is contrary to our beliefs."

"I'll wager you have a knife in your pocket."

"A tool only, I assure you." Brother Asa reached in his pocket and pulled out a small folded knife. He held it in the flat of his palm out toward Officer Neal. "Do you have need to inspect it?"

The officer took the knife, opened out the blade, and held it up to the sun. "A fine bit of workmanship, but not much good for anything but sharpening a quill for writing. Or carving your lover's initials on a tree." The man laughed as he folded the knife up and held it back toward Brother Asa. "Guess as a Shaker man you've never had call to dull the blade doing any of that kind of carving."

Brother Asa laughed along with him as he took the knife but didn't slip it back in his pocket. "For a truth. We give our hearts to God and he has little need of initials carved on a tree trunk. Better to make a fine piece of furniture or a building from the good wood he gives us."

Both men were still eyeing the knife. After a moment, Officer Neal said, "I've been looking for just such a knife."

"Then here." Brother Asa held the knife out to him. "Take this one. A gift in appreciation of your work keeping the peace down here on the dock."

The officer took the knife and polished it against his sleeve. "I always knew you were a generous man, Brother Asa. In return I'll offer you a bit of advice. If you run across that Kingston again, steer wide of him. He's nothing but trouble and I'd hate to have to haul you before Judge Carver. The man has been low on mercy since he lost his daughter. Might be best if you left town and didn't come back this way for a while."

"A wise man listens to good advice."

"That he does." The officer pitched the knife up into the air and caught it in his fist before he jammed it down in his pocket and turned to head back down the riverfront.

Isaac stayed where he was.

Brother Asa tested the tautness of the rope, tying down his load, and then went to check his horses' harness. He rubbed the patient horses' noses as he said, "All right, boys. Looks like we're ready to head home. Could be we'll make it to the east edge of town about the middle of the afternoon. There's a creek there where you can get a little grass and water before we start our journey to Harmony Hill. Could be we might find somebody there who needs some peace in his life. Could be."

The little Shaker never looked toward Isaac's hiding spot behind the barrels, but Isaac knew the words were for him and not the horses. Isaac would be there. What other choice did he have? Leaving Louisville wouldn't mean he'd forget Ella. He would never forget Ella.

6

From the time she was a little girl, Lacey had embraced spring like a miracle in the making as soon as the sun began to warm each year. It was a joyous fever she had caught from her mother. The minute she spotted the first dandelion bloom of the season, her mother would throw open the cabin door to the sun and shuck her high-top shoes and stockings to run barefoot with Lacey and Junie down to the creek. Often as not, their feet turned blue as they splashed through the chilly creek water that hadn't been so quick to give up winter as the bright little yellow flower. But that didn't stop them from doing their spring dance.

Then they'd go back to the cabin and find the warmest spot on the porch to sit in the sun until their feet thawed out, while her mother told them stories about doing the same spring dance back in Virginia with her mother. At last, with their feet pink again and Junie's eyes heavy with sleep, Lacey and her mother would go inside and bake a cake yellow as that dandelion bloom.

After her mother died, Lacey tried to keep the spring dance going for Junie. The first year they just sat down on the rocks in the creek and cried. They tried to make the cake, but it came out of the oven so tough it bounced when they threw it out to the chickens. The second year the Widow Jackson whipped them for getting their skirts wet, but they made mud cakes with dandelion flower icing and both took a bite. The third year Junie was gone to live with their aunt in Virginia, and Lacey stood in the creek and let the water run over her feet until she thought her toes might fall off. She was too sad to do any splashing, but she didn't forget the dance. The next year she was taking care of Miss Mona, and when spring came, her feet felt like dancing again. While there wasn't any creek close by, Miss Mona said it was likely a spring dance could happen anywhere bare feet could touch the ground. Just so long as it was out of sight of Preacher Palmer and the church deacons. And then Miss Mona sat at the kitchen table and stirred up a yellow cake almost as good as the one Lacey's mama made.

While Miss Mona was mixing up the cake, Lacey told her some of the stories her mother used to tell about doing the spring dance back in Virginia. Since Lacey couldn't remember every word, she added a little here and there, but she told Miss Mona some of it was made up. So it wasn't like she was telling lies or anything. Just stories.

"Nothing wrong with telling stories," Miss Mona assured her. "The good Lord himself told stories to help people know how to live. They're called parables."

"Did he make them up?" Lacey asked.

"I don't know. Could be they were stories about real people, but he told them like stories. You remember the one about the prodigal son and how he wanted to eat the pig feed. Or how about that story you read me just the other day about that king who had trouble getting people to come to the wedding banquet for his son? That's a fine story."

"But Jesus was teaching things with his stories. My stories are oft as not just silliness," Lacey said. She licked the batter off the spoon Miss Mona handed her.

"Not silliness. Your stories connect you with your mother and with Junie and your aunt in Virginia and with me. And someday when you have children of your own, you'll be telling them stories that will connect them back to all of us too. No, not silliness at all."

Lacey knew about the parables. She'd heard Preacher Palmer expound on this or that one in sermons, and she'd read a lot of them to Miss Mona from her Bible. But try as she might, she couldn't bring to mind any Scripture stories that might be about doing a spring dance. She told Miss Mona as much.

"What about the parable of the sower?" Miss Mona said with a smile as she handed Lacey the cake pan to put in the oven. "You have to sow seeds in the spring."

After Lacey put the pan in the oven and stoked the fire to keep the stove warm enough to bake the cake, Miss Mona helped her find the sowing seed parable in the Bible. When Lacey finished reading, Miss Mona sat silent a few minutes the way she always did. She never spoke up on the meaning of the Bible words until she'd given them proper consideration.

At last she said, "And I'll pray for you, Lacey, that the seed of the gospel will always find good soil within your heart. That the nourishing rain will fall on your head and the tares won't grow around you. I don't worry about the seed falling on rocky ground. Your heart is too soft to ever be that hard."

Lacey didn't like thinking about that parable now. Not this spring when all was hard ground inside her. On the way to church after a rain in April, her eye was drawn to a spot of yellow in the wet grass. It wasn't the first dandelion of spring. She knew that, but she'd closed off her eyes to seeing any of the others. This one just popped up in front of her eyes before she had time to look another way. Lacey didn't point it out to Rachel, who was walking along beside her. Instead she stepped off the path and stomped down hard on the yellow bloom and then twisted her shoe around like she was killing a wasp.

Even before she lifted her foot up to see the smear of yellow smashed down in the soft ground, she was sorry. She might as well have ground her heel right down on her own heart. And not just her heart, but the hearts of her mother and Miss Mona too. She wanted to fall to her knees there on the wet ground and try to piece that little flower back together. She wanted to pluck it up out of the mud and hold it gently in her hand to show Rachel. She wanted to run to some creek somewhere and strip off her shoes and stockings and remember joy. And even if she couldn't dredge up any of that joy in her own heart, she wanted to plant it in Rachel's heart the same as her mama had once planted it in hers.

But she couldn't. Not right there beside the path in sight of the church house with Preacher Palmer walking two paces ahead of her. He stared back at her impatiently as he slowed to keep from leaving her and Rachel too far behind. She wanted to tell him to go on ahead. He liked to stand in the doorway and greet each arriving member. He didn't want her beside him at the church door. She had to perch stiff and solemn on the front pew, the proper place for a preacher's wife. A place that had been empty since Miss Mona got too weak to make the short walk to the church house some time back. A place that needed to be empty still, in Lacey's mind. On Sunday morning when she sat there letting the preacher's words stream past her ears without taking in any of their sounds, it was like she was sitting on a board with nails poking up through it. Or maybe that was just all the eyes of the church people stabbing into her back.

Those stabs weren't as bad as the preacher's eyes following

her around in the kitchen back at the house. It was getting harder and harder to stay out of the sight of those eyes, even though it was the first thing she prayed about every morning and the last thing she prayed about every night. *Dear Lord, make me invisible.* Not to everybody. Not to Rachel. Just to the preacher and the Ebenezer church people who seemed to be dropping by twice as often as before Miss Mona took flight for heaven. It was like they needed to make sure she didn't find any escape from that prickly spot of having to act like the preacher's wife.

What was it Miss Sadie Rose had told her some days before? "A body makes her bed, she has to lie in it."

She hadn't been talking about Lacey. Not directly at any rate. She'd been pretending to talk about some other poor soul who found herself in a patch of trouble, but Lacey had felt the words pound down on her. Lacey had wanted to tell Sadie Rose that was a bed she'd been keeping out of, but that wasn't anybody's business but hers and Preacher Palmer's. She knew without bringing it up in uncomfortable words that the preacher wouldn't be wanting anybody to know about their strange agreed-upon union. Nearly once every day he turned her Bible open to that passage about a woman cleaving to her husband and left it open so she'd have to see it. She didn't have to ponder on the word *cleave* he underlined to know the meaning he meant her to note.

Lacey could tell their agreement was wearing on the man as the days went by. The furrows between his eyes were getting deeper, and he hadn't preached anything but brimstone sermons for three Sundays in a row.

At midnight the Friday night before she'd seen the dandelion on the way to the church house, he'd climbed up the stairs to where she and Rachel slept in the little attic room. Some of the church folk had fixed up the space under the roof for

Lacey when she first came to take care of Miss Mona. While there was barely room enough for the bed and no place for a grown person to stand up straight with the way the ceiling sloped down on both sides, Lacey had always felt as warm and safe in the little room as a downy chick under a mother hen's wings.

At least until Preacher Palmer climbed up the steep stairs and hunched over to come to the bed. Without the first word, he sat down on the edge of the bed and took off his shoes before he laid himself down next to her.

Once Rachel went to sleep, didn't much short of a booming thunderstorm ever wake her up, but any little noise made Lacey's eyes pop open. She'd heard the first step of the preacher's foot on the bottom stair and hardly dared to breathe as she prayed she was dreaming. She even reached up to touch her eyes in hopes she'd find them closed. But they were wide open, staring out at the grainy darkness, and her heart began to pound inside her chest. Not a good pounding. She felt as brittle as new-formed ice on a pond, and she wasn't sure but what the way her heart was working overtime that it might not just cause her whole body to break into a thousand pieces.

He lay there on the edge of the bed beside her for a long time—or what seemed like a long time to Lacey. She kept up the pretense of being asleep even though she figured her whole body was jumping with the force of her heart pounding in her chest.

Finally when it was all she could do to keep from screaming, he reached over and laid his hand on her stomach. She felt a quiver in his fingers as he moved his hand back and forth across her nightgown in the kind of strokes a body might use to settle down a fractious horse before trying to put a harness on it. She couldn't move away from him. Rachel was on the other side of her with the bed pushed up against the wall so the little girl couldn't roll out.

"You promised." Even though she whispered the words, her voice sounded loud in the stillness of the dark room.

His hand stopped moving. Any gentleness he had been intending drained away, and his hand felt hard on her stomach. She braced herself for the anger she felt gathering in that hand, but she said the next words anyway. "On Miss Mona's grave, you promised."

That wasn't exactly true, but Lacey needed some way to bring Miss Mona in front of his eyes. Even if it did make him mad as old Balaam was at his reluctant donkey in that Bible story before the Lord let the donkey do some talking. She'd take a blow from him before a caress.

But he didn't hit her. Instead he pulled away his hand, and even though he wasn't touching her up close anymore, she could feel how stiff his body got to match her own. After a long moment, he sat up on the edge of the bed and picked up his shoes. He stood up and stared down at Lacey. It was dark, but she could see the shape of his head and knew his eyes must look how they did when he was in the pulpit talking about sinners. Hard. Condemning.

He didn't whisper when he spoke. He said the words right out loud. "I didn't promise forever." The words hung there in the air over her, even after he turned away from the bed and made his way to the top of the narrow stairs.

There he stopped. She didn't look toward him. She kept staring straight up at the ceiling, trying not to think about anything except how the dark air separated and made little circles the longer she stared at it without blinking. The truth was, bringing Miss Mona in front of his eyes had brought an unease to Lacey's mind as well. She couldn't imagine what Miss Mona would think about what was happening. She had loved the preacher. More than she ever loved Lacey. What if she was looking the same kind of condemnation down on Lacey as the preacher was?

The motes of darkness were about to press down on Lacey and smother her before the preacher finally spoke the words she knew he'd stopped there to say. "Not forever, Lacey Bishop. Come summer you'll have to act the proper wife. That will be nigh on a year since Mona passed on. More than enough time for both of us."

"You promised," Lacey whispered again.

He made a sound of disgust and didn't bother trying to quiet his steps as he stomped down the stairs. He didn't go to his bed but went out the front door. It was near dawn before she heard him come back in the house.

That morning he looked at the fried eggs on the plate she set in front of him at breakfast. He poked them with a fork and said, "You got them too done." Then he picked up the plate and threw it against the wall. The plate shattered all over the floor and the soft yolk of the egg ran down the wall.

Rachel stared at him with eyes as big as saucers and let out a yowl like as how a piece of the plate had hit her.

When Lacey started toward her to comfort her, Preacher Palmer grabbed Lacey's arm. "Fix my eggs right first."

She wanted to shake loose of him, but his grip was hard on her and his eyes even harder. When she still hesitated, he said, "You're my wife. Do as I say."

She went to the stove and broke more eggs in the skillet. She thought about catching him looking another way and spitting in them, but it did little good to answer meanness with meanness. She shut her ears to Rachel's wails and cooked the eggs and put them on a new plate. There wasn't an iota of difference in the eggs on the second plate and the first, but when she set it in front of him, he pushed his fork into them and ate.

Lacey sat down beside Rachel and let the little girl climb up in her lap.

"She's too big for you to baby like that," Preacher Palmer said.

Lacey pretended he hadn't spoken as she rubbed the child's back and whispered, "Shh. Stop your crying."

The preacher stabbed a biscuit and smeared butter on it. He pointed his fork toward the egg splattered on the wall and the shards of glass on the floor. "Best clean that up."

Lacey kissed the top of Rachel's head. Then she set her on her feet. "Get me the broom, Rachel."

She was still wiping the yellow yolk off the wall when Preacher Palmer pushed his chair back from the table. She could feel his eyes on her, but she didn't turn to look at him. She just kept rubbing the wall even after no spot of egg was left on it.

"All this is your fault, Lacey. Every bit your fault."

Her spirit fired up at that. She turned to stare straight at him. "A man of God shouldn't fool himself with lies."

She thought for a minute he might sling another plate straight at her head, but then he lowered his eyes and his shoulders drooped. "Our Father in heaven, what is to become of us?" he said softly before he turned and went toward the door.

So it was no wonder that, with the clouds gathered around them so thick, no sign of spring had made its way through. That was why she hadn't been out looking for the first spot of yellow spring the way she usually did. A heart had to be ready for spring, and hers was stuck in winter.

But as she stared down at the crushed dandelion bloom, she felt Rachel's little hand reaching into hers. It wasn't right to keep the spring from her. Wasn't Rachel the reason she'd agreed to this farce of a marriage? Spring came in spite of clouds. Dandelions bloomed and little girls needed to dance in the spring.

That afternoon after Preacher Palmer went out with Deacon Crutcher to visit the sick, Lacey told Rachel to go looking for a dandelion in the backyard. A smile was spread all the way across the little girl's face when a few minutes later she came running back to the porch with a round yellow dandelion bloom clutched in her hand.

"Do we get to do the dance?" Rachel asked her.

Lacey's heart hurt as she stared down at the child's hopeful face and thought about how rare Rachel's smiles had been in the last few weeks. As rare as her own. She'd agreed to wed the preacher to keep mothering Rachel, and now here she was shirking her duty, pulling sadness over on her when there wasn't a bit of need in that. Even if come summer she'd have to attend to the preacher's demands. Married women did as much everywhere. Cleaved to their husbands.

Lacey grinned at Rachel and sat down on the porch steps to start unlacing her shoes. Rachel giggled and kicked off hers too. They danced all across the backyard right out into the edge of the woods to a little wet-weather spring the rain had made. The water was cold, just the way it was supposed to be, as they stomped and laughed. Lacey didn't even look over her shoulder to be sure no church people had come to the preacher's house to check that his wife was attending to her proper place.

With their skirt tails soaked and mud between their toes, they went back out of the woods, but instead of going straight to the house, Lacey led Rachel over to the church house and into the graveyard. She'd been putting off visiting Miss Mona's grave though she'd promised Rachel they'd plant flowers there. It had been too hard to think about Miss Mona in that cold winter ground. Too hard to think about her being gone forever.

They both got quiet as they solemnly walked toward the new grave. Lacey's heart started pounding almost as hard as it had the night the preacher had climbed up to the attic room. Maybe they shouldn't have done the spring dance with Miss Mona so newly gone. The gloom was coming back to sit heavy on her shoulders, when all of a sudden, Rachel jerked on Lacey's hand and started jumping up and down.

"Look, Lacey. Look. Mama's doing the spring dance with us."

Lacey could scarcely believe her eyes. Bright yellow dandelions were blooming all across Miss Mona's grave like as how somebody had sowed them there. A blanket of yellow spring.

It was a sign. Miss Mona was telling her or maybe it was the good Lord who was telling her that spring comes. Even when a person tries to close it out. It comes.

Rachel ran ahead to the edge of the grave and reached down to the dandelion blooms. Lacey started to yell at her not to pick any, but she held back the words as the little girl ran her hands across the blooms like she might be stroking a soft pillow. Lacey sat down right beside her and told the stories about the spring dances her mother told her and about the spring dances with her mother and Junie and the ones with Miss Mona. And finally the story of this spring dance when spring was late to come to Lacey.

"You think Mama's hearing your stories?" Rachel asked as she leaned against Lacey.

"Oh yes. I'm sure of it. That's why all these sunspots sprouted here on her grave. So we'd know it. So we'd know that spring comes, and with the spring somehow things will be all right. Now we've got to go make that cake."

They had the cake in the oven and the mud washed off their feet and their skirt tails drying by the stove before the preacher came home.

The next day the Shaker men came peddling their bean seeds.

7

As Isaac made his way to the outskirts of the city where Brother Asa had promised his horses a rest before starting for the Shaker village, he didn't spot any of the watch. But they could be after him. They might even put a price on his head that would have everybody hunting him. He imagined his description on flyers spread across town like the ones he'd seen for runaway slaves. *Fugitive white male, 25, brown hair, shifty brown eyes. Dangerous. Reward offered for his capture.*

There hadn't been time to print anything like that. Isaac knew that. All the same, he cringed every time he stepped from the shadows into the open. So he slipped down back streets and cut across backyard fences. Here and there a dog chased after him, barking loud enough to raise the neighborhood. Each time Isaac's heart bounded up into his throat as he could almost feel hands reaching to grab his collar and drag him in front of the judge.

When at last he left the city streets behind, he wasn't sure he'd find the Shaker man still waiting, but Brother Asa was right where he said he'd be, leaning against his wagon while his horses picked at the spring grass.

"I was beginning to doubt you'd come," Brother Asa said when he spotted Isaac.

"Yet you waited." Isaac looked up at the sun. It was well past mid-afternoon.

"Yea, so I did. And have you come with your mind made up to seek peace at Harmony Hill?" Asa climbed up to the wagon seat and looked down at Isaac.

"I don't know about peace." Isaac thought that might be too much to ask. "But food and shelter I'll admit to chasing after."

"Then food and shelter you will find. The Ministry will be glad enough to give you a bed in our Gathering Family. We have much need of strong, young men in our midst with the spring planting season upon us." Brother Asa picked up the reins, and the two horses reached for a last mouthful of grass before they raised their heads. "Spring is more often a season of parting rather than joining for those uncertain of the Shaker way."

"I once worked on a farm. I know about planting."

Isaac's legs felt heavy as he climbed up to sit beside Brother Asa. He told himself it was because he'd been running. It had nothing to do with reluctance to leave Ella's town behind. He looked over his shoulder as Brother Asa guided the horses up onto the road and headed them east. There was nothing for him back there. He didn't need to stand beside Ella's grave to keep his love for her alive in his heart. Yet when he turned back to look ahead again and tried to pull up her face, her image kept drifting away from his mind's eye as if this time she was refusing to allow him to carry her away from her beloved Louisville.

He shut his eyes and forced her image out of the shadows of his mind. Her face the day they first met. The day the preacher pronounced them man and wife. The day they left for the West. Her face in death. The memories marched through his mind, some stabbing his heart. But he remembered. There was no reason to stay near her body in the grave. And every reason to get far away from her father. Especially now with the watch searching him out as a thief and a man capable of murder.

They hanged murderers. Not the end Isaac was after. While he had been considering the advantages of dying, he didn't want to partake of those advantages as an innocent man on the gallows. Better to join the living dead. That should be punishment enough.

No chasing after adventure in the West. No loved one to lie down beside at night. No children to swing high in the air above his head. Nothing but work and discipline and preaching. Punishment enough.

Once out on the road, Brother Asa flicked the reins to encourage the horses forward. He didn't look over at Isaac or speak again as the horses settled into an easy pace.

Silence hung over them. Not a good silence. At least to Isaac's ears. He imagined unspoken questions bouncing between them with every jolt of the wagon, but when he peeked over at Brother Asa, he could see no lines of worry on his face. Nor did he slide his eyes over toward Isaac even when a horse and rider galloped up behind them.

Isaac didn't share the Shaker's calm. His heart began pounding again as he imagined one of the watch riding after him. He scarcely dared breathe until the rider overtook them and passed by with nothing more than the slight nod of acknowledgment one traveler gives another.

Isaac eased his grip on the wagon seat and tried to force his breath in and out slow and steady. He'd been poised to leap off the wagon and run for the woods across the field. Until that moment, he hadn't realized how used to staying out of sight in the shadows of the city he'd become. Now here on the wagon seat, he felt exposed to every eye, even when the road was empty and the only eyes were those of the cattle in the pastures.

Brother Asa reached behind the seat and pulled a felt hat nearly identical to his own out of a wooden box. "Here. Your head might need protection from the sun. I took these for sale, but few took note of my wares this trip."

"The sun is sinking," Isaac said as he put the hat on and pulled it down low on his forehead. Not as good as a shadow in the alley, but at least part of his face was hidden.

"Yea, the day is fading, but the moon is nigh full this night. A good time to travel the roads and get us closer to our destination." Brother Asa looked over at Isaac. "Of course, at times there are more scalawags abroad in the night, but we will trust Mother Ann to watch over us and give us safe journey."

Again the silence fell over them. Isaac kept his eyes on the horses' rumps and listened to the sound of their hooves against the hard bed of the road. It should have been a peaceful sound combined with that of the birds singing their spring songs in the trees alongside the road. But it wasn't.

Finally Isaac said, "I didn't stab that man last night."

"I know that, my brother," the little Shaker said.

"How?" Isaac turned to study the man's profile. His face was calm and unworried as it had been ever since they met. "You never laid eyes on me before this morning. And I've already told you I am responsible for a death."

Brother Asa glanced over at Isaac. "So you say, but your eyes say different. The eyes are the window into one's soul. You may have seen death. Of that I have no doubt. But you have never carried desire in your heart to cause such. Even your own."

"That was no more than cowardice. Plain and simple." Isaac looked down at his hands on his knees. The handkerchief was still wrapped around his hand. He slowly uncurled it and stared at the cut. It was beginning to fester.

"If that is so, it was a gift to you."

"The gift of cowardice." Isaac's voice showed his scorn for that. "Not much of a gift."

"Gifts come in many guises. While it may seem that cowardice would not be what one would desire, at the same time it has given you the gift of another chance to be the man the Eternal Father would have you be. Have you never considered that? What path our Lord may have set before you?"

"I was going west. That was the path I wanted."

"Why?"

"There's opportunity there. Land for a man ready to work for it. Fortune perhaps." His words echoing in his head mocked him. The same words he'd said to Ella and her father.

"Fortune." Brother Asa shook his head. "Fool's gold most often. Fortune brings no man happiness. Happiness must reside within one's soul. Then we can reach for fortune in the gifts of the spirit."

"Is fortune one of those?" Isaac asked. "A gift of the spirit?"

"Nay, not fortune as you speak of it. True fortune lies in the likes of these. Love for your brothers and sisters. The desire to give your heart to God and your hands to work. Tasks that satisfy the need to be useful to our society. Worship that fills your being with light. Songs of joy. Peace."

Isaac was quiet a moment as he considered the man's words. Such gifts seemed out of his reach. "Do you have those gifts?" he finally asked.

"I have been blessed with such gifts often in my time with the Believers."

"You've never felt a fighting of the spirit? Nothing that would make you think you might find more in another place?"

"Nay. The Believer's life has always filled me all the way

up to the top." Brother Asa laughed a little. "But could be that's because there isn't much of me to fill to get to my top. Even before I danced my legs off to the knees." His laugh got heartier.

Isaac was surprised to feel an answering laugh swelling up inside him. He hadn't truly felt the urge to laugh since Ella came down with the fever. He never thought to laugh again. He never thought to deserve to laugh again. Not with Ella in the ground because of him. The good feeling shriveled within him as he reached for the gloom and pulled it back around him the way he might slip on a well-worn and familiar coat.

If Brother Asa noticed, he made no comment as they settled into the silence and rode away from the sunset into the long shadows of evening.

They stopped to rest the horses in the deep of the night as the moon began to sink toward the western horizon. The little Shaker offered Isaac his bedroll, but Isaac waved aside his generosity and curled up on the wagon seat instead. He was used to sleeping in corners away from the light. There in the fading moonlight with stars decorating the sky seemed the best bed he'd had for weeks.

At daylight they were back on the road. Isaac expected Brother Asa to preach the Shaker way at him as they rode along, but the man seemed content with the silence. Once when he handed the reins over to Isaac, he said, "It's good to have a companion on such a trip. It's the usual thing to travel in twos, but Brother Andrew came up sick the morning we were to leave."

"Were there no other men who could come with you?"

"Yea, there are many brothers, but they were all about their duties and a bit of solitude is good for the spirit at times."

"I guess I'm spoiling that for you," Isaac said.

"Not at all, my brother. You appear to have a gift for silence. Not a common gift for one so young."

Isaac started to refute him. Deny any gifts. The man was making him into a Shaker before he even got to the borders of the village. Bouncing along hiding under a Shaker hat, practicing the Shaker gift of silence. What other gifts would he have to practice? Would they expect him to dance and whirl the way he'd heard Shakers worshiped?

He thought about Marian and how solemn she'd looked the last time he'd visited her. Nothing like the little sister who'd trailed after him through the first years of their lives, helping him catch toads and grasshoppers. His little sister Marian from those easy years before the steamboat boiler explosion had taken their father—that sister he could imagine dancing and whirling. It was the new sister Marian, the Shaker sister, he couldn't imagine doing the same.

He wanted to ask Brother Asa about that. About the dancing. But at the same time he didn't want to break into the man's reverie. He felt it ungrateful to so quickly throw off this gift of silence Brother Asa had claimed for him. So he just watched the horses plodding on, lifting one foot and then another before doing it all again. Moving forward without any sense of when their journey might be finished. A feeling he shared as the sun rose higher in the sky.

Not a feeling his father would ever share. His father was a man who made things happen, who chased after life. Who knew what he wanted and was ready to risk it all to make it happen. Isaac wondered what his father would think about him now. A man with nothing but defeat perched on his shoulders. A coward hiding under a Shaker hat. Isaac's mother had surely been wrong when she claimed he was like his father.

"Did you know your father?" Isaac broke the silence that had stretched between them for much of the morning.

Brother Asa kept his eyes on the road ahead of them without saying anything for so long that Isaac began to think the man was so deep in his desired solitude that Isaac's words hadn't made it through to his ears. But then he inclined his head a little toward Isaac. "I ever seek to know our heavenly Father, but I'm guessing you are speaking of a father of the world."

"The father you were born to," Isaac said.

"I have no memory of such a father," Brother Asa said. "But Brother Harper was a good father to me once I came to Harmony Hill. Not that he would have called himself such. He was the older brother who guided my way along the Believer's path. Then there was Brother Martin who taught me my letters and how to do sums. And I can't fail to mention Brother Carl who taught me the value of honest labor. No father of the kind you mean, but many brothers who taught me much."

"Do you think your father died and that's why your mother brought you to the Shakers?"

"That could be. Such an end—death—is the lot of us all."

"My father died. Everybody used to say I was like him." Isaac kept his eyes straight ahead.

"And were you?"

"I don't know. I wanted to be. He made things happen."

"Yet he died."

"Not of his own cause."

"Ah. On the steamboat that exploded."

"Right."

"The world is full of such sorrows." Brother Asa shook his head sadly.

Isaac looked around at the Shaker man. "Shakers die too, don't they?"

"That they do." Brother Asa smiled a little. "All men die.

86

But for a Believer it is but a step across a divide from this paradise we have made here on earth to the paradise that awaits us on the heavenly shores. It is not a fearsome step."

"Fearsome." Isaac echoed the word as he looked back out toward the road. Everything he'd done lately seemed fearsome. Even sitting beside this peaceful little man riding back toward his village. Not something his father would have ever thought to do. No, his father would have gotten on another steamboat. His father would have ridden down the river. His father would have found a way to make some more money, to keep alive his westward dream if that was the dream he'd had. But Isaac was not his father. He was a man with a gift of cowardice. Not a gift his father would have been likely to embrace.

"All life has sorrows, my brother, of one sort or another, and while you seem to have experienced a good bit of such in your life, you will come to see that sorrow can strengthen your spirit. Our Mother Ann once said that if we took all sorrow out of life, we would take away all richness, depth, and tenderness. Sorrow is the furnace that melts selfish hearts together in love. And in truth, it is often sorrow that brings new brothers and sisters into our midst where they find that love." Brother Asa reached over to lightly touch Isaac's arm. "You will see."

Isaac didn't know why he was so worried about finding himself in this village of peace Brother Asa kept offering him so freely. So what if he never found that peace? So what if he could imagine his father frowning down on him? So what if his mother's words telling him to live like his father were mockery as they echoed in his ears? At least he wouldn't find the jail or gallows the judge was eager for him to find.

The sun was once more sinking in the west when Isaac spotted the first buildings of the Shaker Village rising up into the sky ahead of them. Brother Asa sat up taller on the wagon seat, and the horses, either noting the difference in the reins or perhaps smelling home, picked up their pace.

"Almost home," Brother Asa said. "A good place to be. Home."

Home, Isaac thought, and wondered what the word would ever mean to him again. He couldn't imagine embracing this place as home, but then Marian had. Marian did. She had been born to the same father as Isaac.

Behind the buildings and across the fields he could see trees, thick and dark in the dusky light. Beyond the woods and down the cliff, the river ran past the village. Marian had written of the landing the Shakers had there and how Isaac could stop to visit her if he was on the river. There were many avenues of escape from the village if a man so desired. If a man wasn't wrapped too thickly in his gift of cowardice. A man different from Isaac.

The village pathways were deserted as Brother Asa drove the wagon through the village and out toward one of the barns. "I had hoped we'd be here in time for the evening meal, but perhaps one of the sisters will take pity on us and bring us a bit of sustenance out of the regular time. If so, you will be expected to eat whatever is offered."

"You'll have no worries there."

"First we must tend to the horses. Then we'll visit the bathhouse and get you some proper clothes before we take you to Elder Homer. He is in charge of the Gathering Order." He pulled the horses to a stop in front of a barn and waited while Isaac climbed down to open the doors.

"Where is everybody?" Isaac looked around while Asa guided the horses inside the barn. Isaac left the doors open to the fading light and went to hold the horses while the Shaker man climbed down from the wagon. "All in bed already?"

"Nay. The retiring bell rings at nine o'clock. Now the brothers and sisters are gathered in each family house for worship practice."

"Practice?" Isaac looked across the back of the horses at the Shaker man who was unhooking the harness. "You practice worship? I thought that just happened."

"We labor the worship dances in good order and the steps must be practiced. Plus there are new songs to learn. This is Tuesday, so the families spend time in worship and practice. If you listen well, you might hear their music."

Isaac stood still and listened. He could hear nothing but the horses making anxious noises for their supper and the bugs and tree frogs beginning their night songs. A clear evidence of spring, along with the fresh smell of the evening air rising up off the new pasture grass. When he left the McElroys' farm, he never thought he would miss the country, but he wasn't sorry to have the sounds of country in his ears again.

"I don't hear any music," he said after a moment.

"Oh well," Brother Asa said. "Perhaps it is only an echo I hear in my heart. Not any real sounds coming down from the upper rooms of the family houses. You will hear the songs soon enough."

They brushed the horses down, led them to the watering trough, and fed them grain. Brother Asa talked to them softly as he worked. At last, as once more the moon had risen to give them light, they led the animals out to a pasture.

"It's a warm night. They will be glad to be in the open." Brother Asa looked over at Isaac. "You have a nice touch with the animals. Perhaps that is another gift that will stand you in good stead here among the Believers."

"I'll do whatever you say."

"The elders and eldresses of each family decide the duties with guidance from the Ministry. But have no worries. The work duties are rotated so no one brother is stuck in a tedious and unwelcome task overlong."

"Family? I thought there were no families." Isaac frowned.

"Not as families of the world. Families of Believers. It may sound odd to you now, but it will become simple in time." Brother Asa put his hand on Isaac's shoulder. "Come, let us go wash the dirt of the world off our bodies. There is still much to do before we can lay our heads down on a pillow this night. And I admit my energy is ebbing."

Isaac followed the little man along the pathway past some smaller buildings that were closed and shuttered for the night. As they came near an impressive brick building rising three stories high and with many windows indicating a number of rooms, Isaac heard the singing Brother Asa had asked him to listen for when they were at the barn. The music of many voices spilled out the open windows on the upper floor of the building, along with the flickering light of lamps or candles.

"I hear the singing now," he said.

"Yea, a fine sound." Brother Asa stopped in the pathway and looked up. "The sound of home."

It didn't sound like home to Isaac. It just sounded odd. Very odd. But oddness he was ready to embrace in order to stop the growl in his stomach. And to keep away from the gallows.

8

The minute she set eyes on the two men, Lacey knew there was something unusual about them. It was more than how they stood side by side in front of the porch dressed as alike as any pair of twins in a storybook. Brown trousers held up by black suspenders, shirts without proper collars and yet buttoned all the way up to their neck in spite of the way the sun was shining down warm on their shoulders, and then those broad-brimmed hats. Even their hair was alike. Bangs cut straight across their foreheads and long hair in the back spilling down out of their hats. But it was more than how they didn't look much like Deacon Crutcher and other Ebenezer men who came to seek out Preacher Palmer. It was the way they stood there waiting for the preacher to invite them to speak. As if the sun had stopped sliding across the sky and they had all the time in the world.

She didn't know they were Shakers. Not until they pushed a couple of seed packets toward Preacher Palmer and asked him if he would be willing to guide them to some of his flock's houses that might be in need of such. They offered free packages of bean and cucumber seeds for his help.

One of the men looked to be near the age of Preacher Palmer. The other somewhat younger. Older than Lacey, but not by very many years. She stared straight at him and had to bite her tongue to keep from asking right out loud what it was like being a Shaker. She might have unloosed her tongue if they'd been alone, even though Miss Mona had taught her such direct questions were considered rude more times than not. Could be the young Shaker thought her stare rude enough without the questions, because he cast his eyes down toward the ground away from her.

Preacher Palmer had been sitting out on the porch reading his Bible since the morning sun burned off the fog. She'd even considered carrying his dinner to him come twelve o'clock, but before she got it out there, he'd come in and sat lonely at the table and ate what she put before him without complaint. Then without a word, he'd pushed back from the table and made his way back out the front door to settle in the porch rocker again.

Lacey figured he felt easier in the spirit outside. For sure she felt easier in the spirit when he was out of the house. He hadn't thrown any more plates or given the first indication of thinking about laying his hand on her again. But the droop was still on his shoulders.

He'd carried it all through Sunday even while he was in the pulpit reading the Scripture. When he'd come back to the house after his Sunday visiting, he'd sat at the table and ate a piece of the dandelion yellow cake in total silence before he opened up his Bible and read the verses Paul wrote about it being better for a man of God not to marry. Out loud in his preacher's voice. Lacey had no idea what he was wanting her to think. She'd been expecting him to read the verses about wives submitting to their husbands, and then he came out with those. It was all she could do to keep from saying it was a little late to shut the barn door once the horses had already got out.

They were married. Legal and proper. It didn't much matter that they weren't acting like most married folk. If he stuck to his word, she had till summer to worry about the cleaving part, and then now here he was talking about a man of God not marrying at all. Sometimes Preacher Palmer was more than she could figure out, and she wished Miss Mona would whisper some understanding in her ear. It was a fact Miss Mona knew Preacher Palmer inside and out.

That morning after she combed her hair, Lacey peered into the old mirror that Miss Mona had let her carry up to the attic room when she first came to live at the preacher's house. The mirror didn't give a true reflection. Lacey could lean a bit to the left and make her nose shorter and her chin longer. So she couldn't be sure if the same sort of droop had fallen on her own shoulders as the preacher was wearing. She didn't want it to. Not after she'd finally brought spring to life for Rachel. But she couldn't deny the droop in her spirit, even if she was determined to do her best to hide it.

The Bible didn't promise no trials. Every life had trials and tribulations. Miss Mona had often reminded Lacey that a person had to trust the Lord to hold her hand anytime she had to walk through one of those valleys. *Come unto me, all ye that labor and are heavy laden, and I will give you rest.*

When Lacey had asked Miss Mona what it meant to be heavy laden, the woman had thought a minute before she said, "It's like a horse loaded down with more than the beast can carry. In a way, we're all beasts of burdens in this life at times as we collect worries and sorrows. But the Lord is willing to lift them from us. And give us rest."

That's what Preacher Palmer offered the two Shaker men when they climbed down from their wagon and walked up to the porch to talk to him. "Come on up and take a few minutes rest," he said. When the men hesitated, he held up the Bible off his lap and added, "We can talk the truth of the Word. Yours against mine."

"We have no desire to war our beliefs with yours," the older brother said as he climbed the porch steps and sat in the only other chair. "But we're more than ready to share that which we believe. The way of the Believers. Is that not right, Brother Jacob?"

"Yea, our truths are meant to be shared with those who want to find the true way." The young brother perched on the edge of the porch, still with his eyes cast down and not even looking at the older brother.

"The true way." Preacher Palmer leaned back in his chair and stared out at the yard. "Every man of God seeks that."

Lacey had been hovering in the shadow of the doorway, and now the older brother looked straight at her. "Why don't you tell your daughter to come out where she can hear better?"

"My daughter? She's too young by far for talk of Bible truths," the preacher said before he followed the Shaker man's gaze toward Lacey. Then a dark frown swept across his face, and Lacey thought he might order the men off the porch and to be gone. But instead he closed his eyes for a brief moment and stroked the open Bible in his lap as if the touch of the Bible page could ease his anger. When he opened his eyes and looked back at the older Shaker, his frown was gone. In its place was a weary look. A heavy-laden look. "Lacey's my wife."

"There is much sin in the world," the Shaker said softly.

Lacey heard his words plain enough, even though he spoke them softly, almost under his breath. She looked across at the preacher to see if he'd heard them too. He had his eyes down on the Bible, and she was about to decide he hadn't when he raised his head to look straight at her. Not at the Shaker man.

"For all have sinned and come short of the glory of the Lord," Preacher Palmer said. There was no doubt he was aiming those Bible words directly at her.

She didn't deny his words. Not even in her head. Nobody in this world other than the Lord Jesus ever lived without some kind of sin sneaking into her heart. And she had plenty of them in there bouncing around right then. Wasn't any reason trying to pretend that wasn't true. At least to the Lord. He knew a person's heart.

On the other hand, Lacey didn't see the first need of peeling open her heart to show these two odd Shaker men how some bad seeds were taking root there. Or to show Preacher Palmer either. That was weeding out that she had to do on her knees beside her bed in the quiet of the night. Trouble was that lately, ever since Miss Mona had passed, the weeds seemed to keep sprouting fresh with the first light of morning.

Lacey had hoped it would be different on this Monday after she'd opened her eyes to the dandelions of spring, but that morning as she'd fried the preacher's eggs, she'd still felt burdened down with the years of living as Mrs. Elwood Palmer stretching out without end in front of her eyes. She'd talked stern to herself. A person didn't have to wallow in discontent. Not with spring in the air. Not with a little child looking to her for love.

Once the preacher left the table to find his Bible reading spot out on the porch, she had let Rachel eat a piece of the spring cake for breakfast with her bacon. Rachel had been hopping around happy as a little bird ever since, begging for Maddie stories and making up silly rhymes while they cleaned the kitchen and did the wash. That was what Lacey needed to think on. Rachel and her need for the sunshine of spring after the sadness of the winter.

She aimed to keep that spring alive for Rachel even if the preacher did preach condemnation at her. She let her eyes slide over to the Shaker man there not an arm's length away from her on the porch and expected his eyes to visit the same disapproval on her. But the man's eyes held nothing but kindness in spite of his words about the sin in the world that he had seemed to be directing toward her and the preacher's marital union. Even the young Shaker looked up to give her a gentle smile. Perhaps because Rachel had come out from the kitchen to lean against Lacey's leg and stare at the strange men with big eyes.

Lacey put her hand on the child's back and rejoiced in the feel of her sturdy body under her cotton dress. She and Miss Mona used to pray every morning and night for Rachel to grow strong and healthy. A prayer the Lord had answered. The child rarely even had the sniffles.

"So this must be the daughter you spoke of, Brother Palmer," the older Shaker said. He looked directly at Rachel. "What's your name?"

When she just stared at him without speaking, he went on. "Perhaps it would be well for me to let you know who I am first. Forrest Carson here to make your acquaintance this fine afternoon, along with my brother Jacob Baylor."

He made a motion with his hand toward the young brother whose smile hadn't faded. It made him look even younger. And again Lacey had to bite her lip to keep from asking more questions than she ought. Her curiosity was no reason to give cause for the preacher to complain about her behavior in front of the strangers.

When the silence stretched and began to twang a bit in the air, he went on. "We're from the Shaker village not so many miles from here. Harmony Hill. We've come to offer our fine seeds to those who might not get to a store until after prime planting time. Our seeds are pledged to grow and produce bountifully if planted in good soil. They are just the same as the ones we plant in our own gardens to feed more than three hundred brothers and sisters."

"Three hundred?" The preacher stared across the porch at the Shaker. "That's a goodly number."

"Many have come to us seeking peace and spiritual rest."

"As they do here at Ebenezer Baptist," Preacher Palmer put in as though they had entered some sort of competition of numbers. A competition the preacher had lost before he opened his mouth. The church had never sheltered more than fifty souls at one time since Lacey had known anything about it.

"Yea," Forrest said as he looked directly over at the preacher. "Many seek but few find such peace in the world." His face stayed gentle and kind, but his words seemed to be yanking the rug out from under Preacher Palmer's feet. "I sense you know the truth of that. Even as you search the Scripture for such peace right now."

The preacher's eyes narrowed and his mouth pursed up in a tight circle, as if considering what words would be perfect for putting the visitor in his place or propelling him off the porch to be on his way in short order. Lacey had seen him look such many times in the pulpit before pronouncing some judgment of the Lord in a sermon. But then the righteous anger visibly slid away from him as he looked down and caressed the pages of his Bible again. His voice speaking the Scripture words was calm and quiet. "And into whatsoever house ye enter, first say, 'Peace be to this house.'"

"Would that it could ever be so in houses of the world," the Shaker man said. "As it is in our village."

A very unpeaceful air crept up on the porch to poke at Lacey, even though the Shaker men appeared unaffected by it. Lacey decided it was time enough to stop dwelling on peace or the lack of it and think on more practical things like slaking the men's thirst and planting garden seed. She spoke up.

"I'm Lacey and this is Rachel," she said, as if the Shaker

man had only just asked the child's name. "We'll bring you out some water."

The Shaker man named Forrest followed her lead. "Rachel is a fine name and we'd appreciate a drink, Mrs. Palmer. The sun has been warm on our journey today."

Lacey smiled toward him before she turned back to the kitchen with Rachel still clinging to her apron. Behind her, she heard the Shaker ask, "Do you have other children besides young Rachel?"

"No. No children at all. Not even that child. The girl was left on our doorstep as a babe. We could do no less than take her in."

"An orphan child then?" the younger Shaker said.

"More likely a child of sin. The result of immoral living."

Lacey hurried Rachel on toward the kitchen, hoping the little girl's ears hadn't been as attentive to the talk out on the porch as Lacey's. She pushed some words out to cover the echo of the preacher's words. "Do you think we should offer them some of our spring cake?" she asked Rachel as she lifted a tray down off the shelf and set three glasses on it.

Rachel looked toward the pie safe that held the remains of the cake. "They didn't look hungry."

"Thirsty, but not hungry. At least for cake, right?" Lacey smiled down at Rachel, who looked up at her and nodded seriously with no answering smile. Tears were gathering in the little girl's eyes and her lip was trembling. Lacey dropped the dipper down into the bucket and knelt in front of Rachel. "What's the matter, sweetie?"

"Have they come to take me away?"

Lacey gathered the child close to her. "No, of course not. Why would you ever think that?"

"Papa's mad at me." Rachel whispered the words against Lacey's shoulder.

Lacey stroked her head. "Papa's mad at everybody right now."

"But I'm not really his, am I?"

Lacey leaned back to look at the child's face. "What do you mean, not his?"

"Jimmy told me so last week after church. He said that I don't belong here. That nobody knows where I belong." Rachel hesitated and then rushed on. "He said that you didn't belong here either. That Papa was sinning. And that a preacher's not supposed to sin. He's supposed to get rid of sin." Her words came out all in a spill as if they'd been building up inside her and now had to burst out like a stream of water breaking through a mud dam.

Jimmy was Miss Sadie Rose's youngest, two years older than Rachel. The boy didn't know how to behave. Nearly every Sunday Lacey was nigh on ready to tweak his ear and teach him a few manners. She would have done more than tweak his ear if he'd been in front of her right at that moment, but she supposed he was just repeating what he'd heard from Sadie Rose and Deacon Crutcher. She held back a sigh. There was no way she could tweak their ears and make them stop talking. She'd just have to stand between them and Rachel.

She put her hands on Rachel's shoulders and looked her straight in the eye. "Now you listen to me and you listen good. It's my words that matter. Mine and the ones you remember Miss Mona telling you and the ones the good Lord puts in our hearts. You belong with me. You will always belong with me."

"Like you belonged to your mama?"

"The very same," Lacey said.

"But your mama left." Again Rachel's blue eyes brimmed with tears.

"I still belong to her. She's watching over me from heaven now."

"The way Mama is watching over us?" A couple of tears trickled out of the little girl's eyes to slide down her cheeks.

Lacey mashed her mouth together and blinked hard to keep back the threat of answering tears. Getting all weepy wasn't going to help Rachel one bit. Better to be strong like her mama and Miss Mona. "They're probably standing side by side holding hands watching us this very minute."

Rachel grabbed Lacey's apron front and pulled on it until the tie around Lacey's neck dug into her skin. The child looked almost frantic. "I don't want you to go to heaven to be with them. Promise you'll stay here."

"I'm not going anywhere." Lacey pulled Rachel close in a hug again.

She wanted to keep holding her and holding her, but the preacher was yelling from the porch. "Lacey, bring on out that water. A man could die of thirst."

Lacey leaned back and wiped off Rachel's face with the hem of her apron. "I'll tell you two Maddie stories after I take them their water."

Rachel tried to smile, but it sort of slid off her face without sticking. "I like Maddie stories, Lacey. But I'd trade them for Papa not being mad at us."

Lacey swallowed down another sigh as she ran her hand down Rachel's cheek and stood up. "Some things aren't so easy to change, but things will get better. I know they will. But you don't have to worry about those men in the funny hats. They've just come to sell us seed for our garden. When they go on down the road, we'll dig up a row out by the onions and plant some of their beans."

Rachel climbed up in the rocking chair and held her Maddie doll close while Lacey carried the water out to the porch. The child still looked worried as Lacey pushed open the door and stepped out on the porch where Preacher Palmer was asking, "So it was your Mother Ann, this woman you say is the second coming of Christ, that told you to live celibate lives as sisters and brothers?"

"Yea, that is the way of the Believer. Man and wife relationships cause too much stress and are the reason for much sin in the world," the man named Forrest said.

"I can't disagree with that," the preacher said. His eyes settled on Lacey as if she were offering him an apple off that tree in the Garden of Eden instead of just a glass of water.

She wanted to remind him that it hadn't been her idea to get married, but what good would that do? If it was a sin for them to be wed, it was a sin they'd committed and there wasn't any way out of it. It didn't matter what these Shaker men told him. It didn't matter what Sadie Rose and Deacon Crutcher said. The words of that old preacher, Reverend Williams, echoed in her ears. *Till death do you part.* Those were the words that mattered.

She took the packet of bean seeds the young Shaker handed up to her when she gave him the glass of water and thanked him kindly. Then she left them to argue what couldn't be argued while she went back through the house with Rachel trailing after her. She let Rachel hold the seeds while she got the hoe off the fence and dug up the ground.

The dirt was dark and rich as she turned it over. Rachel giggled when pink fishing worms crawled out onto her hands. The sun was warm on their backs and dandelions bloomed on the edges of the worked ground.

"See. This is good," she heard Miss Mona whispering down at her, and she remembered the sound of her mother's laughter as they splashed in the creek doing their spring dance. She didn't have the first reason to worry about whatever those Shaker men and the preacher were talking about out on the porch. If they convinced the preacher he ought to be celibate, then she wouldn't have to worry about the summer.

Even so, a niggling worry was waking inside her. She shook it away. Preacher Palmer couldn't be thinking of turning Shaker. Not the ordained preacher of the Ebenezer church.

9

At the Shaker village, Isaac entered a different world. A world where the only loud voices he heard were those singing worship songs. A world where he didn't have to make any decisions. He only had to obey the bells that signaled the times for eating and sleep and work duties that were assigned by the elders.

Isaac stepped willingly into the Shaker cocoon. It wasn't like he was actually one of the odd people passing him on the village walkways. So what if he was answering to Brother Isaac and blending in with the other brothers in like clothes and with his hair chopped across the front and back Shaker style. Alike as trees on the horizon, some short and some tall but bedecked in the same green leaves. Yet at times he felt like a tree split by lightning and standing sparse and broken among all the other trees so peacefully lifting their limbs toward the sun.

Even so, he had the Shaker clothes to wear, a Shaker roof over his head, and a Shaker bed to lie down in when night fell and the bell indicated time to retire. While his feet hung off the end of the narrow bed that was little more than a cot, it was still better than an alley doorway or a hole dug out under the docks. It was good to be clean again and to have his stomach full. It was good to get up from bed in the morning when the rising bell rang with a task to do. Something besides hiding in the shadows and wishing for what could no longer be.

He couldn't go west. Elder Homer said that Isaac's desire to put what he wanted over every other consideration was the reason for the trouble in his life. The elder had taken Isaac aside the morning after Brother Asa brought him into the village to hear his story, to determine if he was sincere in repenting his wrongs, and to decide how Isaac would begin his journey in the Shaker village. Isaac would have preferred to do his talking to Brother Asa instead of the stern old elder, but Elder Homer said such could not be.

"It is not our Brother Asa's duty to guide the novitiates. His gifts lie in bearing the odious duty of trading with the world, and while we need such, those exposed much to the world lack the spiritual purity to hear the confessions of young Believers."

No smile softened the elder's face as he spoke, and Isaac couldn't imagine him laughing about anything, but at the same time his sternness was tempered by a kind light in his eyes as he studied Isaac.

After a minute, Isaac said, "What do you want to know?"

"Naught but the truth, my brother. If you have sin in your life, it is best not to let it hide in your heart where it can fester and spread darkness on your soul. Here at Harmony Hill we believe peace comes from confession, for how can our Father God forgive us if we refuse to admit our wrongs?"

Isaac stared down at his hand, newly bandaged by the sister doctor Brother Asa had taken him to after breakfast. She'd cleansed the wound of the dirt and infection with a bubbling potion. Now the elder wished to cleanse his heart.

Isaac looked up at the man, who had to be in his seventies. "You speak all your sins?" he asked.

"All that we recognize, and we continually pray to recognize more as we move toward a perfect life here in our village. Such is not easy to obtain, but with each sin we surrender and each gift of the spirit we accept, we step nearer that center of perfection."

"I am far from perfect," Isaac said.

"As all of us are when we begin our journey." The elder combed his fingers through his gray beard.

Isaac looked down, but even with his eyes lowered, he could feel the elder's sharp eyes probing him for any crack he might pry open to peer inside Isaac's soul. Isaac decided it was best to be honest. "I have done much wrong."

"Those words are a good beginning, but you must not speak only in general terms. Each wrong must be examined and brought out into the light as you determine to leave it behind and move forward along the true way here in our village."

The elder paused a moment, but when Isaac remained silent, he went on. "But you must also know that although we are separate from the world here in our village, we are nevertheless subject to the laws of the land even as the Christ told his followers they were as well, when he walked among men here on the earth. The same was true with our Mother Ann. If you have committed some illegal act in the eyes of the world, my brother, you must admit responsibility for that crime and accept the punishments accorded for such." His voice held no condemnation. It was easy to tell he'd heard many confessions of wrong without allowing his heart to be burdened down by the sins of others.

Isaac looked up and met the man's eyes. "I have broken no laws of the land. My wrongs were against the ones I loved most. Taking my wife from her family to a place where she got sick and died. All because of what I wanted with no consideration of her needs."

"Selfish desires can wreak much havoc in our lives and the lives of others." Elder Homer nodded and stroked his beard again. "But continue. No wrong is too small to speak. Each uncharitable thought. Each poorly performed duty. Each lust after ways of the world. Only spoken confessions can be forgiven."

"That might take awhile," Isaac said.

Elder Homer's lips turned up in a slight smile. "Each moment of time is a gift and a treasure to be wisely used, for we have none to waste. There is work to be done, but the first task a man must do is make his spirit right within him so that the work he does will shine with the purity of the hands that performed it."

"Where should I start?" The idea of listing every sin he'd ever committed seemed as impossible as counting the hornets storming out of a hornets' nest when all a man wanted to do was run from them.

"At your first memories of doing wrong."

Who could even remember every wrong thought he'd had or deed he'd done? And even if he could, such small slights seemed inconsequential compared to being the reason for Ella's death. That seemed enough to admit. But if the old Shaker elder wanted a confession in exchange for the breakfast that filled Isaac's stomach, Isaac could speak the words.

"When a child, I didn't always listen to my mother. I threw a rock once and hit my sister. I told lies. I shot a red bird for no reason except to see if I could hit it."

As Isaac talked, little sins kept rising up in his head like bubbles in a pan of boiling water. Things he hadn't thought about for years, but that had poked his conscience with guilt when he'd done them. Elder Homer's chin drooped down on his chest and his folded hands stayed motionless on his long beard. He looked like he might be dozing, but Isaac kept talking. If the man wanted sins, Isaac could come up with sins.

Isaac rattled on with this or that wrong. The elder kept his eyes closed and his hands folded. The house was quiet. They were enclosed in a small room on the first floor of the large three-story building. Now and again a banging of pots rose up from the kitchen area deep in the house, but it was muffled and barely noticeable over the sound of Isaac's voice. He wondered how many childhood sins he should recount before moving on to more recent wrongs. He was barely listening to his own words until he said, "I hated my father when he died."

Isaac's voice trailed off to nothing as his words echoed in his ears. Elder Homer opened his eyes and looked at Isaac but didn't speak.

Isaac tried to back away from what he'd said. "I mean I hated it when my father died."

"That's not what you said," the elder said quietly. "But either way you've admitted the wrong of it. And have been forgiven. Are there more?"

The elder slipped his eyes toward the window as though to check on the progress of the sun toward noon. He shifted a bit in his chair and then once more assumed his posture of deep listening or perhaps sleep. Isaac had no desire to trot out more sins of his younger days or to walk through the years with the McElroys when many sinful thoughts had bedeviled him. Including the one of hating his father for dying.

He hadn't hated his father. He'd loved him so much his heart swelled to fill up his chest when he was with him. He wanted to be just like him, with the smile that won friends before a word was spoken, with the courage to chase his dreams even when Isaac's mother worried those journeys might mean not enough food on the table for his family,

107

with the power to never let that happen. He'd been strong and invincible to Isaac.

Then the boiler on the steamboat had blown and his father hadn't been strong enough. He'd left Isaac cold and alone on the riverbank while angry talk circulated among the survivors that the steamboat valves were tied down and hams thrown into the boiler fire to increase the heat. The new owners had a bet with another steamboat on the fastest time down the river. Isaac's father was one of the new owners. He'd gone down below the deck to check on the boilers. He would have wanted to win. He always wanted to win.

"Coming out on top, son. That's the thing," he'd often told Isaac. "Doesn't matter where you start so long as you come out on top."

He wouldn't think Isaac was on top of anything, sitting there with the old Shaker nodding off to sleep while he tried to think of which sin to admit next. "No need admitting anything," his father would have said. "Not even to the good Lord."

If Isaac's mother heard that, she always made sure to add that the good Lord already knew everything anyway. If that was true and Mrs. McElroy's Bible had echoed Isaac's mother's words, then it hardly seemed necessary to spend a morning of sunshine repeating them all again for the Lord to hear by way of the elder's ears.

But there was always a price to pay for anything in life, and Isaac was willing to go along with the Shaker way in order to put his feet under their table for a few weeks. So he skipped right past half his growing up years and didn't mention again his blame for Ella's death and simply said, "I often speak without proper thought and my words sound wrong."

Elder Homer opened his eyes and looked long at Isaac as if expecting more, so Isaac added without proper thought, "And I don't pray as much as I should."

"Did you not pray when your wife of the world fell ill?"

Isaac looked down at his hands. "Those prayers weren't heard."

"All prayers are heard, my brother. Not all are answered as we think they should be, but we must trust in the wisdom of the Father God who may have been using this sorrow to show you the error of your ways and the evils of the world and that is why you now sit here with me."

"A just God would have carried me away with the fever instead of my wife."

"God's justice is not our justice. Such we cannot under-stand." The elder stood up and leaned on the table in front of him as though he needed to give his legs a moment to accustom to standing.

"I don't understand much of anything," Isaac admitted as he scrambled to his feet. He didn't think he should be sitting if the old elder was standing.

"Yea, that is true for many who come among us. You have much to learn, and here you will have ample opportunity to practice the grace of prayer and thoughtful speaking. It is good you have come to be part of our family here at Harmony Hill." The elder's lips curled up a bit in a smile. Nothing like Brother Asa's cheerful acceptance of Isaac as he was—hungry, dirty, and friendless. But nevertheless a smile of acceptance.

"I will try to do as you say," Isaac said.

"You will not always be successful, my brother. But when you fail, your spirit will be cleansed by confession."

"To you?"

"Yea, but not as this has been. We have many new converts. There would not be enough hours in the day to hear the confessions one brother at a time. We will meet in a group with all given the opportunity to rid their souls of sin. Your guide into the Believer's life will tell you when."

"My guide?"

"Yea, each novitiate must be taught the ways of the Believer. And guided in the proper performance of your duties. Come. Brother Verne will be waiting in the hallway to start you in your assigned duties. Planting today, I would surmise, since the sun has dried the fields and it is necessary to get the crops in the ground in a timely manner. We depend on our harvest and the work of our hands." The elder held up large hands that had surely once been strong and able, but now their wrinkled skin was covered with age spots and some of his fingers misshapen with arthritic knots. "Hands to work and hearts to God. With that to guide you, you will do well."

Isaac followed the elder out into the hallway and down the east stairway. A brother was always to use the east doors and stairways while the sisters used those on the west of whatever building they were entering. Brother Asa had made sure he knew that the night before.

"There are many rules," Asa had said after he told Isaac to step on the stairs with his right foot first. "It is a way to feel joined and in union with all your brothers in discipline and service. In time the rules disappear."

"You mean you no longer have to do things a certain way?" Isaac asked.

"Nay, instead you will no longer note them as rules but only as part of your Shaker life."

"Is there punishment if you forget the rules and step with the wrong foot first or go in the wrong door?"

"Nay." Brother Asa smiled broadly. "None of the sort you may be imagining. The punishment would be in the loss of harmony with your fellow Believers."

Isaac had wanted to say that he wasn't a fellow Believer. He didn't even know what the Shakers did believe except the little Marian had tried to tell him. He'd paid scant attention to her words about believing in the second coming of Christ. He hadn't even given much consideration to the first coming of Christ, in spite of his mother's and Mrs. McElroy's admonitions that he would face a life of ruin if he didn't look to the Lord for help.

And now here he was in just such a ruined life, following after Brother Verne to work long hours in the fields, tamping seeds into the ground. Listening to Brother Verne instruct him on precepts of the Shakers' Mother Ann. Learning songs about simple gifts. Practicing dance steps that Brother Verne claimed were worship that would open him up to receive the spirit. Assuming postures of silent prayer upon rising in the morning, before and after every meal, and before lying down on the narrow cot at night. Kneeling on the proper knee first to keep from hearing Brother Verne's displeasure with Isaac's inattention to the rules.

Isaac had yet to determine what spirit the dances would bring. He hadn't been to a meeting in their worship house. Nor did he have any prayer words in his head when he knelt along with all the other brethren. He was empty of prayers. Empty of all thoughts as he obediently followed the unsmiling Brother Verne from duty to duty.

Brother Verne took his task of guiding Isaac along the Shaker pathway with solemn diligence. He was as different from Brother Asa as night from day. Tall and so slim that his shirt hung loose from his shoulders and was only kept from billowing out from his body like a flag in the breeze by the suspenders that held up his trousers. His full head of hair, as dark brown as his eyes, seemed proof he wasn't old, but it was hard for Isaac to think of him being young.

When Isaac didn't restrain his curiosity and asked how old he was, Brother Verne frowned at the intrusive question. "The counting of the years of a man's life seems to me a bothersome custom of the world. The only birthday that matters is that when a man reaches the age to sign the Covenant of Belief."

"What age is that?" Isaac asked, not because he really cared, but just to keep words in the air. That seemed necessary at times or at least better than the heavy silence that often settled over them in between Brother Verne's instructions.

"Twenty-one."

"So you were raised here like Brother Asa?" Isaac asked.

"Nay. I was not so blessed to escape the sin of the world at such an early age as our Brother Asa. I came into the village with the need to cleanse my life of the sin of matrimony."

"You're married?" Isaac couldn't keep the surprise out of his voice. "I didn't think you could be married here."

"You don't listen well, Brother Isaac." Brother Verne looked at him like a weary teacher might a recalcitrant student. "I cleansed my life of that sin when I came into the village and began to walk the Shaker way. My wife of the world and I lived as brother and sister among the other Believers."

"So which sister is she?" Isaac didn't know why he asked. He knew only a few of the sisters' names. The Sister Mae who had brought food to him and Brother Asa on that first night. The ancient Sister Lettie who had treated the wound on his hand with such efficient care.

A few other women's names had been spoken in his hearing, but there were many sisters. Nameless faces downturned and shadowed by their caps as they passed him on the pathways or while eating their meals on the opposite side of the silent dining room. He had a better look at their faces as they practiced their marching dances in the upper room of the Gathering Family House, but even there the men and women shared no words other than the words of the songs as they wound in and out in the dances without ever touching. He'd not yet even seen his own sister, Marian, but such a meeting was being arranged for the next night when the Shakers shared what they called Union night. On those nights Brother Verne had told him brothers and sisters were allowed to meet in small groups to discuss the work of the day.

So Isaac wasn't really bothered when Brother Verne ignored his question. The two were walking to the men's bathhouse to wash off the dirt of the field before the evening meal. While they needed the good dirt to grow their crops, the Shakers didn't believe in carrying any of it into their houses. Everything in the village was brushed and swept as the sisters waged an ongoing war with dirt of every description. They had even practiced a sweeping dance the night before, as they attacked the dirt that might seep into one's heart and soul with pretend brooms.

It wasn't until they were leaving the bathhouse and Isaac had almost forgotten the question that Brother Verne answered. "That sister is no longer here in the village. She turned back to the sinful ways of the world." The man's voice was low, almost as if he were talking to himself instead of Isaac.

"She left?"

"Yea. Each person must choose for himself or herself the proper road. She chose the slippery slope to sinful destruction. Not a slope I want to find my feet on ever again."

"Didn't you love her?"

"Such worldly love is the cause of much sin. Our Eternal Father revealed to Mother Ann that we must relinquish all such ties and seek a life of grace and forgiveness."

"But . . ." Isaac started and then stopped. He couldn't imagine deserting his wife to live among these people, but then Ella's face with tears streaking down her cheeks as they rode away from Louisville came to his mind. In the end he had deserted her needs for far less.

113

Brother Verne peered over at him. "A man's soul is not a trifle to be thrown away for the lusts of the world. Each man must pick up his cross and carry it. Such is the Believer's path away from sin to purity."

For just a second Isaac imagined doubt in the man's eyes, but then the staunch Believer returned. So Isaac bent his head and stared down at his feet as he said the Shaker yea in agreement. For whatever time he was there, he could stop speaking without thought and answer yea to the teachings Brother Verne wanted to force into his head. That was little enough to pay for the food they were giving him and a place to hide away from the judge's eyes. A coward's way perhaps, but then hadn't Brother Asa claimed the gift of cowardice for him?

10

Lacey didn't think things could get any stranger at the Ebenezer preacher's house after the regretful marrying words, midnight attic visit, and breakfast eggs splattered all over the kitchen wall. But that was before the Shaker men showed up with their seeds and stayed with their preaching talk. They came back every day of the week to sit out on the porch with the preacher and go on and on about dancing worship and men and women being brothers and sisters. More than once Lacey wanted to ask them when they aimed to sell the seeds they'd been so anxious to find buyers for when they showed up on that first day.

It was always the one called Brother Forrest, but sometimes the young brother wasn't with him. So maybe he was out selling seeds and tending to their proper business. The preacher didn't buy any seeds from them even though Lacey had asked him to see if they had butterbean seeds. She was particularly fond of the plump, half-moon beans and how a bowl of the beans were filling enough to be all she needed to cook for supper.

Truth was, she was ready to plant anything just so she and Rachel could be out in the sunshine digging in the dirt instead of stuck in the house. She was worn out with overhearing the preacher and his new Shaker friends go back and forth about what this one believed or that one believed on how to set a body's feet on the path to salvation.

Miss Mona could have told them. She could have quoted them Scripture and had them all understanding the way things should be. Especially for Lacey. Lacey hungered for Miss Mona's sensible words in her ears, pointing to this or that Bible passage to help Lacey figure out what she needed to do next. Hiding from the truth of her situation didn't seem to be working, but she kept doing it anyway. The garden was a good place to hide.

On the third afternoon that the Shaker men came to the porch, Lacey carried them water and then took Rachel out the back door over to the graveyard behind the church. There they dug up the ground beside Miss Mona's gravestone to plant some iris bulbs. Purple and white. Miss Mona's favorites. They put them to the side of the stone so the flowers wouldn't cover up the name Reuben Harrison had chiseled in the stone.

Reuben was the nicest man at Ebenezer Church. He never looked crossways at Lacey when he smiled and said, "Good morning, Miss Lacey." The words came off his tongue without the first tinge of condemnation. Sadie Rose would probably say that was because the poor man didn't have enough sense to know right from wrong.

The good man was a little slow in his thinking, but he was at the church every time the doors were open and first to stand up to volunteer for any work that needed to be done at the church or the preacher's house. He was the one who had brought his mule to turn over the sod for Lacey's garden last fall. He was the one who dug out the first shovel of dirt for every grave in the church graveyard. He was the one who spent long hours carefully chiseling the names in the stone markers for those graves.

Lacey ran her hands across the letters of Miss Mona's name. The stone was warm from the midday sun.

Rachel abandoned the earthworm she'd been letting crawl across her hand and came to lean against Lacey's leg. "Is that Mama's name?"

"Mona Wilson Palmer." Lacey took Rachel's hand in hers and helped her trace out the letters on the stone with her finger. "She loved us."

Rachel stared at the stone. "Tell me about how you found me on the back porch." The little girl looked up at Lacey. "The way Mama used to tell me."

"You mean the true story and not a made-up Maddie kind of story?"

"The true story. I was in a box on the porch and I wasn't crying. Angels were watching over me." Rachel started the story she'd heard so often. Miss Mona's words ran through Lacey's mind as familiar as a nursery rhyme.

"That's right." Lacey kept one hand on the stone and the other flat against Rachel's back. But instead of telling the story the way Miss Mona used to, with angel wing embellishments here and there, Lacey told the story as true as she could remember it. "At least you weren't crying right at first. You were all wrapped up in a soft quilt and sucking on your two middle fingers when I went out the door to go draw water from the well. It was early in the morning, and the sun was just peeking up over those trees in behind the house. It was the tenth day of September, and one of those special days with the air so clear and bright that a body just knows something good is going to happen."

"Did you know I was coming?"

"No, but later when I thought back on it, I remembered feeling the day was special as soon as I opened my eyes that morning. I was humming when I came down the steps to help

Miss Mona get dressed. I didn't always feel that way in the morning. Sometimes I wanted to just bury my head under my pillow and sleep a little longer, but that morning it was like the Lord pushed me out on my feet and told me to get with it. That this was a day I didn't want to miss."

"And then what happened?" Rachel looked up at Lacey, her blue eyes eager for this new telling of her story.

"Well, when I got downstairs, there was Miss Mona sitting up in her bed reading her Bible. She looked up at me and said, 'This is the day the Lord hath made. Let us rejoice and be glad in it.'"

"That was out of the Bible, wasn't it?"

"It was. But then Miss Mona told me to get ready for something good to happen."

"Where was Papa?" Rachel asked.

A little shadow drifted over the fun of telling the story, as Lacey didn't want to think about the preacher that day or this day either. But she kept smiling as she said, "He must have been still asleep, because he didn't know about how me and Miss Mona were feeling all crawly with joy even though we didn't know why yet."

"So then what happened? Did you go to the well?"

"I started to the well, but I didn't get there. When I opened up the back door, there you were. A gift from heaven."

"Did I fall out of the sky?" Rachel looked up at Lacey as if she wasn't sure of the answer, even though she asked that very same thing with every telling of the story.

"Oh no. Babies don't fall out of the sky." Lacey didn't stray from Miss Mona's answer but used her exact same words.

"Then how did I get there?"

Miss Mona had always slipped past that question by talking about the angels watching over Rachel, but Lacey didn't do that. She looked straight into Rachel's eyes as she said,

"Somebody who loved you very much put you there. Somebody who knew Miss Mona and me would love you just as much."

"Did you love me right away?"

"We did. Even before I unwrapped the quilt from around you to count your toes." Lacey leaned down and tickled Rachel's bare toes. "They were a lot littler then."

Rachel giggled and pulled her foot back. But then her smile faded.

"What's the matter, honey?" Lacey asked her.

"I wish I knew who put me there." Rachel dug her toes down in the newly turned dirt. "Jimmy says angels couldn't have done it. That it had to be my real mother. The one I was born to. He says everybody has a born-to mother. That even Jesus had a mother he was born to."

"Well, Jimmy's got that right, but sometimes for reasons we can't always know, the Lord gives a baby to somebody else. And then you're born to their heart the way you were to me and Miss Mona." Lacey wrapped Rachel's hand in hers and put it over her heart.

"That's a real purty thought, Miss Lacey."

Lacey jumped a little when the man spoke. She looked over her shoulder to see Reuben leaning against a gravestone closer to the church. They had been so intent on their story that they hadn't noticed him coming into the graveyard.

"Mr. Reuben," Rachel yelled. Her smile came back as she ran toward him. He had a stick of candy pulled out of his pocket for her before she got there.

Lacey straightened up and smiled at him too. He had his rake and shovel.

Her smile faded. "Nobody's passed on, have they?"

"Oh no, miss. I just come to make sure none of the stones had sunk during the winter freezes. We wouldn't want Miss Mona's stone to get crooked."

He followed Rachel back over to the grave. He set each foot down solid and careful as though he planned out where he was going to land each step. He wasn't very tall, but built solid like a tree trunk. Lacey had no idea how old he was. He seemed ageless. A man-sized boy with a generous heart, who was as much a part of the Ebenezer church as any deacon there.

He studied the ground beside the stone for a moment before he said, "If you'd a told me you needed to do some digging, I'd a done it for you."

"We only dug a little to plant some flowers."

"She'll like that," he said. "Miss Mona liked purty things. She'd a liked that story you told about finding Miss Rachel. I remember that morning."

"You do?" Lacey was surprised. He'd never told her that before.

"I saw her on the porch." His words came out slow. Reuben never talked in a hurry.

Lacey looked for Rachel to see if she was paying attention to what Reuben was saying, but she had run over to the church steps. She wasn't taking any chances Lacey would tell her she couldn't eat her candy until after supper. Lacey looked back at Reuben's round face. "The baby you mean."

"I saw the box. I didn't have no way of knowing a baby was in it. I figured it was potatoes or maybe beans for Miss Mona and the preacher. It was her I saw."

"Her?" Lacey suddenly felt very still inside. How come she had never heard about this before?

"The one who brung the box."

"Did you know her?" Her heart thumped up in Lacey's ears as she waited for his answer. Rachel's words echoed in her mind. *Everybody has a born-to mother.*

He shook his head once. "Weren't nobody from church.

120

But I'd seen her talking to the preacher before. Folks come talk to him, you know. When they've got troubles."

"They do," Lacey said. "How did you know she had troubles?"

"She was crying some that day when the preacher was talking to her out behind the church house. I didn't hear nothing she said, because I turned around and went on back home. It ain't right to bother the preacher when he's helping somebody with their troubles. My mam always made sure I knew that."

"Did you tell Preacher Palmer you saw her put the baby on the porch? After you knew it was a baby and not potatoes."

"Miss Mona told me not to."

"Miss Mona?" Lacey wasn't sure she'd heard right.

"She said I shouldn't tell nobody. Not the preacher. Nobody. That whoever the girl was had enough trouble heaped on her without us adding more."

"Did she know who she was?"

"She never said no name." Reuben looked down at his feet and then poked the ground with his shovel. "Guess as how I shouldn't a ought to told you, but somehow it seemed like she was pushing me to tell you."

"Who? Miss Mona?" Lacey frowned a little.

"Now don't go being upset with me, Miss Lacey. I ain't thinking on Miss Mona being a ghost or nothing, but sometimes it's like she's still talking to me in my head. Like she knows I got to talk to somebody. I could always trust Miss Mona whenever I needed help with anything. Like writing out the names for the stones. She always did that for me, but then you had to write out her name. I figure she would want me to be trusting you now."

Reuben couldn't read. He painstakingly copied out the lines of the names on the tombstones he chiseled without knowing which letters made which sounds.

"I could teach you your letters, Reuben."

"Miss Mona tried once. Before you came to live with her. I couldn't keep those markings in my head no matter how I looked at them. But I know my numbers. I can count to a hundred." He smiled up at her. "You want to hear me?"

"Not right now, Reuben," Lacey said and then felt guilty when Reuben looked disappointed. "How about just to twenty-five?"

His face lit up again as he started counting. "One, two, three . . ."

She kept her smile on her face as he said the numbers slowly and carefully, but in her head it was his words about seeing the woman put the box on the porch that she was hearing. And Miss Mona had known. Miss Mona had told him to keep it a secret.

Her candy gone, Rachel came back to stand between Lacey and Reuben as he counted. The little girl threw in a number with him sometimes when he paused, but if it wasn't the right number, he'd shake his head and keep steadily on. He wasn't a person to be thrown off track. A butterfly floated by to distract Rachel from the man's number recitation, and she took off chasing it. At last Reuben said twenty-five.

"That was nice, Reuben. Thank you."

He smiled sheepishly at her praise. "Wasn't nothing to it. I like counting. I count most everything. There's sixty-four graves here, you know, and twenty-three hymnbooks in the church. There used to be twenty-four, but somebody must've took one home and forgot to bring it back. We had forty-six people at church Sunday counting the preacher."

When Reuben paused to consider his next count, Lacey jumped in with a question. "Have you ever seen her again?"

He looked puzzled by her question. "Seen who?"

"The woman you saw bring the box to our porch."

"She weren't no woman. Not much more than a girl like you, Miss Lacey. But no, I never saw her no more. And my mam always said I could remember faces like I can remember numbers. Like I could see you ten years from now and still know you was Miss Lacey."

"I won't forget your face either, Reuben." Lacey touched his arm. "But maybe Miss Mona was right and we shouldn't talk about the girl anymore. Everything worked out the way the Lord intended."

"That's what Miss Mona told me. That it always does. She said the Lord could make a person see sunshine on the cloudiest day."

"And the devil can bring clouds on the sunniest day."

Reuben's smile faded. "Yes, ma'am. I have knowed her to say that too, but she told me to think on the sunshine and not the clouds. So that's what I do. You should too."

"You're right. I should," Lacey said. "I will."

But it seemed like the clouds kept gathering even with the sun beating down on them as she and Rachel walked back to the house. The Shaker men were still on the porch, and she'd no more than set foot in the yard than they were wanting her to come up and sit with them. To listen to their nonsense. She made them wait until she got Rachel settled down for a nap with her Maddie doll. The digging and chasing after butterflies had worn the little girl out, and her eyelids were drooping even before Lacey spread the little coverlet Miss Mona knitted over her legs. She didn't even ask for a Maddie story. So Lacey had no reason to delay going out on the porch.

"Do you need more water?" she asked as she stepped out on the porch and gently shut the door behind her. She tried to smile, but the attempt died on her lips in the face of their solemn expressions.

"Nay," the older Shaker said as the younger one jumped up

out of the chair the Preacher had carried out of the kitchen for him. "Please sit and join us."

Lacey looked at the chair but made no move toward it. "That's kindly of you, but I need to be about my chores." She reached back toward the door.

"Sit," Preacher Palmer ordered.

She looked across the porch at him and wanted to defy him. To tell him to throw his glass if that would make him feel better, but that hardly seemed proper with the two Shaker men there between them. She moved in front of the one called Brother Forrest, who was intently studying his hands spread out flat on his knees, and perched uneasily in the chair. The young Shaker sat down on the edge of the porch with his back toward her. She was having the same bad feeling about this that she'd had listening to Reuben in the graveyard. The clouds the devil was blowing her way were thickening. Served her right, she supposed, for not remembering to pray more for the sunshine.

The silence deepened on the porch and almost clanged in the air as the seconds ticked past. The Shaker men didn't move. They all sat there as though one of them had heard something and now the rest of them were listening to hear it again. A bobwhite call or more likely, with the way they sat stiff and on edge, a mountain lion's snarl. Nobody had heard any of the big cats in this area since before Lacey was born, but Miss Mona said they were prowling the woods when she first came here with Preacher Palmer to start their church in the wilderness.

Actually Lacey wouldn't have minded hearing the big cat scream. It would have taken the men's thoughts off whatever they were waiting for somebody to say and she could go inside, bar the door, and be safe for at least one more night. Of course she couldn't bar the preacher outside or the two Shaker men either. Then there was Reuben over in the graveyard with nothing but a shovel to defend himself. She shouldn't be conjuring up any mountain lions to bring new trouble down on them.

When she peered over toward the church house to see if Reuben was still there, she could only see the front of the church and none of the graveyard from where she was sitting. But there would be a clear view from the back porch. She pushed those thoughts from her mind. One bunch of clouds at a time.

Lacey folded her hands in her lap and waited. She wasn't going to be the one to shatter the silence over them. After what seemed like a half hour, the preacher cleared his throat. When he spoke, it was almost as slowly and deliberately as Reuben, like the words were having a hard time getting from his head to his mouth.

"Brother Forrest here, he says our marriage is an abomination in the eyes of God and his Mother Ann."

Lacey was so taken aback by his words that she forgot to watch her own tongue. She stared straight at the preacher and spoke right out loud with no consideration of the other two men sitting there listening. "Well, for heaven's sake, I could have told you that without you spending three days out here on the porch fussing back and forth."

A smile slipped across the older Shaker's lips, and he raised his hand up to cover his mouth and wipe it off his face. "It seems our young sister already has her feet firmly on the Shaker path to salvation."

That wasn't true at all, and she wanted to deny it outright. But she'd already spoken out once when she should have kept her mouth shut. She wasn't about to do it twice.

11

The next morning Preacher Palmer was up early with his hat on and out the door before he even finished swallowing his last bite of biscuit. They didn't talk about the Shakers or anything else. Words were scarce as hen's teeth between them, but then that was hardly new. Even before Miss Mona passed on up to heaven, Lacey hadn't shared many words with the preacher other than paying mind to his Bible readings and his sermons.

Now it was more a report of this or that church member who had dropped by to give news of somebody sick in the community or stating the need for coffee or flour when the preacher made his trip into the town on Saturdays. One thing Lacey had to say for Preacher Palmer. He didn't deny them any of their needs or ever complain the first time about fetching home yard goods for her to make Rachel a new dress.

Lacey heard him ride his horse away from the house. He wasn't a bad man, she reminded herself as she sat at the table sipping her tea. He hadn't said where he was going, but there was always somebody needing the preacher's ear or prayers in the church community.

Rachel was still asleep up in the attic room. Now with the preacher out and gone, the house was quieter than church at prayer time. Miss Mona used to call such early morning minutes before work had to commence the sweet part of the day. A time when a person could think on what the Lord might be wanting to plant in that person's heart. That was, if a person could push aside all the stray worries that wanted to hang around from the day past.

Lacey shut her eyes and tried to do that. Just clear out her head completely. To go back to a better time before she had to worry about being the preacher's wife. Or not being the preacher's wife in the common way. Again the thought was in her head. Preacher Palmer wasn't a bad man. He was a man chosen by God to shepherd his people. He was a man chosen by Miss Mona to love. Neither one of them would have picked a bad man.

It wasn't him and it wasn't her. Imperfect both of them, but not chasing after evil. It was the knotty situation they had got embroiled in, like a skein of yarn yanked and tangled in a hundred wrong ways until there didn't seem any way to pull out a loose string. A person had to sit down and patiently untangle each knot to make the yarn useful again. But she wasn't sure she could undo these knots she and the preacher had gotten tied up in, no matter how diligently she worked at the untangling.

An abomination in the eyes of God. The words burned through her mind. If she really thought that was true the way she'd told those Shaker men and the preacher, then shouldn't she just stand up and walk away? Wouldn't it be better to go off in the woods and live on roots and berries than be part of something the Lord thought an abomination?

Lacey looked up as though expecting to see some answer coming down to her. But all she saw were the smoke-blackened planks over the cookstove that she should have already washed down in spring cleaning. The ceiling would have never gotten that black if Miss Mona were living to see it. She was an ardent believer in spring cleaning for both the house and the soul.

Lacey could almost hear the dear woman's words in her head. "Sweep out bad thoughts that bedevil you. Knock down the cobwebs of poor attention to the Bible teachings. Mop up any feeling sorry for yourself and cast out grudges like you'd throw out a broken chair that can't be fixed and is taking up room that could be put to better use. A body's spirit needs a good going-over on a regular basis to keep it pleasing to the Lord."

Lacey sighed a little and was glad to hear Rachel's bare feet coming down the stairs, stepping whisper soft, to give her a reprieve from thinking on how she surely needed that spiritual cleaning every bit as much as the ceiling needed washing. The same as every morning the little girl made a beeline for the kitchen to lean against Lacey for a hug. Lacey breathed in her sweet child scent and held her a little closer. A gift from heaven.

She'd been wrong when she'd agreed with those Shaker men. Whatever allowed her to put her arms around this little child and be her mother, that couldn't bé an abomination. A tangled mess for sure. But hadn't Miss Mona told her over and over that there wasn't any mess the Lord couldn't make right if a body surrendered it up to him? That the trouble with most people was they wanted to rush on ahead and try to fix things on their own instead of waiting for the Lord's perfect time. That's what she and the preacher had done. Rushed on when they should have waited.

Now as she turned loose of Rachel to stand up and dip her out a bowl of oatmeal, she could only hope the preacher wasn't rushing on again instead of giving the Lord a chance to untangle their mess. But it was worrisome thinking on how intently he'd listened to those Shaker seed peddlers as they talked about their perfect ways and how their village was like heaven on earth. As if any human being could bring down heaven and live perfect.

If there was one thing Lacey knew for certain, she couldn't. The second thing she was pretty sure of was that the preacher couldn't either. Then while she might not ought to pass judgment on those Shaker people, somehow even without knowing any but the two who had spent three afternoons on her porch, she suspected they lacked some being perfect too. *For all have sinned, and come short of the glory of God.* That was what the preacher had quoted to the Shakers that first day out on the porch. Paul's words to the Romans. Preacher Palmer had without a doubt spoken that verse in church or wherever he was witnessing for the Lord hundreds of times.

All have sinned and come short. Those words kept running through Lacey's head as she went about her chores. Some truths a person just couldn't get away from.

That afternoon she was standing on a chair, scrubbing clean the kitchen ceiling, when she heard somebody coming up the front porch steps. She thought at first it might be those Shaker men back to find the preacher. The last thing she wanted to do was talk to them after she'd admitted being an abomination, and she thought to keep quiet and let whoever it was think nobody was home. But Rachel was in the front room playing with her doll and she ran right for the door.

"Miss Sadie Rose." Rachel squealed and jumped up and down. "Did you bring Maddie's new dress?"

Lacey finished wiping off the planks on the square of ceiling she could reach before she climbed down off the chair. As she dried her hands on her apron and went into the front room, she had the uncharitable thought that she'd have rather seen the Shaker men. At least she could have sent them on their way. Now she'd have to sit down and drink tea and wait for whatever it was Sadie Rose had come to tell her. It wouldn't be good.

They settled on the front porch with the tea Lacey stirred up the fire to brew. They didn't have anything sweet to go with their tea, because crumbs were all that was left of the Sunday spring cake in the pie safe, and Sadie Rose hadn't bothered to bring cookies. But she had brought the promised new dress for the Maddie doll, so Lacey couldn't hold no cookies against her.

At least Sadie Rose hadn't brought Jimmy with her to whisper more of his troublesome words in Rachel's ears. They sat there in the early afternoon sunshine and talked about the sick in the community. Mr. Jarvis had tried to pick up the end of a log and bothered his back. Dottie Whitlow was nigh on ready to birth her fourth baby, and Sadie Rose was lining up women to carry food over to the family during her confinement. And of course she knew Lacey would want to help out. The church windows could use a good washing, and the women needed to set aside a day for some spring cleaning at the church. Like Lacey was doing at the preacher's house. Miss Sadie Rose almost looked approving when she said that.

Lacey listened and waited. Sadie Rose had her work clothes on the same as Lacey. She hadn't even put on a clean apron. That meant she'd taken time out from the middle of her chores for some purpose other than noting the dirty windows in the church building.

The tea was all gone in both their cups and they'd run out of sick people to talk about before Sadie Rose set her mouth in a hard line. She put her cup down on the porch with a clatter and leaned forward a little with her hands on her knees, like as how she was ready to take Lacey on.

"I reckon I should just be out with it, Lacey," she said.

"Miss Mona always thought that the best way. If you want to say something, say it. Don't leave a body guessing."

"Dear Mona." Sadie Rose sighed and looked sincerely sad. "I do miss her and the steadying influence she had on the church. Even when she wasn't able to walk over and meet with us at the church house, we knew she was praying for us and that the good Lord was bending down his ear to hear her and us."

"Do you think he's stopped bending down his ear to listen?" Lacey asked. It was a question she needed answering, because there'd been times in the last few weeks when she'd felt that might be true. But then she reminded herself that a person had to send the prayers up for the Lord to bend down to listen. That's where she'd been negligent since Miss Mona died. She'd think prayers but then let them slide right out of her mind without offering them up proper. It was like she was afraid of the answers the Lord might send down to those prayers.

Sadie Rose's forehead wrinkled up in a frown. "No, no. Of course not. That wasn't my meaning at all. The good Lord pays attention to anybody's fervent prayer. But that doesn't mean I don't miss Mona. Or that Preacher Palmer doesn't. She was a steadying influence on him too." The woman's eyes sharpened on Lacey. "And on you."

Lacey glanced over at the steps where Rachel was singing to her Maddie doll and was relieved to see the child wasn't paying the first bit of attention to any of her and Sadie Rose's talk. Lacey looked back at Sadie Rose, who was still leaning a little forward in her chair as if ready to argue down anything Lacey might say. But Lacey didn't want to do any arguing. Being crossways with Miss Sadie Rose and the churchwomen was just another mess of tangled knots she was in.

Lacey stared down at the cup she was holding and felt a

tear threatening to leak out of her eye as she said, "I didn't want Miss Mona to die."

Sadie Rose let out a breath of air and then surprised Lacey by reaching across to touch her hand. "Of course you didn't, Lacey. We know that. We all know that."

Lacey didn't look up at her. She kept her eyes on the woman's work-worn hand with its calluses and chapped skin. Sometimes it was easier to stay mad at a person than to stand up to her kindness without completely falling apart. Becoming a puddle of tears wouldn't serve any real purpose.

"We know the fault of none of this can be laid at your feet, Lacey. We're seeing that more and more."

Surprise wiped the tears right out of Lacey's eyes as she looked up at Sadie Rose. "How's that?"

Sadie Rose sank back in her chair and didn't meet Lacey's eyes. Instead she studied her hands now twisted together in her lap. After a long moment with the only noise Rachel's chatter to her doll over on the steps, the woman let out a tired sigh. "I've never felt it proper for church members to speak ill of their pastor. Always thought the error in thinking was more apt to be in the church member than the man the Lord called to be his messenger of the Scriptures."

Lacey didn't know what to say to that, so she kept quiet. For a minute she didn't think the woman was going to say anything more, but then she looked up at Lacey before letting her eyes drift to something beyond Lacey's head. Something in the air that might make what she was wanting to say easier to speak out loud.

"We've . . . me and Harold, I mean. We've been hearing some disturbing news about Brother Palmer. We were of the mind to not think much about it, knowing the preacher the way we do. We figured it was some kind of mistaken thinking on them that were doing the talking to Harold, but then this Shaker man came by with his seeds this morning before Harold went out to the field. Jacob, he said was his name. Not much more than a boy and so mixed up on the truth of the Bible. We were all right with that. A person has to make his own choices and we could pray he'd see the light. But then he said our preacher had sent him our way and that he was hoping we'd be as open to the true way to salvation as Brother Palmer. The true way, mind you, like we didn't already know that way. Like we were the ones who didn't know the truth instead of them. Like the Bible didn't tell Adam and Eve to go forth and be fruitful."

Miss Sadie Rose's voice had started out calm enough, but with each word it rose a little, like as how she was trying to outtalk a thunderstorm only she could hear. Rachel looked up from playing with her doll, then deserted Maddie on the steps to come lean against Lacey and stare at Sadie Rose with big eyes. Lacey figured her own eyes were every bit as big. She didn't try to say anything to stop the stream of words coming out of Sadie Rose's mouth. She just listened.

"That they—we're supposing he meant him and others of those Shakers—had been talking a right smart to the preacher and thought that come Sunday Brother Palmer might be bringing us all the truth of how Christ hadn't just come to earth once, but how he had to come back as that woman they go on about over there in that Shaker town."

Sadie Rose's eyes came back to Lacey's face. She didn't pay any mind at all to Rachel and try to moderate her words as she went on. "I'm telling you, it sounds about half crazy when you hear them talk about it, and then there he was telling us that the preacher—our preacher, mind you—was going to tell us how it was all true. That he'd had a vision. A vision of ruin, according to that Shaker boy. Something about the church falling down. That the roof was just going to fall down on top of all our heads or something foolish like that. Harold and the other men put that roof on over there." She nodded toward the church building. "They built it sound."

Sadie Rose stopped talking to breathe in and out a couple of times in an attempt to compose herself. "Anyway, Harold told me to come over here soon as I could get away from my chores to see if anything that Shaker boy said was true."

"Maybe Deacon Crutcher needs to ask the preacher about that himself," Lacey said as she rubbed her hand up and down Rachel's back.

"Oh, he will. Don't you worry. But that Shaker boy said Harold wouldn't find him today. That Brother Palmer was over visiting their place. Is that so?"

Lacey picked her words carefully. "I don't know. The preacher doesn't normally tell me where he's going. But he has been talking some to them. I'm thinking everything that's happened lately has put him under a strain."

She didn't know why she was trying to protect him. If he was having visions and going Shaker, it wouldn't be secret long. Not secret like the way they were living. She thought about telling Miss Sadie Rose about that. That maybe it would make her not look so hard on the preacher, but then the woman would be back to looking hard on Lacey. Some messes didn't allow for the first bit of untangling but just kept getting more knotted up.

Miss Sadie Rose stared at her with her mouth hanging open a minute as though Lacey had just confirmed all her fears. "Then don't you think he ought to be talking to his Lord about his worries or maybe his deacons who've been worshiping faithful with him for more years than I like to number?"

Lacey didn't have any answer for that, nor did Sadie Rose expect her to. They just sat there and looked at each other.

Two women without answers. Lacey was used to the feeling. She hadn't had answers for some time, but she could tell it was different for Miss Sadie Rose. She thought she already knew the answers. She wasn't expecting the man she'd sat in church and listened to for years and years to suddenly be saying those answers might be wrong. That he was coming up with new answers that might shake the foundations of the church. Make the roof fall in on top of them all.

After a long minute, Miss Sadie Rose spoke again in a quiet little voice. "All right, Lacey. Answer me this. Do you think he's considering what they've been telling him? Seriously considering it."

Lacey couldn't do anything but tell her the truth. "I'm thinking he might be."

Sadie Rose twisted her mouth in concern. "To actually go live in their village?"

"I don't know. He's been pointing out to me the part of the Bible that says a man of God shouldn't be married."

Sadie Rose huffed a breath of air out her nose and stood up. "They don't believe in families, you know. Divide a man and his wife. A mother and her children." Her eyes fell on Rachel. "Of course that might not be such a problem for you with no borne children of your own. But it wouldn't be a path I'd want Harold to follow the preacher on."

"You think he might?" Lacey wrapped her arm tighter around Rachel as though to shut out Sadie Rose's words denying the true connection between her and the child. Born to or not didn't matter all that much.

"Men can get some strange ideas sometimes."

"But over there they say it was a woman that started them. A woman that told them to live like that."

"I've heard the same." Sadie Rose's face brightened at the thought. "Harold won't go for that. No matter what the preacher might preach to him. Not that he should get his gospel from a woman. The Bible speaks strong against that." She reached over, grabbed hold of Lacey's hand, and squeezed it hard. "We'll just have to pray about it. Pray for the preacher that he'll come to his senses."

Lacey looked up at the older woman and nodded. Wasn't that what women were always left to do? Pray.

"Before Sunday," Sadie Rose added as she lightly touched Rachel's head and stepped past them toward the steps.

Lacey watched her until she was out of sight and then went back to cleaning the kitchen ceiling. Each time she dipped her cleaning rag back in the water and wrung it out, she said a silent prayer. *Lord, watch over us. Me and Rachel and Miss Sadie Rose. And the preacher too.* It didn't seem right not to throw the preacher in there with them in her prayers. She thought about mentioning the Shaker men, but they were the ones causing the trouble. Then she knew it wasn't just them. The trouble had been there in the house before they ever showed up with their seeds of discontent.

That night the preacher came home with a packet of butterbean seeds. That seemed proof that he'd been to the Shaker town to do some more talking, but at the same time he brought in the seeds. That had to mean he expected Lacey to plant them and watch them grow into the summer. He didn't talk about it and she didn't ask him.

But come Sunday morning, he did more than talk about it. He got right up in the pulpit and preached about it. He talked about that vision of the church falling down around them because they weren't living right lives. Folks stirred a little in their pews with that, but it wasn't uncommon for a preacher to talk about wrong living. Then he started talking about the Shakers and their Mother Ann being God's daughter. Three families stood up and walked right out the back door without waiting for the final prayer. That just brought on more fervent preaching and dark warnings of condemnation.

Lacey sneaked a look over her shoulder to where Sadie Rose sat with her two youngest boys on the pew behind Lacey and then at Deacon Crutcher over on the men's side of the church with the older boys. Lacey didn't think Sadie Rose had to worry about the Shaker thinking cracking through the deacon's stony face, and Lacey was glad that maybe her prayers for Sadie Rose had been answered the way Sadie Rose wanted.

Lacey turned back to look at Preacher Palmer. On the other hand, it didn't look like she was ever going to pick the first butterbean off the plants from those seeds she and Rachel had put in the ground the day before.

12

"There's no reason to delay when you see a thing needs doing. No, more than see it needs doing. When the Lord shows you in clear and certain ways that it must be done. A man sins who doesn't obey his calling." Preacher Palmer spoke the words with a surety, like he was declaring a truth anybody ought to understand.

He stared across the table at Lacey with a strange light in his eyes that she wanted to blame on the reflection of the oil lamp on the table between them, but some things were hard to pretend. She looked away from his face and stared at the kitchen window open to the night air. Moonlight flowed in it so bright that she could have gone out on the back porch, picked up her hoe, and gone to work in her garden. But if any of them came by, the church people would think she was crazy out there chopping in the moonlight.

Bad enough that they already thought the preacher had taken leave of his senses. The deacons had come to him one by one on Sunday afternoon after he'd preached about the Shakers' perfect life. Then they'd all come together on Monday morning. Left their plows in the field on a sunny day and congregated to save their preacher. The Shaker brothers had been there on the porch standing beside the preacher when the deacons showed up. Brother Forrest and the young one Jacob along with an aged man they called Elder something. There was a lot of talk. Most of it not so pleasant. Lacey hadn't even offered any of the men a drink. She didn't have that many glasses.

Tuesday nobody had come knocking on the door. Nobody at all. That somehow seemed as strange as all the comings and goings the day before. And now the preacher was telling her they were going to the Shaker town. That he was giving up the church he and Miss Mona had started when they first came to these Kentucky woods. The church he'd let Miss Mona name.

Here I raise mine Ebenezer. Hither by thy help I'm come. Lacey could hear her singing the song about the fount of blessings and showing Lacey the chapter in Samuel where the prophet had placed a stone and called it the name of Ebenezer for how the Lord had chased off the Philistines with a great and mighty bang of thunder. The prophet Samuel's Ebenezer stone in the Bible first. The Ebenezer church next. The Ebenezer community last.

Lacey didn't say anything, even though the preacher had quit talking. It was like he was taking a pause in preaching, and it wouldn't be right to interrupt his thinking. Besides, she didn't have the first idea of what to say anyway. But he kept sitting there looking across the table at her until she knew he was waiting for her to say something, and the only word rising in her head was no. That was the word she should've said to him some weeks back when he talked on how they had to get married.

More minutes crept by and she had to fight the temptation to leave this sorry moment behind and go off in her imagination to think up a story to make things better. To somehow change what was happening into a story with no more bothersome problem than getting past a snake on the porch step. That was the story she'd told Rachel the other day out on the back porch while the little girl was letting her latest fishing worm pet curl up in the palm of her hand.

Rachel liked something worrisome in her stories, and since her fondness for worms didn't carry over to snakes, the mere thought of a snake in her path was plenty worrisome. But this snake had turned out to be the talking variety, although not the Garden of Eden trouble-making kind. Her story snake had been a right handsome fellow with black rings who had come very politely asking for help for his sister who'd fallen down in the well. In the story they'd gone right out to let the bucket down in the well so the sister snake could crawl in it and be pulled up to slither away with her brother.

Lacey mentally shook her head. It wasn't a time to be fading out into the world of make-believe. Preacher Palmer wasn't one to encourage flights of fancy. His dark eyebrows were almost meeting over his eyes as he stared at her.

"Well, aren't you going to say anything, girl?"

Finally the word she wanted to say came out. "No."

But of course her real meaning of it was lost from delaying so long. He just thought she wasn't arguing against the move. And she supposed she wasn't, seeing as how her words all seemed stuck in her throat. His eyebrows settled back in their proper places and he looked relieved.

"That's how I thought your thinking would be," he said. "Since you've been crossways with this union we might have entered in a bit too hastily for your peace of mind. The Shakers believe in a different sort of union. A union of peaceful living without the distractions of worldly living."

"I've been told they don't believe in families." She stared at the flame burning steadily inside the glass chimney of the lamp.

"Nay, that's not true at all," Preacher Palmer said.

Nay. He was talking like those Shaker men with their yeas and nays. She let her eyes go to the preacher's face. He had already stepped across the divide into the willingness to follow their ways.

He kept talking. "They believe in family in a better way. A more united way where none are excluded and all are brought into proper fellowship with one another and the Lord. Brothers and sisters, all. Just as the Bible commands. Love thy brother."

"And sister," Lacey said in a voice not much above a whisper.

He must have heard something in her voice then. Some reluctance to accept his word. "I thought you would welcome this."

Lacey didn't look down even though she wanted to. She kept her eyes on the preacher's face as she said, "They divide families."

"We're already divided. Have ever been. You told them our marriage was an abomination. You can't be sorry to wipe that away."

"But what of Rachel?"

His eyes pierced her in the lamplight. "What of Rachel?"

"She needs me."

"The Lord takes care of little children. And so do the Shakers. They have many orphans among them."

"Rachel isn't an orphan."

"How can you say she's not? A child abandoned on a doorstep with no mother to claim her."

"I claim her. Miss Mona claimed her. You claim her."

"I never claimed her." He put both hands flat on the table and leaned toward Lacey as he continued speaking, each word getting a little louder. "Never. She has never been more than an abandoned waif in need of care. Care she will abundantly receive among the good Shaker sisters. She has nothing to do with me. Or you. You are not her mother."

She wanted to tell him how wrong he was, but the fire in his eyes burned away her words. She stared down at her hands and prayed for courage to speak. After a minute she said, "What if I don't want to go with you?"

"Lord, grant me patience," he whispered under his breath. He sat back in his chair, and when he next spoke, his voice sounded tired. "You don't have to go with me. You're my wife, but you can go to town and file to have the union dissolved. I don't know what might happen to you then. You can't stay here. The church owns this house. I own a bit of land to the south, but that will go over to the Shakers when I sign the Covenant of Belief. That won't be right away. There's a trial period, they say. But there's no house on the property. Mona and I had hopes once of building there, but the church built this house for us close to the church building first. I suppose you might go to your father if you can find him or perhaps hire out to someone. That might have been what you should have done before."

"Except for Rachel," Lacey said quietly.

"You will have to choose whatever way you think best, but I will choose Rachel's way. She has never called you mother."

"What difference does a name make?"

"True enough." He leaned his head against his hand and rubbed his forehead back and forth. "'Art thou loosed from a wife? Seek not a wife.' Oh, that I had attended to the apostle's words. You carry the name wife, but it's a word without meaning for the two of us. That you cannot deny. Nor can I."

Lacey felt a blanket of guilt fall around her shoulders. He was right. She had denied him the rights of a husband. She had driven him to this decision. She swallowed hard and forced out the words as she peeked up at him. "I can change. Be the wife you asked me to be."

"You would prostitute yourself for the child. A child conceived in sin and clothed in temptation." His eyes burned into her, condemning her words. "The Lord sent the Shaker brothers here to keep our feet off that sinful path. 'For our transgressions are multiplied before thee, and our sins testify against us.'"

Lacey not only knew he was speaking Bible words, she knew they carried truth. She looked back down at her hands folded in her lap. She was beaten. Her sins were testifying against her. She was clinging to what she wanted without opening her heart to what the Lord intended for her. The way she was fighting against humbling her spirit was doing nothing but trapping her in a deeper quagmire with every word.

But the Lord couldn't want her to give up Rachel. The preacher, yes. She could give him up without a second thought. The preacher's house, yes. But not Rachel. She couldn't give up Rachel. She'd just have to turn this mess over to the Lord. To trust him to make it right while she kept walking the path set before her, even if she couldn't see where it was leading her.

What was it Miss Mona always told her when she was worrying over something? There wasn't no need in borrowing trouble from tomorrow. If such was laying in wait, it would get to her soon enough. Best to keep praying. Keep hoping the trouble would slide off in the shadows before she reached the valley. *Yea, though I walk through the valley of the shadow of death, I will fear no evil: for thou art with me.*

The preacher pushed his chair back from the table and stood up. "You have to decide, Lacey."

"When are we going?" She looked up at him, surrendering her will.

He nodded a bit in acknowledgment of her decision before

he said, "The Shakers are bringing a wagon to pack our things in tomorrow."

"We'll be using our things then at this new town?"

"Nay. All will be given over to the Shakers. They'll use what they can, sell or give away what holds no use for them. All property there is owned in common."

"But what if we don't stay?"

"We'll stay." His shadow in the light of the lamp reached all the way to the just-washed kitchen ceiling. He looked as fierce as she had always imagined the Old Testament prophets when they made their pronouncements of the Lord's coming punishment for evil behavior, but then he changed his words. "I'll stay."

"The church here will have no leader." The thought made Lacey sad.

"Those who want a leader will come with us. Those determined to continue on the wrong way have rejected leadership."

"Are some others convinced to try the Shaker way?"

"The Whites and the Barlows, they're considering it. And others may follow in the weeks ahead when they acknowledge the error of their ways."

"It's a way you taught them."

"A man must stand ready to follow the leading of the spirit. If I were to turn from this, I'd be tormented with failures. My sins."

"They don't sin at the Shaker town?"

"They remove all reason for sin and are ready to confess their wrongs. You will see." He stepped back to the table and twisted down the wick of the lamp until the flame guttered out. He stared down at her in the moonlight flowing through the window. "Our house will be cleansed of sin. A cleansing we need. You will see."

The next morning when she told Rachel they were leaving the only home the child had ever known, she looked at Lacey with enormous eyes and hugged her Maddie doll tighter, but she didn't cry. She trusted Lacey the way Lacey was telling herself to trust the Lord. Neither one of them mentioned the preacher closed up in his room doing his own packing or soul cleansing or whatever. He hadn't even eaten his breakfast. Just came out for a cup of coffee and carried it back into his bedroom with barely more than a grunt of greeting.

There wasn't any reason for talking anyhow. They'd done that the night before. Lacey just set his plate of eggs and biscuits in the warming oven and ate her oatmeal with Rachel. She didn't bother with feeding the fire in the cook-stove. She'd cooked her last meal on that stove in Miss Mona's kitchen. She turned her mind from that thought before tears could steal into her eyes and kept spooning in her oatmeal to set the right example for Rachel. Food wasn't to be wasted.

It didn't take long to pack up the dishes, even with the way her fingers wanted to linger, tracing the rose pattern on Miss Mona's Sunday plates. If the preacher was right and they weren't going to be able to use them in the Shaker town, then she should have let Miss Sadie Rose carry them home. At least that way Miss Mona would be remembered. But none of the church people had come around. Lacey supposed they'd given up fighting the preacher's vision of truth.

Lacey stood up and stretched. Rachel was pulling all the pans out of the bottom of the cabinet, enjoying the clatter they made. Lacey peeked out the back window toward the church. The roof looked sturdy as ever. Not in the least bit of danger of falling down. But she supposed there was more than one way for a roof to fall in on a church. Certainly the preacher turning from the beliefs he'd been preaching since before the church roof was built was a way none of them might have ever imagined.

The clock in the front room bonged out the hour. Ten strikes. She didn't have time for woolgathering, but she didn't bend back to her work at once. Instead she looked from the church roof down to the graveyard. The sun was bouncing off the headstones. Markers testifying to lives lived and lost. What marker would there be to show her time here? Would the echo of her footsteps on the stairs up to the attic room haunt the next people who lived here? Would her foolish dreams of someday knowing true love stay captured in the mirror where she'd watched her face go from a child to a woman? No need mourning those dreams now. They'd died the day she'd stood in that preacher's parlor in the town and let them think she said "I do."

She could see Miss Mona's headstone. She wanted to just forget the packing chores and walk over there to see if Miss Mona might speak some wisdom out of the grave to her. Lacey stepped out on the porch where she could see the grave better. The yellow dandelion blooms had all turned to fluffs of white. Thousands of seeds waiting for the breeze to carry them away. Not caring where, but ready to take root and bloom wherever they found themselves next spring. Maybe that was Miss Mona's wisdom to her. To be ready to take root and bloom no matter where the winds of life were blowing her.

Rachel came out the back door to lean against Lacey. "Can I dig my worms up out in the garden and take them with us?"

Lacey smiled down at her. "No, they wouldn't want to leave their home dirt."

"We don't want to leave either." Rachel looked up at Lacey. "Do we?"

"Think of it as an adventure. Something new." Lacey kept the smile on her face and the worry out of her voice.

"Like in a Maddie story?" Rachel looked hopeful. "She has adventures."

"She does."

Rachel's hopeful look faded. She stared down at her bare feet and worked her toes against the wooden porch. "I'm not as brave as Maddie."

Lacey stooped down to look directly in Rachel's face. "Neither am I, but we'll be brave enough."

"Will you help me be brave, Lacey? The way you did when Mama died?"

"I will. And the Lord will help us both. Your mama always said we could count on that." Lacey touched Rachel's cheek. "Another thing you can count on is that there'll be worms in the gardens at the Shakers' town. I've even heard tell that they have worms that make silk. Can you imagine that?"

Back in the house Lacey took the rose-patterned plates out of the packing crate and set them up on the kitchen shelf. Miss Sadie Rose would find them. It didn't take long to pack up the rest of the kitchen things.

After she fed Rachel a slice of bread and honey at noon and the preacher finally ate his cold eggs, she sent Rachel out to the garden to tell her worms goodbye. Preacher Palmer went out to the horse shed and left Lacey alone in the house. She was looking through Miss Mona's books when a man spoke behind her.

"You might as well leave those here. The Shakers don't have any use for storybooks. They'll let you keep the Bible maybe. Nothing else."

13

When the young woman on the floor visibly jumped, Isaac wished his words back. He hadn't meant to startle her. Or discourage her. From the look on her face as she jerked around to stare up at him, he'd done both.

Her wide brown eyes studied him with no hint of shyness. She was very pretty. He felt a flash of guilt for noting that, as if the thought made him unfaithful to his beautiful Ella with her light blue eyes and china-doll pale skin. This girl had no fear of the sun. The scattering of freckles across her nose was proof of that. She was sitting on a bright rag rug with her faded yellow skirt hiked up to reveal bare feet and a generous portion of leg. A fact she seemed totally unaware of, since she made no attempt to yank her skirt down to regain her modesty. Books lay all around her on the floor. Some in stacks. Some open so the words could spill out to her eyes. Isaac hadn't seen that many books just tossed about since he'd left home after his father died.

His father had liked books. Carried one with him everywhere he went in case he had a quiet moment. When he was reading, no matter where that was, he would read snippets out loud to whoever was close by, as if the words were such a treasure they had to be shared. Isaac always watched his father's face to decide if he should embrace the beauty of the words or chuckle at their cleverness.

At the McElroys', books other than the Bible were considered a waste of time and money. Then at Ella's house, books abounded again, but mostly law volumes lined up in handsome rows on the judge's library shelves with no expectation of anybody other than the judge pulling them off. Ella's thin volumes of poetry and weepy romance tales were stashed neatly away on a shelf in the morning room.

Isaac spotted a few of the same titles in the girl's books in front of him. None of the stories of frontiers conquered that had fed Isaac's imagination and led him down the sorry path that had caused so much grief. Perhaps it was better to read only the Bible as Mrs. McElroy had insisted and now the Shakers were telling him. The Bible and the teachings of their Mother Ann that would help him abide by the many Shaker rules.

He was surely breaking some of those rules now as he stood above the girl near enough to touch if he reached toward her. Definitely a sin in the eyes of the Shakers who kept men and women forever at a distance for fear that even the incidental brush against a sister's arm in passing on the stairs might plunge a brother into sin.

He supposed a proper Shaker novitiate would turn and go back out to the porch to wait as Brother Verne had told him to do. But instead he stayed where he was and waited for the young woman to say something. Since he'd had no way of knowing anyone was in the house when he stepped inside to find a drink of water, being near the young woman wasn't an intended breach of the rules. Intended or not, he would have to confess his disobedience of not staying on the porch. Obedience was highly regarded among the Shakers. Especially by Brother Verne.

It wasn't that Isaac didn't want to keep the Shaker rules. In the time he'd been at Harmony Hill, he had surrendered his will in a dedicated attempt to live as they instructed. He no longer allowed himself to dream of the West and the adventures that had once beckoned him. He had destroyed enough people already with those foolish dreams. He had learned to kneel on his right knee first at the many prayer times. He had conditioned himself to begin every climb up the stairs with his right foot and to keep in mind the proper door for the brothers to enter the buildings. He rose without complaint at the sound of the rising bell and worked diligently at whatever task they set him to. He filled his stomach with the Shakers' good food and thought it only right to expend his muscle power in payment. He even dutifully listened to their sermons and practiced their dances and confessed enough sins to satisfy Elder Homer. But he wasn't a Shaker. Not the way Marian was.

The week before, he had talked with Marian in what the Shakers called a Union meeting. Six sisters across from six brothers in the brothers' room, sitting in the plain straight chairs made by the brothers. The rows of chairs were placed far enough apart that there was no danger of the brothers and sisters touching. The sisters had shed their aprons but wore their caps and the wide white collars over their bosoms. Marian was the youngest among them, but in spite of the bloom of youth on her cheeks, she too looked plain as if that was part of the uniform costume. Beauty of the spirit was to be desired. Outward beauty meant nothing. Or so Brother Verne had told him more than once.

She was well satisfied with her life there, Marian assured Isaac before adding that she hoped he too would find the same satisfaction in time. After the other women nodded their approval of Marian's words, they moved on to talk of the week's planting and how the strawberries were beginning to ripen and who had received the gifts of the spirit. Some young sister at the Children's House had claimed to be visited by angels and had neglected her chores to frolic in the meadow with these heavenly visitors, but none of the sisters or brothers seemed upset about that or to doubt the truth of the young sister's vision.

Isaac said little. What was there for him to say? The questions he might have liked to put to Marian were not for the ears of any sister or brother other than his birth sister, and especially not for Brother Verne to hear. The man had a way of sifting and measuring each and every word out of Isaac's mouth for signs of worldliness and improper thought.

Brother Verne would be sure to condemn him for speaking to the young woman in front of him instead of slipping unnoticed back out to the porch. He could have. With her head bent, she'd been totally absorbed in her books as she stroked their covers and opened one to run her finger across a line or two inside. He watched her a moment before he spoke, imagining his own hands holding those books, his own eyes receiving the gift of their words.

But it wasn't only the books that held his eyes. The girl had too, even before he spoke and she looked up at him. She looked so vulnerable with her hair falling forward to reveal the delicate skin on her neck. He wanted to help her even before he knew what help she might need.

That didn't mean he had forgotten Ella. It had only been six months since she died. Six years could pass and he wouldn't forget her. Every night when he lay down on the narrow Shaker cot, he fought off sleep long enough to bring Ella's face up in front of his eyes. While he had left her body in the cold grave on the Louisville hillside, he would never desert her memory. No matter how much time went by. Atonement

demanded as much from him. He could never look at another
woman in the same way he had looked at Ella.

And yet something about the girl sitting there on the floor
staring up at him with sparkling brown eyes made him want
to smile at her and see her smile back. He wanted to sit
down beside her in the middle of the books and forget the
Shakers. Forget everything and go back to a time before guilt
weighed down his shoulders. A time when he could take joy
in made-up stories.

"I can't take any of them?" she asked. There was no rebel-
lion in her voice, only disbelief.

"Could be I'm wrong," Isaac said. Not because he believed
he was, but because he didn't want to be the reason for her
unhappiness. "Maybe you should ask your father."

"My father?" She looked puzzled. "I don't know what
you mean."

"Your father. The preacher. Maybe Brother Forrest has
told him what you can bring or not bring."

She laughed. She seemed as surprised by the sound as he
was. She put her hand over her mouth to smother the laugh,
but still it worked its way out between her fingers. It wasn't a
good laugh. Not the kind that cleared sorrow and cheered a
person. And then with no pause between, she had her hands
over her face, and a sob choked out the laughter. She was better at stopping the tears than the laughter. The one sob was
all that escaped her as she rubbed her hands across her eyes
and down over her face before picking up the book again.

She closed the book with a snap before laying it on top of
one of the piles. He thought to offer her a hand to help her
up, but she was already on her feet before he reached out to
her. She was nearly a head shorter than he was, but with a
sturdy strength in the set of her shoulders. Again nothing like
Ella, whose shoulders had curved forward almost begging for

an arm around her to support and hold her. To protect her from the dangers of life. This woman looked capable and ready to knock such dangers aside on her own.

It was a look he admired and then as quickly felt shame, as if he was betraying Ella's memory with the comparison. He shouldn't be making such comparisons. This woman was nothing to him. He didn't even know her name. Ella was everything.

"Are you one of them?" the woman asked. "I guess that's a silly question when it's clear as day you are. Dressed how you are."

"I live with the Shakers," Isaac admitted.

"You don't say that like you're all that sure you want to." She looked down at the books scattered across the floor and didn't wait for him to answer. "But then plenty of us have to do things we aren't all that sure we want to. Our feet can get set on some strange roads in this life." She glanced up at him with a little frown of worry. "None of the books? Do they not believe in books?"

"They believe in their own books. The ones that teach you about the Believers and Mother Ann. Not storybooks."

She let out a sigh and dropped her head as though his words were blows. "How can they not like storybooks? They dance when they worship."

He wasn't sure what to say to that, so he kept quiet.

She looked up again. "Do you dance with them?"

"Sometimes. If I've learned the dance well enough not to take a wrong step and mess up the union of the dancers."

"A wrong step. I've taken plenty of those. And I'm thinking I'm about to take another one." She breathed out another sigh before she straightened her shoulders. "But I shouldn't be burdening your ears with my sorrows."

"I don't mind."

"You're being polite. Something I fear I'm neglecting." She smoothed down her apron and pushed a little smile out on her face. "I'm Lacey Bishop." The smile wavered a little, but she didn't let it disappear. "Lacey Palmer now. The preacher and me, we got married six weeks ago today."

"The preacher? The one outside?" Isaac thought of the older man who had come out of the shed to speak to Brother Forrest. The man had to be more than twice as old as the girl in front of him.

She laughed again. A short sound that held little humor. "The very one. No storybook romances around here." She looked down at the books. "Even in the Bible there are storybook romances. Did you know that? Jacob working fourteen years for Rachel. Ruth and Boaz. Of course he was older than her or at least I always imagine that to be so when I think on the story of her out gleaning the grain, but then again she was a widow. At least I'm not that. A widow. The preacher is. Not a widow, but a widower."

With color rising in his cheeks, Isaac tried to think of something to say that wouldn't make what he'd already said worse. He should have stayed on the porch. "I'm sorry," he finally stammered.

"Me too," she said as she reached down to pick up a Bible from among the books. "Very sorry."

He had the feeling she thought he was expressing sympathy for the preacher's loss and not for his careless words, but he didn't know how to change that.

She looked up at him then and noticed his flush. She pushed out her lower lip and blew air up across her face to ruffle the stray strands of hair falling down on her forehead. "I've embarrassed you with all my talking. And about things you being a Shaker would rather not hear. Talk of marriage and such. I can't see how I'll make much of a Shaker."

"I was married."

"Married before you went to the Shakers but not now?"

"I wouldn't be at the Shakers if I was still married. My wife died."

"Oh." She studied his face. "Now I'm the one who's sorry. I can see you're still sorrowful. The preacher is too in his way. For sure I'm thinking he's sorry we got married. That's how come your Shaker talk fell on such willing ears."

"Your ears weren't so willing?"

"Willing in some ways. Not so willing in others." She didn't wait for him to respond to that. "Do you like it there? With the Shakers?"

"There's plentiful food."

"You have to work for it though, don't you?"

"You don't look afraid of work."

"That's true enough."

"But you're not sure you want to go." Isaac didn't make it a question. Her reluctance was plain to see. He'd seen the same look on Ella's face when he'd told her they were going west. So now he said the words to this woman that he should have said to Ella. "If you don't want to go, don't go."

"A married woman has to do what her husband says."

"You won't be married among the Shakers," Isaac said.

She frowned again. "How can all those men and women be together and none of them think on marrying?" She didn't wait for him to answer. She didn't expect an answer. "It's a puzzle for sure."

"Romantic love is forbidden." Isaac wasn't sure why he said that. Again it would have been better to stay silent.

She shook her head a little with a knowing smile. "Lots of things are forbidden among church folks. That doesn't mean they don't sometimes happen."

He was saved from having to respond to that by a child

running in from the back of the house. "Lacey! Lacey! Those men are here."

The little girl's eyes, as blue as the woman's were brown, flew open wide at the sight of Isaac. She skidded to a stop in the doorway as if afraid to come closer to him. Her hair was dark as night and her cheeks very pink. She didn't favor the woman who held a hand out to her. The child crept forward and grabbed hold of the young woman's skirt pulling it in front of her.

"It's all right, Rachel. He's one of the Shakers. Brother . . ." She stopped and looked over at Isaac. "I can't recall you telling me your name."

"Isaac. Isaac Kingston."

The woman called Lacey put her hand tight against the little girl's back and pressed her close against her leg. "How about that, Rachel? A Bible name just like yours." She looked down at the child and then back at Isaac. "This is Rachel. She doesn't take to strangers."

"Your little sister?"

"Do you always jump to conclusions about how people are related when you meet them?" Lacey said with a smile that took the sting out of her words. "We aren't sisters. And before you ask, she's not exactly my daughter, but she's mine. Every bit mine. I'd try explaining it all, but it's complicated and would take awhile. So instead of storytelling, I guess I'd better go on and pack up these books to leave here for the church people if I can't take them with me." She glanced down at the books. "I'm beginning to wonder what's the use of packing anything. Could be we should leave it all for the church folks here to fight over."

"Will they?"

"Will they what?"

"Fight over it. Fight over those books and whatever else you leave."

"Of course they will. Church folk fight over everything even when they're pretending not to. Don't they do that over there where you live? At that Harmony Hill place?"

"Not so you notice. Everybody follows the rules."

"Rules." Lacey looked at him with a puzzled frown between her eyes. "What rules? The Ten Commandments?"

"Those too I suppose. But more. Shaker rules." The ones he was breaking, he thought, but there was no need telling her that.

"Oh, you mean like the no-storybook rule. And the no-romance rule. Who makes up all those rules?" Her frown grew darker, and the little girl peeked up at her before burying her face in the woman's skirt.

"The Ministry. Or so I've been told." Isaac wondered if he should warn them about more rules. Something about the way the woman gently stroked the child's head stabbed Isaac's heart with loss. Not only for the child he and Ella would now never have but for the two in front of him. The Shakers would separate them. Their rules not only separated husbands and wives but mothers and children. But what good would it do to tell her? It would just bring the sadness sooner.

"A bunch of their preachers, you mean?"

"Their leaders anyway. They don't exactly do church like most people around here."

"I guess not if they just hand down rules and don't let their people have any say in it. Our church people here aim to have a say in nigh on everything." One side of her mouth twisted up in a little smile and her eyes sparkled. "For sure, I can't imagine getting them or any body of church folks to agree to that one about the no marrying. The Bible we read speaks plenty about a man taking a wife and being fruitful."

"The Shakers have a different way of looking at those parts of the Bible, I suppose."

"You think they're right?" Her smile disappeared as she waited for him to answer.

"It's what they believe." He avoided an answer, but she didn't let him slip past her question.

"But what do you believe? Isn't that what we need to figure out? Not what they think, but what we think." The child eased the woman's skirt away from her face to peer at him as if she wanted to know his answer too.

"Me, I'm not worried about that kind of fruitful. Not since my wife passed on." Isaac felt the familiar stab of sorrow and regret mixed with guilt.

Her face seemed to reflect some of the same sorrow and regret back to him as her shoulders sagged a little. "Guess as how I'm not either, with how I've been living here with the preacher. But if everybody lived that way, believed that nobody should be fruitful, there wouldn't be any babies." Lacey tightened her hand on Rachel's back as her voice took on a pleading tone. "That can't be what the good Lord wants. It just can't."

Isaac heard the men coming into the house, but there was no escape from their notice now. It was going to take a lot of confessing to get Brother Verne's forgiveness for this lapse of obedience.

The man's voice was harsh and condemning. "Brother Isaac, you were told to wait out on the porch."

Lacey spoke up for him. The very worst thing she could have done. "He was doing no harm. Merely explaining your beliefs."

Brother Verne turned his scowl on the young woman. "It is surely impossible to explain that which one has no understanding of himself. Obedience is the first duty."

Lacey met his stare with no give in her own as she asked, "Duty to who? You or God?"

"That's enough, Lacey," the preacher said, his voice every bit as harsh as Brother Verne's. "You speak out of turn."

She turned her eyes to the man she'd claimed as her husband, and for a second Isaac thought she was going to defy him too. But then she shut her lips tight together and bent her head before she muttered, "Sorry. Forgive my rudeness."

In the uncomfortable silence that followed her words, the child began to sob. The woman pulled the little girl around in front of her and held her tightly against her apron.

The preacher looked completely disgusted with them both as he said, "Rachel, stop that noise right now." He raised his hand as though he might be thinking of striking the child to make her hush.

Brother Forrest spoke up quickly. "We must all keep in mind that kindness is as much a duty as obedience." Brother Forrest's voice was soft with no censure as he looked at Brother Verne.

A bit of color climbed into Brother Verne's face. "Yea. Forgive me as well, my sister and brothers."

Brother Verne looked over toward Lacey, who acknowledged his words with a barely perceptible nod and then at Isaac. Brother Forrest and Brother Jacob were looking at Isaac too, expecting him to ask forgiveness as well. To bring peace back among them. So he said the expected words asking forgiveness for his disobedience, but what he really wanted to say as Lacey raised her eyes to meet his for a brief second before she turned away was *don't go.*

He'd told her that once already when she'd asked how he liked living among the Shakers, and it had been plain from the look on her face that she had little desire to go to the Shaker village. The words, ill advised then, were impossible to speak again in front of this man who was her husband. It was just as she had answered him earlier. Of course she had to go. She was the man's wife. The same as Ella had been his wife.

14

Blessed are the meek: for they shall inherit the earth. That verse kept running through Lacey's head. Words straight out of the mouth of Jesus, telling folks gathered on that Bible mountain how to live. Miss Mona had taught her the blessed verses early on. She'd told Lacey a person might not understand them all exactly, but that didn't mean there weren't lessons to be learned and attitudes to be sought.

Lacey had trouble with the meek part. Not understanding it. She knew what meek meant. It was the being it that was hard for her. She didn't know why. If anybody had reason to be meek, it was her. A girl whose father had the same as given her away instead of standing up to his new wife. A girl who had to depend on the kindness of others for a place to live. A girl like that had no reason to be anything but meek. And yet her spirit resisted any hint of meekness.

Even when she bent her head there in front of the Shaker men and the preacher and pretended meekness, her insides knew better. She wanted to stare right into the face of that Shaker brother with his condemning attitude and talk some Bible at him. "Judge not that ye be not judged" and the like of that. But then the meek verse had slid through her mind and the "turn the other cheek" part of that mountain sermon

160

and the "so far as a body is able live in peace with one another" verse.

Miss Mona was surely pelting her with those bits of Scripture straight from heaven. And if that was true, then Miss
Mona must be telling her to go on and set her feet on this
new path without fighting against it inside or out. Besides,
she didn't want to get the young brother in deeper trouble
with the frowning brother. He seemed nice. The younger
one. Isaac.

If you don't want to go, don't go. That was what he'd said.
She wondered why. He was there living with those Shaker
men learning obedience. And kindness, she reminded herself.
Brother Forrest was that. Kindness on foot. So could be there
were more brothers and sisters like him at this village Preacher
Palmer was determined to take them to than those like that
other brother with his frowns and grudging apologies.

That's what she would have to hope for, because she didn't
have the first choice except to follow the preacher wherever
he went. He was her husband, in the sight of God and man.
Didn't matter if he acted like a husband or she acted like a
wife. They were married. She'd stood up in front of a preacher
and promised to love, honor, and obey till death do them
part. Against her better judgment perhaps, but the vow had
been made. While she hadn't done the first two so well, she
could manage the last one. Especially since to do any different would mean being parted from Rachel.

After the Shaker men started carrying the furniture out to
the wagons they'd brought with them, Lacey hushed Rachel's
crying and mopped up her face with her apron. Then she and
the little girl carried the storybooks to the kitchen and stowed
them away on the shelves next to the rose-covered plates.
She'd leave Miss Sadie Rose a note telling her everything
left on those kitchen shelves was to go to the churchwomen

in memory of Miss Mona. Maybe they wouldn't fight over it that way, in spite of what she'd told that young brother about church folk fighting over everything. Maybe they'd remember that "meek inheriting the earth" verse and divide it all up with no cross words or hurt feelings.

Meekness. That was what she was going to dwell on. That and the verse about how the good Lord would never desert those who followed after him. She should have told the young brother that. His eyes had been so sad when he talked about losing his wife. Just the thought of a man loving a woman that much made Lacey feel all soft inside. That had been the kind of love she'd once dreamed of knowing while reading those storybooks the Shakers didn't believe in. The kind of love a body could read between the lines in some Bible stories. The kind of love she'd likely never have a chance to know.

She shook away her wayward thoughts about love and turned back to emptying out drawers and packing. She added Miss Mona's fans and recipe box to the kitchen shelf pile for the church people. Brother Forrest said there wouldn't be any need for either at the Shaker village.

Each piece of furniture they carried out made the house echo with a little more sorrow. When Rachel melted into tears for the fourth time, Lacey grabbed the little girl's hand and pulled her out the back door past the garden where the onion tops were beginning to fall over on the dirt and the corn was practically knee high. Another thing the church people could share, or maybe by the time the corn was ready to harvest they'd have a new preacher and his wife in the house. She wasn't bothered by the thought of some other woman pulling the ears of corn off the stalks she'd planted. No need in her labor being wasted.

"Are we going to pick flowers to put on Mama's grave?"

Rachel asked when they went through the gate into the little cemetery.

"We won't have to. Look." Lacey pointed toward the grave where dandelion fluffs were so thick they made a bed of cotton. The yellow flowers hugging the ground had been transformed into fluff balls sticking up their heads to catch a breeze. Lacey bent down to softly touch one of the white fluffs and seeds took flight to leave nothing but the empty stem. So quickly gone through its cycle of life.

"Can I blow one, Lacey? Will Mama care?"

"She'd tell you that's what you're supposed to do. Blow the seeds. Open the door for new flowers."

Rachel blew the seeds off one of the stems and giggled as she carefully picked another to do the same. Lacey put her hands on the warm gravestone. She shut her eyes and thought on meekness again. Miss Mona had been meek yet strong. And so good. *Blessed are the pure in heart: for they shall see God. Blessed are they that mourn: for they shall be comforted.* She skipped around in the "blesseds," saying whichever came to mind.

She didn't realize she had spoken them aloud until she opened her eyes and saw Reuben standing there beside her. "Was you praying, Miss Lacey? Or just practicing reciting? They was Bible words, weren't they? I stayed real quiet so as not to disturb you."

"Thank you, Reuben." She smiled a little at him before her eyes sought out Rachel chasing some of the dandelion seeds floating on the wind across the graveyard. "I was praying for help."

"Help? I can help you. My mam always said I was good at helping."

"That you are, but this is different help. Spirit-strengthening help. The kind you have to get direct from the Lord."

"I can help you pray for it." Reuben put his big blocky hands flat together under his chin and bent his head.

"You can, Reuben. Thank you. And I'll pray for you too." When she reached out to touch the man's arm, his face lit up. She looked straight into his eyes and said, "I'm going to miss you."

His smile faded away. "Do you have to go away, Miss Lacey?"

"I have to go where the preacher goes."

"But he shouldn't ought to go either. He's always been here. Since before I can remember." Reuben's broad face looked worried.

"I know, but sometimes things change." Lacey kept her voice soft.

"Even when you don't want them to?"

"Even then."

He let out a heavy sigh and stared down at the ground. "My mam said that too. After she took sick and the Lord started calling her home to heaven. She said things was gonna change, but I'd have to keep going down here."

"And you have."

"But I'm sad sometimes." He peeked up at Lacey. "I'm gonna be sad when you aren't here no more to help me with my letters the way Miss Mona did." He reached over and ran his fingers across Miss Mona's name on the tombstone. "I won't be able to carve the names."

"Yes, you will. Miss Sadie Rose will help you with that."

He shook his head. "She don't make them all square and straight the way you do. The way Miss Mona did. The way I have to have them."

Lacey stared at the letters of Miss Mona's name and tried to swallow down the sorrow that was making tears creep up in her eyes. Why did everything have to be so hard? The man before her knew nothing but meekness and service. Where was the earth he was supposed to inherit? She held in a sigh and stared down at the white cloud of fluff on Miss Mona's grave. New beginnings in every ball of seeds. But every seed didn't have to fly off to a new spot to begin. Some could take root right where they were and stay the same.

She looked back up at Reuben. "The Shaker town is not all that far from here. Somebody passes on and nobody in the church can write out the name so you can see it right, you bring me the paper with the name on it over there and I'll do the letters for you same as always."

Relief exploded on his face as he grabbed her in a bear hug.

Lacey couldn't keep from gasping a little as she tried to push him back. "Not so tight, Reuben."

Reuben turned her loose at once and cast his eyes down at the ground while his cheeks burned red. "I'm sorry, Miss Lacey. I shouldn't have done that."

"It's all right, Reuben. Everybody needs to hug somebody now and again." Lacey wondered when the last time was that she'd hugged anybody besides Rachel. Never a man, except maybe her father when she was a little girl. Certainly not the preacher. And now that she was going to the Shakers who didn't believe in romance of any kind, the only embraces she'd have much chance of experiencing would be in her stories. Nothing but a figment of her imagination. How funny that the only man to ever actually hug her as an adult woman would be the childlike Reuben.

His face was flaming red. "My mam told me not to hug on you church ladies. That it wasn't nice. I forgot."

"We all forget sometimes."

"I saw Preacher hug that girl. But preachers are different. Mam told me that too."

"Preacher Palmer?" Lacey stared at Reuben. She couldn't remember ever seeing the preacher hug anybody. Not any of the church people. Not Rachel. Not even Miss Mona. But Miss Mona's health had always been so delicate. A body worried the little woman was too fragile at times to withstand a touch much less a hug.

"He's the preacher. Mam said he started the church afore I was born. My mam liked Brother Palmer. She said he was a man of God and me seeing him with that girl didn't mean nothing. She told me preachers was appointed by God to comfort them that was in need of comforting, and it weren't our place to judge who was needing comfort."

"What girl?" Lacey couldn't keep the question from tumbling off her tongue.

"That one I told you about. That put that box on your porch back when Rachel come to you."

Rachel, hearing her name, stopped blowing the dandelion fluffs and came to lean against Lacey. She'd been practically attached to Lacey's leg for three days now. Ever since the preacher started talking serious to those Shaker men.

"Well, you said she was crying when you saw him talking to her. That was a pretty good sign she was needing comfort."

Reuben peeked over at Lacey with an odd little grin that made Lacey wonder if he was quite such an innocent as she'd always thought. "It weren't that day," he said.

Lacey stared at Reuben and didn't know what to say. Especially with Rachel there listening. Rachel knew Lacey had found her on the porch in a box, but she'd never asked about how she got in that box. Lacey wasn't ready to try to answer that question today. Not with everything else that needed answers. Why in the world had Reuben picked now to tell her about seeing the girl after all this time?

Reuben was as much a part of the Ebenezer church as the preacher. More now, Lacey supposed, since the preacher was turning his back on his congregation to go to the Shakers.

Reuben was rooted as solid in the church as the oak tree out in the churchyard. The church people were his family. The tending of the graveyard his mission. At every service, he showed up with his boyish smile and drifted around the edges of the fellowship ready to pounce on any chance to talk. And yet he had hidden this secret for years. How many other secrets did he know?

Lacey pushed a smile out on her face. The curiosity Reuben's words had awakened inside her was nothing but a poison she didn't dare let spread in her mind. Curious imaginings about other people put a body's feet on the path to trouble.

"It's a preacher's duty to comfort his sheep on any day they need help," she said.

"Deacon Harold says he's trying to scatter the sheep." Reuben's brow wrinkled with worry.

"The Lord will take care of you, Reuben. He'll take care of all of you. He won't let you be scattered."

"But you're going, Miss Lacey. You're gonna be a lost sheep. You and Rachel." He looked ready to cry.

"No, no, Reuben. The good Lord isn't confined to one place. You know that. He'll be right there with us wherever we go, the same as he is here with us now." She lightly touched his arm. "We won't forget you." Lacey looked down at Rachel, who was staring up at Reuben with sad eyes. "And Reuben won't forget us either, Rachel."

They left him standing there by Miss Mona's grave. Lacey tried to leave the questions that wanted to circle in her head because of his words there with Miss Mona too, but they trailed along after her like bits of a spider web she'd run into and couldn't get wiped off. She didn't need to pile on worries about things in the past atop the ones that were fresh and new.

Miss Mona used to tell her the Bible said each day had its worries and that was enough to keep a person busy without borrowing from yesterday or tomorrow. That was sure enough true on this day with leaving this place she'd called home these many years and going to somewhere she didn't know the first thing about except they danced in church. What a thing to know! That sort of rumbled around in her head and made her feel almost dizzy.

She pulled in a deep breath and straightened her shoulders. Whatever it was, she could handle it. "Blessed are the meek" popped up in her head again, but she didn't let the words linger there. Meek wasn't going to work. She was going to have to stiffen her spine and face whatever was coming head on. She'd done that plenty. And it appeared she was going to have to do it plenty more.

"Lacey." Rachel pulled on her apron.

Lacey looked down at her. That was going to be the hard part. Not being able to keep some of those hard times from Rachel. She'd thought she could by agreeing to marry the preacher, and look where that had got them. Stuck down in a deep hollow of unhappiness. It had been her intention to keep sunshine pouring in on Rachel, but there wasn't anything but worriment on the little girl's face as she looked up at Lacey.

Lacey asked, "What's the matter, sweetie?"

"Did Reuben know the mama I had before you found me on the porch?"

"He said he saw her, but he didn't really know her."

"Did Papa? Did you?" Her eyes were trusting. She didn't seem worried about what Lacey might answer. More like she was just asking what happened next in one of Lacey's stories.

"No, I didn't. But she must have been very pretty because you are." Lacey leaned down and hugged the little girl. "How about a Maddie story while they finish loading the wagons?"

Rachel's face brightened. Stories were always an easy way

to distract her from things not going right. Lacey too. What would she have done all these years without her stories?

"Not a Maddie story. Tell me about the angel Mama saw. The one that came and peeked in the windows to make sure you and her could take care of me."

"That's not my story. That was Miss Mona's story."

Rachel yanked on Lacey's apron. "But you can tell it. You know it. I like the part where the angel dances on the roof to get you to go outside and see me before I got too cold."

"That's not real, Rachel. Your mama just made up the angels to make you smile."

"Please, Lacey. Please." She stared up at Lacey with pleading eyes. "There could be angels, couldn't there?"

Lacey relented. "There could be. An angel told the shepherds about baby Jesus for sure." She looked toward the wagons. They weren't completely loaded, so she just sat down in the grass next to the garden and pulled Rachel down beside her. The sun warmed their shoulders as she told the story about the angels that Miss Mona liked to tell Rachel. Miss Mona liked talking about angels. She said they were everywhere all around them. Ready to lift them up and keep them from dashing their feet on a stone in the path. She said that if a person paid proper attention and had her spirit open to the Lord, that sometimes, just sometimes, that person might feel the flutter of wings. That was the way she always ended the story and that was the way Lacey ended it too.

And then she held Rachel's hands in hers and wished hard that Miss Mona's angels would follow them to the Shaker town.

15

It was good Lacey fed Rachel some bread and cheese back home at the preacher's house before they climbed into the buggy with Preacher Palmer to follow the wagons to the Shaker town. Lacey had thought about cooking the eggs that wouldn't be needed for breakfast, but the fire was out in the stove and there wouldn't have been time to wash the dishes. She wasn't about to leave dirty dishes for the churchwomen to find.

It was a long ride and past dusk before they came to the village. A silent ride as the preacher spoke not a word. His grim silence stilled Lacey's tongue and that of Rachel's as the child held tight to her Maddie doll and leaned against Lacey's side. More than once Lacey wished they could be riding on the back of one of the wagons where the two of them could have marveled out loud over the sights along the road. Houses with flowers blooming in the yards. Mares with new foals running beside them out in the pastures. The scent of lilacs on the breeze. A stand of trees with dogwood blooms lingering among them.

Of course there were dogwood trees in the Ebenezer woods. And lilacs in the people's yards and horses in the fields, but somehow everything looked different along the road. New and strange and, from the way Rachel scrunched up against Lacey, a little scary.

Lacey could understand that. She'd traveled this same road when her father delivered her to the preacher's house. She'd been frightened then, just the way Rachel was now, not knowing what lay ahead. But Miss Mona had been at the end of her journey. Lacey took hold of Rachel's hand and sent up prayers that somebody just as kind might be at the end of this journey. The Lord could make good come of everything. Even tangled messes like the one she and Rachel were in.

She did her best to hang onto that hope as they rode into the village. The buildings loomed up in the near darkness, larger than anything Lacey had ever seen. The wagons turned to the side and stopped in front of a brick building that could have held the preacher's house and the church twice over with room to spare. And that was only one of the buildings. Brother Forrest helped them down from the buggy and led them along a road between two white buildings. One was built out of white stone that seemed to have gathered the sun's light and was continuing to radiate it now even though night was falling. On the other side of the road was a white frame building not as big but one that Lacey would have thought large if she hadn't just seen the other two buildings.

"Our meetinghouse." Brother Forrest nodded his head toward the smaller building.

"Where you dance." Lacey was sorry for the words as soon as she spoke them. They seemed to hang in the air and echo disrespect for their ways. Ways she was going to have to learn.

"Hush up, Lacey." Preacher Palmer's voice was harsh.

"Worry not, Brother Elwood. The young sister is right. That is where we go forth in exercises of worship. It is a gift to worship so."

After that, Lacey made sure she didn't open her mouth again even when Brother Forrest directed her and Rachel to go up separate steps and through a different door into yet another large brick building while he and the preacher went in the opposite door. For a few seconds Lacey had the crazy idea to grab Rachel and run. But where would they run? So instead she took Rachel's hand and climbed the stone steps into the building where three Shaker sisters and the elder who'd been at the preacher's house on Monday were waiting. Waiting to take Rachel away from her.

Miss Sadie Rose had warned her. She'd told her straight out the Shakers didn't believe in families in the usual sense, but somehow Lacey hadn't eyeballed the truth of that. After all, in the telling, stories oft as not got skewed a bit. Instead she had gone on thinking that she and Rachel could keep being the way they were back at the preacher's house. Together.

That might have happened for a few more days, even weeks, if not for Preacher Palmer. The minute one of those strange-looking Shaker women named Sister Janie took hold of Rachel's hand to lead her away, the little girl started wailing every bit as pitiful as she had the morning Miss Mona had passed on. The sound like to have broke Lacey's heart. She grabbed Rachel close and stared down the Shaker woman until she dropped the child's hand and stepped back. Sister Janie looked at the other Shaker women, and Lacey could almost see them thinking on maybe changing their minds about taking Rachel from her. Not that she was going to let any of them peel her arms away from Rachel anyway.

"Perhaps we need to give them a little while to adjust to the Shaker way," Sister Janie murmured.

Lacey felt her breath coming a little easier with the words. They weren't heartless.

But Preacher Palmer was. He turned cold eyes on Lacey.

"Let the child go, Lacey. Right now. We've come into this community to leave things of the world behind and do as they say."

Lacey held Rachel against her even tighter. "But she needs me." She spoke barely above a whisper.

"She needs discipline. And so do you."

Lacey stared down at Rachel's head and wanted to lean down to kiss the sweet part dividing her dark hair. With her face pressed tight against Lacey, the child stopped crying but stood stiff, taking tiny breaths like as how she might escape the notice of the people around her if she could only be quiet enough. Lacey felt the same stiffness inside, along with a swelling of pain in her chest. They wouldn't listen to her over the preacher.

Why hadn't she paid more mind to what Sadie Rose had said about them separating mothers and children? It just hadn't seemed like something they'd really do. Not to a child as young as Rachel. She wasn't much more than a baby and she'd already lost two mothers. It wasn't right to force her to lose another one.

Lacey should have stayed back at the preacher's house. She and Rachel could have sat there on the kitchen floor in front of the shelves full of Miss Mona's things that had no place in the Shaker village and waited for the churchwomen to come divvy up what had been left behind. The churchwomen would have took pity on them. More pity than the preacher, who was glaring at Lacey with eyes hard and full of fire, like some Old Testament prophet calling down doom on the Israelites for forgetting the Lord.

Even the Shakers standing around her and Rachel looked on them with kinder eyes than the preacher. Especially Brother Forrest. He and the bearded old man they'd called Elder Homer stood to the side of Preacher Palmer. Then there were the three women in like dresses with wide white collar scarves lapped across the front and tucked under the waistbands of the aprons that still covered their blue and gray skirts, though it was well past supper-cooking time.

After a long moment of strained silence, Brother Forrest came to her rescue once more. He looked at the older woman dressed in gray. The one they had called an eldress.

"Eldress Frieda, the two young sisters have had a long day of work and are surely tired from their journey here. Perhaps it would be well to allow them to sleep at the Trustees' House tonight and let them begin their new life with us in the morning sun."

"There's not the least need in that," Preacher Palmer said. "They will do as I say."

Lacey kept her eyes away from his face, not anxious to see the anger that would be there. Anger that surely grew fiercer when the eldress spoke. "This is not a decision for you to make, Brother Elwood. Nay, we will do as Brother Forrest suggests, but there are beds here we can use on this night so as not to bother those at the Trustees' House with this minor predicament."

Lacey peeked up at the woman. It was obvious she expected no argument from anyone in the room. Not even the preacher when she turned her steady eyes on him. With the way the color flooded the preacher's cheeks, Lacey wondered if he might be rethinking his decision to follow the Shaker path. Most of his adult years had been spent telling others what they should do, with the full power of the pulpit behind his orders. Now a woman was telling him that he would have to humble his will and do as she said.

He clamped his mouth together and stayed silent, but Lacey could see the effort it took. She bit the inside of her lip to keep a smile from creeping out on her face. It wasn't a time for smiling. Because the truth was that even though they had won this night together, come morning the eldress would be just as firm in separating her from Rachel, and there wouldn't be a single thing she could do about it.

Brother Forrest led the preacher up the stairs to the right. Doors opened and closed. Voices were quiet but firm. Still in the entrance hallway, the Shaker women eyed Lacey. One of the sisters, the one named Drayma, stepped between Lacey and the door.

"I will do as you say," Lacey said quietly.

"Yea, so you say, my sister." Eldress Frieda pinned her with stern eyes. "But you have already refused that, have you not?"

"I suppose so." Lacey looked down. *Blessed are the meek*, she reminded herself.

"It is best to not suppose, but to know. Only then can we deal with our wrong thinking."

"Your ways seem strange to me and contrary to what I have always known."

"Yea, that is true for many who come from the world. You will not be expected to understand everything at once. We will explain it to you, and then you will see that it is a better way. A way written of in the Bible."

Lacey looked up. "Where?" She and Miss Mona had read clear through the Scriptures more than once, but Lacey couldn't remember one verse that said a mother shouldn't take care of her child. In fact, babies seemed to be a major way the Lord blessed folks in the Bible.

"The Christ speaks of it in the gospel of Mark. He promises no man—and our Mother Ann completed the message to make us understand the words mean no woman as well—shall leave house or brethren or sisters or father or mother or wife or children for the way of truth and not be richly rewarded. As those among us have been." Eldress Frieda's voice softened.

"But it is plain to see that you and the little sister are near exhaustion as Brother Forrest pointed out. Bible truths are better understood by a rested mind. Sister Drayma will find you nightclothes and show you where you can pass the night until the morning bell rings."

"And then what?" Lacey asked.

"Then if you stay among us you will have to abide by the rules that stand us in good stead here and eliminate the stress that bedevils the lives of those who choose to live in the worldly way." Her face was stern.

"What if I can't?"

"'Can't' is not a word that we should dwell upon, my sister. We can do what the Eternal Father wants, if we are willing to turn our will over to him."

"Blessed are the meek," Lacey whispered.

"Indeed. You will do well to think on meekness." The eldress smiled, and she suddenly looked years younger and not so forbidding.

"And if I can't?" Lacey asked.

"Again you speak that word 'can't' when surely what is more often true is 'won't.' But Sister Lacey, don't give up before you have even started," the eldress said. "However, if that does hold to be the truth and you are not able to surrender your will for the union of the community, then we do not keep those unwilling captive. All are free to come and go as they wish. Our village is not a prison."

"And Rachel?" Lacey asked softly as she rubbed her hand up and down the little girl's back.

"As I understand it, the child's mother died some months ago and then you married her father. So you can claim to be her stepmother."

The woman's voice wasn't exactly condemning Lacey, but it did wipe away any hope Lacey had been clinging to that she could get them to see a better way. Lacey's way. "I've been with her since she was a tiny babe in arms."

Eldress Frieda took a minute to consider Lacey's remark before she said, "The child's path will be determined by her father. That is the accepted way of the world and one we recognize here in our village."

But her father doesn't love her the way I do. Lacey held back her words. It would change nothing to say them aloud, only bring Rachel sorrow. There was enough of that lying in wait for them along this Shaker path without adding more. So Lacey bent her head and thought on the meekness Beatitude. What in the world could the Lord have meant about the meek inheriting the earth? The meeker she tried to be, the more things were pried out of her hands, until it didn't seem she had hold of anything but air.

Think on the promises of the Lord. Miss Mona's words whispered through her head after the Shaker sister called Drayma got Lacey and Rachel bedded down. She'd given them plain, soft nightgowns. Rachel's swallowed her, but that was because they didn't have children's clothes in this house, according to the sister. There was a special children's house where all the youngsters lived together with some sisters and brothers overseeing their upbringing and welfare. It was on the tip of Lacey's tongue to ask to be one of those tending sisters, but she knew that wouldn't be a job they'd let her do. Not unless she was able to swallow the Shaker way, and the more she was hearing about that way, the bigger the wad was getting in her throat until it was nigh on choking her.

She lay there on the narrow bed and rubbed Rachel's back. They hadn't started out in the same bed, but as soon as Sister Drayma shut the door behind her, Rachel slipped out of her bed to crawl in beside Lacey. The room was small, barely big enough for the three beds that were little more than cots. No one slept in the third bed.

Rachel had fallen right to sleep as soon as she cuddled next to Lacey. She trusted Lacey to take care of her. A trust that was going to be broken come morning. As Lacey stared out at the dark air that surrounded her, she tried to think up what she would say to Rachel come morning. What words could ease their parting. What promises could she make and be sure to keep.

Think on the promises of the Lord. The words whispered through Lacey's mind again. Miss Mona would tell her it wasn't this earth she had to worry about inheriting. It was the Promised Land she needed to be seeking. That all people needed to be seeking. So maybe that was the earth the Lord was talking about in that meekness verse. But Lacey wasn't exactly ready to step over to heaven's shore. Somehow she was going to have to find a way to live in this strange place where what seemed to be the natural way of life was denied. Not that she'd been living in any natural way with the preacher in the weeks since their marriage.

It kept coming around to that. To how she'd aimed to fashion and shape life to suit her will instead of accepting things as they were. She had no idea why she thought she could do that. It had never worked before. She hadn't wanted her mother to die. She hadn't wanted her father to marry the Widow Jackson. She hadn't wanted to watch Junie ride out of her life back to Virginia where it was likely she'd never lay eyes on her again. She hadn't wanted Miss Mona to move on up to heaven. She had never had the first thought of ever marrying Preacher Palmer. And yet she had. Stood up right beside him and surrendered every hope of knowing love like she imagined it could be. The way she dreamed it should be. And now come morning she was going to have to surrender this last person she loved.

She could make up a hundred stories, whisper a thousand wishes, and cry a million tears, but it wasn't going to change a thing. Not one earthly thing.

The best she could do was think up words that might make the parting easier for Rachel. She'd have other girls to play with. Other women to mother her to whatever extent the Shakers believed in mothering. She would get to sing and dance in church instead of sitting still as a mouse. She would be safe. And Lacey would never stop loving her. That was a promise she could make with no worry of not being able to keep it.

Lacey kissed the top of the child's head and then smoothed the hair back from her face. Each moment seemed extra precious as the night slipped past. Too precious to waste in sleep.

Once in the deep of the night, Rachel cried out and grabbed for Lacey as though she'd lost her footing on a cliff. Lacey tightened her arms around her and then to sweeten the child's dreams began whispering a story into the dark air pressing down on them.

"Once upon a time, there was a little baby in a box and angels watched over her." A tear slipped out of Lacey's eye and dribbled down her cheek, but she didn't quit whispering the story. "Those angels were the fastest flyers, because the Lord knew that baby was going to grow into a little girl who did the most amazing things. Her and her doll, Maddie, and her pet worm, Silas."

Lacey didn't know why she'd thought up a pet worm, much less given him a name, but a smile pushed some of the worry out of her heart. Stories had always done that for her. A gift, Miss Mona had said, as long as she stayed clear on which were the made-up parts and which were the real parts and didn't mix them up. But there in the dark with Rachel's hair tickling her chin, Lacey couldn't help wondering which was harder to believe. The made-up story or the one that was truly happening.

16

Rachel didn't cry the next morning when Sister Janie took her hand before breakfast to take her away to the Children's House. Lacey had awakened the child at the first hint of daylight to prepare her for what was going to happen.

"It won't do the first bit of good for us to cry and carry on," Lacey told her. "All that will do is make our heads hurt and your mama up in heaven ashamed that we're forgetting to trust in the Lord to take care of us. He will, you know." She tried to sound extra sure of that. If she kept saying it, maybe she could start believing it the way Miss Mona did. "The good Lord has something in mind for us. Something good."

"Can't we just go home, Lacey?" Tears were in Rachel's voice, but none slipped out of her eyes.

"Not now, sweetheart." Lacey pushed Rachel's dark hair back from her face.

"Tomorrow?"

She looked at Lacey with such hopeful eyes that a lump jumped up in Lacey's throat so big she could barely squeak out an answer. "We can pray about it, but it might be awhile before we can go home." Lacey tried to smile, but her lips wouldn't turn up.

Rachel stared at Lacey's face a long minute before she said, "We don't have a home anymore, do we?"

Lacey swallowed down the lump in her throat and spoke her next words fiercely. "We may not be able to ever go back to our old house, but that doesn't mean we don't have a home. We'll always have a home together if nowhere but in our hearts. You in mine and me in yours." Lacey took Rachel's hand and placed it over her heart and then placed her own hand over the child's heart. She imagined its steady thump under her hand. Life continuing.

"That sounds too hard." Rachel lay her head over on Lacey's shoulder.

Lacey stroked the child's hair and let her rest there for a moment until a bell began tolling in the village. Measured and loud. No doubt a signal for the Shakers to rise. She had no idea how much time they had before the Shaker sisters would come for them. The only thing she knew for sure was that they would come. She took hold of Rachel's shoulders and pushed her back from her so she could look into the child's face.

"You can do this, Rachel. You have to do this. We both do."

"But I don't think I can keep from crying." The little girl's bottom lip trembled.

"You can blink those tears away. It's not like we won't see one another. We're both going to be right here."

"Will you still tell me stories?" She held up her Maddie doll. "About Maddie?"

"Every chance I get. We'll get Maddie into so many pickles you'll think there will be no way she can get out of trouble. But she always finds a way, doesn't she?" Lacey pushed a smile out on her face.

An answering smile touched Rachel's lips, but then disappeared as quickly as it came. "I wish we could be like Maddie and think up what we want to happen next."

181

Out in the hallway Lacey heard footsteps. She wanted to shut her eyes to block out the daylight pouring in the window and delay the morning, but she couldn't stop time. They would have to face the day. "All right. Let's do that. Think up what's going to happen next."

"How?" A little frown wrinkled the skin between Rachel's eyes.

"Think about it. What happens every morning?" Lacey pointed at the window where the first hint of sunlight was creeping into the sky.

"The sun comes up." Rachel smiled. "Mama said the sun always comes up no matter what else happens."

"That it does. And then one of the Shaker sisters will come and bring us new dresses."

"Will mine be blue? I like blue."

"Could be. Sister Janie's was blue, wasn't it? And she was the sister who was going to take care of you."

"I didn't like her." Rachel stuck her bottom lip out a little. "She looked mean."

"That's just because you were worried about what was happening. She didn't look a bit mean to me."

"She did to me. I want to stay with you."

"I know you do, but right now that can't happen." Lacey remembered the eldress taking her to account for using the word "can't." But no other word fit. "But you know I love you. My love wraps all around you and nobody can take it off. Nobody."

Rachel settled her soft cheek against Lacey's chest and was quiet for a long moment. Finally she said, "Lacey, can I call you Mama?"

Lacey caught her breath in surprise. While she knew in her heart she was Rachel's mama, she had never expected to hear Rachel call her that. Sometimes Lacey wondered about the good Lord's sense of humor. Here with them about to be parted, he had put in Rachel's mind to recognize Lacey as her mama. "Why are you asking that now?"

"Because Mama told me that mamas never stopped loving their little girls. No matter what." Rachel peered up at Lacey with intense blue eyes. "And I want you to have to keep loving me forever, Lacey." She shook her head a little and changed her last word. "I mean, Mama."

"You don't have to worry about me stopping loving you, sweetheart. Ever." Lacey hugged the child close and kissed her forehead. "It doesn't matter what you call me. Lacey or Mama. I'll always love you."

"More than all the rocks in the creek?" Rachel leaned back to ask.

Lacey smiled and played the "more than" game Miss Mona had taught Rachel. "More than all the pebbles in the river."

"More than all the stars in the sky?"

"More than the moon and all the stars put together."

Rachel thought a moment before she said, "More than all the bees in a field full of daisies?"

"More than all the worms wiggling under the ground."

Rachel giggled at that and ended it the way Miss Mona had taught her to. "Then that's enough. Not as much as Jesus loves me, but plenty enough."

Lacey held her a minute before she said, "Don't ever forget that, Rachel, and somehow, someway, things will work out."

"Papa will take us home? We can be happy again?"

Lacey didn't know how to answer that. Home was never going to be the same for them and happiness was something that seemed out of reach. At least for her and Preacher Palmer, but maybe not for Rachel. "You will be happy again," she promised her. She let a little prayer wing up in her heart that it was a promise the good Lord would honor.

The door opened and Sister Janie and Sister Drayma came into the room with dresses draped over their arms to get them started on their new lives. Rachel didn't cry as Sister Janie led her away, but her face was sad as she looked over her shoulder at Lacey, who managed to keep a smile on her face until the child was out the door. Then it slid away from her lips like one of Rachel's worms crawling back into the dirt.

That left her alone with Sister Drayma who didn't appear to favor smiling overmuch anyway. The Shaker woman reminded Lacey of some of the churchwomen back at Ebenezer. Those who looked worried that if they smiled at church, they might look to not be taking the business of the Lord serious enough. It was more than obvious that Sister Drayma was taking the business of being a Shaker plenty serious enough, and making Lacey into a Shaker sister was her part of that business on this day.

Gray hair peeked out around the edges of Sister Drayma's cap and her faded blue eyes were squinted as if she had to narrow her eyes down on something to see it clear. When Lacey gave in to her curiosity and asked her how old she was, the Shaker woman claimed not to remember the exact number of years. She said a Believer didn't think on her worldly birthday that much. The important day to celebrate was the day one signed the Covenant of Belief and for her that was thirty-two years ago in March.

"What's the Covenant of Belief?" Lacey was feeling as full of questions as Rachel on a walk through the woods.

"That's your promise to live the perfect life in union with your brothers and sisters."

"Oh." Lacey eyed Sister Drayma and decided she couldn't have been all that young even then. "But what about before then? You must have been older than me when you came here."

The woman frowned at Lacey. "My worldly life ended and

my new life began on the day I came into the village. Just as it will for you."

Lacey slipped the Shaker dress over her head and shoved her hands out through the sleeves. She pulled her hair free of the dress neckline and picked up the broad white scarf. "But were you married? Did you have children?" Lacey asked as she draped the scarf around her neck.

"You ask questions of the world. Things that do not matter." Sister Drayma narrowed her eyes even more on Lacey before reaching over to yank the edges of the scarf straight and even on Lacey's shoulders. "Now pull the corners down in front. Your apron will hold them in place."

Lacey wrapped the apron around her waist and reached behind her to tie it. She knew how to put that on without help. "But how can being married not matter? The preacher that spoke the vows for me and Preacher Palmer said something about what God has joined together, let no man put asunder. Till death do the two part."

"Nay, those are the words of a preacher with worldly beliefs. The Lord revealed a better way to our Mother Ann. One of purity and peace. The man and wife relations of the world bring naught but worry and upheaval into our lives."

"But what of children? They are a gift from God."

"Yea. We treasure our children. In union with all. Young Sister Rachel will be much loved by all the sisters and brothers. Such love as she could never know in the world."

"Nobody could love her more than I do." Lacey straightened up and stared at Sister Drayma.

Sister Drayma met her stare and spoke with the confidence of one expecting to be obeyed without question. "So you may think, but now you will be sharing that love in union with all who are like-minded in our village. In time you will come to see how your love can change from a selfish, narrow feeling to something that can encompass all your brothers and sisters. 'Tis a gift to know such love."

She reached her hands up in the air and gazed toward the ceiling. Lacey might have thought she was praying if she'd closed her eyes, but instead she kept her eyes wide open like she was searching for words written up there above her head. She reminded Lacey of an old tree with only a few branches left coming out of its thick trunk but rooted solid where she stood. She wasn't exactly fat. Just thick through the middle the way a lot of older women got when the years piled on. Miss Mona hadn't, but then she'd been afflicted with those weak spells that took her appetite.

When Sister Drayma started shaking her hands back and forth, Lacey spoke up to try to bring her away from whatever she was seeing up on the ceiling. Lacey wasn't sure she was ready to witness one of the shaking dances just yet.

"Love is good." She pushed the words out tentatively, but they worked.

The woman dropped her hands and was back to stern Sister Drayma. "Proper love," the sister said. "Love you will gladly embrace when you learn more."

"Love's embrace," Lacey whispered.

But the old sister had turned away to gather up Lacey's discarded clothes and didn't show any sign of hearing her. It was just as well. Lacey's thoughts weren't on brotherly love. Instead she was thinking she might never know a true embrace of love. One that made her heart quicken and stole her breath. The kind the young brother she'd met the day before had surely known with his treasured wife who had died too soon. Brother Isaac. He'd had such nice eyes. Just the thought of them made Lacey feel a little trembly inside as she took the cap Sister Drayma handed her. She could imagine loving a man like that. Just not the preacher.

She sighed softly as she twisted her hair and shoved it up under the cap. Her hands shook as she straightened the cap. She told herself that had nothing to do with the young brother's face sticking in her head or her thoughts of love that would never be. It had more to do with the truth that she hadn't eaten since her bowl of oatmeal the morning before. That was what brought the trembles on. Only that.

As the days passed, Lacey didn't mind the work they expected her to do. A body needed to be busy. Even the practicing of the dancing they did in the evenings wasn't bad. The up and back steps were curious but entertaining enough. Often as not, Lacey's foot tapped to the beat of the songs while she sat and watched. Sister Drayma said it was best to watch for the first week or two so she wouldn't mess up the lines.

No, it was the plethora of Shaker rules that piled on Lacey like thick woolen blankets until she could barely breathe. That was what she wanted to throw off. She'd been prepared for some of the rules. The "no men except as brothers" one. Everybody knew the Shakers had that rule. She didn't know as how she believed on that with the way the Bible read, but she was more than ready to go along with it. Thinking on the preacher as a brother was better than thinking on him as a husband. She wasn't so willing to go along with how they spirited Rachel away from her and then refused to let her so much as see the child. Sister Drayma claimed such a visit would be a hindrance to Rachel being able to settle in to the Shaker way of living.

Lacey argued against that, but Sister Drayma turned a deaf ear, simply saying, "When you chose to come into our community, you chose to abide by the rules that have served us well for many years."

Lacey wanted to tell the Shaker woman she didn't choose any of it, but then there she was. Right in the middle of the Shakers. So that meant a choice had been made. To keep from thinking on the sorrow of that choice, she said, "How many years?"

They were walking back to the Gathering Family House after a day of working in the washhouse. Lacey had done most of the work, with Sister Drayma directing her every move. As if she didn't know already how to scrub clothes. That was something she'd been doing since she was big enough to reach into a tub of water. Of course, back then or at the preacher's house either, she didn't have the washing machines the Shakers had invented nor the water piped into the house. That should have made it all easier, but here hundreds of Shaker people were dirtying up clothes. A scrub board with only one pair of britches and a shirt and dress or two to scrub down sounded easier than all those Shaker clothes, no matter if water did pour out of a pipe instead of being packed into the house in a bucket. Lacey was wishing for the bucket and her rain barrel back home.

"It is good to know our history." Sister Drayma gave Lacey an approving look as though just asking the question meant she was starting to believe in their ways. "Mother Ann came to America before the Revolution and began sharing the truth of the Believers' way."

"Here? She was here in Harmony Hill?"

"Nay. She has only been here in spirit to deliver us messages of love. Our beloved mother was never in the frontier states. It was not until some years after her death that the Ministry sent the first Shaker brothers here to the west. The eastern communities heard of the great revival workings at Cane Ridge and felt Mother Ann leading them to come plow the fertile spiritual fields here. The village was established here in 1805."

"Forty years ago."

"Yea, we have prospered much in those forty years. So many converts. So much building. When we do as Mother Ann directs and give our hands to work and our hearts to God, good things happen. Every day." Sister Drayma's face took on that strange shine Lacey had come to expect when she talked about their worship. "Many marvelous things are happening now during this time of Mother's work."

"What things?"

"Signs and wonders that come to us from the spirit world."

"What sort of signs and wonders?" Lacey eyed Sister Drayma a little uneasily. She wouldn't have been a bit surprised to see the woman go into a shaking frenzy, even though she hadn't seen so much as a tremble from any of the Shakers so far.

In spite of what Lacey had heard about their shaking dances, everything in the village seemed strictly ordered as the Shaker people went about their business with solemn intent. Even the business of eating was solemn with a rule of silence reigning over the tables and the only noise the clanking of forks on plates. Prayers were silent too. Numerous and far from spontaneous, as each Believer knelt upon rising in the morning and prior to retiring at night as well as before and after every meal. A lot of praying opportunities, and Lacey had plenty to talk to the Lord about, but often as not her mind couldn't settle down to pray before everybody was standing up and going about the next ordered thing.

Now Sister Drayma's voice sounded oddly high-pitched as she answered Lacey. "Songs and dances. Wondrous drawings. Spirit dreams and directives. Angels coming to dance among us." The woman looked toward the sky and threw her hands up as though indicating angels gathering around them that very instant. Then as suddenly as the glow had come upon her, it was gone as she narrowed her eyes on Lacey once again. "If you choose to surrender your spirit to the truth and stop holding back your belief, perhaps you will witness these wonders. But it is plain to see that you resist our way."

"It seems too much to understand and believe in such a short time," Lacey answered honestly.

"Nay, not for someone with a contrite spirit. Something you appear to lack. A person who seeks to understand would confess the sin in her life and vow to do better on the morrow. You must admit the wrongs you harbor in your heart." Sister Drayma turned her sternest look on Lacey. "As Brother Elwood has done."

"Has he?" Lacey had seen the preacher at the practice sessions and on the men's side of the dining room. She had wondered if he was chafing against the rules being set for him instead of being the one to explain the rules to his church people. But it appeared that was not the case.

"We are told he is progressing in his understanding. He is learning the simple way to true peace. A way you should consider, for it is a gift to be simple."

"Simple. How do you make things simple when nothing seems that way?"

"But it is simple, my sister. As simple as shrugging off the ways of the world and embracing the rules that keep life simple."

"You mean like which foot to step up on the stairs first?"

"Yea. Always step with the right foot first. Such disciplined obedience keeps you in union with your brothers and sisters."

And makes you a sheep, Lacey wanted to say, but she bit back the words. Not that being a sheep was wrong. The Lord spoke of his sheep knowing his voice. Perhaps Sister Drayma was right. Perhaps she was resistant to the spirit. There was no doubt she was nursing a contrary spirit here in this Shaker village, the same as she had clung to a contrary spirit as the preacher's lawful wife. She could fess up to her contrariness when next Sister Drayma asked her to number her sins. But confessing sin didn't necessarily mean she had turned from it. She could imagine nothing but contrary feelings as long as they kept Rachel from her.

That didn't mean she had to be contrary in every small thing. So when she came to the steps into the Gathering Family House, she lifted the proper foot up on the first stone step. She could at least set her mind to abide by the common rules, even if some of them didn't seem to matter the first bit. What in the world difference could it make to the good Lord above which knee hit the floor first when she knelt down to pray or whether or not she was holding a handkerchief in her hand when she dropped to her knees? But she could do those things as Sister Drayma instructed. And save her contrariness for the big things.

She could listen with a meek spirit to Sister Drayma harping on obedience and contrite spirits and the telling of how to do every little thing, even if it did make Lacey's head spin with rules and regulations. But she would never be able to keep her heart from aching for some sight of Rachel.

On the first Saturday after they came to the village, Lacey was in the garden planting beans when she heard the children's voices. Sister Drayma wasn't beside her. She was too old for garden work, she said before she left Lacey at the garden to work through the day. The six sisters worked in teams as one dropped the seeds a hand's width apart and the other covered the seed with dirt and tamped it down with her hoe.

It was good to be in the sunshine and away from the suds and dirty clothes and a relief to not have Sister Drayma's preaching words in her ears for a few hours. The sisters in the garden plot talked only of the work and how hot the sun was on their bonnets and what might be on the table at evening time. Lacey kept her silence, for Sister Drayma had warned her idle chatter was not allowed and that, although she wasn't with Lacey, other eyes would be watching.

And then Lacey heard the children passing by the garden. She stopped dropping the bean seeds in the row and stood up to peer across the way at the little girls following after a sister like ducklings trailing their mother duck. She spotted Rachel almost immediately walking in the line with her head bent and her shoulders rounded. A picture of sadness. Lacey took a step toward the edge of the garden, but a hand on her arm stopped her.

"You can't go to her, Sister Lacey." The sister's voice was barely loud enough for Lacey to hear.

"Why?" Lacey looked around at the sister. It wasn't Sister Nina, who had been following her with the hoe and covering the seeds. This sister had stepped over from another row. Sister Aurelia. A woman about the same age as Lacey with wisps of black hair escaping her cap and eyes as blue as Rachel's.

"It is not allowed." She spoke the words as if they explained everything. And perhaps they did. Follow the rules. Do this. Don't do that. Stop living life and become a sheep.

"But she needs me." Lacey looked back at the line of children who were disappearing from sight. It was all she could do to stand still and not run after them. How in the world had she ended up in such a place?

"She has others now."

Sister Aurelia reached for the hoe Sister Nina held. The sister gave it over without a word and stepped across to the next row to begin dropping the beans in Sister Aurelia's place. The other sisters began their planting dance again. Lacey wanted to throw her cloth bag of beans down on the ground and let the seeds fall where they may, but instead she leaned over and placed a seed in the row and then another.

Sister Aurelia covered it over and tamped down the dirt with her shoe. When she spoke, her voice was so quiet that Lacey had to strain to hear the words. "They tell me you have the sin of marriage to Elwood Palmer to overcome."

Lacey looked up at her, but the sister kept her eyes on her hoe as she covered the next bean. "Who tells you?" Lacey asked.

"Such things are common knowledge." Without raising her head, she glanced to the side. The other pairs of sisters had moved ahead and were not close. Even so, she didn't look directly at Lacey as she said, "Keep dropping the bean seeds so that Sister Ruth won't have cause to separate us."

Lacey did as she said, dropping a handful of beans one by one in the row before she said, "I do have that sin to overcome." Lacey thought she might not have spoken truer words for weeks.

Sister Aurelia said, "When did his wife die?"

"Last November."

"He didn't grieve long."

Lacey looked up at Sister Aurelia, but the woman's face was void of expression. "No."

"Nay. It is good to learn to say our yea and nay. It demonstrates unity of spirit," Sister Aurelia said. She covered several seeds and tamped them down before she spoke again. "And yet he seemed devoted to her."

Lacey stared at the Shaker woman. She couldn't remember ever seeing her before, but then she could have known Miss Mona before Lacey came to Ebenezer. And the preacher led meetings at different churches in the area. "So you knew Miss Mona and the preacher?"

"Yea, I knew the preacher."

193

Lacey dropped more seeds in the row. Sister Aurelia covered them over as they planted the rest of the row without more words. But Lacey felt no comfort in the silence.

Finally as they started up a new row, Lacey said, "I shouldn't have married him."

"Yea, some sins are harder to overcome than others."

17

Isaac watched for the new sister. He didn't know why exactly. Maybe because of how she'd run her fingers over the books around her when he'd told her that she wouldn't be able to keep them once at the Shaker Village. Like they were old friends she was about to lose.

He understood the sorrow in that touch. He did miss opening a new book and the promise of the words it held. The only books Brother Verne allowed him to read were Shaker books. He had read the story of Mother Ann coming to America and of her visions of a perfect life apart from the world. He read the Shaker books of rules and the reasons for them. A Believer must avoid anything that might tempt him back to the worldly ways of selfish living and greed. Books of songs were plentiful, but reading the choruses tended to make Isaac's eyelids droop.

No books of adventure or derring-do were allowed. Except for the Bible where Isaac found stories of man's struggle with sin in his quest for God. He read about Jacob's flight from his brother Esau, and David fighting the giant. And then there were Joseph's harrowing adventures after his dreams so raised the ire of his brothers that they sold him into slavery, where he went from slave to prisoner to keeper of the kingdom's stores. The Lord's plan with man's detours.

Isaac could see no plan of the Lord's that had him in the Shaker village. No reason for him to be there other than hiding from the law. Brother Asa had assured Isaac that even that was no longer necessary. After his last trip to Louisville for more building materials for the West Family's barn, Asa had cheerfully reported to Isaac that he was not a wanted man with leaflets carrying his description spread about the town. The man who had been stabbed on the riverfront had lived to point out his actual attacker. Isaac could return to the world. He could go wherever he wanted to begin his life again. As long as he stayed away from the judge's town, he had little reason to worry about ending up in prison for a crime he didn't do, the way Joseph in the Bible story had.

Yet he stayed at the Shaker village even though it meant enduring Brother Verne's sour humor and harping sermons during the day and being tormented by dreams at night that, unlike Joseph in the Bible, he had no idea how to interpret. His Ella dreams were often foggy and just beyond his recall, but he would wake from them with a beating heart and a terrible weight of guilt. He was the reason she was dead.

You killed her. The judge's accusing words rang in his head until Isaac wanted to bang his fists against his ears to block out the sound. Often in those dark moments on his narrow Shaker cot, Isaac recalled the pull of the water as he'd stood on the docks back in the spring and wondered if the Lord had favored him or cursed him with Brother Asa's hand on his arm.

Then to keep the darkness from overwhelming him, he'd turn his mind to other things. The tasks of the day behind him. The new novitiates that had appeared on the Shakers' doorsteps. He'd think of the new sister with her brown eyes like his, though his were dark and hers seemed to have captured a flicker of sunlight. And he would wonder how she was adjusting to Shaker living.

She was not Ella. She was nothing like Ella. Except for the sadness that hovered over her now when he spotted her in the dining room or along the walkways. Perhaps she had loved her home as much as Ella had. But he couldn't believe she had loved the old man who had claimed her for a wife in the world. Brother Elwood.

He slept in the same retiring room as Isaac. A long frame of a man who knelt by his bed and prayed so long in the morning upon rising that his Shaker guide had to touch him on the shoulder to stop the prayers so that their work could be accomplished. The man's prayers were just as extended at night, and most of the brothers in the room were long asleep before the man began snoring.

Toward the end of May, he and Brother Elwood shared the same duty of planting a late crop of corn. It was the first time they had worked together.

Isaac was rolling a wheeled device the Shakers had invented to make seed planting go faster. Following behind it a man only had to press the dirt down over the seed with his foot and the planting was done. But there was need for more seed often as the workers moved down the long rows. Brother Elwood had been assigned the duty of carrying the seed. The heat of the sun and weight of the sack reddened his face until it looked as if his cheeks might spurt blood. Isaac offered to exchange tasks with him, but the man refused.

"Nay, Elder Homer assigned this task to me. I will do it." He had to stop to gather his breath.

"They allow adjustments when one is unable to carry out the duties. Brother Verne has been given other duties today due to his ailing back."

"I am not ailing. I am able," Brother Elwood said shortly. He set the sack of corn down on the dirt with a thump. "Fill your seeding wheel."

Isaac didn't hurry as he filled the chambers on the wheel. He told himself he was being kind to his brother and giving him an extra moment of rest, but in truth he was curious about the man. And about his wife. Isaac looked to the side to see if any of the other brothers were near enough to hear before he asked, "How come you to join with the Shakers, Brother Elwood?"

"I have always been one to search for the truth." He did not look at Isaac, but kept his eyes on the sack of corn. "And what of you, Brother Isaac? Is that not why you came among these people as well? In search of the true way."

"Nay," Isaac said. "I admit to being in need of food and shelter when Brother Asa came across me, and my feet fit well under the Shakers' table."

Brother Elwood leveled a disgusted look at Isaac. "Such words sound sinful to my ears."

It was easy to imagine him in the pulpit calling down judgment on his wayward church members and just as hard to think of him and the young sister lying together. Isaac pushed that image from his mind and tried to move back to safer ground. A common ground that would take the fire from the man's eyes. "I ask your forgiveness and will confess my wrong words to Brother Verne."

"Confession brings no forgiveness to an unrepentant heart."

"I feel great sorrow for my sins, but you are right that I have yet to find forgiveness." Isaac looked straight at the older man. "Nor do I ever expect to find such. How about you? Have you never done anything that burned a hole in your heart like an ember of fire settled there that no amount of sorrow can extinguish?"

"Nay," the man said almost before Isaac got all the words out. "Nay," he repeated even louder.

Fire shot out of the man's eyes, but Isaac didn't back away from it. "Not even with the young sister?"

Brother Elwood clenched his fists as his face twisted in anger. "Nay. She is the one who brought the sin down. Not I. I was about the Lord's work."

"And now you gave that up, your calling to the Lord's work, to come here." Isaac didn't know why he was tormenting the man with his words. It was like someone else had taken over his tongue. A chill moved through him. The Shakers claimed something the same happened to them in meeting when they spoke as if departed saints were controlling their mouths. Or angels. That was not happening to him. He wouldn't let that happen to him. He was just there because his feet fit under their laden table.

"I know you." Brother Elwood's eyes narrowed and his voice became icy. "You were the brother at my house who knew no discipline. The one Brother Verne speaks of as having a wayward spirit that works to bring disharmony among us. It is a fearsome thing to allow the devil to control your tongue."

"And what of you?" Isaac thought to clamp his mouth shut and go back to turning the wheel to plant the corn, but the words kept pushing out into the air. "You condemn Sister Lacey and not yourself?"

"Sister Lacey?" A puzzled frown flashed across Brother Elwood's face. "I have never done anything to Lacey. She has known only kindness under my roof."

"Brothers!" Sebastian, the brother in charge of their planting, walked up the row toward Isaac and Brother Elwood with fast, determined steps that made deep indentions in the soft ground. His forehead wrinkled in a worried frown as he spoke. "Such exchanges are not allowed, my brothers. Surely you have been told that such is not our way. Nor is the anger I note on your faces allowed among us as brothers. You must love your brother and have only good intentions one for another. We seek the gifts of peace and harmony in all we do. Both of you must beg the other's forgiveness."

It was a matter of a few words to restore the peace and harmony Brother Sebastian sought. At least the words satisfied Brother Sebastian and brought calm back to his face. The same could not be said for Brother Elwood, who continued to scowl every time he got close to Isaac the rest of the day. A scowl that found a twin on Brother Verne's face the next morning when he caught up with Isaac as he was carrying the slops down from the sleeping rooms.

"Brother Isaac."

Isaac knew as soon as he heard the man speak his name, he was in trouble, and the thought that a morning could actually get worse for a man carrying out slop buckets made a smile edge out on his lips. A smile that surprised him. It made him remember his father saying that when a man hit bottom, there was nothing for him to do but laugh at where he was while he tried to find a handhold to start the climb back up. He imagined telling his father that it was hard to start climbing with slop buckets in both hands and that made a laugh bubble up inside him. He couldn't remember the last time he had felt such an urge to laugh. To just sit down on the bottom step of the stairs and laugh until tears came to his eyes. Maybe before his father died. Certainly before Ella had.

With the thought of Ella, the familiar sadness welled up inside him, but it didn't completely push aside the desire to laugh. Perhaps he was losing his mind. Laughing when nothing was funny. But then in his haste to catch up with Isaac, Brother Verne tripped on the stairs and had to grab the railing to keep from tumbling into Isaac and his slops. The man ended up on his backside on the steps. That was funny. Isaac coughed to disguise the hiccup of a laugh he couldn't swallow and turned away to keep the man from seeing him smile. It was a good feeling to smile.

Brother Verne didn't share in the good feeling. "Surely you do not laugh at the sight of your brother's stumble."

"Nay." Isaac bit his lip to hide any trace of the smile that still wanted to curl up his lips. He set the slops down and offered his hand to Brother Verne to help him up.

Verne ignored his outstretched hand as he grabbed the railing to pull himself up to his feet. "Adding falsehood to your amusement at my misfortune only doubles your sin." He brushed off his britches and straightened his suspenders.

"Forgive my lacks." Isaac didn't feel the need for forgiveness, but he had no problem saying the expected words.

The brother frowned at him. "Your lacks in proper behavior seem to increase daily."

"I will attempt to do better in the day ahead of us."

"It takes more than words, Brother Isaac. It takes a proper spirit of contrition, and that appears to be your biggest lack."

Every thought of laughter flew from Isaac's mind. "Nay, that is not true. I carry much contrition in my heart."

"So you say. Again only words. Actions are what prove the words."

Isaac didn't say anything more. Instead he bent his head and turned to pick up the slops to continue his morning's duties. The breakfast bell would ring soon and the chores needed to be finished by then.

"Wait, I am not through with you." Brother Verne stayed on the steps.

Isaac turned back to him. Suddenly he was very weary. Too weary to speak.

While the Shaker man was not quite as tall as Isaac, now standing on the step enabled him to look down at Isaac. "It has come to my ears that you disrupted the harmony of the work in the cornfields yesterday." Brother Verne's face was dark with disapproval, but at the same time a glimmer of pleasure at catching Isaac in such wrong sparked in the man's eyes.

"I had plans to make confession of my transgressions this evening."

"Some confessions should not wait the scheduled hour."

"It appears they did not since Brother Sebastian reported my error to you already."

"Nay. It is Brother Elwood who spoke to me this day. He says you have sinful curiosity about his wife from the world."

"Sister Lacey?" Isaac set the slop buckets down again. "Why would he say that?"

"Perhaps because it is true." Brother Verne narrowed his eyes on Isaac.

"Nay."

Brother Verne paid no attention to his denial. "Do you deny you have noted our new sister's beauty?" He rushed on without waiting for Isaac to answer. "Any eye that is not blind can note that, but it is the beauty of the spirit that matters here in our village. Not beauty of the face. Purity is what we need. A man can't give up his salvation because of the temptation of a pretty face. A man must carry his cross."

He paused to gather his breath, but Isaac stayed silent as he studied Brother Verne's face. The man's words carried too much passion. It was almost as if he was trying to convince someone besides Isaac. But no one else was on the steps. No one else in the hallway. Just Brother Verne preaching from the steps and Isaac listening.

Upstairs a door opened and closed and footsteps whispered

along the upstairs hallways toward the stairs. No doubt one of the sisters making sure not a speck of dirt escaped her broom so the good spirits Mother Ann claimed could not live where there was dirt would not desert their buildings. Nor could good spirits live in a heart that was weighted down with sin and temptation. Or with guilt and grief.

"Well, what do you have to say for yourself, Brother Isaac?" Brother Verne finally asked.

"I carry my burden," Isaac said. "Every day."

"A burden of sin you do not wish to lay down. You cling to the worldly sins rather than pick up the cross of right living."

"And what of you, Brother Verne? Is your cross growing too heavy?" Isaac knew he should stop there from the storm that was gathering on Brother Verne's face, but he did not. The same as in the cornfield when he'd spoken the words of conflict to Brother Elwood, his mouth seemed to form the words on its own and let them out into the air. "Your eye is not blind. Or do you have a beam in it while you are trying to get the speck out of mine? Perhaps you do not have the proper brotherly feelings toward the new sister yourself."

"Get thee from me, Satan." Brother Verne pushed his hands out toward Isaac palm first. "Brother Elwood is right. You are allowing a wrong spirit to dwell in you."

"Can you say my words are wrong?" Isaac stared at him. "Without the sin of falsehood you accused me of earlier?"

The tip of Brother Verne's long nose turned as red as the skin stretched across his cheeks. "You have no right to accuse me of wrongdoing. You who cling to the world and cast lustful eyes on your sisters. You who spoil the harmony of our village. You who run after evil. You who . . ."

Isaac picked up the slop buckets and ignored the brother's accusing words that were spilling around him every bit as repulsive as the contents of the slops. A noise in the upper hallway drew his eye as he turned away from Brother Verne. The new sister, Lacey, had paused in the middle of her sweeping motion at the top of the sisters' stairway. Isaac expected her to be upset, even frightened by Brother Verne's vehement outpouring of condemning words, but she didn't seem bothered. Far from it. With a smile, she leaned the broom handle against her shoulder and put both hands over her ears. Isaac was so surprised that he felt an answering smile want to slip across his own face, but he held it back until he went out the door. Brother Verne's words followed him, but so did the new sister's smile. The smile won.

Elder Homer was waiting for Isaac when he carried the empty slops back into the house. Brother Verne was nowhere to be seen, but it was evident that he had reported Isaac's impenitent spirit to the elder. Sister Lacey must have finished sweeping the stairs and taken her broom and smiles on to another task.

"Come, Brother Isaac," the elder said as the bell signaling the morning meal rang. "We will talk as we walk. Or I will talk and you will listen."

"Yea." He stashed the empty slop pails under the stairs and followed the elder out the brethren's door.

"You have disturbed Brother Verne's inner calm, and we feel it is better for you to stay away from him and not bother him with your words for a few days. Perhaps longer." The elder looked over at Isaac. He didn't appear to be angry. A bit weary perhaps, but his eyes remained kind. He pulled on his beard. "It is best if we do not let accusing words upset our harmony. Silence is often a virtue."

A virtue Isaac decided to practice. It would do little good to speak of Brother Verne's angry words and accusations. He was a covenanted Believer. Isaac was a novitiate with no plan to join anything. He had no thought of achieving spiritual or physical purity. Not with what he'd done. His sole aim upon rising each morning from the Shaker bed was that of exchanging honest labor for meals and a bed. A meal it appeared he was going to miss this morn as they walked away from the eating room instead of toward it. So he kept his eyes on the ground in front of him and tried not to think of his empty stomach as he said, "Yea."

The elder walked on a few steps in silence as well. The village was quiet with all the brothers and sisters inside their family houses eating their biscuits and applesauce and eggs. There would be no bacon or ham since the New Lebanon ministry council had forbidden the eating of pork a few years back. What they decreed, every Shaker village practiced.

"We are missing the morning meal," the elder said as he turned back toward the Gathering Family House. "Not my intention, but a missed meal is better than a broken peace among our brothers. Do you not agree, Brother Isaac?"

Isaac could not truthfully say he preferred peace with Brother Verne over breakfast, and while it hadn't bothered him to lie to Brother Verne, he didn't want to do so to Elder Homer. So he sidestepped the question and asked one of his own. "What would you have me to do, Elder?"

"You avoid the question of peace, my brother." The elder let out a small sigh as he ran his fingers through his beard again. "But perhaps in time you will be able to answer as you should. As for now, Brother Asa has spoken up for you. He has asked that you be allowed to work with him during this time of adjustment in your understanding of our ways. He came to me last week with this request."

"Last week?" Isaac peered over at the elder. "Brother Verne only got angry with me this morning."

"Yea, that is true, but Brother Asa had a dream of you that troubled him. He feels responsible for you in many ways since he brought you into our society. And responsible to the society."

"That sounds like you think I might do harm to someone here. I promise I have no thought to that."

"So you say. And I believe your words come from your heart, Brother Isaac. At the same time we can wound others with careless actions or selfish thinking. Or thoughtless words." The elder looked straight into Isaac's face. "Such can be forgiven, but the wounds have still been inflicted."

"Yea, you need not remind me of that truth." Isaac closed his eyes and saw Ella's face in death. A wound that would never heal, but it did him no good to dwell on it. He pushed thoughts of Ella away and concentrated on the elder's words.

"Brother Asa is working in the barns with the animals. You will do well to listen to his instructions. We never fail to treat our dumb animals with kindness." Elder Homer stopped on the walkway before going up the steps into the Gathering Family House. "I trust I will hear of no more disruptive words from you."

"Nay, you will not."

Isaac had no worry making that pledge if Brother Asa was going to be his Shaker guide. Perhaps his life as a novitiate was about to get better. The promise of being free of Brother Verne for a few days was enough to make up for missing the morning meal. As the elder turned away from him to climb the steps into the house, yet another smile crossed Isaac's lips. And with it came the memory of the new sister's smile that had taken the sting from Brother Verne's words. Could it be she had the same contrary spirit that dwelt within Isaac?

18

Sister Aurelia saw angels. At least so she told Lacey. Actually she did more than see them. She talked to them. And danced with them. She claimed not to be the first bit afraid of these angelic creatures. That was what had Lacey wondering and doing some doubting. She thought back over all the Bible stories she and Miss Mona had read. All the ones she could remember about angels coming down to talk to people face to face, every last one the very first thing the angel told them was "Don't be afraid. Fear not."

And who wouldn't feel her knees knocking together if a great shining angel, who might have just the minute before been getting his marching orders from the Almighty himself, was now standing right in front of her? Just thinking about it made chills chase up and down Lacey's spine.

She'd imagined plenty of unusual happenings. Fairies and such. Plus those angels Miss Mona had told Rachel were scrambling around on the roof to get their attention the morning she was a baby in a basket out on the back porch step. Such made for good storytelling, but Lacey hadn't believed angels were really out there tapping on the roof. And she hadn't thought Miss Mona did either. Not the kind of angels a body could actually lay her eyes on and see.

Miss Mona was of the opinion angels were real, and Lacey wasn't doubting that either. Anybody who believed the Bible spoke true words would have to believe that. But at the same time, angels didn't just come down to say howdy. Even in Bible times. When angels started talking to people, they always had some sort of powerful message. Like telling Abraham and Sarah they were going to have a baby. Or Zechariah to name his boy John. Or Mary that she was going to have a baby even without knowing a man.

When Lacey thought about the Bible angels, it seemed like a heap of their pronouncements had to do with babies, and for sure, that wasn't going to be the kind of news any of the Shakers were expecting to hear. Not so long as they stayed true to their Shaker vows. Virgin births weren't all that common. One in an eternity, the way Lacey had it figured, and that one had already happened.

But Sister Aurelia had a different way of believing about angels. She thought they did come down just to say howdy or to whisper secret messages in her ear. And she wasn't the only one. She said that angel visits fell on the Shakers like raindrops in the spring and that Lacey would witness the power of that once she got to go to meeting.

The first Sunday she was in the village, Sister Drayma had decided Lacey wasn't spiritually ready to attend the meeting, but she had seen them practicing their steps and songs after the supper meal on several weekday nights. The songs they practiced weren't a thing like the ones she'd sung back at the Ebenezer church, even though some of them were written down in books with the music notes. Only one note per word. Everybody was supposed to sing on that same note. For unity, Sister Drayma claimed. Some of the Shaker songs were a dozen verses. Others a mere chorus of a few lines, begging love from their Mother Ann sung over and over a dozen times.

No fiddles or Jew's harps or pianos were on hand at the practices or in the meetinghouse when Lacey lined up with the rest of the Shakers to worship on her second Sunday in the village. Sister Drayma told her the music all came from the people. Even the marching and dancing music. The steps back and forth looked to be easy enough in the practice. The leaders put marks on the floor to help the dancers remember where to turn and start off another direction, and they managed not to bang into one another. Lacey figured that would be severely frowned on, seeing as how a man and a woman couldn't even be on the same stairways or go in and out the same doors for fear of an errant touch. But could be the dancing was different.

A lot was different about the Shakers' Sunday morning meeting, although the bell ringing to get the people out of their rooms and started toward the meetinghouse was some the same.

They walked in lines. Men and women separate the same as any day. Singing as they walked to the meetinghouse. That was different from the church, but Lacey liked the joyful sound of the Shakers' voices. A "glad to be going to church" sound. Better than the solemn silence that fell over folks back at Ebenezer when they approached the church. Preacher Palmer had always set the somber mood with his grave greetings to the church members at the door. The Shaker Believers did fall silent as they came into their meetinghouse, but the ones outside kept on singing until the last one of them stepped through the doors.

Once inside, the women perched on benches on one end of the meetinghouse and the men on the other. Lacey searched through the Shaker men until her eyes landed on the preacher, dressed in like clothes to the rest of the men and looking odd without his black preaching suit and his Bible tucked in the crook of his arm. He shifted a little on the bench and looked as nervous as a fresh-shorn sheep pushed back out into the field with no wool. Shorn to look like all the other sheep with nothing about the field familiar.

The place didn't even look like a church, with no pulpit or offering plate table or anything else that spoke church the way Lacey and the preacher knew it. No picture of Jesus. Not even a Bible. Just the big bare room with lines of benches on the wooden floor and those Shaker peg strips all around the walls with hats hanging on them. Things got even stranger when a woman stood right up in the middle of the floor and spoke about how strong the spirit had been the last few meetings and how they all needed to be ready for more of Mother's work.

Lacey sneaked another look over toward the preacher. Brother Elwood. Sister Drayma had told her that was what she needed to call him now. It sat odd on Lacey's tongue, but she didn't have much need to speak his name here in this place. He was sitting straight with his hands on his knees just like the two men on each side of him. Fitting in. She supposed she ought to try to do the same, but she felt like a sharp-edged rock in a pile of round pebbles.

And the truth of the matter was, the preacher was looking like some of his sharp corners were showing too as he stared at the woman speaking right out in church. That wasn't something that would likely be happening back at the Ebenezer church when they gathered to worship without their preacher on this Lord's Day. The churchwomen would be doing plenty of talking out in the churchyard or in their sitting rooms or on their front porches, but in the church building it would be the men who spoke up.

The preacher didn't look her way. Never looked over at the sisters' side of the room at all. Kept his eyes right where he was supposed to—on the preaching sister. While Lacey watched, he slid one hand up off his knee and yanked on his collar like it was cutting off his air. Lacey almost felt sorry for him. Almost. Until she let her eyes wander to the side where the Shaker children were sitting. Rachel wasn't among them. No children as young as her were there.

Lacey shifted uneasily on the bench. Her legs were itching to stand up and walk out of this building and search through the other houses until she found Rachel. And then maybe just grab her hand and walk on out of this village with all its against-nature rules and women preachers and angel visions.

They wouldn't let her, of course. Somebody would step in front of her and try to push her back into the fold. She could fight them and probably outrun those nearest her, but what good would that do her? They'd just pitch her out of the village. Without Rachel. And then the little girl would be lost to her forever. Lacey wasn't willing to risk that. She'd have to figure out a better way. One that wouldn't get Sister Drayma's or Eldress Frieda's neckerchiefs all in a twist.

Sister Drayma sat on Lacey's left and Sister Aurelia on her right. Sister Aurelia had been practically attached to Lacey's side since that day in the garden when she'd stopped Lacey from chasing after Rachel. She was on every work detail with Lacey and had taken over Sister Drayma's duty of showing Lacey how to properly perform the Shaker tasks. Lacey didn't mind. Aurelia didn't preach so much as Sister Drayma. She mostly talked about the angels who whispered in her ears and danced with her.

So far Lacey hadn't heard the first echo of angel feet dancing, but the angel talk was easier on her ears than Sister Drayma's constant harping on rules about what she couldn't do and rules about how to do what was allowed. There had to be hundreds of rules. More than once Lacey had wanted to ask if the Shakers hadn't ever read the part in the Bible where Jesus had reduced all the rules to two. "Love the Lord with all thy heart and love thy neighbor as thyself." But there were times it was smarter to keep her mouth shut.

This appeared to be one of those times, as Lacey peeked over at Aurelia and then folded her hands in her lap to match. Conform, she told herself. Make them think she was following the rules and they might quit watching so closely. Then she could slip away and find Rachel to tell her those Maddie stories she'd promised her. In spite of the watchers Sister Drayma had made sure Lacey knew about early on. Shakers who stood at the upper windows or even on the roofs to watch the village pathways and shadows to make sure no wrongdoings were going on.

In fact even sitting there in the middle of their meetinghouse while the little Shaker preacher woman kept going on and on about the mighty works their Mother Ann had been sending down to them from heaven, Lacey felt somebody watching her. When she was a little girl, she used to imagine her mother peering down on her from heaven, and these last few months, she often felt some the same about Miss Mona. That she might be watching her with loving eyes. Wishing her the best. Reminding her to pray. And to love the Lord.

But here in the middle of a pile of Shaker sisters, she didn't have that benevolent feeling. It was more like all the churchwomen back at Ebenezer watching her to be sure she acted like a proper preacher's wife. It had been a good thing they couldn't see behind closed doors. Or inside her heart. She hadn't been any kind of proper preacher's wife.

She let her eyes slide back over to the brothers' side of the room, thinking maybe it was Preacher Palmer's disapproving eye on her, but he was sitting straight as a fence-post with his eyes still fixed on the Shaker sister doing the talking. Other than fretting that her contrary spirit might cast a shadow on his quest for perfection, Lacey doubted he'd given her the first thought. Or Rachel either. He'd been more than ready to disavow them both, once those Shaker men had shown up peddling their seeds and their peculiar way to salvation.

She shifted her eyes a little to the side and right into the eyes of that Shaker brother who had told her not to come to the Shaker village. Brother Isaac. The one who had loved his wife so much that the thought of it made Lacey's heart go soft. The one who strange Brother Verne had been browbeating on the steps the other morning.

She'd chanced Sister Drayma seeing her hold her ears and shoot a smile down at Isaac that morning and been rewarded with a lift of his shoulders and the beginnings of an answering smile. Now as if he had read her mind across the room, he moved his head slightly to the side and up as he motioned with his eyes. She followed the direction of his look. A small peephole opening toward the top of the wall above a closed doorway. Eyes peered out the hole straight at her.

Lacey looked down at her folded hands. She wanted to look back over at Isaac and smile, but didn't dare with eyes watching her. And him. How could he have guessed what she was thinking? Or maybe he had just thought to warn her when he noted her wandering attention. She wished they could talk again. Be in one of those union meetings Sister Drayma said the Shakers sometimes allowed, where the sisters sat in a line across from the brothers and they talked of planting the crops and weaving baskets or whatever tasks their hands were engaged in that week. But they wouldn't be able to talk about the odd Shaker rules about books. She wouldn't be able to ask him about the wife he'd lost and how he'd ended up in this place. That was the kind of talking she wanted to do. She couldn't care less how many cows were eating the grass in the back pasture or whether the strawberries were turning red.

The Shaker preaching sister's voice got louder until her words were ringing off the walls. "Next Saturday is Feast Day when we will go to our holy Chosen Land to worship as the spirit leads. Prepare your hearts this day as you labor the dances so that we can be refreshed and ready for Mother's sweet gifts on that day." The little woman reached her hands toward the ceiling. "Let us labor now to bring down Mother's love."

The men and women stood at once and began moving the benches to the side. Clearing the floor. Sister Aurelia took hold of Lacey's arm and pulled her over to the side benches. "You won't be able to labor the regular exercises yet, Sister Lacey. You can watch from here and sing the songs in chorus if you know the words. Unless a whirling gift falls on you."

"A whirling gift?" Lacey raised her eyebrows at Aurelia. She wasn't thinking on doing any whirling.

"Or a shaking one. The spirits have been strong among us lately. They could take over your body the same as mine. The angels don't only dance with me."

"I don't know much about dancing. With angels or not," Lacey said.

"But the angels know enough for all of us." Aurelia smiled and touched her arm. "You should see your face, my sister. Rest assured you have nothing to fear from these gifts that might fall down on you if you will only open up your spirit to receive them. It is ecstasy to come under operations and be an instrument of such love."

Aurelia looked over her shoulder as one of the sisters began singing a tune with no words, only tra las. Others joined in, and after a moment they all began singing words.

Come Mother's sons and daughters,
We want a full supply of the holy waters
That are never, never, dry.

The men and women formed lines and moved up and back in a shuffling dance. They moved one direction for a while and then turned as a unit and began going in the opposite direction. The lines of brothers and sisters passed but never joined, even when they began to dance in circles. Lacey could see why they had to spend so much time practicing. The steps were ordered and the formations precise.

The dance grew even slower and more solemn with a change of song.

Step on, turn around, back and turn in order.
Step on se len ven ve in holy order.
Forward go se len ven vo, back in holy order.

Lacey listened closely, but she couldn't make sense of some of the words. Nobody else seemed the least worried about that as they moved up and back, keeping the lines straight and square. Then just as the dance and singing had slowed, it changed to what sounded to Lacey's ears like a jig. That changed to a sweeping song. All the dancers started pretending to sweep. Even the men. It was a sight to behold and a laugh climbed up in Lacey's throat. She clamped her lips together, determined not to give Sister Drayma any reason to find fault. Or the watchers through their peepholes. So far Lacey hadn't seen any sign the Shakers had a bit of appreciation for the gift of laughter.

Brother Isaac danced past her, wielding his pretend broom with awkward thrusts that didn't look much like sweeping. She ran her hand over her mouth to hide her smile, but he must

215

have seen it anyway because the corners of his lips turned up as he lifted his shoulders in a slight shrug. The watching eyes might think it was part of his sweeping motion, but Lacey knew better. He was feeling as foolish as she thought she would feel whenever it was deemed she must take part in the exercising of the dances.

Following close behind him was a short little brother who was sweeping with the spiritual fervor Isaac lacked.

> Sweep, sweep, and cleanse your floor.
> Mother's standing at the door.

By the time they started singing about hopping and jumping, Lacey's head was spinning and her ears ringing. She was thinking she knew why they didn't call it a church. Nobody would act with such total abandon in a church. But it was a fact that their faces had a kind of holy glow, and the Shakers who danced and whirled past her did look as if they were getting a full dose of spirit. At the same time, she didn't have the first desire to stand up and add her feet to the others that were hammering down on the floor. Not all of them looked swept away by the spirit. Brother Isaac didn't as he stood to the side and let the dancers with more fervor have the floor. The little Shaker woman preacher wasn't stomping and whooping, but she was looking pleased with those who were.

All at once one of the sisters let out a shriek. Lacey jumped clear up off her bench, but nobody else seemed the least bit worried as they started singing words that no ear could understand. Except maybe this Mother Ann they kept talking about. That made sense, Lacey supposed. She'd been able to understand Rachel's baby chatter a long time before any of the churchwomen could. Mothers had that gift. If only she could be using it.

Lacey bent her head and tried to pray that the Lord would help her reclaim Rachel, but no prayer words would come in her head with all the Shaker noise banging against her ears. These people were making her jumpy as a dog trying to corner a snapping turtle.

If she was feeling out of place, she couldn't imagine how Preacher Palmer, or rather Brother Elwood, would be feeling so far removed from the solemn services at Ebenezer Church. There he was the only one who ever did any stomping or shouting, and that only when he was warning of damnation for wrong living. She looked across the floor to where a few men were sitting out the dances the same as she was. The preacher wasn't among them.

It took a minute to find him with all the people on the floor whirling and twirling and stomping and carrying on in a frenzy of spirit catching. She blinked her eyes twice, not sure she was seeing right, but there he was. Standing right out on the floor shaking like a willow tree in the wind. Somehow seeing that, seeing the preacher under operations, as Sister Aurelia called it, brought a tremble to Lacey. But not with the Shaker spirit. She might not have ever loved the preacher, but she had trusted him to know the truth of the Bible. Miss Mona had trusted his "thus saith the Lord" preaching. And now he was out there shaking and throwing all that aside. So what was she to believe as she sat in the middle of the madness that had overtaken the staid Shakers? And the preacher too.

She thought things couldn't get any crazier, but that was before Aurelia whirled out to the middle of the room and began talking in a voice that sounded twice too loud for her. The Shakers around her ceased their whirling as silence fell like a thick blanket on every one of the worshiping Shakers except Aurelia.

"I am the angel Esmolenda sent by Holy Mother Wisdom

to condemn those among you who have done wrong. Wrongs that you have not confessed. It is a fearful thing to reach for the spirit with an unclean soul." Aurelia kept her eyes on the ceiling and her hands straight up in the air. She moaned slightly as she swayed back and forth a few times and then went as stiff as a towel frozen in the winter wind on a clothesline. Even her eyes seemed fixed open. The only thing that moved was her lips. "A perilous sin. There are those among us who know."

Several Shakers dropped to their knees at her words and began to mutter prayers. Aurelia's face and body stayed stiff, as though more words might break her apart. Here and there some of the Shakers watched Aurelia with a wary look on their faces, and Lacey decided this wasn't the first time they'd seen her deliver a message from her angels. Lacey wondered if it was always of doom. An uneasy feeling settled in her stomach as she began to think it might not be all that good a thing to have a friend who was on such close terms with angels.

The thought had no more than tripped through Lacey's head when Aurelia lost her stiffness like mist disappearing in the sun and began whirling straight toward Lacey. If there'd been any place to run, Lacey would have been out and gone before Aurelia could touch her, but instead she sat like she didn't have good sense and let Aurelia grab her hand and pull her to her feet.

"Fear not, my sister. Whirl your fears away and shake free of the worldly sins that shackle you in unbelief. Speak of the sins you've witnessed."

Lacey tried to jerk her hand free, but Aurelia's grip was too tight. "Don't resist the spirit," Aurelia hissed toward her. "The truth will be revealed through visions and song."

Lacey's heart pounded and her mouth went dry as Aurelia

tugged her toward the center of the floor. Lacey hated having every eye in the place plastered on her, but Aurelia appeared to be reveling in it. Or the angel—whatever her name was—who was supposed to be speaking through her. Lacey was feeling some doubts on that. Why would an angel come down out of heaven to grab her hand, to make like she, Lacey Bishop, had a message for these strange Shaker people when the good Lord above would know of a certainty that she didn't have the first word to say? She tried to ignore all the Shaker staring eyes and pinned her own eyes on Aurelia to try to figure out what she was up to.

Aurelia yanked her closer so hard that it came near to jerking Lacey's shoulder out of its socket. "Speak, I say. Do not hide sins with your silence."

"Let me go, Sister Aurelia," Lacey said in a fierce whisper. She didn't want to accuse her of faking the angel act in front of the assembly, but at the same time she had no desire to be part of Aurelia's show.

"Aurelia is not here. I am Esmolenda, angel of truth and power."

Aurelia tightened her grip until Lacey's knuckles were mashed together, even though she had stopped trying to pull her hand free. Aurelia did look strange. Like she was in some kind of trance. What if she really had been taken over by an angel? One that had special powers. The whole bunch of the Shakers appeared mesmerized by her. Lacey wasn't above trying to use that.

"If that's true, let me see Rachel," Lacey demanded. "Show me where my daughter is."

Aurelia glared at Lacey as though she spoke blasphemy that couldn't be forgiven. "You have no daughter."

19

Isaac never knew what to expect at meeting when the staid and solemn Believers seemed to transform themselves into children playing a game of worship with no rules. They sang and danced. They whirled and jabbered. They hopped and skipped and entertained strange imaginings. But when Sister Aurelia grabbed the new sister's hand and pulled her out on the floor, it seemed different. No longer innocent and harmless. Or loving.

Everything about meeting was supposed to be loving. Love for the brothers and love for the sisters. Love from the spirits and the Lord. Love from Mother Ann. All love. While Isaac hadn't exactly embraced their idea of love, he had no argument against it. He was content to roll along with their ways, pretending to sweep away sin, keeping his hands busy and his stomach fed.

He didn't deserve more than that. He didn't deserve that much. Not with Ella in the grave. But then his eyes would catch on the new sister again. It wasn't just that she was pretty. She was that. Even with the sisters' cap covering her brown hair that had fallen so softly around her shoulders back at her house. But it was more the sensing of her contrary spirit there among the Shakers. A contrary spirit that matched his own, even if he was dancing and working and acting the Shaker role. The contrary spirit that had her covering her ears and smiling down at him while Brother Verne was berating him. A contrary spirit that had him wanting to smile, even while holding the two odorous slops full to near overflowing.

So when Sister Aurelia grabbed hold of the new sister and pulled her out on the meetinghouse floor, he tried to catch the young woman's eye with the same kind of contrary smile, but she was staring at Sister Aurelia with a look near panic.

It wasn't the first time he'd seen Sister Aurelia under operations. She often whirled away from the other dancers and began the angel talk. But Isaac had yet to be convinced that she or any of the Shaker Believers claiming visitations had really been taken over by spirits from the beyond.

Because he lacked faith, Brother Verne told him. As if that was some kind of revelation. Isaac sometimes thought it would be nice to have faith, to believe love could fall down out of heaven in balls pitched by angels, but then he'd remember Ella burning with the fever and calling for her mother. He'd remember how his love hadn't been enough.

Sister Aurelia wouldn't let the new sister go. Sister Lacey. The name fit her. Lacey. He kept his eyes on her, but she didn't look toward him. Instead she had stopped trying to get away and stood with her head bowed as Sister Aurelia shouted in her angel voice and demanded Lacey name some sins.

The Shakers were big on speaking sins. Elder Homer was always urging them to think hard to recall the slightest wrongs in order to cleanse their consciences and their hearts when Isaac and the five other novitiates met to confess their sins each week. Isaac had taken to making up a few lapses just to satisfy the elder's need to hear wrongs. He wondered if the other brothers did the same, but doubted it. They didn't appear to have his contrary spirit. The wrong spirit would be what Brother Verne would tell him he needed to confess. And the way he wanted to walk out onto the floor and rescue the new sister from Sister Aurelia's hold. That would lose his place at the Shaker table in a heartbeat. Doing battle with an angel spirit for a sister. A sister who, even if she wasn't a Shaker, was married. To the old preacher.

Isaac looked over at Brother Elwood. He'd seen the man shaking earlier. More of a Believer already than Isaac would ever be. Ready to shake all that was carnal away from him. But he looked stricken now as he stared out at the two sisters. His face was pale and his mouth dropped open a little as if someone had just punched him in the stomach. Then with small wary steps he eased back behind two other brothers and bent his head to stare down at the floor. He appeared to want nothing to do with the scene playing out in front of him.

Isaac was surprised when Lacey spoke up. He didn't know why, since it fit in with her contrary spirit to challenge this angel that was rebuking her. He wasn't surprised that she asked about her daughter. He'd seen the love she had for the child that day they'd packed them up and moved them to the village. A pure love that made him think of his own mother's tears the day he'd gone to live with the McElroys after his father's death. Change and sorrow so often came into a person's life hand in hand. The strong survived, his mother had told him that day as she blinked away her tears. And those who put their trust in the Lord.

She'd boxed his jaws when he told her the Lord hadn't proved too trustworthy so far. Then she had held him against her so tightly that he thought she might never turn him loose. "Oh my son, don't lose your faith. It was man's folly and the explosion that took your father. Not the Lord's design."

"What is the Lord's design?" He remembered leaning back from her and watching her face in hopes she would tell him

222

something he could carry away with him. Some bit of faith that would see him through, the way it was seeing her through. And Marian too. His sister had not shed the first tear when she left for her new home with the Shakers the day before.

"That we put our hand in his and trust him to show us a way. It's as simple as that."

He had carried his mother's words away with him, but Isaac hadn't found it simple at all. He still didn't find it simple. Perhaps the Shakers were right when they sang their song about it being a gift to be simple. To step out in simple faith instead of trying to shoulder and push against the world to make his way. That was why he was there in the meetinghouse. Not because he was reaching for faith, but because he was tired of pushing against the world. He was hiding every bit as much as Brother Elwood, who was ducking down behind the other brothers across the floor from Isaac.

"You have no daughter." Sister Aurelia shouted the words at Lacey and then raked her eyes across the Shakers watching her. Her voice took on a strange timbre as she began to whirl, yanking the new sister with her. "The sin is not yours, but another's."

Without thought, Isaac stepped forward to rescue the new sister from the grip of Sister Aurelia's vision. It was one thing to chase after a gift of the spirit with fervor that threatened one's own life and limb, but it couldn't be right to drag an unwilling sister along with her. A brother's hand caught him to keep him back. Sister Aurelia began whirling even faster, nearly pulling Lacey off her feet before suddenly letting go of the new sister's hand and dropping like a stone. Lacey spun across the floor like a top turned loose and would have fallen into the benches if Isaac hadn't jerked away from the hand restraining him and stepped forward to break her fall.

She knocked against him with more force than he expected,

and he stumbled back with his arms still around her. He couldn't catch himself and ended on the floor with the girl on top of him, her face inches from his. Her eyes widened in surprise. He thought his staring back at her must surely be just as wide. She was soft in his arms like Ella, but at the same time nothing like her. Female but not helpless as she caught her breath and pushed back from him. For one crazy moment he tightened his arms around her. Two bright spots of red lit up her cheeks as she looked down at him and did not fight to free herself.

An audible gasp went through the Shakers and then hands were grabbing at them both. A brother shouted out, "Woe, woe." Across the room a sister began singing.

> Come, holy angels, quickly come.
> And bring your purifying fire;
> Consume our lusts in every home,
> And root out every foul desire.

Some voices picked up the cry of woe while others sang the song.

He had the strangest urge to laugh at the commotion their fall was causing as he reluctantly dropped his hands away from her. Two sisters snatched her off him and jerked her to her feet before they began hitting at her dress to brush away his sinful touch. They glowered at him, as though he had assaulted the new sister instead of merely breaking her fall. It was plain to see they would have been better pleased to see their sister bash her head into the benches than end up crashing into him.

He shook off the brothers' hands grabbing at him and ignored their frowns as he got to his feet. He had done no wrong. He would have done the same for any of the sisters who might have been falling. Even old Sister Phoebe, whose face looked like a wrinkled prune. Of course his arms might not have impulsively tightened around Sister Phoebe. He let his eyes slide back over to Lacey as she endured without protest the fervor of the sisters who even yet were beating at her skirt like they expected snakes to fall out of her petticoat.

As though she'd been waiting for him to look her way, she met his eyes, but only for the barest second. But in that second he caught the smile buried there. She stepped back from the beating hands of the sisters and said quite calmly, "What about Sister Aurelia? Shouldn't you see to her?"

Sister Aurelia was stretched out in the middle of the floor as stiff as the plank seat of one of the benches. She hadn't fallen that way. She'd collapsed in a heap of skirts, but now she lay like a tree felled with her skirts laid out as straight as her arms by her side. The angel must have arranged her so before the heavenly creature departed for heaven. Again Isaac had to twist his mouth to keep from letting a smile touch his lips. For a man who had almost forgotten how to smile, he seemed to be having to hide a pile of them. Maybe he had been taken over by a spirit himself. A mischief-making spirit who had him wanting to throw up his hands and laugh in the face of the woes and scowls, in spite of the fact that would cause him much trouble.

Brother Verne was staring holes through him. Angry holes. And even Brother Asa was giving him a quizzical eye. But it was Elder Homer he would have to answer to. Mischievious spirit and all. And what of Ella? Had the mere touch of another woman thrown aside his sorrow?

His thought of smiling vanished as his guilt settled back around his shoulders like a well-worn cloak. Perhaps the condemning looks were right. He was nothing but sin. He was almost glad when the singers switched to a new song.

Come, let us all unite to purge out this filthy, fleshy,
    carnal sense.
And labor for the power of God to mortify and stain
    our pride.
We'll raise our glittering swords and fight. And war
    the flesh with all our might.
All carnalities we now will break and in the power of
    God we'll shake.

Some sisters dragged Sister Aurelia out of the way as the
Shakers took their places on the floor again, shaking and
stomping to chase away the temptation of the devil that had
come into the meeting. Lacey went over to kneel by Aurelia.
Brother Elwood, his face still pale, stared at the two sisters a
moment before his arms began quivering. Brother Asa took
hold of Isaac's sleeve and pulled him out on the floor.

So he shook as they expected, but he felt nothing. To him
it seemed nonsense, but it had ever been so. Faith eluded him.

Then as he reached his hands up in the air and pretended
to shake the carnality out of his body, he turned and looked
directly at the new sister again. She was watching him. No
smile lurked on her face or in her eyes now. Instead she looked
sorrowful. Perhaps she was thinking of the daughter they
had taken from her, but her eyes were on him. Probing him.
Wondering and denying at the same time. Doubting his dance.

He had no answers for her. He had no answers for anyone.
Not even himself. Especially not for himself.

She bent her head then in an attitude of prayer, and it was
his turn to wonder about her. Perhaps faith did not elude her
as it did him. And he suddenly wanted to stop his farce of
shaking and pretending to seek the Shaker way to go kneel
beside her. He wanted to let her take his hand and pray for
him.

20

By the time Lacey left the meetinghouse, she was of the mind that the whole bunch of the Shakers had been into some cider gone hard. She thought back to when Miss Mona had claimed witnessing the Shakers' worship had scared Sadie Rose. Lacey hadn't understood then how a church service could scare a person, but she was beginning to now.

Not that she had exactly been frightened by the Shakers' carrying on. At least not until Aurelia had grabbed her. It wasn't right to stand in judgment of other Believers and how they acted. A person could find that truth often enough in the Good Book. Certainly she couldn't cast the first stone at anyone after the wrongs she'd done. But then again, she'd never stomped and screamed and acted like a complete heathen inside the walls of a church.

The dancing was odd, but the Lord gave people feet and the itch to dance. There were places in the Bible where King David did some worship dancing. Plus she'd heard folks talking in tongues back at Ebenezer. Not often, but a time or two. Singing songs with words no ear could decipher wasn't all that different. But to go into shaking fits and stomping till the whole building had to be doing some shaking of its own, that was worse than odd. It had to border on sacrilege. She couldn't imagine Miss Mona disagreeing with her in any fashion, even with the way she never liked to find fault with anyone.

And there had been Preacher Palmer right in the middle of them, shaking and quaking and giving her the eye like as how she was the evil he was trying to shake off him. Lacey's cold heart after they married must have driven him to the brink of madness.

She wasn't too sure she wasn't tripping along that crevice rim herself. She'd always thought of herself as practical about the things that mattered. Oh, so she did her spring dandelion dance, a gift from her mother, and it wasn't all that different from the Shakers' whirling dances. The same as the gift dance Sister Aurelia had said might fall on Lacey and take over her feet. And she dreamed up her fanciful stories about animals that talked and fairies that twittered around like dragonflies. She'd even spent some time imagining how true love, the kind she read about in storybooks, would feel. But underneath all that dreaming and wishing, she'd always stared straight on at what was actually happening in her life. Especially after she'd stood up with Preacher Palmer in front of his preacher friend and nodded her *I do*.

But there in the middle of the Shaker meetinghouse with Sister Aurelia thinking she was some kind of angel and all the Shakers staring at them both, Lacey had lost her grip on practical common sense and felt like she might never make sense of anything again.

Her head was already spinning before Aurelia jerked her along in a mad, whirling circle. When she had turned her loose with a hard fling, Lacey stumbled across the floor trying to catch her balance. The next thing she knew, strong hands were grabbing her, but that didn't stop her falling. She ended up right on top of that Brother Isaac and wondering if she might not be just dreaming it all. That any minute she'd wake

228

up in the narrow Shaker cot and have to get up to sweep and clean before going out to plant beans or some such chore.

She'd looked right into the brother's eyes and he'd looked right into hers. Her heart started beating even harder than it was before, while she was out there with all those eyes watching her and Sister Aurelia. Plenty of eyes were still watching her. And him. Eyes more shocked by a woman stumbling against a man than they'd been by an angel coming down to take over one of their sisters and shout out about sins.

Lacey wasn't so dizzy that she didn't know that falling on top of the brother would be the height of wrongdoing even before she heard the mournful woes declaring it so. She pushed against Isaac's chest to right herself, but instead of scrambling away from her, he'd tightened his hands around her waist. And right there and then, Lacey's world shifted.

Nothing about what was true changed as some sisters jerked her away from Isaac and began beating on her dress to remove any trace of his touch. She was still married to Preacher Palmer, who had brought her into the midst of the oddest bunch of people she could imagine. No wonder she was losing her grip on good sense. At the same time while nothing changed, nothing was the same. A smile sneaked into her eyes when Isaac got to his feet and looked toward her. A smile that had no right to be there. She was a married woman, even if the preacher was over there on the fringe trying to shake every carnal thought of her out of his head and body.

Aurelia was still prostrate on the floor, but when the dancers started spilling back out on the floor, a few of the sisters lifted and dragged her over to the benches like she was no more than a piece of furniture in the way. A little Shaker man not even as tall as Lacey took hold of Isaac's hand and led him out as the singers started a mournful "stop lustful sinning" song.

Lacey knelt by Aurelia and took her hand. It was limp and her face was stiff, but Lacy had the almost uncontrollable urge to reach over and poke the woman in the ribs to see if she would jump. But she restrained her hand. She'd caused enough commotion in the Shaker meetinghouse for one Sunday. Besides, she liked Aurelia and didn't want to go back to being preached at by Sister Drayma through every daylight hour. So if Aurelia wanted to play at courting angels, then who was Lacey to deny her the fun? Just as long as she didn't pull her along into her vision. She'd make sure Aurelia knew that before the next time they gathered in the meetinghouse.

She raised her eyes from Aurelia's stonelike face and looked out at the dancers. They weren't exactly dancing steps. Just shaking to rid themselves of the carnal burst of the world that had visited their meeting. Isaac was shaking too, the same as all the rest. Had she imagined that tightening of his hands around her waist? That hint of a smile in his eyes? He looked as much a Shaker as any out there. Shaking off her touch.

During the final dance that was a march up and down with no shaking, Aurelia opened her eyes and claimed to remember nothing of the angel speaking through her. Lacey didn't believe her. Any more than she believed an angel had come down from heaven to pluck Lacey off her bench and spin her in circles. With a flush crawling up into her cheeks, Aurelia looked entirely too pleased when some of the sisters clustered around to touch her like they hoped to get some leftover angel sparkle on their fingers.

Nobody said the first thing about the sinful colliding of Lacey with Brother Isaac. Even to speak of such would have them sharing Lacey's sin. A sin that it appeared had to be confessed before another hour passed. Eldress Frieda pulled Lacey aside as they were on the way back to the Gathering

Family House for the time of contemplation and rest before the evening meal.

Lacey followed the eldress into a small room equipped with a desk and chair. Another chair hung on the peg rail, but Eldress Frieda didn't suggest Lacey lift it down as she settled in the chair behind the small desk. So Lacey stayed standing with her hands clasped in front of her and her head bent in a posture of compliance. It would do little good to defy the good eldress. Better to pretend to accept the Shaker yoke of obedience.

The room wasn't much bigger than a closet, but a small window let in the late afternoon sunlight. Only a few dust motes floated in the air, a tribute to the Shakers' war against dirt. On the first day that Lacey had swept out the Shaker sleeping rooms, Sister Drayma had made sure she knew the importance of cleaning every nook and cranny.

"If you do not sweep out the corners of a room when cleaning it, that is the way the corners of your heart will look." Sister Drayma had stooped down to run her hand over the floor to make sure Lacey hadn't missed even a smidgen of dust. She stared at her hand almost as if disappointed not to find a trace of dirt there before she stood up, brushed her hand off on her apron, and went on with her sermon. "Good spirits will not live where there is dirt. Mother Ann taught us thus."

Now from the look on Eldress Frieda's face as she considered Lacey standing in front of her, she seemed to be having the same kind of doubts of Lacey's sweeping ability. And yet her eyes weren't condemning Lacey but simply waiting to see what would be said in confession.

Lacey was waiting too. She had no idea what the eldress was expecting. She'd made confession several times. She'd offered up regret for bad thoughts and for dropping too many seeds in a garden row and not bending down to pick them out. With no truth in her words, she'd claimed sorrow for resisting the Shaker beliefs and then with more conviction confessed to sometimes not speaking the complete truth. But those confessions had been made to Sister Drayma who accepted them grudgingly. She had not spoken with the eldress since that first night when she had clung to Rachel and won one more night to hold her close. That had been ten days ago, and suddenly the need to see her child brought tears to her eyes. Tears the eldress misunderstood.

"You are new to the Believers' way, my child, so it is easy to understand and forgive when you stumble." Eldress Frieda's wrinkled face looked kind in the light from the window.

"I did stumble, Eldress. I had no intent of disturbing your meeting."

"Your meeting too," the eldress said softly.

"Yea." Lacey was glad she'd remembered to use the Shaker word to agree. "But I wanted to stay on the side to watch, since I know so little of your ways. I did not want to hinder the spirit."

A small frown appeared between Eldress Frieda's eyes. Her cap very neatly covered all but a white crown of hair around her forehead. Everything about the eldress was neat and contained. "Yet the angel singled you out. Why would that be?"

Lacey had no answer for that. Other than saying she thought Aurelia had faked it all. The truth of the other sister's vision was between Aurelia and the eldress with no need for Lacey to get in the middle of that. She'd already been too much in the middle. She let a little silence build before she opened out her hands in a gesture of puzzlement. "I have no idea."

"Hmm." The eldress studied Lacey's face.

Lacey shifted a little and the floorboards creaked to reveal her uneasiness as she waited for Eldress Frieda to go on.

Finally the eldress said, "I sense a doubting spirit in you, my sister."

When Lacey opened her mouth to ask what she meant, Eldress Frieda held up a hand to stop her. "Nay, it is a time to listen, not speak. I am not condemning you, my sister. Merely saying what I sense. Sister Drayma has reported to me that you are a hard worker, diligent in your chores, but at the same time she says it is plain to see you resist our ways. Many do who are brought into our community of Believers from the world by others. As you were brought to live here by Brother Elwood. It was a decision made for you and not by you."

The eldress dropped her hand back to the table and let the silence gather around them. Lacey didn't know whether the eldress expected her to keep listening or maybe start talking now, but she wasn't ready to chance getting it wrong. So she just kept her head bent as she stared at the older sister's hands.

The woman's hands were not unlike Miss Mona's. Slender with skin so transparent it was easy to see the blue trace of veins across their backs. Her fingernails were cut blunt across to keep from interfering with her work, for Sister Drayma had told Lacey that all who were able-bodied in the community worked. Even those in the Ministry, although they lived secluded lives and had a separate workshop. When Lacey had asked what work they did, Sister Drayma had acted like the question was tantamount to blasphemy. The Ministry was not to be questioned.

Lacey had the feeling it was the same with Eldress Frieda. Whatever she said, Lacey would have to do. What other choice did she have? If she refused the Shaker ways, she would have to walk out of the village and give up Rachel. She couldn't do that. She couldn't. Even if they wouldn't let her see Rachel, at least here in their village she might get a glimpse of the child from time to time.

The silence continued. Lacey could hear Eldress Frieda's breathing in and out as well as her own stomach complaining because her dinner was delayed. To go from the bedlam in the meetinghouse to this silence so deep Lacey could almost see it hanging in the air between her and the eldress was a little unnerving. Lacey started counting in her head to keep her mind disciplined so she wouldn't blurt out some wrong word. She was up to forty when the eldress spoke.

"Do you have naught to say?"

Lacey considered the woman and tried to guess at the right thing to say. Yea? Nay? Beg for forgiveness? She might have guessed what Sadie Rose or some of the other churchwomen back at Ebenezer wanted to hear and come out with words to soothe their ears, but not here. She pulled in a breath and stopped trying to speak to please. "I don't know exactly what you want to hear. It wasn't my doing for Sister Aurelia to grab my hand and spin me around. I had no intention of knocking into anybody. I was dizzy and fell. The brother caught me. I see no sin in that. It was nothing but an accident."

"So you feel you have done no wrong that you need to confess?" Eldress Frieda's eyes stayed kind even as her voice seemed to take Lacey to task.

"I am not without sin." Lacey managed to keep from sighing. Why did her spirit have to be so contrary to their ways? It would be easier to simply beg pardon for being clumsy and be done with it. "So please forgive me for the wrong I've done."

Eldress Frieda's frown appeared between her eyes again. "Confessions should be from the heart, Sister Lacey. Not mere words uttered to tickle the ears of your listeners."

"I am truly sorry if what happened was upsetting to the sisters and brothers at the meeting." She had no problem speaking those words sincerely.

"And what of your words that seemed uttered to challenge

234

the angel Esmolenda?" She spoke the strange name easily without hesitation.

"You know the angel?" Lacey stared at the eldress. Maybe Aurelia hadn't been making it up after all. "Is she like Gabriel or Michael to you here?"

"There are legions of angels. We meet the ones Mother Ann sends down to us."

"And this Esmo . . . Esmolenda has been here before, talking to you?"

"Nay, but you stray from the question, Sister Lacey. What of your words demanding the angel let you see Sister Rachel?"

Lacey was suddenly so overcome with sadness and exhaustion that she gave no thought to whether or not the eldress would approve of her words. "I would do anything to see Rachel. I had not spent one hour away from her since she came into my life before she was stripped from me here. If I could call on angels to make that happen, I was ready to put out the call."

"You tread on shaky ground there, my sister. Would you also be ready to call on evil forces to bring your desire to fruition?"

"I said what I said. I would like to believe I wouldn't surrender to the devil's lures, but at the same time, my arms ache for my daughter." Lacey sent a silent prayer up from her heart without taking her eyes off Eldress Frieda. She was a woman. Surely she had once loved a child or been loved by a mother. "I promised I wouldn't desert her. To a child her age, ten days must seem like forever. Please, would it break so many rules to let me visit her?" She was not above pleading. With her hands on the edge of the desk, she dropped to her knees. "Please."

"Come, my sister, your sorrow is misplaced. The child is well." The eldress rose and came around the desk to lay her hand on top of Lacey's cap with gentleness. "Gather yourself and surrender your will to the Eternal Father. Only then will you know peace in your heart."

"I do believe in the Lord."

"But not as we do here."

"Nay, but is not my Lord, the Lord I have prayed to since I was a child, the same Lord you worship?" Lacey looked up at the eldress. "The Creator of the world? The God of love and mercy?"

Eldress Frieda dropped her hand away from Lacey's head. Her words were stiff and unyielding. "And the God of judgment for those who choose worldly lives of sin."

"How can it be a sin to love a child?"

"To love the Lord and do his bidding is the duty of all, and the Eternal Father revealed to Mother Ann how the selfish relationships of husband, wife, and children hampers the development of mutual love and order among his people. Our way is the best way. Nay, the only way to live a perfect life as is demanded of us."

"I have no hope of perfection this side of heaven."

"So it is with those of the world," Eldress Frieda said. She put her hand under Lacey's arm to encourage her to stand. "But here we are no longer of the world."

Lacey got slowly to her feet. "I feel as though I am floating somewhere between, unable to set my feet in either place. The world there or your world here."

Eldress Frieda surprised Lacey by smiling. That was the last thing she expected. "Perhaps you are moving closer to our ways since the angel chose you out of our number. We shall pray that is so. And it is also true that you are not yet one of us. If a mother from the world comes to see a child given over to us, we do not deny her that right. Neither will we deny you as you float between worldly thoughts and right beliefs. It will be arranged. After the evening meal on the morrow,

I will take you to the Children's House. There you will see that Sister Rachel is well cared for, and perhaps then you will be able to turn loose your worldly thinking."

Lacey wanted to grab the eldress and hug her, but the woman stepped back to put distance between them. That was the way of the Shakers, Lacey thought. They wanted distance between them all, as though they could walk in their own individual circles without inviting any other person into the circle with them. Only the Lord and their Mother Ann were welcomed to step nearer. So Lacey restrained her impulse to hug the woman in gratitude. Instead she clasped her hands together to hide the way they were shaking with excitement and merely said, "Thank you, Eldress."

"Your understanding of spiritual things is like that of an infant, Sister Lacey."

"I have read much in the Bible," Lacey answered in mild protest. She knew the Bible. Miss Mona had taught her and taught her well.

"Yea, Sister Drayma has told me so. Perhaps that is why the angel reached for you. To help you see the truth that you have not gleaned in your times of studying the Bible in the past."

Lacey bent her head in submission, even as the stories of love in the Bible that were rewarded with children came into her mind. It was not a time to be contrary. Not when she had been granted the answer to her most fervent prayer. What was that verse that Miss Mona had sometimes quoted to her? Lacey searched through her memory for it as she followed Eldress Frieda out of the small room to join the line of sisters going into the eating room.

It came to her as she knelt for the silent prayer before the meal. *Delight thyself also in the Lord; and he shall give thee the desires of thine heart.* A joyful prayer of thanksgiving took wing from her heart. She was going to see Rachel.

21

Monday morning Brother Asa was uncommonly quiet as he and Isaac headed toward the barn. The bell would summon them back to breakfast in an hour, but by then the horses would already have their feed and be ready to go to work in the fields as soon as the Shaker brethren had their own feed.

"I prayed for you last night, my brother," Brother Asa said with no sound of a smile in his voice.

The sun was not yet up, and the dawn air hung around them like thick gray curtains they had to keep pushing aside. While not as cold, it reminded Isaac of the morning they'd met on the dock in Louisville. He had no river to swallow him up here, and when he looked within, no desire now to rob himself of his next breath. He liked looking across the fields and seeing the cows nursing new calves. He liked breathing in the fresh air. He liked Brother Asa's voice in his ear, even when he noted the edge of concern there. He liked thinking about the new sister smiling at him.

The last thought brought him up short and he made himself think of Ella. But in spite of the all-too-familiar stab of guilt, it was getting harder and harder to keep his feet sunk in that pit of sorrow. He had no right to climb out of it. He knew that. Not when Ella would never climb out of her grave.

But still the sun was pushing fingers of pink light up over the trees on the eastern horizon, and up ahead in the barn, a couple of horses nickered in anticipation of their feed. He liked working with the horses and cows.

Isaac brought his mind back to Brother Asa's prayers for him. "I have need of prayers," he said.

"As do we all." Brother Asa gave the expected response, but Isaac heard an unusual coolness in his voice that had to be because of what had happened the day before.

"I didn't intend to upset you or any of the brothers and sisters at meeting yesterday." Isaac tried to set things to right with his brother. "I was only trying to keep the new sister from falling."

He'd already confessed his sins to Elder Homer at the elder's insistence after the meeting the day before. Some sins were too big to allow to fester and infect one's soul with worldly desires, Elder Homer had said as he stroked his beard and waited for Isaac's words of contrition. Words Isaac had felt no need to speak, but the elder had great patience. He would sit with Isaac till the retiring bell rang if necessary. So Isaac asked forgiveness for disturbing the meeting with carnal thoughts whether the thoughts were Isaac's own or that of others led astray by the sight of a man and woman holding on to one another. It mattered not that the sister had fallen into him and he'd had no intent of embracing her. That was what Isaac claimed. But there had been those few seconds where his hands had tightened quite intentionally around the new sister's small waist. That he did not confess to Elder Homer or see any need of mentioning now to Brother Asa.

"Yea, so it seemed, my young brother." Brother Asa looked up at Isaac. "But do not forget I was near enough to clearly see your face. Her nearness was a temptation to you. Do you deny that?"

239

"Nay. I have not fully become a Believer," Isaac admitted. He bent his head and studied the walkway of stone beneath his feet. Some other Shaker men had gathered the stones and laid the walking path. Some other men who had no doubt struggled with sin the same as he did.

"She too carries the odor of the world and has not bent her spirit to the Shaker way."

"What makes you think that?" Isaac looked up at Asa.

"I have been much in the world, my brother, and I have eyes and ears that work as they should. Ways of the world are not hard to discern. Her spirit still lusts after those ways. Even if I had not seen it in her face, I would have heard it in her voice when she asked about her child with blame in her voice."

"Blame?"

"She counts being separated from her child a wrong done to her."

"She did appear to care deeply for the little girl on the day we helped move them to the village. Isn't it too much to expect such feelings to just fade away in a few days?" Isaac looked away from Brother Asa out toward the fields again where the sun was touching the tops of the trees now. Was he letting his feelings for Ella fade away?

"She will be given time. The same as you are being given. No one is forced to make a decision before his or her heart is ready. But the child won't be unloved. I can vouch for the truth of that. Love of many quickly healed my loss of a worldly mother."

"Do you think that will be so of the child? That she will forget Sister Lacey's love?"

"Perhaps not forget. More to not need it among her new family. But in truth, all are not meant to be Believers. If they were, we would have to build many more houses." Brother Asa's smile bounced back on his face, his good humor restored

240

as he stepped in front of Isaac to pull open the barn door. The horses whinnied and moved impatiently in their stalls. "But enough preaching. We must be about our work. The horses need their feed. Hands to work. Hearts to God. That takes care of all problems."

When the bell rang an hour later, they were already headed back to the Gathering Family House for the morning meal. Isaac was eager to Shaker his plate. Eating every bite of whatever was set in front of him was the one Shaker rule he had no trouble obeying with enthusiasm.

They were nearly close enough to catch the aroma of freshly baked biscuits in the air when a brother alone in front of them suddenly climbed up on the fence beside the pathway and tried to walk across the top rail like a tightrope performer. With his arms wobbling out to his sides, he made two, then three steps before he lost his balance and fell flat on the ground.

The man scrambled to his feet and climbed right back up on the fence. It was Brother Elwood, the new sister's preacher husband. Once more he fell before he had taken four steps and this time landed hard on the stone walkway. Isaac ran ahead of Brother Asa to see if the man was hurt.

Brother Elwood held his palm out to stop Isaac when he reached toward him. "Nay, keep away. I have no need of aid from one such as you."

Isaac dropped his hands and stepped back. The man had a strange look in his eyes as he stared fiercely at Isaac. He'd seen the same look on men's faces along the riverfront, but it wasn't a look he'd expected to see here. "Are you drunk, Brother Elwood?"

Anger flooded the man's face. "Nay. My body is pure. Pure I say. Else the spirits wouldn't speak to me."

Brother Asa came up beside them and asked in a gentle voice, "What is it the spirit is telling you to do, Brother?"

"Balance. I must lift myself up between the earth and heaven and find balance there." He climbed up on the fence again. "Sweet, holy balance."

When the man began wobbling on the edge of the top plank of the fence again, Isaac started to step forward to help him, but Brother Asa grabbed his arm. "It is best not to impede the spirits," he said quietly.

Isaac stopped, but it was all he could do to keep from saying that it looked to him like the spirits had all gone crazy. Then again, what did he know about the spirits? He couldn't even figure out his own spirit.

"He's going to fall again," Isaac said.

"Yea, perhaps." Brother Asa moved a bit closer to the man swaying on the fence rail and raised his voice. "May I advise you, Brother Elwood, in your quest?"

When the man gave no answer, Brother Asa went on as if he'd received permission. "In time, sweet, holy balance comes to all who believe. You have taken a good step toward such belief and the balance you seek, but now it is time for the morning meal. A proper Shaker must feed not only his soul but also his body in order to perform his duties well and contribute to the good of all. So Mother Ann has instructed us."

Brother Asa reached up to encourage the man to climb down from the fence, but Brother Elwood kept his eyes forward and ignored the little Shaker completely. Brother Asa kept his hand outstretched and spoke in the firm voice he used when working with one of the more fractious horses. "Come, Brother Elwood. Take my hand and climb down."

The man turned to stare at Brother Asa's hand for a long moment without reaching for it. Instead he blinked his eyes a couple of times before he jumped down from the fence. He stumbled when he hit the ground but didn't fall. Once he recovered his footing, he stood on the walkway staring down at the ground with his shoulders humped forward and didn't move.

"Come, Brother, it is time to go eat." Brother Asa took the man's arm. "When we kneel before our meal, we will pray for you to find the balance that will bring peace to your heart, will we not, Brother Isaac?"

Isaac nodded, although he was blank of prayers for himself. He certainly knew nothing to pray for this man with his tormented spirit.

"Prayers won't help," the man muttered. "She won't let them help."

Brother Asa frowned. "Nay. Mother Ann rejoices in our prayers. She delights in sending blessings down on us. Such gifts of love will soothe your troubled spirit."

Brother Elwood looked up at Brother Asa as if his words made no sense to him. "She has no love in her heart for me."

And even while Brother Asa was assuring the other man of the mother's love, Isaac knew it wasn't the Shakers' Mother Ann whose lack of love was tormenting Brother Elwood. It had to be Lacey. With her name came memory of the feel of her waist in his hands and the smile in her eyes, and Isaac was glad she had no love for the man before him.

Isaac lagged behind the two men. He didn't want Brother Asa to see his face and guess his unkind spirit. Or worse to somehow divine his thoughts and see how the new sister's face was not only lodged there in his mind but welcomed. A temptation he sought. Just a few weeks before, Isaac entertained no thought of such a temptation even being possible with his heart still full of Ella. He could not let himself look on another as he did Ella.

Guilt flooded him now. And yet Lacey remained in his thoughts in spite of the guilt. In spite of the fact that she was this tormented brother's wife. Wives meant nothing in this village. Such were disavowed and turned into sisters. But she was to be his sister too. Certainly it was a sin to think of her in any other way.

He'd had a wife. He would still have a wife if he hadn't spurned her father's advice. Being trapped under the judge's thumb would have been no worse than being separated from the world in this village. And Ella would still be leaning on his arm, smiling up at him, depending on him for her happiness. But he had not put her happiness before his. Not before it was too late to offer his life for hers.

Could the same guilt be torturing the man walking with Brother Asa in front of him? It did not seem the same. His Ella was dead. This man's wife, the new sister, was very much alive. Exercising her contrary spirit that seemed to so match Isaac's own as she resisted the Shaker way. He could not see her giving in to despair. Instead she let smiles slip out that poked at Isaac and made his lips turn up in answer.

Isaac was glad when they met Brother Forrest on the walkway coming to find Brother Elwood. He took him on toward the house to take their place in the line to the eating room. Brother Asa fell back beside Isaac once more. Since they had not yet entered the house, the rule of silence was not over them.

"Do you think he will find the balance he seeks?" Isaac asked as he watched the two men go up the steps to the brothers' door.

"That is not an easy question to answer. It would appear the poor man is soul sick." Brother Asa shook his head slightly before he went on. "For such there is no cure that can be given by another. That cure has to come from within or from the heavens. Something the man seems to realize and why he thinks the spirits are telling him to climb into the air."

"You don't think he's receiving a true spirit message?"

"Nay, I did not say that. Any among us can be an instrument of the spirits. But when the spirits torment instead of bringing joy, then a Believer must be sure he is allowing the proper spirits access to his heart. There are evil spirits as well as those sent by Mother Ann." Brother Asa stopped at the bottom of the stone steps and stared at the door above them. The other two men had already disappeared inside. "On the anvil of life we are forging the chains that link us to heaven or to hell."

"How can we change what we've already forged?"

"Those evil chains can be broken and new chains forged. With confession comes forgiveness and changed hearts. There are none too evil to be forgiven."

"But he was a preacher in the world. Surely he had done nothing so evil to link him to hell before he came here."

"So it would seem, but that we cannot know. Each man— you, me, Brother Elwood, all of us—must face his personal demons and find his own peace with the Eternal Father. The Christ himself faced the demons of temptation while on earth, as did our Mother Ann. None are free from such temptations. But in our village we shut away the world with its sinful enticements. Here a Believer can put his feet on that path to a perfect life in union with his brothers and sisters and find the peace that lets us live without sin."

A perfect life. Isaac didn't think that was possible. Mrs. McElroy's Bible had said Jesus had lived without sin. Isaac had no reason to doubt the Bible's words, even if he'd never let them seep down into his heart. But he did doubt that he himself could ever live a perfect life or if any of the Shakers he'd met could either. Even Brother Asa, who wore his faith like a shield against the arrows of sin.

Brother Asa must have seen the shadow of a frown on Isaac's face, because he smiled and put his hand on Isaac's

245

elbow to urge him toward the steps. "Some things are difficult to understand, my brother. But this is an easy truth for you to know. If we don't hurry, we will miss our breakfast."

They fell silent as they entered the brothers' door and slipped into their places in line to go into the dining room. When they knelt for the silent prayer before the meal, Isaac did offer up words for Brother Elwood. *Forgive this man his sins.* Isaac had no idea if he had used proper prayer words. He wasn't even sure he should be praying for another man's forgiveness when he'd never prayed for his own. But at least he'd kept his promise to Brother Asa.

As he got to his feet, he thought he could have prayed the same prayer for himself. For any man. Who didn't need forgiveness? A bit of a prayer his mother had taught him when he was just a boy came into his mind. *Forgive us our debts as we forgive our debtors.* For just a second he did think about whispering the prayer again for himself, but he pushed away the impulse as he reached with his right hand to pull out his chair at the same time as the others around him. The chairs scraped against the floor to break the silence in the room as the men and women settled in for the serious business of feeding their bodies.

When all had cleaned their plates, they pushed back their chairs in union again and stood before once more kneeling to pray. Another chance to pray for himself. At least eight times a day he knelt in the posture of prayer. Why had he never said the words for himself? He felt the words welling up inside him, but he turned his mind from them. He had no right to forgiveness. None. Better to think about the fence they needed to mend or the heifers that Brother Asa worried might have problems calving.

He was glad when the time of prayer was over and they could be about their duties. Without intent, as he stood up, his eyes fell on the new sister getting up off her knees across the room, and for no reason other than that she was in front of his eyes, his spirit lightened. She must have felt his eyes on her and looked across at him. She looked happy. Not the look of everyday contented happiness that many of the sisters wore. Her face was alight with joy. No small secret smile the way she had looked at him the day before in the meetinghouse. This smile lit up the room and she sent every bit of it his way. A fact that did not go unnoticed by the older sister beside her, who jerked on Lacey's sleeve and frowned displeasure at her. Even that didn't dim the new sister's smile. Isaac wouldn't have been a bit surprised to see her spin out away from the other sisters in a whirling dance.

He looked away from her before he found himself smiling back and earning them more trouble. But her smile lit up his heart and he found himself wishing he knew the prayer of her heart.

Isaac glanced around for Asa, but the little man was behind him in the line. He could only hope the brother hadn't noted Isaac's wandering gaze. But he wasn't the only one looking improperly toward the sisters' side of the eating room. Brother Elwood was standing to the side and not falling into line with the other brothers as they prepared to leave the room. He seemed unaware that the line was even forming as he stared across at the sisters.

He didn't seem to be looking toward Lacey. Instead he looked to be staring at Sister Aurelia, who had brought down the angel at the meeting the day before and started the commotion. At first Isaac thought the sister unaware of the man's stare, but then she turned her head slightly toward Brother Elwood. Her eyes only touched on the man for a brief second before she pulled on the corners of her cap and stared straight ahead again with the slightest of smiles. Brother

Elwood stayed rooted in his spot until Brother Forrest took his arm and moved him toward the line.

Once outside, the men split off in pairs and groups to go to their duties, as did the women who were spilling out the women's door of the building at the same time. Spring brought much work. Strawberry patches were red with berries to make jam. Weeds were rearing their unwelcome heads in the gardens already planted. Ground had to be readied for more beans and corn. It took acres of productive fields and gardens to supply the village with the necessary food for the Shakers and their stock and still leave abundant seeds to gather for next spring's planting and to package to sell to those of the world.

At Harmony Hill, idleness was not allowed in any fashion. Just the day before, Elder Homer had warned Isaac that an idle brain was the devil's workshop and that an empty soul tempted the devil to come take residence. Isaac didn't doubt the elder's words or the judgment he'd seen in the man's eyes that Isaac's soul might be tempting the devil to move in. But it was beginning to look as if his soul wasn't the only one tempting the devil in the Shaker village.

22

The strawberry patch stretched out in front of Lacey so far a person might pick all day without finding the end of one row, but on this day Lacey didn't mind. She didn't even mind how the sweat was rolling down her face from the edges of the wretched bonnet she had to wear all the time, or how her dress was sticking to her back as she filled her baskets with the plump red strawberries.

She didn't let it bother her that it was forbidden to eat any of the strawberries off the vine, when everybody knew that strawberries tasted the very best with the sun warming their sweet flavor. Not once did she try to catch the other sisters with their heads turned away so she could sneak a berry into her mouth. This day she would be a dutiful Shaker and abide by the rules, for when the strawberries were picked and the evening meal had been eaten, she was going to see Rachel.

If it hadn't been for the worry of squashing a few berries, Lacey might have done a few steps of her dandelion dance. She bent down to pluck another strawberry from the vine to hide the smile that wanted to spread clear across her face. Sister Drayma had already taken Lacey to task for the way she had smiled with too much abandon in the eating room. It had been on the tip of Lacey's tongue to say that Aurelia's angel Esmolenda was dripping smiles down on her, but then Sister Drayma would have given her the lecture on lying. A well-deserved one at that, because no angel was smiling through her. She was doing every bit of the smiling herself.

In fact she had almost laughed out loud when she'd caught the eye of the young brother, Isaac, who had caused such a stir in the meetinghouse on Sunday when he reached out to catch her. It hadn't exactly worked since they'd both ended in a heap on the floor and shocked the stuffing out of the assembly. If the woes were still echoing a bit in Lacey's head, then they were probably sounding ten times worse in his. So it was no wonder he'd looked surprised to see her grinning from ear to ear like she didn't have a care in the world. He had surely thought she would be downcast from all the finger-pointing and blame that had gone on at the meeting. Blame for something as innocent as a clumsy fall. Or an angelic push. Either way, a totally innocent happening as far as she and the brother were concerned.

Certainly nothing she'd planned, even if something about Isaac did jerk on her heartstrings. She couldn't pay any attention to that. She didn't have any loose heartstrings for anybody to be jerking. But if she did, if she wasn't Mrs. Reverend Palmer, if she wasn't living right in the middle of a bunch of people who thought being Mrs. Anything was the biggest sin a person could commit, then she might hope, might even dream of falling against that young brother again. Without a few hundred eyes looking on.

She could almost hear Miss Mona whispering in her head, *If wishes were horses, beggars would ride.* So it was better to stay focused on what was and not be pondering what wasn't. She *was* the lawfully wedded wife of a man who had lost all touch with reason ever since those seed-selling Shakers had landed on his front porch. That was what was. This morning the poor man had appeared sickly, standing there in the middle of the eating room looking for all the world like a blind sheep in need of a good shepherd to prod him along the proper path.

She'd known it wasn't going to be easy for Preacher Palmer here with these people. He was used to declaring the gospel, not hearing it from others. It was still beyond her how he could have swallowed what these people preached. That the Lord had to come back again like he hadn't gotten the job done right the first time. And then to come back in a woman. While Lacey could almost wrap her mind around that even as crazy strange as it sounded, she couldn't see the preacher ever being able to do so. Not with what he'd always preached from his pulpit. Yet the day before, he'd been shaking and quaking and losing all grasp on his sanity, from the looks of things.

There wasn't the least thing she could do about it. Even if the way she'd acted toward him after they'd spoken their vows might have been the first shove toward his downward slide, she couldn't change that now. She didn't like to think about what Miss Mona would tell her if she were still breathing, but then if Miss Mona had still been breathing, none of this would be happening.

It was all a tangle. That was for sure. Such a tangle that she just pushed it to the side and gave up pulling any strings to untangle it. She was going to see Rachel. That was what she needed to think on. That and how the sky was a robin's egg blue and the strawberry juice on her fingertips was sweet and Sister Drayma was way at the other end of the patch. Too far to hear any careless word Lacey might let escape her mouth to bring on one of the woman's lectures.

Aurelia was there beside her, picking one strawberry to Lacey's four. She kept smiling too. Some the same as Lacey. But some different too. Not big smiles like the ones Lacey kept having to bite back when she thought about seeing Rachel. Aurelia's smiles were a bare lift of the corners of her lips, like as how she knew where the mouse had hid the cheese. And she was the only one who did. The only one who ever would.

Lacey supposed that might be the way of it after an angel stepped down inside a person. That person might feel things a bit different for a spell. Even if a person was making the whole thing up, the fact that she'd fooled so many people might keep a smile lurking for a day or two.

Idle chatter wasn't encouraged while they worked, but a few words now and again were overlooked. Besides, nobody was close enough to know if they were talking about strawberries or what.

"Are you feeling all right, Sister Aurelia?"

"Yea, I am fine. I might claim even better than fine." Sister Aurelia lay the strawberry she'd just picked gently down in her basket. Then she moved it to the side as though each strawberry had its assigned place in her basket before she looked up at Lacey. The corners of her lips turned up a bit more and her eyes looked ready to laugh. "Why do you ask, Sister Lacey?"

"You just seem a little off kilter this morning. Like maybe you'd been spinning some this day like as how you did in meeting and it was keeping you from thinking straight."

"Spinning." Aurelia did laugh then, a sweet whisper of a laugh, as she held her arms out away from her and looked ready to do a turn or two. She dropped her arms back to her side and bent down to the berry row again. "I'm so glad you came here, Sister Lacey. You are an answer to prayer."

"Me?" Lacey stopped picking and stared at Aurelia. "What prayer?"

"The better question might be, whose prayer?"

"All right then. Whose prayer?"

"Whose prayer indeed?"

252

"I think that's what I asked you."

Lacey waited for Aurelia to answer, but she just kept smiling mysteriously at Lacey with no words forthcoming. Like maybe she was trying to get under Lacey's skin. If so, it was working.

With a shrug, Lacey smashed down her irritation. "I don't know what bee you've got in your bonnet this morning, but I don't see any need in letting it sting me." She turned her attention back to the strawberry plants and searched through the thick growth of leaves to locate every ripe berry. She didn't look at Aurelia as she went on. "And if prayer brought me here, then could be prayer will see me away from here."

Aurelia leaned over to find another strawberry too. Her head was very near Lacey's and her hand swept through the same plants that Lacey had just picked clean. "Don't you like it here, Sister Lacey? With the angels? With me?"

"There's ways I'd rather live. That doesn't have anything to do with you or the other sisters either. It just doesn't seem natural." Lacey moved a short way down the row. There wasn't the least bit of sense of them picking in the same spot. She looked back at Aurelia. "What about you, Sister Aurelia? Do you like it here? With your angels?"

"Some people don't have any choice."

"That's God's own truth," Lacey said. "Plenty of times life don't give a body much choice." One by one she picked off a handful of strawberries to drop into her basket. Out of the corner of her eye she saw Aurelia pick a green strawberry and then stare at it as if she could make it turn red before she dropped it on the ground and quite deliberately stepped on it.

"Nor do the angels," Aurelia said as she leaned back over to the strawberry plants in the same place, the already picked place, and began searching through the leaves again.

"I think we've already got the ripe ones there," Lacey said. "Maybe you should move up the row a little."

Aurelia paid no attention and Lacey picked back through the strawberries between them so none of the ripe ones would be missed. Aurelia certainly couldn't be relied on to find them. Not on this day when her mind seemed on anything but strawberries. They worked in silence for a moment with Aurelia continuing to rake her fingers through the strawberry leaves, checking the ones with just a blush of red over and over before leaving them on the vine.

Lacey had almost forgotten her question about the angels by the time Aurelia decided to answer. "They're not my angels. More like I'm their mouth and hands. Can you understand what I mean by that?" Aurelia looked over at Lacey. "How if you had no voice you might have to borrow someone else's. That's the way of the angels. They have to borrow my voice, my body. I am their instrument."

"Is it a good feeling? Seems like it might be scary to me." Lacey had her basket heaped up. No little sister was close to fetch her an empty basket. That was their duty in the patch, but there were many pickers and only a few children. So she dropped her handful of berries in Aurelia's basket. Aurelia wasn't ever going to get it filled up the way she was going anyway.

"Angels are creatures of love. A vessel filled with love keeps a trace inside the way a jar of honey can never be completely emptied without leaving behind the film of sweetness." Aurelia finally stepped up to the row and picked a ripe strawberry. She gazed at it for a moment before she put it in her mouth rather than in the basket without even a glance around to be sure no one was watching.

"Whatever was talking through you didn't appear all that loving to me," Lacey said as she dropped another handful of berries into Aurelia's basket.

Aurelia grabbed Lacey's wrist just as she had at the meeting.

Her eyes went cold as she said, "You should not speak ill of angels."

"Turn me loose, Sister Aurelia." Lacey kept her voice even and didn't try to jerk free of the sister's hold. Instead she met her eyes fully and said, "I wasn't speaking ill. Only the truth. I think an angel can bear up under the truth. And so can you. Whoever was talking through your mouth yesterday wasn't talking love, but sin."

"Sin." Aurelia whispered the word and dropped her hand away from Lacey's wrist. A look of distress crossed her face. "You cannot hide from sin. Even when you hide it from everyone else, the angels know."

"The Lord does for sure." If Aurelia kept up with these angel carryings-on, Lacey might look more kindly on going back to hearing Sister Drayma's sermons in her ears. She glanced down toward the older sister who was still too far away to hear them, but she was standing with her hands on her hips watching them. Lacey stooped down beside the strawberry row to give her back a rest. "We'd better get back to filling up our baskets before Sister Drayma decides I'm not working diligently enough. I wouldn't want them to change their minds about letting me see my daughter tonight."

Aurelia squatted down across the row in front of Lacey. She didn't even make a pretense of berry picking now as she said, "You have no daughter. Isn't that what the angel told you?"

Lacey sat back on her heels and considered Aurelia. "I thought you didn't remember anything the angel said." She didn't know why she was surprised. She had never really believed an angel was talking through Aurelia.

"At times the angel's words hover in my mind and come back to me later. As now. Am I not right? She did not accuse you of the sin, but didn't she tell you that you have no daughter? Wanting a child to be your child does not make it true."

255

"Rachel is my daughter." Lacey spoke the words slow and true.

"But didn't you tell me she does not call you mother? That she called another such and that one was not her mother either. Not her natural mother."

Lacey had told her that, but coming out of Aurelia's mouth the words sounded different. Like they had nothing to do with a real child. More like the pronouncement of a judge on a guilty party. "It doesn't matter about names or who gave birth to her. It matters how I feel."

"And yet you deserted her here. Just as she was deserted by her first mother. Just as she was deserted by her second mother." Aurelia's voice was harsh.

"No, that's not true." Tears spilled out of Lacey's eyes. The baskets of strawberries were forgotten. Sister Drayma storming up the row toward them didn't matter. Nothing mattered but Aurelia's words that had stabbed through Lacey's heart. "I didn't want to be parted from her. I had no choice. Why are you saying these awful things?"

"Can't you bear up under the truth, Sister Lacey? As the angels can. Do you think the first mother had a choice?" Aurelia leaned closer to Lacey. "Do you?"

"I don't know," Lacey whispered. "How could I know?"

Sister Drayma was only a few steps away. Her frown was fierce as she called out to them. "Sisters, what is the meaning of this?"

Neither Aurelia nor Lacey turned to look at her. Instead their eyes were locked on one another, and all at once tears appeared in Aurelia's eyes to match Lacey's. She reached across the row to lightly touch Lacey's hand. "I am sorry, Sister Lacey. The sin is not yours. It has never been yours. Please forgive me." Then a tremble shook through her as she sank down between the strawberry rows.

Lacey sprang up and across the row, but she couldn't catch her. She sat down in the dirt beside Aurelia to lift her head and shoulders up on her lap. "Aurelia. Are you all right?" The woman's eyelids twitched but didn't open. Lacey loosened the strings of the woman's cap and slipped it off to begin waving air with it down toward her face.

"Was she having a vision?" Sister Drayma asked. The crossness in her voice was gone, replaced with a hint of awe. Angel visions obviously took precedence over duty.

"Perhaps. She seemed not herself," Lacey answered.

Other sisters were clustering around them now, all the baskets forgotten for the moment.

Sister Drayma asked, "Was it that angel again? Esmo something."

"She didn't call any names," Lacey said. "It might be no more than the sun too hot. We need to fetch her some water."

"The sun is hot on us all and none of the rest of us are falling prostrate in the patch." But Sister Drayma looked around and ordered a young sister who wasn't much bigger than Rachel to bring a dipper of water.

Rachel. Lacey had to take charge of this confusion to make sure Eldress Frieda's promise wouldn't be taken from her. That might happen if Sister Drayma decided Lacey was the reason for the disruption in the strawberry patch instead of Aurelia. After all, nobody expected Lacey to be seeing any angelic visions. Least of all Lacey.

But maybe Aurelia was being visited by angels. Or thinking she was. She hadn't seemed herself. Lacey pulled up the corner of her apron and gently wiped the dirt streaks off Aurelia's damp cheeks. And she had pleaded for forgiveness there before she'd started playing possum. She knew her words wounded Lacey.

Lacey could forgive her. That was easy enough with her

head lying in Lacey's lap and her face as pale as the sliver of moon that sometimes hung in the sky during the daylight hours. But why had she said them? Why did she or this angel keep saying Lacey had no daughter? If angels were love, as Aurelia claimed, those angels would know that love was a bond as strong as any forged by blood. And how could the Shakers not believe that when they spoke continually of love without the strictures of the natural blood relationships? If Sister Drayma had told her once, she'd told her a dozen times that all were of a family in the village. All in union. All loving one another as their Mother Ann and the Christ directed.

Sister Betsy got back with the gourd dipper of water, no more than half full since she'd spilled much of it in her haste to bring it. Lacey raised Aurelia's head and Sister Drayma tipped the dipper up against her lips. The water dribbled out the corners of her mouth and down on her dress.

"It might be well to carry her to the infirmary," one of the older sisters in the circle around them suggested.

"She will be heavy," another spoke up. "We should call the brethren to help. They could bring a stretcher."

"First let me try to give her another drink," Lacey suggested. Aurelia's eyelids were twitching again. Lacey thought it might be according to whether Aurelia liked the idea of being carried to the infirmary how soon she decided to let them open.

Sister Drayma handed over the dipper. With no warning of what she planned to do, Lacey threw the little amount left in it directly into Aurelia's face. The woman gasped and jerked straight up from Lacey's lap. It appeared angels didn't care a whole lot for water.

23

"Perhaps you could fetch another dipper of water, Sister Betsy. I think Sister Aurelia could use that drink now." Lacey held the dipper out toward the young girl, who took it with a notable lack of enthusiasm. She didn't want to go off to the water pail at the end of the patch and miss whatever was about to happen with Aurelia who was looking mad as a wet hen. An apt description, in spite of the fact there couldn't have been more than a cupful of water in the dipper that Lacey had splashed on her face. Aurelia swiped at a few wet strands of black hair falling down on her forehead and snatched her cap out of Lacey's hands.

"Sister Lacey, that lacked kindness." Sister Drayma frowned.

"Yea, you are right, Sister Drayma." Lacey was ready to make amends. "I should have dipped the corner of my apron in the water and brought our sister back from her faint more gently." Without looking at either Aurelia or Sister Drayma, Lacey cast her eyes down at her empty hands, but she could feel Aurelia's angry stare. "But our sister is back among us in body and spirit now and can perhaps walk on her own feet to the infirmary while the rest of us continue in our duty of picking berries."

"There is good sense in what our sister says." One of the older sisters clustered around them spoke up. "The berries do not jump into our baskets on their own, and Sister Aurelia has no need of us all attending to her. Come, Sisters, back to picking before the rain that might come in the night sours the berries in the patch."

As the older sister turned back to her row, she caught Lacey's eye with a quick smile that flashed approval. All the other sisters except Sister Drayma and the little sister holding the dipper reluctantly followed the older sister back to their deserted baskets.

Lacey didn't allow any hint of an answering smile to slip out on her face as she gathered her courage to look straight at Aurelia. She wasn't anxious for another confrontation with the sister's angel. "I beg your forgiveness, Sister Aurelia, for the way I splashed the water in your face. That was wrong of me and did not show proper thought or consideration. Will you forgive me?"

Perhaps Aurelia heard the echo of her own words before she fainted in Lacey's words now. Whatever the reason, her face softened as she wiped her face with her apron before saying, "Yea, it would be sinful to withhold forgiveness in the face of your confession of wrong." She positioned the white cap on her head and tucked her hair up under it.

"Very well, Sisters. That is good." Sister Drayma slapped her hands together and then pointed Sister Betsy back to the water bucket. The child went willingly enough, since the drama seemed to be at an end with the forgiveness words.

Lacey got to her feet and brushed off her skirt. Aurelia made no move to follow Lacey to her feet but stayed on the ground between Lacey and Sister Drayma.

"Come, Sister Aurelia. Let us help you up." Sister Drayma sounded more concerned than impatient as she reached down toward Aurelia. "You can lean on me as we walk to the infirmary. Sister Lacey will fill your basket."

"You can't expect her to fill her basket and mine as well," Aurelia said as she took Sister Drayma's hand and got to her feet. She staggered back a step and Lacey put her arm around the sister's waist to steady her.

"I will work double quick," Lacey said.

"Perhaps you can." Aurelia looked at Lacey so long that Lacey was beginning to worry her angel was coming back to torment the both of them. But then she went on. "You seem to be gifted at taking over the duty of others."

"What duties are those? Other than the picking of these berries."

"Don't keep pestering Sister Aurelia with questions." With a stern look toward Lacey, Sister Drayma stepped to the other side of Aurelia. "You can see that she is weary."

"Yea." Sister Aurelia leaned away from Lacey toward Sister Drayma. "It is true that though the visitations of the angels leave me joyful of spirit, they also empty me of strength and leave me with tremors outside and in." She held out her hand to show how her fingers were trembling. She covered her hand with the other and pulled it back against her waist.

Lacey watched the two women move away, stepping carefully across the rows to do the least damage to the strawberries. Once at the edge of the patch, Aurelia leaned against Sister Drayma as they headed toward the middle of the village where the infirmary was located. With both her Shaker guides gone, Lacey was alone for the first time since she had put on the Shaker dress.

Of course she wasn't really alone. Plenty of other sisters were scattered about the strawberry patch filling their baskets, and the little sisters were up and down the row collecting the filled baskets and offering drinks of water. But no one was

261

in her ear. No one was preaching the Shaker way to her or instructing her on the proper way to pick strawberries, as if that was something that took teaching.

The silence was good. Being alone was good. She thought a moment about leaving Aurelia's half-full basket and stepping across the rows out of the patch the same as Aurelia and Sister Drayma had. She could keep walking until she found Rachel, and then together they could leave this strange village behind.

They won't let you take Rachel. The words slammed into her head. True words she had no way of changing.

Lacey bent back down to the strawberry row. She could pick double fast. Miss Mona had always told her she was quick about everything she did. Or maybe it just seemed so to Miss Mona, who at times was too weak to comb out the bed tangles in her own hair or even take the caps off a handful of strawberries for her morning's breakfast. They'd never tried to grow their own strawberries. The little patch of garden ground where Lacey planted the corn and beans and potatoes was too small. None of that precious space could be wasted on strawberries.

But this or that churchwoman had brought fresh-picked berries by at times, along with the sugar cakes to eat with them. Lacey missed the churchwomen. Her hand stopped in mid-pick at the thought, and she shook her head a little at her contrariness. Back at the preacher's house, she had at times thought those very women were the bane of her existence, but that was before Sister Drayma and Aurelia's angel started pushing the sin words at her. Miss Sadie Rose's unsought advice seemed sweet in comparison.

Then again without Sadie Rose and the other women's gossipy talking, she might never have spoken vows with the preacher. They might still be living unbothered back at the preacher's house with poor Preacher Palmer in his own pulpit armed with the word of the Lord instead of shaking and quaking and falling apart here in this place.

A sigh swept through Lacey down to her toes. She couldn't figure everything out. Certainly not angel visitations or the way Preacher Palmer was acting. Or even her own mind that hopped about like a grasshopper on a hot cookstove. Worry could do that to a person, Miss Mona had told her once. She'd said it was all right not to know all the answers and it was proper to leave some things up to the good Lord. That he could take care of the things Lacey didn't understand. What she was supposed to think on was what she could figure out. Like filling up her basket with strawberries. Like thinking on seeing Rachel. Like praying about those other things so maybe the Lord would open up her own understanding.

Praying. That was what she ought to be doing right at that moment while she was pulling off the strawberries. The berry picking occupied her hands, but not her head. She could ask the Lord to help her make sense of Aurelia and her angel talk about sin, but yet she edged away from offering up that prayer. She couldn't seem to keep her mind focused on any prayer. It seemed so useless. She couldn't get out of being married to the preacher. She couldn't get out of this village. At least not without giving up Rachel. What was the use of bombarding the Lord with requests for things that couldn't happen?

Don't think of prayer as a wish list to hand up to the Lord. You'll be robbing yourself of Spirit power if you do that. Prayer is more than a list of things you get in your head and think you want. Miss Mona's voice echoed in Lacey's ears plain as if she was standing right beside her. *Prayer is for asking the Lord to help you deal with whatever befalls you. And plenty is going to befall you. It befalls us all. But the Lord is only a prayer away.*

A prayer away and yet Lacey couldn't seem to get past *Dear*

Lord in heaven before the prayer words evaporated out of her head like water in a hot frying pan. She'd made the mistakes. She'd have to live with them. Of course she could surely find a thankful word for Eldress Frieda giving permission for her to see Rachel when the day's work was done.

She didn't stop and close her eyes. She didn't lift her face to the sky or hold her hands up in supplication. She just kept picking off berries as she whispered, "Dear Lord in heaven, thank you for your blessings." Even to her ears the words sounded like something she was throwing out in the air with no more thought or feeling than speaking about the color of the strawberry in her hand. A person had to be open to prayer.

Maybe that was the sin Aurelia's angel kept seeing in her. But then she'd said it wasn't Lacey's sin. Lacey dumped another handful of berries into the basket. It was almost full and she stood up to rest her back as she waved at one of the little girls to bring a new basket. She watched the child walking up the row toward her. Not Rachel, but with the same bounce to her step. And the joy awoke in her again over the prospect of holding Rachel against her bosom once more. She pushed Aurelia's confusing words out of her head. Maybe angel talk was just something that Lacey would never understand.

At the evening meal Aurelia's place was empty at the table. Lacey wanted to ask Sister Drayma about her, but no words were permitted in the eating room. And afterward, Lacey had to hurry to meet Eldress Frieda. She didn't want to be late.

The eldress was waiting in the hallway and led the way out the door and down the steps. She didn't speak until they were walking along the path toward the Children's House. "I am told the angel came to speak to you again."

"To me?" Lacey whipped her head around to look at the eldress.

Eldress Frieda met her look with a deep calmness. "No one else was nearby."

"Sister Aurelia was there."

"Yea, but she was the instrument to deliver the message." Eldress Frieda was silent for a few steps before she went on. "Do you fear the angel's message? Does it disturb you?"

"The thought of an angel coming down out of heaven to talk especially to me worries me some," Lacey admitted.

"I suppose that might be the normal reaction of one of the world. But here you should feel blessed to be so selected by the angels."

"Selected? I'm not sure what you mean by that."

The eldress smiled over at her. "Worry not, my sister. It is good to be selected. To be thought of as worthy of singular attention to bring you into our fold. Mother Ann must have some special work in mind for you once you embrace our ways. Once you become a covenanted Believer."

Only barely did Lacey bite back the words denying the possibility of that ever happening. She was but a few minutes from seeing Rachel. Not the best time to slap the eldress in the face with contrary words. Instead, Lacey bent her head to stare back down to the pathway to hide her total disbelief. But the eldress must have caught a glimpse of her face anyway.

"You think that can never happen," the eldress said with the sound of a smile in her voice. "I once felt something the same."

"You did?" Lacey didn't try to hide her surprise as she looked back up at the eldress.

"Yea, it is so. I came into the Believers much as you. At the bidding of my worldly family. Not to this village but to one in the East."

"You were married?" Lacey's surprise grew.

"Nay. I did not have the sin of matrimony to shake from

me, but I had dreamed of that being my way along with many other worldly thoughts. I refused to bend my spirit to the Shaker way. I resisted our Mother Ann's sweet love." All trace of a smile disappeared from the woman's face as she sounded almost sorrowful as she confessed. "I had a stubborn will."

"Why didn't you leave?"

"I harbored that sinful desire for many months, but such is not so easy to do when there is none in the world to take you in. I was yet young. Only fifteen at the time. I might have slid down the slippery slope and been sucked into the miry pits of sin if a man of the world had sought my hand." Eldress Frieda looked up toward the treetops. "I am eternally grateful Mother Ann protected me against my own sinful lusts by enclosing me within a loving community of Believers. By the time I turned twenty-one, my heart and my will had changed and I was ready to step into the life of loving service and peace Mother Ann had ready for me. In time she opened the way for me to come to this western village that has been my home for so many years now. A good home."

"Did she send messages in visions to you?" Lacey was almost afraid to ask the question.

"I was visited with dreams. Such can be visions. There is evidence of that in the Good Book."

"You mean Joseph."

"Yea. The moon and stars bowing down to his sun was a prophetic dream."

"I was thinking of the other Joseph. The one who married Mary. Angels kept showing up in his dreams."

"So they did." Eldress Frieda inclined her head in agreement as they walked past the meetinghouse.

On down the road, Lacey could see the roof of the Children's House. Her heart began beating faster. She wanted to run on ahead, but she made her anxious feet keep matching the pace of the eldress who moved without haste as she kept talking about angels and their visitations and dreams.

"But the plethora of angel visits that are enriching our spirits and worship now only began a few years ago. It is a special era of Mother's work. Many among us here and in the villages all across the country are being visited with manifestations of the spirit. Some are gifted with songs. Some with drawings. Some with visions. Some lend their bodies to the angels or those who have stepped over the divide but wish to bring us some word of encouragement. Many of these come in dreams."

"Nothing like any of that has ever happened to me." Lacey pushed out of her mind the times when she'd felt Miss Mona near after she'd passed on. That was just Lacey's wishful thinking. She went on quickly. "I never can remember my dreams after I wake up. And I'm married."

Lacey didn't know why she added that last unless she wanted the eldress to know she couldn't be the reason the angel was showing up in Aurelia. If an angel was showing up in Aurelia. Lacey couldn't keep from entertaining some doubts about that.

"Married in what way, my sister? I sense little attachment between you and Brother Elwood." The eldress paused on the walkway and fixed her eyes on Lacey. "It has been told to me that you yourself admitted to Brother Forrest your union was sinful."

Lacey stopped beside the eldress even though her feet itched to keep walking toward Rachel. She tried to answer the woman honestly, to get the conversation finished so the eldress would move on toward the Children's House. "It was. Sinful in that it was wrong for me to marry him instead of trusting in the Lord to make a way for me. For us. Sinful in that I drove him to sorrow by not acting the proper wife."

"Yea, such sins of the world can bring much sorrow. We can have no true unity of spirit one with another if we cling to the selfish worldly relationships of a man and his wife and children. The Bible instructs us to love all in a practical, unified way and not in small worldly families but in the one family of God. That is how we prove we are true disciples."

"Yea." Right then Lacey would have agreed with anything the eldress said just to get her to start walking again. Besides, the eldress had a way of saying things that came across as holy even when Lacey wasn't sure what she was preaching about. But Lacey knew about the Bible talking about love. She didn't have any arguments about that. What she couldn't understand was how the Shakers tried to limit love by shoving it into a little box that had only one label on it. The brotherly love label.

But a mother's love, that was surely something the Lord had a hand in putting inside a person the same as the love between a man and woman. That love was the good Lord's design from Adam and Eve on down through the ages to bring children into the world. All that seemed plain as day to Lacey, but not to the Shakers.

The sound of young voices singing drifted out the open windows in the Children's House down the pathway toward them. It was a good sound. A happy sound. Lacey started to turn toward it, but Eldress Frieda laid her hand on Lacey's arm to stop her.

Where before there had been the bare hint of a smile, now Lacey saw a flash of worry. Not something she'd ever seen on Eldress Frieda's face. Normally she floated along on a visible sea of content even when others were naming their wrongs of the week.

"Before we go on, you must keep in mind that all things change, Sister Lacey. It is the way of life. All people change.

We grow. We adjust. We move on with the days assigned to us. Especially the young ones. Children have a way of adapting and learning and leaving the old life behind with much more ease than one would suspect."

Lacey tried to concentrate on what the older woman was trying to tell her, but the children's voices pulled at her. She wanted to hear Rachel's voice. She wanted to feel Rachel's small hand in hers. She threw another yea of agreement out into the air.

The eldress breathed out a slight sigh and looked upward as though wishing for divine inspiration. Lacey eyed her uneasily and fervently hoped the woman wasn't about to have a visitation that would delay their progress to the Children's House even more.

After a moment the eldress began walking again. "Come. Sister Janie will be waiting with the child and we must return to our dwelling before the retiring bell rings."

Finally they climbed the steps up to the sisters' door. The children were in the upper gathering room practicing the same as the Shaker brothers and sisters were doing in the other houses. But Rachel's voice wasn't among them. She and Sister Janie were waiting for Lacey and the eldress in the schoolroom.

The skirt of the long blue Shaker dress covered all but the toes of Rachel's sturdy black shoes as she perched on the schoolroom bench like a lost little bird. Her hands were folded in her lap and her head was bent, staring down at them in a prayerful pose that hid her eyes and face. All Lacey could see was the white cap that hid Rachel's curly black hair. She didn't look up even after Sister Janie greeted Lacey by name. What had they done to her? What had Lacey let them do to her?

Lacey would have rushed across the floor to grab up the little girl, but Eldress Frieda stopped her with a hand on her shoulder. "You must not attempt to disturb the child's spirit of unity. Sister Janie says she has made much progress in the days she has been here."

Spirit of unity. All at once Lacey felt queasy. She and Rachel were the ones with a spirit of unity. It had been thus since she'd lifted her as a tiny baby out of the box on the back porch of the preacher's house. It would be thus forever. She was her mother. Rachel was her child. The Shakers could not change that. She would not let them change that.

24

"Rachel?" Lacey's voice sounded hesitant and unsure even to her ears. She cleared her throat and repeated. "Rachel. Aren't you going to say hello?"

At last the child raised her head, but she didn't look at Lacey. Instead, she stared at the wall over Lacey's shoulder. "Good evening, Sister Lacey." She spoke politely as though to someone she barely knew. The kind of polite greeting Lacey herself had taught her to say to the churchwomen back home when she wasn't feeling friendly.

Lacey pushed a smile out on her face. Not the kind of smile she had worn all through the day when she thought of seeing Rachel. That smile was curling up inside her and dying like one of Rachel's pet worms on a hot rock. "It is a good evening," she said. Then she turned to Eldress Frieda. "Can we have a few moments alone?"

"Nay, that is not possible," the eldress said. "I must attend to some other duties, but Sister Janie will stay here with you until she deems the visit is over. We have granted you this privilege. In return I expect you back to your room long before the retiring bell rings. Remember there are those who watch the pathways."

"Yea. So I have been told." Lacey didn't care about the

watchers. She only cared about the small girl sitting across the room from her who seemed only a shell of the child she had surrendered to Sister Janie just days ago.

"Very well."

After Eldress Frieda left in a rustle of skirts, silence fell over the room. Two weeks ago Lacey would have never believed that Rachel could sit so still and quiet. Or have such veiled eyes.

Sister Janie smiled slightly as she broke the silence. "Sister Rachel has adjusted well. She was somewhat distraught at first, but I have discovered that children are very resilient. Even the youngest ones. And they understand the truth when it is spoken to them. Sister Rachel has been very attentive to the stories of Mother Ann. Haven't you, Sister Rachel?" Sister Janie's smile warmed as she turned toward Rachel.

"Mother Ann loves me." At last Rachel showed a spark of life. She looked straight at Lacey and added fiercely, "She will always be my mother."

Forcing her lips to keep smiling, Lacey went over to sit on the bench beside Rachel. She was beginning to understand. So it didn't bother her when Rachel yanked her skirts away to keep Lacey from touching them. She placed her hand on the bench between them, palm up inviting Rachel to reach for it.

"I will always be your mother too." She kept her voice barely above a whisper with the hope that Sister Janie might not hear her words across the room. "Nothing can ever change that."

"Nay. You would not have brought me here if that was true." Rachel folded her arms across her chest and turned her eyes toward the wall. "Sister Rella says you didn't want me anymore. That you were tired of taking care of me."

"I don't know who Sister Rella is, but she's wrong. Very wrong." Lacey put force in the words, but Rachel mashed her lips together in a stubborn line and wouldn't look at Lacey. "Who is this Sister Rella?" Lacey looked up at Sister Janie, who had moved closer to better hear their words.

"I don't know." Sister Janie appeared to be truly puzzled. "None of the sisters who stay with the children have a like name to that. Unless she speaks of Sister Loretta, who sometimes works in our kitchen." Sister Janie shifted her look from Lacey to Rachel. "Is that who you mean, Sister Rachel? Sister Loretta?"

Rachel shook her head. "Not Sister Loretta. Sister Rella. She comes to me at night and tells me things."

"In your dreams?" Lacey asked.

"She wakes me up. The first time I got scared, but I'm not scared now. I like it when she comes. She tells me about angels."

Was the child falling into the Shakers' spell so much that she was entertaining angels like Aurelia? "What does she tell you about them?"

"It's a secret. Between me and Sister Rella. She says we have a lot of secrets."

"Secrets are not the Shaker way." Sister Janie's voice was stern. "We share all things with our brothers and sisters and don't deny them the joy of gifts presented us by the angels."

Rachel's lip trembled a little, but she kept her arms tightly crossed and didn't look at Sister Janie. Lacey welcomed the evidence that the Shakers hadn't completely conquered Rachel's stubborn streak any more than they had overcome Lacey's own contrariness. Her Rachel was still there under the pouting lips and angry arms. But who was this Sister Rella?

"We used to have a few secrets." Lacey couldn't stop herself any longer. She reached over and stroked Rachel's arm. The little girl didn't act as if she noticed, but at least she didn't jerk away from Lacey's hand.

273

"Sister Rella says those secrets were all made up. That you made up things like you made up stories."

"How did she know I made up stories?"

"Sister Rella knows everything. The angels tell her."

"Oh." Lacey let her hand rest on Rachel's shoulder. She wanted more than anything to gather her close and hold her until she turned back into the little girl who had clung to her and called her mama on their first night in this village. But Rachel needed to come to Lacey's lap of her own will. "Is your Sister Rella pretty?"

Rachel's voice changed, sounded more like Lacey's Rachel. "She is pretty. She tells me I'm pretty too."

"Our outward looks are not important, Sisters. It's the inner heart and soul that matters," Sister Janie said.

Lacey ignored the woman's preachy words and kept her eyes on Rachel. "What does she look like?"

"She has black hair and eyes that can see in the dark. Her fingers are long like mine and never cold." Rachel held up her hands and wiggled her fingers back and forth. "She sings to me the way you used to when I couldn't go to sleep back before . . . " She stopped and suddenly looked sad.

"Before?" Lacey asked. "Before what?"

"Before you quit loving me and brought me here." Rachel's eyes filled with tears.

"I will never quit loving you, Rachel. Ever. I promised you that on our first night here. It was a promise that could never be broken. Will never be broken."

"You said you'd come tell me Maddie stories." Rachel slowly turned toward Lacey. She still had her arms clenched across her chest. "You promised, but you didn't come."

"I wanted to," Lacey said, but her words didn't seem to be getting through to Rachel.

Tears began spilling out of the child's eyes. "They took

Maddie away from me. Sister Rella said because of you. All because of you." Rachel opened her mouth and began sobbing. The sound mixed strangely with the muffled singing drifting down from the room two floors above them.

"Here, here, Sisters." Sister Janie waved her hands back and forth as she scurried the rest of the way across the room toward them. "Nay, nay. This will never do."

Lacey slipped to her knees in front of Rachel and put her hands on the little girl's wet cheeks and made her look at her. "That's not true, Rachel."

"Sister Rella says it is." Her words were a wail of sorrow.

"But she's mixed up on that. I'd never do anything to hurt you. Never."

"Leave the child be, Sister Lacey. You're upsetting her and undoing all the good we've done." Sister Janie tried to pull Lacey away from Rachel, but Lacey refused to budge as she kept staring into the little girl's eyes.

Rachel looked almost ready to drop her head down on Lacey's shoulder. Another minute and she would have had her in her arms, comforting her. But Sister Janie reached around Lacey to jerk Rachel off the bench and yank her toward the door.

When Rachel started crying even louder, Sister Janie gave the child's arm a firm shake as she said, "Hush your crying right now, Sister Rachel. Such out-of-control behavior will not be tolerated."

Rachel shut her mouth and wiped her arm across her nose and eyes as she tried to swallow her sobs.

With her heart about to break, Lacey spun around on her knees to grab for Rachel, but Sister Janie hustled her out of reach. But she couldn't stop Lacey's words from getting to Rachel's ears. "I love you, Rachel. More than all the stars in the sky."

"Sister Lacey, I told you to leave the child be." Sister Janie looked ready to explode as Rachel pulled against her hold to look back toward Lacey.

Lacey paid no attention to the older sister's warning but kept her eyes on Rachel. "And more than all the worms under the ground."

For a moment Lacey had hope the little girl was going to accept her words, but then Rachel stuck her lip out and raised her chin up a little. Lacey had seen her do the same thing dozens of times when she was determined to have her way even in the face of punishment. Her voice was shaky from the tears as she said, "Sister Rella loves me more."

The words slammed into Lacey like a fist ramming into her stomach. She could barely force her voice out above a whisper as Sister Janie herded Rachel on out the door into the hallway. "No, no, it's Jesus who loves you more." Lacey lowered her head and spoke more to her hands than to Rachel. "Only Jesus could love you more."

Sister Janie hesitated at the door to frown back at Lacey. "Take control of yourself, Sister Lacey, and remember your duty to do as Eldress Frieda instructed you. You can be sure she will hear of this."

"Yea." Lacey slowly got to her feet.

That seemed to satisfy Sister Janie, who turned to whisk Rachel out of sight toward the stairs. With the sound of their footsteps going away from her pounding into her ears, Lacey stood in the middle of the floor and stared at the empty doorway. She felt unsteady in mind and body.

The children's voices kept coming down from the upper floor as they sang the Shaker songs, and then all at once the thunder of stomping feet overpowered the voices. They had to be stomping out evil, chasing away the devil. That would be what they were teaching Rachel, only she, Lacey, would be the

276

evil they would want to keep away from the child now. Sister Lacey who wasn't following the Shaker way. Sister Lacey who got visitations from angels that, instead of singling her out for service as Eldress Frieda had thought, could be pointing her out for the disharmony she was bringing into their midst. All the fingers would be pointing at her now instead of the one they should be pointing toward. This Sister Rella who was poisoning Rachel's mind against Lacey. She was the real evil.

Lacey forced her feet to walk through the empty door and out into the hallway with its two stairways reaching away from her up to wherever Sister Janie had taken Rachel. Away from her. The stairs were empty. No one at all anywhere in sight while the stomping dance went on over her head. She wanted to climb the steps, open all the doors, search out Rachel, and force her to listen. Force her to understand. Make her realize this Sister Rella was lying to her. But Rachel was only four years old. How could Lacey expect a child so young to understand what she herself couldn't understand? Angel visitations. Devil stomping dances. The preacher shaking like a willow in the wind. Family love forbidden. Lies whispered in the night to a child.

Lacey blew out a soft breath of air and squared her shoulders. She had to pull herself together the way Sister Janie had said she must. Not to turn into the compliant Shaker sister who did only as she was told. No, she had to pull herself together so that she could find a way to leave this place. With Rachel.

Without thinking about this door or that, she went out the one nearest her and down the steps. It was only when she was stepping off the bottom step onto the pathway that she realized she had gone out the wrong door, the one reserved for the brethren. She looked around to see if any devout Shaker was going to descend on her and point out her error, but the pathways were as empty as the hall and stairs had been inside the Children's House.

What difference did it make which door she went through? Her skirts hadn't been scorched as she went through the doorway. No angel with a sword guarded the door, waiting to slay her the way the angels had lain in wait for Baalam if his donkey hadn't seen with more holy eyes than his. It was just a door the same as any other door.

Man had put the rules in place in this village. Not the Lord. It was the Lord's rules she needed to remember. Pray and seek his face. He cared for her. Isn't that what Miss Mona had told her time and time again? A constant help in time of trouble. It was a sure thing Lacey had trouble. Once a body started down the wrong path, it seemed like she could just keep getting pulled along and find more and more trouble.

But that didn't mean she had to give up. That didn't mean the Lord wouldn't help her. The Lord could forgive just about anything if a person asked with a contrite heart. Lacey's heart couldn't be much more contrite if that meant sad and sorry. She was sorry for the wrong steps she'd taken with the preacher. She was sorry for the wrong thinking that had landed her in this mess. She was sorry that she didn't know who this Sister Rella was so she could go set her straight.

"Can you help me with that, Lord? Show me who this Sister Rella is," she whispered and then felt ashamed she couldn't pray a better prayer. Like the kind Miss Mona used to pray that brought the Spirit down. Lacey's prayer in comparison felt like nothing but empty words that just bounced right back at her and didn't find the Lord's ear. Maybe that was because the Lord was telling her that some things she had to do herself. Like finding out who this Sister Rella was.

If there was a Sister Rella. It could be she only existed in

Rachel's mind. After all, Sister Janie hadn't known anyone with that name. And they kept the doors locked at night. Lacey knew that, because on one of the first nights she'd been in the village, she had slipped out late one evening on the pretense of going to the privy but had gone to the Children's House. The doors had been locked. Even the back door that led to the kitchen. Sister Rella would have to live in the house with the children to visit Rachel at night, but if that was so, then Sister Janie would know who Rachel meant.

Somehow the thought that this Rella might only be a figment of Rachel's imagination made Lacey even more sorrowful. It was all because of her, as Rachel said the mystery sister had told her. Lacey had brought the sorrow down on them heavy and thick. She should have never agreed to come here with the preacher. It didn't matter if she was married to him. Words spoken with no feeling. As Eldress Frieda said, there was no connection between them. None but the one they'd tried to concoct out of feelings that had as much chance of holding them together as reins of thread had of holding a horse to a hitching post.

Real or imagined, Lacey would still have to find a way to battle this Sister Rella. Lacey looked around to get her bearings. She'd been walking without paying the first bit of attention to where she was going. She had turned the wrong way out of the Children's House and was in front of the Farm Deacon's shop. Again no one was about, with the work of the day over and done. She stared down the road. She could keep walking. Just surrender Rachel for the time being. She could come back later for her after she was free herself. But could she ever be free of tears if she gave Rachel up so easily? Rachel was her child. It mattered not that she hadn't been born of her body. She was her child. The desperate mother who had left her on the preacher's back step had given her to Lacey. Miss Mona had given her to Lacey. The Lord had given her to Lacey.

"Dear Father in heaven, help me," she whispered as she turned back the other way to walk to the Gathering Family House. She shut her eyes tightly and imagined her prayer spiraling away from her up toward the heavens. She stood still on the pathway a moment to see if an answer would fall back down to her. She wanted an answer, but all that came to her mind was that Beatitude verse. *Blessed are the meek, for they shall inherit the earth.* She didn't want to inherit the earth. Just have Rachel's arms sliding back around her waist.

Maybe it was the meek part she needed to be dwelling on. At least the appearance of meekness while she was facing up to Eldress Frieda and confessing her wrongs. All the while plotting more wrongs in the eyes of the Shakers.

25

The day after Lacey had smiled so joyfully at the morning meal, Isaac sneaked a look back over to the sisters' side of the eating room to seek her out again, but her back was to him. The stern sister sat across from her. The one whose face was creased by frown lines. Drayma. That was her name. When she caught Isaac looking where he shouldn't, her scowl grew even fiercer.

Isaac quickly turned his eyes back down to the food on his plate. That was where the leadership expected him to keep his attention. On the tasks at hand. Forks scraped against plates and spoons clanked in bowls. Next to him, Brother Jonas smacked his lips as he noisily enjoyed his biscuit smeared with fresh strawberry jam. At the end of the table, one of the brothers belched loudly and then couldn't ask for pardon since no talking was allowed in the eating room. A tiresome rule to Isaac's mind. Only one of many.

It wasn't until they were lining up to leave the room that he chanced another look toward the new sister. She stood stiff and straight in the sisters' line, staring forward at the door as was the rule. No trace of the joyful smile from the day before remained on her face. Where then she'd looked ready to bounce with joy, now she appeared to be cloaked in darksome thoughts.

He kept sneaking peeks at her as they walked out their proper doors to begin their assigned work. In the normal world, he could have simply gone up to her to ask what had so changed her demeanor in such a short time. In the normal world. But not in the Shaker world. Nothing was normal in the Shaker world except work.

Outside the house, the lines broke apart as the men and women headed to their workplaces. Sister Aurelia stepped up beside Lacey, and the two sisters moved away from him. Probably to pick strawberries or make jam. A simple chore, surely as normal here as outside the village. But then again even work was different here. While the tasks of feeding the horses or planting corn or dovetailing the joints of a bureau drawer might seem the same, the Shakers didn't just work to get the horses fed, put corn in their cribs, or make a place to store their undergarments. Each task however mundane was considered worship. Hands to work. Hearts to God. He'd heard that at least once a day since coming to the village.

"Surely it would be a sin to do less than our best as we work to honor the Eternal Father," Brother Asa had told Isaac last week when they first started working together in the barns. "Mother Ann instructs us to do our work as if we had a thousand years to live, and as if we might die tomorrow."

"A thousand years?" Isaac protested Brother Asa's words. "Nobody can live a thousand years. Some people don't even live twenty-five years." A vision of Ella's face frozen forever in death pushed into Isaac's thoughts.

"Yea, you are right. Nor do the most of us expect to die on the morrow," Brother Asa agreed amiably. "But that doesn't mean we shouldn't work with careful, dedicated hands and minds to finish our tasks in a timely manner. Will your contrary spirit argue with that?"

Isaac had looked up from the clean straw he was scattering in the barn stall with worry that he might see the same shadow of displeasure on Brother Asa's face that so often darkened Brother Verne's whenever he tried to pull Isaac along the Shaker way. But no frown lines marked Asa's face. He seemed to look on Isaac's contrariness as no bigger problem than the horsefly buzzing around his head that he easily waved aside.

"Nay." The Shaker word spilled naturally out of Isaac's mouth after his weeks of practice. He picked up more straw with his pitchfork. "I can find no reason to argue that."

"Then see, that is one foot set upon the path of a Believer. The hands to work. Now to give your heart to God."

"What gives you reason to think I haven't?" Isaac straightened up and looked out of the stall at Asa. The little man had yet to go off to wield his own pitchfork but instead was watching to be sure Isaac knew how to properly muck out a stall the Shaker way.

"Have you? As a Believer?" Brother Asa peered at Isaac's face. "If that is so, I should be talking to you about signing the Covenant."

Elder Homer had told Isaac about the Covenant. A confession of faith and an agreement to abide by the Believers' rules. Isaac couldn't do the confessing or the agreeing. Brother Asa was right. His spirit was too contrary.

"Nay, not yet." Isaac bent back to his work of evenly scattering the clean straw before he stepped out of the stall.

"I thought not," Asa said.

"I'd like to believe." Isaac opened the door of the next stall and the odor of fresh horse droppings and urine rushed out to him.

"I can see that you speak from your heart, but I hear in your voice that you think belief will be too hard. That believing will be an onerous duty, when in truth it will lift you up and make you feel light as a bird taking wing with the wind and using no effort at all."

The little Shaker man leaned his pitchfork against the wall and waved his hands up and down almost as though he thought he might lift up off the barn floor. Isaac wouldn't have been too surprised if he had. At the same time his own feet grew so heavy that it was all he could do to step into the stall and begin turning the straw. No birds were taking wing in his spirit.

When Isaac didn't say anything, Brother Asa let a sigh whisper out of his mouth. Not a sound he made often. Isaac kept his eyes on the straw in the stall. He didn't want to see disappointment with his contrariness on his friend's face.

But then Brother Asa suddenly slapped his hands together. "But enough of sermons for this day. Another thing that our Mother Ann said was that none preaches better than the ant and it says nothing at all. So today I will be an ant and teach you through my faithful performance of my duties."

"But there is more than work. There is also worship."

"Yea, we do go forth in exercises at our meetings to strengthen our spirits, but the work of our hands, that is worship just as much. Even more."

Isaac shook off a fork full of soiled straw into the wheelbarrow outside the stall.

Brother Asa looked up at him and laughed. "If you could see your face, Brother. What is it that confounds you so?"

"It's hard for me to think about cleaning horse apples out of a stall as worship. I thought you had to be in church for that or reading the Bible or praying maybe."

"Nay, nay, the best worship is that done with your hands."

284

Asa held up his hands and then reached for his pitchfork. "Even the sort of thing you are thinking of as worship—the world's idea of worship—can happen anywhere. Such holy moments don't only occur in a church or meetinghouse. Think of the Christ who had many holy moments along his road of life as he helped those he met."

"As you helped me," Isaac said. "Pulling me back from the river's edge. I wouldn't be here if you hadn't seen me there in the fog that morning."

"That could be true or not. The good Lord might have sent you another helper if I had refused his leading that morn. But we are duty-bound to do good if we can."

"I am glad to be alive," Isaac said.

"Yea, a day such as today can bring that joy to one's heart. So perhaps your heart is ripe and ready to be harvested for our Eternal Father." Brother Asa must have seen the doubt on Isaac's face, for he smiled a little as he went on. "Our holy Feast Day is coming when we will march out to our Chosen Land to feast on love and gifts of the spirit. Many hearts are altered at our feasts. Yours could be one of those."

"Chosen Land? Where's that?" Isaac began sifting through the muck in the stall to dip out the rest of the horse's leavings.

"Not far from here. A spiritual place of angels. With a fountain stone where the Believer can wash in heavenly waters and be cleansed."

Isaac frowned at Asa. "There's a fountain of water there? You mean a spring?"

"Nay, a spiritual fountain. A fountain of holy water visible to those with pure hearts. But any who are unworthy or have unconfessed sins should not wash in the waters."

"What happens if they do?"

"Some things are best not tested." Brother Asa's voice was grave and full of warning.

"You don't have to worry about me. I won't be dipping into any spiritual water."

"In time you may have a clean spirit and a heart made ready by belief and confession. Once you sign the Covenant."

Isaac had turned back to his task of cleaning out the stall. That he could clean. His spirit was a different matter.

Now with the holy feast only days away, Isaac could see the excitement build among the Believers. Excitement Isaac couldn't really understand. It all sounded too strange. Holy fountains with spiritual water. A place searched out and prepared by specially chosen instruments under the guidance of angels. Feasting on nothing but spiritual food. He had pantomimed eating a few invisible apples that sisters at the meetings were wont to pretend picking and passing around in baskets. That had been odd enough, but to plan a whole feast of imaginary food seemed the next thing to lunacy to Isaac.

He'd watched the Shakers come under operations. He'd seen them shaking and dancing and stomping. He'd heard those claiming to be instruments deliver messages from some long-dead person or an angel the way Sister Aurelia had done at the last meeting. And although he never spoke it aloud, he didn't believe any of it was holy.

But then perhaps he didn't recognize holy because he had never reached for such in his own life. His mother had. Mrs. McElroy had. Even Ella had, begging him to attend church with her at the fort before the fever came on her.

He wondered what Ella would think of the Shakers. She might like Brother Asa. She'd be nervous around Elder Homer in spite of his peaceful countenance. But men like Brother Verne with his dark frowns and piercing eyes would send her into panic. One peek at the glowering Shaker would have sent her running to hide behind her father.

It could be she should have taken one look at Isaac and run to her father. From the first day of their marriage she had seemed to look backward with regret for what she'd left behind. Isaac's love hadn't been enough to wrest her away from her father. Not truly. Now even in death Isaac thought of her belonging with the judge and her mother and not with him. Perhaps if they had been married longer. Perhaps if he could have changed and surrendered his dream of adventure and lived the life she'd wanted, he might have taken over first place in her life in time. Perhaps.

A man could drive himself crazy thinking about perhaps. There was no perhaps when it came to death. Ella was dead. Nothing would ever change that.

But other things did change. He changed. Winter gave way to spring, and with the change of the seasons, he couldn't deny that he was ready to put his grief behind him. To start living again and let spring awaken in his heart once more. He was shamed by that. Ella had only been gone seven months. But grief could lengthen the days into weeks and the weeks into years.

He had no right to do so, but he was turning Ella loose. He could no longer recall the scent of her perfume. He no longer felt the sharp stab of pain when he thought about taking the combs from her silky dark hair to let it fall down around her shoulders. Instead there was only the kind of lingering sadness he felt when he thought about his father dead these many years.

Brother Asa told Isaac it was good that he was forgetting Ella and his sinful bonds of marriage. He need never entertain the errant thought of a wife again. All women were sisters to him. Including the one named Lacey.

Asa didn't mention her by name. While Asa had voiced his suspicions of Isaac gazing wantonly on the new sister when she fell against him at the meeting, he had not continued to poke at Isaac's denial of sin to see if he could find a soft spot of untruth. Unlike Brother Verne who kept watching Isaac with hooded eyes of suspicion. Eyes that were more able to note that sin because he had looked at Lacey with other than a brother's eyes himself. Brother Asa knew nothing of the power of that temptation. He was every inch a Believer. A brother to all.

Even to poor Brother Elwood, who appeared ready to escape reason at any moment and chase after the balance he claimed the spirits were ordering him to find. As if walking along a fence rail could give him spiritual peace. So perhaps he too was tormented by the new sister who had been his wife in the world. Or by the message of Sister Aurelia's angel who had shouted out words of sin at Lacey. Maybe he'd felt those words bouncing off her toward him as her sinful husband. Condemnation that as a preacher he might never have known in the world.

There he was the one holding the holy book. The one interpreting the message for his people. And now he was only another of the novitiate brothers trying to shake off lustful sins of the world. Isaac had seen him shaking. Intently serious. Not as a mere exercise to satisfy those watching, as Isaac sometimes shook his hands at his side.

Unlike Isaac, Brother Elwood earnestly sought the Shaker belief. Even after weeks with them, the only part of the Shaker life that called to Isaac was their laden tables of food in the eating room. He had come to hide among the living dead, but he knew now he would not stay in their village forever.

He might have already gone if not for Brother Asa. And the new sister. He shook away that last thought. Nothing but trouble lay in that direction. It was best not to wonder what had made her smile so completely vanish this morning. Better to think about his work duties and find the missing heifer ready to calve.

"She may have wandered into the woods in search of a spot of solitude for calving," Brother Asa told Isaac as he handed him a coiled rope. "Here, you may need this. It's the young heifer's first calf. I had thought to put her in the small pasture the end of this week where there are no trees for hiding, but it could be we miscalculated her time. You'd best search her out."

The sun, hot for late May, beat down out of the cloudless sky on Isaac as he crossed the pasture field, counting the cows grazing there. Still one short. The heifer hadn't come back to the herd. He'd done plenty of cow hunting while working for the McElroys. Those cows, scrawny stock compared to that of the Shakers, were prone to wander far afield in search of better pasture.

The herd bull the Shakers imported from England was the difference, according to Asa. "Whichever brother picked the name 'Shaker' for him must have had a bit of a sense of humor, don't you think?" he had told Isaac with a smile spread across his face. "Considering the animal's purpose. But old Shaker has made our cows throw some mighty fine calves."

Isaac stepped into the deep shade of the woods, took off his hat, and wiped the sweat off his brow. With no Shaker brother around to upbraid him, he didn't bother shoving the hat back on his head as he moved through the trees, keeping an eye out for cow signs. Squirrels chattered at him overhead, and he spotted the bushy tail of a fox slipping out of sight behind some trees. He needed a dog. A good herd dog could make the search easier, but that was something the Shakers didn't keep. No dogs. No cats either.

"A Believer has no need of pets," Brother Asa had told

Isaac. "An animal has to earn his keep. Like the cows and the horses."

"Dogs could help with the herding of the cattle and cats keep down the mice."

"It is not our way to turn the violence of one animal on another."

"But how do you keep the mice from eating up your corn?" The McElroys had several cats to keep the mice out of their barn.

"We have traps for the mice."

"Seems it would be better to let the cats kill them for food than to do it with a trap."

"Nay, you don't understand. Our traps are not lethal. One of our brothers made them so we can capture the mice to turn them loose far from the barns."

Such a strange people, Isaac thought as he made his way between the trees. Not wanting to pet a dog on one hand and not killing a mouse on the other. Claiming peace while warring with the natural impulses of life. Shouting and dancing in worship. Not saying a word during meals or prayers. Planning to the point of excited frenzy to have a pretend feast and to take a pretend bath in a pretend fountain.

The rustle of a bush caught Isaac's ear and he stood still to listen. At first he thought he might have come up on the missing cow, but then he caught sight of a white cap. A sister out in the woods. Probably gathering roots for their potions. Isaac stepped off the path behind a tree to keep from startling the sister. Or sisters. She wouldn't be in the woods alone. He peered around the tree but saw only the one cap coming through the trees. She had her head bent, watching her step, but then she stopped and looked up to get her bearings. The new sister. Lacey.

He stepped back up on the path and waited for her to spot him. Perhaps Elder Homer would not consider it too great a sin for Isaac to ask the sister if she'd seen the lost cow. Or if she herself was lost. It would surely be wrong not to offer help to a lost sister.

26

A cloud hung over Lacey the morning after her visit with Rachel. No matter how much she told herself Rachel was just angry at her for deserting her to the Shakers and that love remained underneath the anger, Lacey's heart broke a little more every time she heard the echo of Rachel's words. *Sister Rella loves me more.*

Who was this Sister Rella? Lacey tried to recall every word Rachel had said about the sister who came to her in the night. One minute Lacey would be sure there was no real Sister Rella. The next she wanted to guard Rachel's retiring room door to watch for the woman who was whispering lies in Rachel's ears.

The few times Lacey had fallen into a fitful sleep the night before, she was beset with nightmares of sisters surrounding her bed, taunting her. In her dreams, when she tried to rise up off her pillow to see who the sisters were, hands pushed her down as they intoned the word "woe," just as she'd heard it at the meeting after she'd knocked poor Isaac off his feet. She tried to peer at their faces, to know who they were, but she could see nothing but dark shadows under their caps.

The morning bell had rescued her from the nightmare sisters. She had risen and knelt by her bed to pray as was required. *Blessed are the meek*. The words came to her mind, but they were no help. She didn't want to be meek. She wanted Rachel. *Blessed are the merciful; for they shall obtain mercy.* Maybe that was the Beatitude she needed to let rest in her mind.

But she wasn't feeling merciful or meek or pure in heart or like a peacemaker. Poor in spirit. That sounded right. What was it the poor in spirit were promised? The kingdom in heaven. Lacey had never understood why being poor in spirit should get a body anything. Miss Mona had been some puzzled by that one too but had ended up telling Lacey she supposed the Lord didn't want anybody to get all puffed up and proud of how fine they were for believing.

For certain, Lacey wasn't puffed up with believing anything as she bent her head over her clasped hands resting on her narrow Shaker bed. She was poor in spirit on this morning. Did that mean there was no chance of her finding happiness this side of heaven? She tried to reach for some prayer words. *Our Father in heaven*. Then nothing came to mind except Rachel. Rachel turning away from her.

She was glad when Sister Drayma shook her shoulder to let her know prayer time was over. She couldn't stay on her knees praying this or that blessed all day. She had to stand up and put on her Shaker dress. She had to take the broom and sweep out the retiring rooms the same as every morning she'd been in the village. She moved by rote and without any awareness of the sun rising in the east.

The morning meal was no better. The faces around her all kept chewing, lost in their silent thoughts. Perhaps thinking of no more than whether the eggs were cooked the way they liked them or of how sweet the new jam was from the berries just picked. Or perhaps like Sister Drayma with their eyes casting about for some wrong to note. Or like Lacey with too much sorrow in their hearts to speak even if no rules of silence were in place in the eating room. Lacey slid her eyes past the ones who looked as sorrowful as she felt. *Blessed are the poor in spirit*, she repeated in her head as she stared down at the biscuit on her plate. In time they would all be happy in heaven. As happy as she'd been the day before when she was looking forward to seeing Rachel. But the happiness in heaven would endure. Strange, unknown sisters wouldn't steal it away.

When Aurelia nudged her with an elbow and nodded a bit toward Lacey's plate, Lacey realized all the sisters around her had cleaned their plates and were waiting for her to finish. Why ever in the world had she put that biscuit on her plate when the last thing she felt like doing was eating? A Shaker wasn't allowed to leave anything uneaten on her plate, so Lacey picked up the biscuit and bit into it. The morning before she'd eaten the biscuits with pleasure, but today her body rebelled against the thought of food. She wallowed the doughy bread around in her mouth, not wanting to swallow, but she did anyway. She had to. Didn't she always do what she had to do?

She looked at the biscuit in her hand. It looked bigger than when she'd picked it up, and her stomach heaved at the thought of forcing more of the biscuit down her throat. She pretended to take another bite and then, when Sister Drayma looked away, quickly palmed the remainder of the biscuit and dropped her hand to her lap while chewing the air in her mouth with a seemingly hearty appetite.

A moment later when they rose from their chairs and knelt for the after-meal prayer, Lacey slipped the rest of the biscuit into her apron pocket. Do what she had to do to follow the rules or at least pretend to until she found a way to break the rules and talk to Rachel.

They were on the way to the strawberry patch when Sister Aurelia threw all the rules to the winds as she pulled Lacey off the path. "Come with me," she whispered.

When Sister Drayma glanced back at them, Aurelia smiled and waved vaguely toward the privy. None of the other sisters paid them much mind as they passed by on their way to their assigned chores for the day. Their eyes on the path, minds and body ready for work. Following the Shaker rules. Doing their duty. But Aurelia's mind wasn't on duty. Or on any call of nature.

"What are you doing?" Lacey asked her.

"You look peaked this morning. You don't really want to pick berries all day again today, do you? I know I don't."

"You didn't pick many berries yesterday. You spent the day in the infirmary."

"Yea, so I did. Berry picking might have been better. Sister Drayma hovered over me all day, trying to get me to tell her about the angels." Aurelia made a face.

"Why didn't you tell her then?"

"I did tell her. Over and over. But she wants me to make her see them, and the angels only dance with those they choose. They have not chosen Sister Drayma." Aurelia veered off the path and through a gate into a field. "Come on. Hurry."

"Why the hurry?" Lacey asked as she walked faster to keep up with Aurelia.

"We don't want to keep the angels waiting."

"How do you know they're waiting?" Lacey peered over at Aurelia, who had an odd shine in her eyes.

"They told me, of course." Aurelia spun around in the middle of the field until her skirts stood out in a circle, before grabbing hold of Lacey to keep from falling from the dizzy spin. She laughed out loud, a sound so unexpected in the quiet village that Lacey jumped.

"You don't have to fear the angels, Sister Lacey. They like you. They want to dance with you."

Lacey looked around. "Here? Now?"

"Nay. Not yet. We have to go meet them in the woods. They like dim places."

"I thought angels were bright, glowing."

"Very bright. Very glowing. But an angel has no need of the sunshine to stay that way."

Aurelia started walking toward the trees on the other side of the field. Lacey hesitated before hurrying after her.

"Does anyone see angels other than you?" Lacey asked.

"They say they do." Aurelia looked over at Lacey with a bit of a smile before she added, "I'm sure they do."

"You don't sound so sure."

"Don't I?" She raised her eyebrows at Lacey and laughed softly. "Maybe I should say I believe them every bit as much as you believe me."

Lacey looked down at the lush pasture grass under her feet. "I don't know what to believe anymore."

"You must turn loose of your fearful worry." Aurelia threw out her hands and shook them as though such worry could be shaken off as easily as dust. Then she touched Lacey's shoulder. "The angels will tell you what to believe. That's why they want to dance with you." She grabbed Lacey's arm and pulled her toward the trees.

For a minute Lacey wanted to dig her heels into the ground and not follow Aurelia into the shadow of the trees. She should be doing her duty, picking strawberries, thinking of how she was going to talk to Rachel again, anything but chasing after Aurelia and pretending to dance with angels. That's all it would be for Lacey. Pretense. Even if she believed Aurelia could call down the angels, she would never believe that she could see them. Hadn't she already messed up enough of her life by pretending to be someone she wasn't? Like the preacher's wife. Like Rachel's mother. But no, she was Rachel's mother. The Lord had given the child to her. She had to believe that. She had to.

"Are you thinking of Sister Rachel?" Aurelia's hands still held Lacey's arm. "Your visit didn't go well?"

"She was angry with me for bringing her to the Shakers."

"But it wasn't you who brought her. It was her father, wasn't it?"

"In her mind, I was the one who deserted her. Preacher Palmer, I mean Brother Elwood has never acted as a father to Rachel. Miss Mona had to talk him into letting her keep the baby when we found Rachel on our doorstep."

"Who talked Miss Mona into keeping the baby? You?" Aurelia stared at Lacey as she tightened her fingers around her arm. "Or the angels?"

Lacey frowned at Aurelia. The woman's cheeks were flushed and her eyes so glassy that Lacey wondered if she was being overtaken with a fever. "Perhaps we should go back to the infirmary. I'm not sure you are well, Sister Aurelia."

"You are not sure of many things, Sister Lacey. Me. Brother Elwood. The angels. They frighten you, don't they? But you don't need to fear them. The angels bring joy. Peace. Understanding. You'll see. The angels will open your mind to truth. You have no reason to be afraid of the truth." Aurelia paused for a moment before she asked, "Do you?"

"Nay." Lacey was surprised the Shaker word came so easily to her tongue. Was that because it was easier for her to lie when she was pretending to be a Shaker sister?

"Then come with me. The angels await."

She let Aurelia pull her into the trees then. A shiver walked up and down her spine as she went from the bright sunlight into the deep shade. She thought again of turning and going

297

back to the village. But Aurelia had let loose of her arm and was running down a faint path through the trees. She couldn't leave her there alone when she was giving every indication of being ill. "Wait, Sister Aurelia!"

Aurelia looked back over her shoulder. "Hurry, Sister. The angels are impatient with our slowness. Run." Aurelia started running faster.

"I'll trip on a rock," Lacey called after her.

"Nay. The angels will lift you up and keep you from dashing your feet on the stones. Such is the promise in the Scriptures."

"I don't think that meant when you were running through the trees like a fox with his tail on fire."

Aurelia's laugh drifted back to her. "Trust me, Sister Lacey. Let go of your fear and run." She was already almost out of sight ahead of Lacey.

"I'm not afraid," Lacey muttered. "I am *not* afraid." She gathered up a thick handful of skirt and took off down the trace of a path after Aurelia. She kept her in sight for a while, and even when she disappeared into a thicker stand of trees, Lacey chased after her by following the sound of brush rustling as Aurelia made her way through the woods.

But then the angels must have run on ahead with Aurelia and forgot to leave somebody behind to lift Lacey up and carry her along. Lacey stubbed her toe on a rock in the path and fell flat. Her cap flew off as she caught herself with her hands. If this was what it was like to dance with the angels, she hoped the music would end soon. She sat up slowly and bent her wrists to be sure they were still in working order as she tried to catch her breath. She pushed up off the ground. She wasn't hurt except for a little scuffed-up skin on the heels of her hands. Nothing to be bothered about, but where was her cap?

"Sister Aurelia. Wait," she called as she spotted her cap

in the middle of a patch of poison ivy. She gingerly snatched up the cap and hastily stuffed her hair back up under it as she called out again.

Lacey listened for an answer but heard nothing but birds singing and the chatter of a squirrel high over her head. She shut her eyes and concentrated on listening. Surely Aurelia couldn't have gotten so far ahead that Lacey could no longer hear her running through the trees, but nothing except the whisper of a breeze rustling through the leaves came to her ears. Aurelia had to know she was not behind her anymore. She'd come back and find her. Unless she was so entranced with dancing with the angels that she had no thought for anything else.

Lacey let out a long breath and looked around. What she'd thought was a path earlier when she'd been running after Aurelia seemed to melt away before her eyes. She had no idea which way to go to follow Aurelia or to return to the pasture field. She wasn't exactly worried about being lost. It might take some time, but she'd find her way back to the village even if Aurelia didn't come back for her. It might be good to be lost and alone for a while to have time to think.

Blessed are the lonely and lost for they shall be comforted. She could almost see Miss Mona frowning at her and telling her it was a sin to add or take away from the Scripture. So many sins to watch for. But it shouldn't be a sin to seek comfort. And being lonely and lost wasn't that much different than mourning.

The scrapes on her hands were stinging and seeping a bit of blood. She reached into her apron pocket for her handkerchief and instead pulled out a handful of crumbs from the biscuit she'd stuffed in there at the morning meal. She felt like Hansel and Gretel with naught but bread crumbs to mark their path in the woods so they could find their way home.

They'd ended up getting fattened up for the witch's oven. A foolish fairy tale. But was it any more foolish than running after a woman who claimed to be going to dance with angels?

Lacey flung the biscuit crumbs out into the woods. Let the birds eat them. The way they did in the fairy tale. Her path hadn't been marked with crumbs. She'd have clear marks where she'd crashed through the woods like a mad cow. There would be broken branches, stomped plants. Lots of trail signs.

She hadn't walked far when the signs disappeared the way the path had seemed to do earlier. Maybe the angels were wiping it out. Maybe instead of dancing with Lacey, they wanted to lose her. Forever. Or perhaps that was only Aurelia's plan.

"Stop being silly. Aurelia might be a little strange, but she's not mean." Lacey spoke the words out loud as if she needed to hear them as well as say them. Aurelia hadn't lost Lacey on purpose. She would be aggravated with Lacey for not keeping up.

She'd find the path again. She just had to look for it. She moved to her left, but the underbrush seemed to get thicker that way. Nobody would be able to run through that. She was turning to go back the other way when she heard a noise.

"Aurelia?" she called.

A cow raised its head up over the bushes. Lacey jumped back and then laughed at herself. Of course there could be cows in the woods, since the pasture ran right up to the trees. But they'd passed the herd in the field. This one must be as lost as Lacey was.

Lacey stepped around the bush to get a closer look at the little cow down on its side. It stared at Lacey with panicked eyes as it tried to get up. But then the cow's head plopped back down as its stomach heaved. The poor thing was trying to have a calf. A little hoof appeared and then disappeared back inside the cow again. Lacey had heard men back at the church talk about pulling calves when a cow was having trouble, but she had no idea how to do that or even if she could. She'd have to go for help.

Before she started back through the trees, she called for Aurelia again, but it was a waste of breath. Aurelia had run on ahead to dance with her angels with no worry about leaving Lacey behind. If she did decide to come back for Lacey, maybe she could get her angels to point the way. It should be easy as pie for them to find Lacey.

But just in case Aurelia and her angels didn't show up, Lacey tried to mark her trail by breaking the ends off a few branches and pushing up little piles of last fall's leaves. It wouldn't do much good to find one of the brothers to help the little cow if she couldn't point out where the animal was.

Intent on marking her path, she didn't know Isaac was there until he stepped out in front of her. She was so startled that she tripped over her own feet and he reached out to steady her.

"Whoa," he said. "I didn't aim to scare you."

"You didn't," she said as she stepped back away from him and stumbled again. This time she fell flat on her backside.

"Are you all right, Sister Lacey?" He stooped down in front of her, a concerned look on his face.

She sat there a minute, not sure whether to cry or laugh. To her surprise the laughter won out. "You must think I'm the clumsiest person you ever met," she said.

"You do seem to have a problem staying on your feet." He smiled as he stood up. A nice smile.

He held his hand down toward her, and with no thought of whether it was improper or against the Shaker rules, she let him help her to her feet. "Thank you. And thank you for keeping me from falling into the benches at meeting. I figure that probably brought you a good number of frowns from your Shaker brothers."

"Brother Asa understood. I'm not much worried about what any of the others think." He was still holding her hand. She tried to ease it away, but he tightened his grip on her fingers as he held her hand up to look at her palm. "You've hurt your hand."

"It's nothing. Just a little scrape." She pulled her hand free and hid it under her apron. She could feel the color rising in her cheeks. "You won't believe this, but I fell." Then she looked up at him and couldn't keep from laughing again. "Or then again, maybe you will believe it."

He laughed too. The sound seemed to fit with her laughter and land softly in her ears. Not like Aurelia's laughter earlier that had seemed so jarring and out of place in the Shaker village. But they weren't in the Shaker village now. They were alone in the midst of the trees with no spying eyes watching from the high windows or from the fenced walkway on top of the Centre Family House. Built to give the watchers a good view of the whole village. But the watchers couldn't see through the trees.

27

Isaac had the strongest desire to reach for the new sister's hand again. And to not let her pull her fingers away from him this time. To instead pull her closer to him. To where he could look into her beautiful brown eyes. To where he could feel the whisper of her breath on his cheek.

He remembered feeling this way once before. With Ella. Swallowed up by her beauty even though there was little in the young woman's face in front of him that was like Ella. Brown eyes instead of blue. Soft brown hair instead of raven black. A scattering of freckles across her nose and upper cheeks that would have sent Ella into a panicked frenzy of creams. Standing there with an aura of toughness that Ella would have never known. That Ella hadn't needed to know. Not with her father protecting her. Not depending on Isaac to continue that protection.

The all-too-familiar flash of guilt burned through him, but then when it was gone, Lacey was still standing there, her eyes not shying away from his even though her cheeks were flaming. "Are you alone?" he asked.

"I was with Sister Aurelia, but she ran ahead and I lost sight of her." She glanced around as though she thought she might yet locate the other sister. "Then I saw this little cow. So I was trying to find my way back to the village to tell someone." She turned her eyes back to Isaac's face.

"You found the cow?" Isaac didn't wait for her to answer. "That's why I'm out here. To search for a heifer ready to calve."

"That must be the one I saw. She appeared to be having some trouble."

"Can you show me where she is?"

"I think so. I tried to mark my path." She turned away from Isaac and hesitated a moment before heading back the way she'd come through the trees.

He followed after her along the faint path and thought how unlikely it was that he and the new sister would stumble across one another in the woods. And that she would have seen the cow. It seemed Providence somehow, the same as Brother Asa appearing out of the fog on the river docks to help him keep breathing.

Providence. What was it Mrs. McElroy said about Providence? That it was the Lord taking care of a person. But why would the Lord be taking care of him? A man who had never reached for help or forgiveness. Who deserved no forgiveness. Instead of the Lord's providence, it could very well be nothing but sinful temptation, and he should be doing the Shaker stomping dance to keep back the devil. But he didn't stomp once. He just followed after the young woman, glad for whatever had made their paths cross.

When she stopped to get her bearings, he stepped up beside her. "Have you lost your way?"

"Sister Drayma certainly thinks so." She looked up at him with a wry little smile. "And I don't doubt the truth of that. Ever since I stood up beside the preacher and said the marrying words, my way has been muddled."

It seemed she had purposely misunderstood his question—

or perhaps she hadn't. Perhaps his true question had come from his heart. "None are married among the Shakers," he said.

"I am not a believing Shaker. I hold to the ways of the world."

"As do I."

"Even in the world, it would be wrong for me to feel pleasure in standing here so near you." She didn't look away from his face. "To wish to be loved the way you loved your wife who died. It has to be wrong for me to speak such words aloud to you. Or to think them either."

"Yea, some things are judged wrong both in the world and among the Shakers." He curled his hands into fists and forced his arms to stay by his side. He wanted to touch her hair, to offer to love her as he had loved Ella. No, not the same love. A different love, but one that would fill his heart just the same. Not to push Ella out, but to open a door to a new room in his heart.

"And wrong in the eyes of God." She looked sorrowful as she softly added, "What God has joined together let no man put asunder."

"Do you love him?"

"Love has little to do with the promise I made him. But it was a promise made before God." She looked away from Isaac up toward the treetops. "A promise not kept. I haven't been a proper wife. Our marriage is nothing but a sham. A sham that I fear has affected his sanity. It worries me when I see him now."

"Does he love you?"

"He loved Miss Mona. His first wife. She died last year. Just as your young wife did." She let her eyes barely touch on his face before she whipped them away to the trees again. "But no, he doesn't love me. He had other sorts of feelings for me. He told me that being a preacher didn't stop him from being a man."

"Guess that takes becoming a Shaker." Isaac hadn't thought her cheeks could get any redder, but they did.

"So Brother Forrest told him. That being holy meant putting that kind of thinking clear out of his head. The preacher swallowed the whole bit about marrying being a sin. The whole bit, even though might near every married couple in Ebenezer stood in front of him to hear the binding words spoken." She looked like she was still trying to puzzle out the strangeness of the preacher's change of thinking. "And I'm not arguing that me and him marrying wasn't sinful. That's the good Lord's own truth, but to say all marrying is sinful? That can't be right."

"So what does he, the preacher, think now?"

She blew out a long breath of air. "I have no way of knowing that. I've only seen him across the room at mealtimes and at your meeting. But it looks to me that he hasn't found any more peace here than we were finding back at the house. At least there he could do what the Lord called him to do. Preach the word. And I could hold Rachel and dig in my own garden and cook on my own stove. Here I feel like one little broom straw stuck in with a whole passel of other broom straws to make a big broom that somebody else is sweeping with."

"A spoke in a wheel," Isaac said.

"No." She frowned. "I'd think each spoke would be necessary to the strength of the wheel while a broom straw could break free of the others and the broom would keep on sweeping just the same. Would probably sweep up that broken broom straw and throw it away. That's me here. I'm that contrary broom straw that refuses to do what I was grown for."

"You mean be useful?" Isaac offered.

"That might be your spoke in the wheel again. The useful, necessary thing. Is that you? A useful spoke in the wheel here with the Shakers?" She looked at him. "Instead of a contrary broken bit of broom straw."

"Useful and necessary? It's true I'm here because of the necessary need to eat. I was hungry. Brother Asa promised plentiful food here in exchange for some useful labor, and so I came to put my feet under their table." He studied her face a moment. "Why are you here?"

"Because the preacher came looking for that peace Brother Forrest said could be found here. I heard him promising Preacher Palmer he'd be able to capture peace like as how it was a dove fluttering down to light on his hand. But that didn't happen. From the looks of the poor man, it doesn't appear he's found a lick of peace here at Harmony Hill."

"Maybe he's too tormented by things he's done wrong to get still enough in the spirit to let that peace come down."

Isaac's words bounced right back at him. Peace. Who was he to pretend to know anything about peace? As far as he was concerned, it was nothing more than a vague promise on the wind that no one ever captured. But then Brother Asa seemed to have a good grasp on it, along with many of the other Shaker brothers and sisters in the village. Even those who had never felt compelled to walk a fence rail to seek it. The Shaker peace had fallen on them like rain and melted away their contrary corners.

"What things?" Lacey asked.

"I don't know." Isaac shrugged a little. "I guess that's for him to answer and not me. I just have to worry about my own wrongdoings."

"Like talking to a sister hidden in among the trees?"

"A sin of the first order here in this place," Isaac said, but he didn't feel sinful at all. He felt better than he had for weeks.

She looked down as the color bloomed in her cheeks again. "Sister Drayma will not be happy with me. I should be picking strawberries."

He smiled. "You ran away from your duty?"

Her face cleared as she looked up to smile back at him. "But then I found the cow, so maybe my wrong will be forgiven even if Sister Aurelia will be angry that I couldn't keep up with her." She looked around again and turned away from him. "I think it's this way."

"Why did Sister Aurelia want you to come into the woods with her?" he asked as he followed her.

Her shoulders stiffened a bit as she kept walking. He had about decided she was going to ignore his question when she spoke without looking back at him. "She told me the angels wanted her to dance with them and that they were wanting to dance with me too."

"And did you?"

She peeked over her shoulder at him then. "Did I what?"

"Dance with them."

"No. I fell flat on my face instead. I'm thinking they probably prefer more graceful dancers."

"Like Sister Aurelia?"

"They do seem to call to her."

"But you don't believe it?"

Again she looked back over her shoulder at him, slowing her step a bit. "What makes you say that?"

"Your face at meeting when Sister Aurelia or perhaps her angel was pulling you out on the floor. Your voice now."

"I believe in angels. I'm just not expecting any of them to come down to talk to me the way they do Sister Aurelia." She turned away from him back toward the path as her voice changed, sounded sad all of a sudden. "Do you think angels can want to hurt you?"

He wished the path was wider so he could step up beside her. He wanted to see her face. "I don't know. That might be something you should ask Sister Aurelia."

"Maybe I'm afraid of what she will answer." Lacey's voice

was so soft he could barely hear her. Then she seemed to shake off whatever was bothering her as she pointed up ahead. "The cow was right over there. On the other side of those bushes."

The heifer was down on her side, exhausted from the effort of trying to push out her calf. She raised her head and scrambled to a sitting position when she saw them but didn't stand up.

"Can you help her?" Lacey asked.

"Maybe. If she stays docile." Isaac slipped the coil of rope off his shoulder and fashioned a loop in it. "I'll see if I can get this over her head. Stay back in case she gets excited."

Lacey stepped back and Isaac moved closer to the heifer, talking softly to her. "Easy girl. We just want to help you."

The Shaker cows were used to being handled, so she let him step up beside her. She threw her head to the side when he reached down toward her, but he got the loop over her head on the second try and then quickly twisted the rope in another loop around the heifer's nose. As the cow scrambled to her feet to get away, Isaac wrapped the other end of the rope around a tree a couple of times and held it tight until she quit pulling against it. Then he handed the rope to Lacey. "Here, hold this and try to keep it from slipping."

She took the rope with a worried look. "Do you think I'll be able to hold her?"

"The tree will do most of the holding. Just make sure you don't get your hand between the rope and the tree."

"All right." She grasped the rope with both hands.

The small hoof sticking out of the heifer's vulva was right side down. That was a relief. There should be two, but at least the calf wasn't upside down in the birth canal. Isaac kept talking to the cow softly as he rolled up his shirtsleeves and moved around behind her. He'd helped Mr. McElroy pull calves back on the farm. It had usually taken every bit of the strength of both of them, but sometimes a little change in the position of the calf could make a big difference. For sure the calf wouldn't have much chance if he had to go fetch Brother Asa. That would take too long.

He put his hand up inside the cow to feel for the position of the calf. The heifer tried to jerk her head around toward him, but the rope held. Isaac shot a quick glance over at Lacey, who had braced her feet and was holding the rope taut around the tree. He turned his attention back to what he was feeling inside the heifer. The position of the calf's head seemed all right, but one of its legs was doubled back. With care to keep the sharp hoof from injuring the cow, Isaac pushed the calf back down the birth canal to give the leg room to uncurl. He eased the curled leg forward until it seemed to be in the right position. The heifer's head went down again as she started a new contraction. Working with the contraction, Isaac tugged the calf's foot forward gently and then waited until the heifer's muscles relaxed to pull his arm free.

He held his breath and felt a prayer want to take wing in his heart. For a cow. He couldn't believe he was wanting to pray for a cow. If Brother Asa had been there, he would have been praying. He'd tell Isaac the Lord was in little things as well as big ones. And helping a poor dumb creature have a calf might very well be one of the big things.

The seconds ticked by. Became a long minute and then two. Nothing happened. He bent his head, not sure what he should do next.

"Are you praying?" Lacey asked. When he didn't answer right away, she went on. "I am."

"Do you think he'll answer a prayer about a cow?"

"He'll answer. Miss Mona used to tell me the Lord always answers. It's just that we don't like the answer sometimes."

She was quiet a few seconds before she went on. "I'm not going to like the answer this time if it isn't that poor calf getting born right."

"I prayed when my wife was sick," Isaac said. "She died just the same."

"Miss Mona used to say we got good out of the prayer even when we didn't like the answer. That the good Lord helped us through."

Isaac glanced over at Lacey. "You know what your Miss Mona believed, but what about what you believe? Do you know that?"

His words came out harsher than he'd intended and she looked near tears as she answered. "I used to know. Before Miss Mona passed and everything got in such a tangled up mess." Then she flattened her lips in a thin, determined line. "But I'm going to figure it all out again, and I don't care what you say. I think the Lord doesn't mind a bit that I'm thinking on praying for this cow here. Or that other prayers are rising up in my heart. If he's knowing how many hairs I've got on my head like the Bible tells us, he knows what I've got in my heart, don't you think?"

"I'm sorry. I didn't mean to upset you," Isaac said. "I'm the one who doesn't know what to believe. Or what I should be praying about."

Her mouth softened. "How about I just say a prayer for both of us. The kind Miss Mona would say." She didn't wait for his answer, but instead shut her eyes and kept talking. "Dear Lord, please help this little cow have her calf. And help me and Brother Isaac know what we believe. Amen."

"I thought praying was more complicated than that."

"Sometimes. But other times we can just be out with what we want to be telling the Lord and that's good enough." Lacey nodded toward the cow as she eased her hold on the rope enough to let the cow lay back down. "Look, I think she's trying again."

This time both feet appeared and then the head was out, still wrapped in the birth membrane. Two more minutes and the calf was out on the ground. When the cow started clambering to her feet again, Isaac told Lacey, "Let her go."

He yanked the makeshift halter off the cow's head before she got all the way up. The cow gave Isaac a wary look before mooing softly and turning to her calf to start licking it. Isaac pulled his handkerchief out to wipe off his arm as he watched her.

"Come on, little fellow," he said under his breath. "Talk to your mama."

Lacey stepped up beside him, the slack rope still in her hand. "Is it all right?"

"I don't know. But the mama hasn't given up."

"Mamas don't," Lacey said.

Something in her voice made Isaac look over at her. He had the feeling she was talking about more than the cow, but just then the calf raised its head and shook its ears free of the birth sac. Isaac let out a little whoop and grabbed Lacey and swung her around as she laughed out loud.

"The angels told me you found someone else to dance with," a voice said behind them.

28

Lacey almost fell again when Isaac hurriedly set her down at the sound of Aurelia's voice. She staggered backward to get her footing, and Isaac had to grab her arm to steady her. It had to be her dizzy day. For sure all the talk of angels and then getting lost and now the little cow mooing and licking her calf was enough to make a person's head spin. That didn't even take into account how the terrible sadness of Rachel turning away from her mixed so strangely with the good feeling of talking to Isaac. She didn't know how a person could want to laugh and cry at the same time, but she did.

She shot a little grin at Isaac before she stepped away from his hand. She was steady on her feet as she turned to look at Aurelia, leaning against a tree not far from the one Isaac had wrapped the rope around. She was still almost half hidden and Lacey wondered how long she'd been there, listening and watching. Had she been waiting to catch them doing wrong before she spoke up to let them know she was there?

Aurelia didn't wish her ill, Lacey told herself as she pushed the uncharitable thought to the back of her mind. Aurelia wasn't only her Shaker sister. She was a friend. Besides, Lacey didn't want to think about Shaker rules and spying eyes. Watching the little calf spill out into the world and then shake its head with life was too fresh in her head. Isaac grabbing her had been a spontaneous reaction to his joy in seeing the calf alive. A moment of celebration. That's all. A celebration Aurelia could join in and share.

"Look, Sister Aurelia. The calf. It's trying to get up." Lacey beckoned to Aurelia and then looked back at the calf. With the cow still licking it, the calf pushed up on its front legs to raise its head. It wobbled there half up and half down before it plopped down again. Worried, she glanced up at Isaac. "Is something wrong with its legs?" She'd seen new calves in the fields around the church, but never one so new. Those calves were always running all around the mother cows.

"Nay," Isaac said. "Keep watching."

The little cow mooed softly and nudged the calf with her nose. The calf pushed its front legs up again before raising its rump up on its back legs. A few wobbly steps and it instinctively headed for the cow's udder. After nursing a couple of minutes, the calf's tail began flicking back and forth.

"He'll be all right now." Isaac picked up the rope and began winding it up.

He was still smiling.

Aurelia moved up beside Lacey. She looked as bedraggled as Lacey felt, with strands of hair escaping her cap the same as Lacey's. A few sticktights clung to the bottom of her skirt, and her collar was a bit askew. But at least her mess was all on the outside. And not on the inside like Lacey's. Then again she thought she danced with angels. So who could say what the stranger mess was.

"What happened to you, Sister Lacey?" Aurelia said with barely a glance toward the calf. "The angels weren't happy when you didn't come."

"I fell down. By the time I got up, you were too far ahead. I couldn't find you."

"You should have let the angels lead you."

"If they'd come down and took hold of my hand, I'd have been glad for them to show me the way. But I didn't happen to see the first one of them." Lacey didn't bother to hide her irritation. Aurelia couldn't be running off losing her in the woods practically on purpose and then blaming her for getting lost. She had plenty to take blame for what she'd done. She wasn't about to take blame for what she hadn't done.

"Perhaps that's because your eyes were too full of other things." Aurelia frowned toward Isaac.

"I walked some way before my eyes saw Brother Isaac, if that's what you're trying to say. All I was seeing were trees and bushes. And then I found this little cow trying to have a calf. I was trying to find my way back to the barns to tell somebody when I ran into Brother Isaac, who just happened to be hunting this very cow. I guess that was a lucky thing."

"What does a Believer have to do with luck? A Believer leaves nothing to chance. Each and every day is planned and arranged," Aurelia said.

"And yet we didn't do the duties planned for us on this day. We ran off to the woods."

"Nay, there are many duties. It is as much a duty to listen to the angels as to pick strawberries. We were called to the woods by the angels."

"Did you find them?" Lacey peered at her and wondered whether Aurelia would have found the angels if Lacey had been able to keep up with her. For sure Lacey didn't believe she would have seen a single one.

"They found me and they would have found you too if you hadn't tried to find your way by yourself."

"She found the cow instead," Isaac spoke up. "And a good thing too. Else I might not have gotten to her in time to help her deliver the calf while it was still alive."

315

Aurelia looked at Isaac. "Do you call that luck, Brother Isaac?"

"Nay, not luck, Sister. Providence. The Lord's providence. And a calf to show for it." Isaac pointed to the calf with evident pride.

"Is the calf a heifer?" Aurelia looked toward the calf for the first time. It was still suckling and the mother looked oblivious to them watching her.

"Not a heifer," Isaac said.

"Then the poor animal's fate will be to end up on your plate in time," Aurelia said as her lips turned down. "Its hide will become shoes on our feet."

"For the good of the Society," Isaac said.

"Yea, the Lord's providential care. We do our duties and we labor our worship and we eat and sleep and the Lord sends down his love. It doesn't matter if there are prayers that go unanswered. Days that are naught but clouds. Miracles that fade away at sunrise."

"Are you all right, Sister Aurelia?" Lacey had never heard her sound so bitter.

"I'm right as rain. How could I not be all right after dancing with the angels?"

"I don't know. You don't sound like yourself."

"Then perhaps it is not me. Perhaps an angel lingers inside me. Perhaps several angels. They guided me back to you, you know. The angels are very interested in you, Sister Lacey."

"Why?"

"Some questions are to be asked, but they have no answers."

"You're talking in riddles today, Sister Aurelia."

"Riddles are not the Shaker way. Come, Sister, we must return to our duties and let Brother Isaac continue his."

"As you say, Sister Aurelia." But Lacey hesitated as she

looked back at the calf and then at Isaac whose smile had disappeared. "Will you take the cow to the barn?"

"I'll wait awhile, and then encourage her back through the trees toward the barn."

"Perhaps we should stay to help you drive her." Lacey was reluctant to leave the little calf. And Isaac.

"Sister Lacey." Aurelia's voice was sharp as she turned away from the cow and calf and took a few steps before she stopped to say, "Sin lies in wait to overtake us."

"Surely not with your angels all around to protect you. To keep us from dashing our feet on a stone."

"They do look on me with favor, but they might not feel so kindly toward you right now since you spurned their dances." Aurelia held her hand out to Lacey. "Come. It is not good for sisters to be at odds. We must seek peace between us. Our brother can tend to the cow or such a duty would not have been assigned to him."

Lacey hesitated there between Aurelia and Isaac. She knew which way her feet wanted to move, but it was perhaps true that sin was lying in wait for her in that direction.

"She's right," Isaac told her. "I can see to the cow. But when you get back to the village, it would be good of you to get one of the brethren to let Brother Asa know all is well."

"All is well." Lacey echoed his words. If only that were true.

His eyes softened on her. "Thank you for holding the rope, Lacey. I couldn't have done it without your help."

She took one last look at the calf. It had stopped nursing and was staring toward her with big moist eyes. She still wanted to smile when she looked at it standing there by its mother. A gift of life. *Blessed are the meek: for they shall inherit the earth.* She didn't know why the Beatitude came to mind, but it made it easier for her to turn away and follow Aurelia into the trees away from the place she wanted to stay.

"Do you know your way back?" she asked Aurelia when she caught up with her.

"Of course I do. The path is clear." Aurelia pointed ahead of them. "Don't you see it?"

"Nay, but I will trust that you do."

"It could be that you trust too easily, my sister," Aurelia said.

Lacey didn't know what to say to that, so she stayed silent as she followed along behind Aurelia. A silence that Aurelia seemed to embrace as they made their way through the trees.

It wasn't until they stepped out of the woods into the pasture field that Aurelia spoke again. She stopped then and looked straight at Lacey. "The angels seem to be throwing you and Brother Isaac together."

"I can't see what the angels have to do with me getting lost in the woods and stumbling across him today. I thought they wanted me to follow you."

"Perhaps they did. Perhaps they didn't."

Lacey had had enough of Aurelia's riddle talk. "Look, Sister Aurelia, I don't know what's going on with you today, but I know what I've done and what I haven't done. I helped Brother Isaac get that calf born. I didn't do anything wrong. I got lost. That's all."

"And then found," Aurelia said. "You say you did nothing wrong, Sister Lacey, but I saw your face as he swung you around. You had no wish for that to end. And I heard him call your name. Lacey. Not *Sister* Lacey. He does not see you as a sister."

"Even if any of that's true, and I'm not saying it is, but even if it is, it doesn't matter. I am married to Preach—Brother Elwood."

"Your marriage vows mean nothing here." Aurelia stared hard at Lacey. "If they ever meant anything."

318

Lacey dropped her eyes to the ground. *Blessed are the meek.* She let the words whisper through her mind. "I will confess my sins to Sister Drayma," she said without looking up.

They stood there for a long minute as the silence built around them before Aurelia said, "Nay, I don't think that would be wise."

Surprised, Lacey looked up at her. "But I thought I was to confess all wrongs."

"You say you've done no wrong, and if you truly believe that, then sometimes it is best to keep a few things secret. Sister Drayma might not understand the innocence of your meeting the brother in the woods and refuse to allow you to go to the spiritual feast Saturday. Plus your confession might cause trouble for our brother."

Lacey didn't care about the Shakers' spiritual feast, but she didn't want to be trouble for Isaac. "I wouldn't want that to happen."

"Nor would the angels. Not if they are the reason behind this." The hint of a smile played around Aurelia's lips and then was gone. "The angels have many secrets."

"That they tell you?"

"Perhaps they speak them through me. But if they did, they would no longer be secrets, would they?" She reached out and wrapped her fingers around Lacey's upper arm so tightly that it hurt. "Trust me, and when the time is right, I will share the secrets I know with you. And I will keep your secrets."

Just as suddenly as she'd grabbed Lacey, she let her go and then turned to start across the pasture. "We've missed the noon meal, but if we hurry we might be able to pick a basket of berries and keep Sister Drayma from frowning too much. Especially if I tell her about dancing with the angels. That is not secret. I'll say you danced too."

"That would be a lie." Lacey rubbed her arm. Keeping her meeting with Isaac a secret didn't bother Lacey, but telling a lie did.

"If I don't say who you danced with, it won't be exactly a lie." She smiled over her shoulder at Lacey. "Now will it?"

"Bending the truth is a kind of lie," Lacey said as she hurried to keep up with Aurelia.

"True enough," Aurelia agreed. "But didn't you tell me that you used to make up stories for your little girl? What are stories but many lies strung together?"

"Stories are just stories. For fun. Not lies."

"So you say, but do I say the same?"

Lacey let out a sigh. "You are a mystery today, Sister Aurelia, with your secrets and your riddles."

"Indeed. That is a truth we can agree on. We both have our mysterious secrets." Aurelia laughed so loudly that the cows on the other side of the field raised their heads to stare toward them.

Once they were across the field and back in the village, Aurelia stopped on the pathway to adjust her cap and collar. She gave Lacey the once-over. "You'd best fix your cap too, Sister. A Shaker sister's hair must be hidden. We would not want to break any rules."

For a minute Lacey thought Aurelia might be joking, but her face was serious with all signs of her earlier laughter gone. "We've done nothing but break rules all day," Lacey said, even as she obediently stuffed her hair up under her cap.

"But now we will not."

Lacey gave up trying to figure out Aurelia and just followed after her toward the strawberry patch. Aurelia stopped the first brother they met and gave him Isaac's message as though they had simply happened upon him with the cow and calf in the course of performing some assigned duty in the woods instead of being out chasing angels. Lacey was beginning to doubt the sister's sanity. And her own.

The next minute she was doubting her eyesight as well when she spotted the man leaning up against a fencepost alongside the road. Not a Shaker brother, but then the main road went straight through the village. It wasn't uncommon to see men not in Shaker dress taking a moment's rest beside the road at times. But she wasn't expecting to see this man.

"Reuben. Is that really you?" She ran ahead of Aurelia in her hurry to speak to him.

29

At the sound of her voice, he pushed away from the post and stepped out on the path in front of her. "I've been watching for you, Miss Lacey, but I don't know that I'd a known you with that bonnet on."

He looked so much like home she wanted to hug him, but with the now serious Aurelia behind her watching and other eyes peering down on them from who knew what spying spots, she held herself back. But she didn't hold back her smile. "It's so good to see you, but what are you doing here? Not thinking on becoming a Shaker like the preacher, are you?"

"Oh, no, Miss Lacey." He stepped back and held his broad hands palm out toward her, as though to keep the very idea of that away from him. "I couldn't leave the church. Who'd take care of things?"

"I don't know, Reuben. Nobody as good as you. That's for sure." Lacey reached out to touch his arm softly, and the unsettled look her words had brought to his face went away. But he didn't smile.

"You told me I could come find you here if I needed to." His face grew even more somber.

Lacey's heart sank as she remembered why she'd told him that. "Somebody died."

A tear slid out of the corner of Reuben's left eye and down his cheek. "I couldn't ask Miss Sadie Rose like you told me. It's little Jimmy. He was trying to ride this horse he shouldn't a been riding and fell off. Hit his head and never came to. Died last Friday."

"Not Jimmy." Lacey shut her eyes and the little boy's face popped up before her. So full of mischief and life. He couldn't be dead.

"That's what Miss Sadie Rose keeps saying too. She's taking it hard. He was her baby, you know."

"I know." Lacey pulled in a deep breath and swallowed down her tears as she pushed open her eyes and looked at Reuben again. "You need me to write out his name?"

"They're gonna get a stone and I want to be ready to do my part soon as they do." He reached into his pocket. "I brung the paper and a pencil for you. They said his real name was James. That's what Miss Sadie Rose will want. His real name. James Crutcher. And the numbers of his years. 1838 to 1844. And whatever else you think is good."

"'Beloved son of Sadie and Harold Crutcher.' Is that too many letters?" Lacey asked.

"I can work on it however long it takes. As long as you make the letters nice and clear. Wouldn't want to chisel in a wrong line."

Lacey took the paper and glanced around for something to lay it on to write out what Reuben needed. Aurelia was hanging back on the path with her face turned away from Reuben as though she feared a mere look at a man from the world would propel her into sin.

"This is Reuben," Lacey told Aurelia. "From the Ebenezer church. He won't do you any harm."

"No, ma'am." Reuben peered past Lacey toward Aurelia. "My mam taught me not to bother any of the ladies. At church or anywheres else."

Aurelia kept her eyes on the pathway. "That is good. The same is taught here," she said very softly.

Lacey had never heard Aurelia sound so timid. But then today Aurelia might be anything. So Lacey just skipped right to the matter at hand. "I don't know how much you heard, but Reuben chisels out the names on the gravestones back at the church, but he has to have something to go by. Brother Elwood's first wife used to do it for him, and then I did it when she died. So I told him he could come here if he needed help with his lettering."

"She knows how to make the letters the way I need them like Miss Mona did," Reuben said. "Most people don't, you know."

"So somebody died?" Aurelia still didn't look up.

Perhaps it was a Shaker rule that Lacey had yet to be told that a sister had to keep her eyes downcast when around a man of the world, but it was odd talking to the top of Aurelia's cap.

"Yea, it's very sad. A little boy in the church a couple years older than Rachel." Lacey remembered with a pang of guilt her irritation at Jimmy for telling Rachel she didn't belong with Lacey. And now his life was gone. Poor Sadie Rose. Lacey's sorrow over Rachel's anger at her seemed trivial in contrast. At least Rachel was alive and well. Perhaps not happy, but breathing.

"Six then?"

"Six. Rachel is four."

"Yea, that I know. So young," Aurelia murmured.

"We just need a flat place so Miss Lacey can make the letters nice and clear." Reuben pointed toward the meetinghouse down the road ahead of them. "We could go in there and lay the paper on the floor."

"Nay, not in there," Aurelia said, her voice stronger.

When Reuben looked puzzled, Lacey explained. "That's the Shaker meetinghouse."

"You mean like a church?" When Lacey nodded, he went on. "Well, I wouldn't care for somebody laying a paper down on the floor or the pews at Ebenezer Church and writing out letters. Maybe you need to come back there, Miss Lacey."

"It's a long walk, Reuben. I see you rode your horse." Lacey nodded toward the animal tied not far from where they stood.

"You could ride with me."

"But both Rachel and I couldn't. I couldn't leave Rachel here alone."

"She's hardly alone among us, Sister Lacey. But this gets us nowhere. There are many other hard surfaces." Aurelia raised her eyes off the ground to point toward the Centre Family House across from the meetinghouse. "You can use those steps."

Reuben didn't look where she pointed but instead stooped over a bit for a better look at Aurelia. "I thought I knew you."

"Nay, you don't know me." Aurelia turned her face away from Reuben's eyes.

Reuben stepped off the path onto the grass to keep peering at her. "I know faces. My mam always told me I was good at knowing faces. The bonnet fooled me for a minute the same as with Miss Lacey, but I've seen you. You're that girl." Reuben looked back at Lacey. "The one I told you about, Miss Lacey. The one that—"

"Nay, I do not know you." Aurelia cut off Reuben's words as she stepped up close to him to stare directly into his face. Her voice was cold and sure. "Nor do you know me. It is wrong for you to say so."

Reuben backed away from her, a puzzled frown on his face. "But . . ." he started, when a sister walking past the Centre Family House let out a shriek. All three of them whirled around to look toward her.

"Oh, merciful heavens, Sister Abby must have seen a snake." Aurelia sounded irritated.

"Where?" Reuben started toward the shrieking woman, more than ready to spring to the rescue. "I'm not a scared of snakes. I'll take care of it."

"Wait, Reuben. You don't need to." Lacey grabbed for his arm to stop him, but he was already gone.

Who knew what the Shaker rules were about snakes, but she was pretty sure they wouldn't look favorably on a man from the world running to the rescue of a screaming Shaker sister. When Reuben gave no sign of hearing her, she hurried after him to keep him from causing trouble. She glanced back over her shoulder at Aurelia, who stayed rooted to the pathway with her hands on her hips. She appeared to be every bit as reluctant to follow Lacey running after Reuben as Lacey had been earlier to chase after Aurelia going to meet her angels.

But it wasn't a snake. Instead the sister held one hand flat against her chest and with the other pointed toward the rooftop where one of the brothers was climbing up on the low railing around the middle flat part of the roof.

"What's he doing?" the sister said breathlessly.

The house was three stories high with a chimney on each corner and a windowed cupola in the middle of the roof for the watchers. But this brother wasn't a watcher. He was looking up at the sky and not down at them as he held on to one of the chimneys and wobbled back and forth on the railing.

"Is that the preacher?" Reuben squinted his eyes and stared up at the man.

"The preacher? What preacher?" Sister Abby said. She

turned to look at Reuben, then gave another little shriek and stepped back when she saw his worldly clothes.

Reuben didn't act like he noticed as he kept looking up. "That is him, isn't it, Miss Lacey? Sure as we're standing here in this spot."

Lacey felt sick as she stared up at the man. His face was turned away from her, but Reuben was right. It was the preacher. "The man's lost hold of his senses since he came here," she said.

She didn't know what to do. If she called out to him, that might startle him and make him fall. If she didn't call out to him and he fell, then she'd always wonder if she should have yelled some words to him that might pull him back to sanity.

"Is he thinking on jumping?" Sister Abby whispered.

"He wouldn't do that," Reuben said quickly. "That would be a sin that he couldn't never get forgiveness for. I've heard him say as much in the pulpit more than once. If you kill yourself, there ain't no way to ask forgiveness for the killing. Because you're dead."

"Whether he throws himself off or simply slips and falls, the ground will be every bit as hard either way." Aurelia walked up behind them.

"Shouldn't we do something?" Sister Abby whispered, her hands fluttering on her chest again. "Perhaps call out to him. Let him know we're watching and don't want him to fall."

"Yea, why haven't you called out to him already, Sister Lacey?" Aurelia asked.

"I feared startling him and making him lose his footing," Lacey said.

"Is that what you choose to believe?"

Lacey looked from the preacher to Aurelia. "I don't want him to fall."

"It would free you."

"Free her from what?" Sister Abby asked.

"Her sins."

"Miss Lacey ain't doing no sinning," Reuben said. "She's a good woman."

Lacey ignored Reuben as she looked back up at the preacher trying to balance on the railing like a crow on a fence rail. "I don't want him to fall," she repeated. "It is wrong for you to think I would."

"Yea, the angels were only testing you, Sister. They don't want him to fall either," Aurelia said. "You can call out to him. It will pull him away from his torments so that he can step back to safety."

Lacey cupped her hands around her mouth and called up to the preacher. "Brother Elwood, be careful. We fear you might fall."

For a minute she didn't think he heard her, but then Aurelia added her call to Lacey's. "Yea, be careful, Brother Elwood."

Aurelia was wrong. He was startled by their voices as he looked down toward them. He teetered there for a moment before he grasped hold of the edge of the chimney. Even then, Lacey wasn't sure he was going to be able to keep himself from falling. Another brother appeared on the roof and ran to grab his shirt and tug him back down on the roof. They fell backward together.

Lacey's knees felt weak as she blew out a breath of relief. Reuben clapped his hands together, shut his eyes, and started praying out loud. After waving air toward her face with her apron hem, Sister Abby glanced toward Lacey with a trembling smile before she went on up the steps into the house. Aurelia kept staring up at the rooftop as though expecting something else to happen. Perhaps her angels to appear to take credit for the preacher's delivery from death. But all that happened was the man who had appeared on the roof helped the preacher to his feet and guided him toward the cupola.

"For the wages of sin is death," Aurelia said barely above a whisper.

"But all sin." Lacey kept her voice low too, as beside her Reuben kept pouring out his thanks for Preacher Palmer not falling.

"And all die," Aurelia said.

"The Lord promises us forgiveness."

"Do you think every promise is kept?" Aurelia's eyes bored into Lacey. "If you do, then you are even more innocent than the angels think."

"The Lord keeps his promises. Your angels have to know that. Every Believer believes that."

"And so, have you become a Believer?" Aurelia raised her eyebrows at Lacey. "Are you ready to sign the Covenant of Belief? To become one of us?"

"I am not a Shaker, but I do believe."

"And what do you believe?"

It was the second time in one day she'd been asked that question, and once again she didn't have a ready answer. What did she believe? Beside her Reuben stopped praying as though he too was listening for her answer. She could claim what Miss Mona believed. But she needed to find her own words of belief. Blessed are the poor in spirit. Was that her? Poor in spirit, but still believing. Depending on the Lord to somehow make a way for her and for Rachel. Trying to step away from sin. "I believe I am blessed."

Aurelia's lips turned up the barest bit. "Gifted with blessings. That is not a bad thing to believe." She turned to walk away. When Lacey didn't follow, she glanced back. "Aren't you coming?"

"Nay." Lacey held up Reuben's paper. "I must do Reuben's letters first."

"Then write out the letters of the dead child's name. And think in your heart whether that mother feels blessed on this day."

"Blessed are they that mourn: for they shall be comforted," Lacey said.

"Words easy to speak. Ask our Brother Isaac about mourning. Ask him if comfort is easy to find." She turned and began walking quickly away.

"I do know her." Reuben spoke up beside Lacey. "No matter what she says. Well, maybe not know her like I know you with your name and all, but I saw her. More than once. I never forget a face."

"Pay her no mind, Reuben," Lacey said. "This place can get in a body's head and spin it around. Like it's done the preacher. Like it's doing mine."

"You think he really wanted to jump?"

"I don't know, Reuben. He's not himself. We shouldn't have ever left Ebenezer."

"Could be he's still grieving Miss Mona. I mean, I know he married you and all, but he loved Miss Mona a lot."

"You're probably right." Lacey smiled at him. "You wait here on the road and I'll go write out the names over on that step." She pointed toward the Centre Family House.

Lacey said a silent prayer that no Shaker sister would come out the door and ask what she was doing while she sat on the steps and printed out the letters. Then she prayed that the trembles that were besetting her would go away so she'd have a steady hand. She took a deep breath as she carefully unfolded the paper and began blocking out the letters. J-A-M-E-S. She made them nice and square with the straight lines Reuben liked except for the S. He knew about S. With each letter she said a prayer for Miss Sadie Rose and Deacon Crutcher and tried not to think of anything else. Just the letters and the prayers.

But other thoughts kept sneaking in. The joy of the little calf getting born and the thrill of Isaac whirling her around. Aurelia's mercurial personality changes from happy to quarrelsome to doomsday saying. How could she have thought that Lacey would want the preacher to fall? She might not love him as a wife should, but she was still his wife. Bound by wedding vows to love, honor, and obey. In sickness and in health.

In sickness. The words echoed in her head as she began printing out the letters for "Crutcher." In sickness. That's what it was. The preacher wasn't well. The poor man had taken leave of his senses. It happened to people. Sometimes they got better after a spell and sometimes a family had to lock them away so they wouldn't do harm to themselves or anybody else. O dear Father in heaven. She was the preacher's family. She was responsible.

She kept printing the letters, filling up the whole page with what Reuben would chisel on the stone of little Jimmy. B-E-L-O-V-E-D S-O-N. She could imagine how Sadie Rose's arms were aching to hold that beloved child. She had a beloved child she was aching to hold too. But at least her child was alive. She concentrated on drawing the letters perfectly and on the prayers rising up out of her heart. Now not just for Sadie Rose and Deacon Crutcher but for the preacher and her too. If anybody had ever been in need of prayer, she was.

The good Lord honored her first prayer. The door stayed closed and the steps empty until she had all the letters drawn clear and dark. The very second she stood up to carry the paper out to Reuben, the bell began to ring summoning people from their duties to their time of contemplation before the evening meal. Soon there would be many people spilling out of their workplaces onto the pathways.

"I'm much obliged, Miss Lacey." Reuben stared down at

331

the paper. "You made the letters just the way Miss Mona used to do them for me."

"About little Jimmy, you let Miss Sadie Rose know how sorry I am." Lacey brushed away a tear that slipped out of her eye.

"You ought to come tell her yourself."

"I can't right now. She'll understand."

"That other one didn't understand. The one I knew. I wasn't aiming to cause trouble for you, Miss Lacey."

"If you're talking about Sister Aurelia, she'll be fine tomorrow," Lacey said.

"Aurelia. I never heard of that name before. But it was her. She looks like her, don't she? The eyes and that dark hair. Just like your Rachel."

"Like Rachel?" Lacey stared at him with his earlier words echoing in her head. The words he'd said before Sister Abby screamed and took their attention to the preacher on the roof. "She was the one I told you about."

"I guess she knew you and Miss Mona would take good care of her baby." He folded up the paper and carefully slid it back in his pocket. "I'd better be going on home before the dark catches me. Anything you need, you just let me know, Miss Lacey. I'll be asking the church folk to pray for the preacher."

He untied his horse and walked him down the road a ways before he mounted. When he turned back to call a farewell to Lacey, she just waved. She couldn't do anything else. The truth she'd been staring at for days and not seeing had knocked any words right out of her.

30

Aurelia's place was empty at the supper meal. Later at the evening gathering in the top room, Lacey searched through the sisters for sight of her, but Aurelia was nowhere to be seen. She couldn't stay hidden forever. But now with Sister Drayma frowning her way, Lacey tried to quiet her runaway emotions and pay attention to the leaders talking with growing excitement about the Feast Day coming up on Saturday. They practiced a special song of prayer that one of the sisters told Lacey they only sang on the two feast days held in May and September. That didn't take much learning for Lacey since the words were the Lord's Prayer. *Our Father who art in heaven.* While she'd never sung it before, she'd spoken the words hundreds of times. Miss Mona had taught Lacey that prayer first thing after Lacey came to stay with her, and Lacey had been teaching it to Rachel.

Rachel. Would she ever be able to kneel with Rachel by her bed as she recited the words of the prayer again? *Lead us not into temptation, but deliver us from evil.* Lacey looked around for Aurelia again. She had no doubt that Reuben was right about Aurelia being the one to leave Rachel on the preacher's back porch, but she wanted to hear it from Aurelia herself. Aurelia was Rachel's mother. Birth mother. She had carried Rachel in her womb. She had given her to Miss Mona. To Lacey. That was what she needed to hear come out of Aurelia's mouth. That Aurelia had given the child to Lacey to love and keep.

The next morning, Aurelia's place was empty yet again at the breakfast table. After the meal, as they left the eating room, Sister Drayma stepped up beside Lacey. "You will work with me today."

"Where's Sister Aurelia?" Lacey asked.

"She has special duties to prepare for the Feast Day on Saturday."

"What duties?"

"Things we need not question, but that are necessary for her to prepare to be an instrument of the spirits. Others who have shown such gifts in the past are doing the same." Sister Drayma looked over at Lacey. "You have seen with your own eyes the way our sister gets drained of energy when the angels speak through her. During the feast time the angels come with great energy to distribute many holy gifts of refreshment."

"Have you ever entertained angels, Sister Drayma? Seen them with your eyes or felt them in your spirit?"

"I will." Sister Drayma's face became fierce. "Yea, I will. Sister Aurelia promises me that the angels will reveal themselves to me in time. My belief is strong." She tightened her hands into fists and squeezed her eyes shut, as though she could force the angels to appear through sheer desire. After a moment she opened her eyes to glare at Lacey. "Much stronger than yours. And she tells me the angels have danced with you."

"She has told me the same," Lacey said.

"What do you mean?" Sister Drayma's eyebrows almost met over her eyes.

"That if there have been angels dancing with me, I haven't caught sight of any of them." Lacey had not promised Aurelia

334

to lie about the angel dancing. Too many lies were already floating around their heads. But she did attempt to soften the denial a bit. "Sister Aurelia sees the angels for me."

Sister Drayma's face lifted. "And for me." She almost smiled. "I had doubts one so new to our ways as you would be so blessed by the angels. Or gifted so abundantly by our Mother Ann."

"You see things truly, Sister," Lacey said. "Worldly thoughts still trouble me."

They picked up their baskets and started toward the strawberry patch. It took many berries to feed so many.

"Yea," Sister Drayma said as they walked. "As they do poor Brother Elwood. It is said the poor man can't keep his mind on his tasks and is wont to escape Brother Forrest to run after forgiveness for his wrongs. He keeps being compelled—by the spirits he claims—to climb up on some precipice to balance between the earth and heaven. He claims that until he can achieve that perfect balance he cannot be truly forgiven." Sister Drayma clucked her tongue and shook her head slightly. "Such a shame. He showed such promise when he first came among us. The poor soul is misguided."

"What do you mean misguided?"

"That is not hard to understand. Even for one new to our ways." Sister Drayma's frown was back. "The spirits don't prompt us to do things that threaten life and limb. All our brother need do is confess whatever sins are bedeviling his soul and accept the peace the forgiven find in such abundance here in our Society."

"What makes you think he hasn't admitted his wrongs and asked forgiveness already?"

In sickness and in health. The words circled in her head.

"Sometimes, Sister Lacey, I think you block the truth from your mind of a purpose." Sister Drayma gave Lacey

335

an exasperated look and then spoke her next words slowly as though Lacey were dimwitted. "If he had done so, if he had confessed and repented of his sins, he would not have reason to hear the spirits tell him to climb on precarious rooftops." She stopped at the edge of the strawberry patch where the berries lay ripe in the rows waiting for them and the other sisters, but instead of leaning down to begin their task at once, she kept talking. "They say he came near to falling from the Centre House roof."

"Yea, so he did."

"That's right. You and Sister Aurelia were witnesses to his folly. Along with Sister Abby."

"I'm thinking his mind is troubled," Lacey said.

"Then as I just got through telling you, he should shake free of his sin and embrace forgiveness." Sister Drayma peered over at Lacey. "As you should as well. I will expect you to ask forgiveness for speaking to your acquaintance from the world without proper permission to do so. We don't deny our brothers and sisters visitors, but we do expect the visitors to abide by the rules and ask to see you in the proper manner. Not just wait alongside the road to waylay you."

"Reuben is harmless."

"The world is not." Sister Drayma stepped out into the strawberry row. "You will need to make confession during the rest time before the evening meal. In two days we will be given our heavenly garments for the Feast Day. Such garments would not sit well on shoulders that carry unconfessed sin."

Lacey wanted to ask why she couldn't just confess right then and there and be done with it. While she would never believe in the Shaker way, she didn't have a problem admitting she'd done wrong. At least to Sister Drayma's eyes. She'd broken Shaker rules of which there were many. She wouldn't have been surprised to find out there were rules on which eye to wink with first or instructions on the proper way to lick the strawberry juice off her thumb. She was beginning to think the whole bunch of them had troubled minds just like Preacher Palmer with their talk of heavenly garments and peace. *Blessed are the peacemakers: for they shall be called the children of God.*

Peace was good. She bent down to join the other sisters in the duty of picking the ripe berries. She'd told Aurelia she believed she was blessed. Blessed are the meek. Blessed are the poor in spirit. Blessed are those who mourn. So many ways to be blessed. Blessed with faith. Blessed with love. Blessed with forgiveness. Blessed with hope.

What would it be like to gather those blessings and fill the basket of her heart the way she was filling her strawberry basket? Then she could take some and hand them out to Sadie Rose or Aurelia or Isaac. Or poor Preacher Palmer.

That afternoon before the bell rang to signal the evening meal, Lacey pretended to confess her wrongs, at least enough of them to satisfy Sister Drayma's need to hear repentance. Aurelia was back in her place at their table, but she kept her eyes either on her plate or on a spot in the distance that no one could see but her. As soon as they left the eating room, she melted away and was gone. Lacey was about ready to believe her angels were spiriting her away.

The next two days, Aurelia didn't even show up for meals. Sister Drayma said she must be eating with the angels in preparation for their spiritual feast. Lacey bit back her doubting words as she worked alongside Sister Drayma in the strawberry patch. It would do no good to bedevil the sister with the questions boiling up inside her. The answers she needed could only come from Aurelia. So Lacey filled her baskets with strawberries and her thoughts with prayers for Rachel while biding her time. The Feast Day would come and go, and then Aurelia would return to her daily duties. Lacey would have her questions ready.

On Friday night amid the flickering candlelight, the elders and eldresses stood at either end of the upstairs meeting room. Lines formed with the brothers on one end of the room and the sisters on the other. Again she could not find Aurelia in the lines of sisters, but she did spot Isaac in the brethren's lines. He was watching her in return and smiled when he caught her looking at him. Lacey wanted to smile back but instead she turned away. *Blessed are the pure in heart.* A pure heart did not chase after sin.

The lines moved slowly as each member of the Gathering House family went forward to kneel, the men in front of Elder Homer and the women in front of Eldress Frieda. They in turn pretended to sort through chests of clothes before pulling out some imaginary garment to drape around the shoulders of the sister or brother kneeling in front of them.

"Then," the sister next to Lacey whispered instructions in her ear. "Then the person stands and lets the angels help adjust the clothing before bowing low four times."

"I don't see any angels. Do you?" Lacey whispered back.

"Nay, but it is best to pretend to do so. And some sisters say they feel the angels' hands straightening the collars of their holy dresses." The sister whose name Lacey thought was Wilma shuffled forward to wait her time to pretend or perhaps to hope that this time she would feel the flutter of angel wings so near her. Her eyes were gleaming with excitement.

Lacey went through the pantomime, bowing as instructed. She felt like she was back at the preacher's house telling Rachel a pretend story about talking snakes. That made about as much sense. But it wasn't time to be contrary. It was time to play along, do what they wanted until she could figure things out. *Blessed are the meek.*

On the other side of the room, the brothers were doing the same. She caught sight of the preacher shuffling along beside Brother Forrest. He looked hardly aware of where he was. *In sickness and in health.* The words circled in her mind. How could she keep denying her responsibility? Keep refusing to pick up her cross and carry it? *Come unto me, all ye that labour and are heavy laden, and I will give you rest.* The verse, a favorite of Miss Mona's, popped up in Lacey's head. But the verse was speaking to her now. Telling her that she could do whatever had to be done. The Lord would help her. Hadn't he always helped her? Even when she was trying to run ahead of him to untangle her messes herself and just getting everything in a bigger tangle.

Long into the night, she lay on the narrow Shaker bed and stared out at the darkness. Around her the other sisters were breathing softly in sleep. She should be sleeping too, but her thoughts kept springing first one way and then another. Aurelia and her angels. Isaac and the little cow. Isaac lifting her so easily off the ground with joy. Reuben saying little Jimmy was dead. The preacher out of his head. Aurelia Rachel's mother. The whole group of Shaker brothers and sisters playing pretend like children playing paper dolls.

"Put on this beautiful dress spun of pure gold, Sister Lacey, with emeralds for buttons." Eldress Frieda had actually spoken those words to Lacey as she pretended to drape something over Lacey's head. Then she had turned and offered the sister beside Lacey a gown bedecked in diamonds.

The next morning the sisters rose at the sound of the morning bell, dressed in their Shaker dresses, and then went through the ridiculous pantomime of slipping on the heavenly garb the eldress had given them the night before. A couple of the sisters even asked Lacey to help fasten their dresses but to be sure to take care with the jeweled buttons. Lacey wanted to tell them to just pretend their arms were longer and do up their buttons themselves, but she quelled her contrary spirit and pretended to fasten their buttons. Perhaps if so many worries hadn't been besetting her, she too could have enjoyed the break from the solemn Shaker duties of work.

After the morning meal the whole village assembled at the meetinghouse and then began to march toward whatever place the angels speaking through their instruments had designated consecrated ground. A place called Chosen Land according to Sister Lena, who had stepped into the missing Aurelia's place to instruct Lacey on the proper behavior for their Feast Day celebration as they had swept out the sleeping rooms that morning. Just because they were planning a celebration didn't mean they could ignore the dust that might accumulate in the corners or under the beds if vigilance was not practiced in the war against dirt.

Now somebody began singing and other voices joined in as they marched.

How happy pretty little angels are, O how happy.

They repeated the same words over and over until Lacey felt like the song was plowing a deep furrow in her brain that she might never climb out of. Happy. Happy. As though singing the word could make it so.

Lacey had been instructed to keep her eyes straight ahead, but she sneaked looks toward the columns of men marching alongside the sisters. Preacher Palmer was there, his mouth spilling out the song, but even as he sang the happy words, his eyes were darting about as though on the lookout for something else. Something to climb perhaps. Not far behind him she spotted Isaac. Marching and singing like the rest. She wondered if he'd asked forgiveness for talking to her in the woods. If he had and Sister Drayma heard of it, Lacey would have some confessing and explaining to do. Saying Aurelia told her not to speak of it would be a lame excuse. Akin to Eve in the garden, blaming the serpent for her sin.

She didn't see Aurelia, but Sister Lena told her the instruments of the angels would be leading the way, followed by the Covenant-signed Believers. Lacey was in the last group of marchers, those on the fringes of belief in the Shaker way. Or unbelief.

The song suddenly changed, flashing through the marchers like a grass fire.

> To the Chosen Land we are going as our voices
>   praises sound.
> Our hearts unite in rejoicing as we enter this sacred
>   ground.

Lacey stopped even pretending to sing. She shouldn't be there pretending to believe something she didn't. Pretending to see angels. Pretending she had no choice but to play along. And still her feet kept moving forward with the others. Those who did believe that angels had brought down dresses of gold and robes of purple to ready the Shakers for whatever was going to happen next. The singing trailed off as the Believers began to circle around a stone enclosed inside a low fence, the men on the east side and the women on the west. When the circle around the enclosure was complete, a new circle formed behind it.

Without any discernable signal that Lacey could note, a profound silence fell over the Shakers as every man and woman there became perfectly still. The air was so charged with anticipation that Lacey could almost see a glow hovering over the heads of the Shakers gathered closest to the rock.

The fountain, or so Sister Lena had called it that morning as they had swept out the sleeping rooms.

"There's a marble stone in the middle and out of it holy water flows so that those free from sin can wash themselves clean," she'd said. "Of course, it's spirit water that can only be made real by how much you believe."

"And everybody does this?" Lacey asked.

"Oh nay. As I said, only those free from sin. There's a warning from the angels written in the stone for any who might defile it by trying to wash in the fountain's water while yet in sin."

"I won't be trying it for sure," Lacey said.

"You couldn't anyway. Not as a novitiate. But you can partake of the spiritual fruit and drink of Mother's wine. And then maybe next Feast Day you'll be Covenant signed and able to wash clean at the fountain."

Lacey paused in her sweeping and looked over at Sister Lena swiping out the corners with the brush the Shakers made especially for that task. Small and birdlike in her movements, she had told Lacey she'd been a Believer for so long that she could barely remember her years before coming into the village.

"Have you washed in the fountain?" Lacey asked. It all sounded so strange coming from the mouth of Sister Lena, who seemed every bit as full of common sense as Miss Mona had been.

"Yea, what a gift. Three years now. One cannot begin to explain the feeling." Sister Lena stood up and looked out the window. A strand of iron gray hair escaped her cap and she absentmindedly tucked it back out of sight.

"Did you see angels?"

"Oh my, did I see angels! Glorious winged creatures whose very presence burned even the least remnant of the desire to

342

sin from my heart." She turned toward Lacey with a smile all across her tiny face that made her wrinkles vanish. "That can happen to you at the feast as well, Sister Lacey, even if you can't wash in the fountain. The angels sometimes choose a young Believer. As they did Sister Aurelia a few years ago when she'd only been with us a short while." Her eyes sharpened on Lacey. "Like you."

"Nay, I think not."

"Don't naysay the spirit, little Sister. Let it shower down on you and fill your heart. Those troubles that you have carried here from the world will vanish like mist on a summer day."

When Lacey didn't say anything, Lena sighed. "Perhaps in time you will be ready to accept the abundant gifts laid out for you here in this place."

"You don't have to be a Shaker to receive gifts of the Spirit," Lacey said.

"So many do think." Sister Lena shook her head sadly. "But Mother Ann has shown us the true way. If your feet aren't set firmly on the path that she has made for us, then they are surely on the slippery path of destruction. A woeful path. One that I am sad to say many of our young sisters and brethren step upon, but I will pray that you follow after Sister Aurelia instead and find joy among us here."

Sister Aurelia. A shining light among the Shakers. Now she and other instruments of the spirit gathered in front of the fountain area where they were sprinkled with spiritual incense and draped in mantles of strength, according to an elder who narrated the events. Then Aurelia spun out away from the others and began singing while passing around the fountain.

> I sing for the angels who come down from above
> And bring us bounties of blessings of love.

343

Blessings sent from our mother to land on us like a
dove.
Strength and power abound on this holy ground.

She made a complete circle of the fountain and then did
it once again. Lacey hadn't heard Aurelia singing by herself
before, but she had a beautiful voice that walked shivers up
Lacey's spine. It was easy to see why the Shakers thought
the angels sang through her. But did they know she was the
mother of a child? Without the sanctity of marriage. Had
she confessed that to the Shakers and been forgiven? What
had Eldress Frieda told Lacey? That all sins could be forgiven.
Perhaps only those truly forgiven were given the powerful
gifts of the spirit.

With the blessing song complete, a lively dance broke out
among the Shakers. No circling in fine order or marching up
and back with straight lines. Instead the men and women
began jumping and shouting while clapping their hands. Some
bowed low. Others reeled and staggered about as though
dizzy with drink. A few fell down on the ground and began
rolling around like dogs having fits. Lacey, along with others
new to the feast, stood back out of the way of the spiritual
mayhem. It was frightening and wondrous at the same time.
Not because she would ever believe as they did, but because
they believed so completely to surrender every inch of their
body to their spiritual ecstasy.

Sister Drayma was there whirling and spinning. Sister Lena
was hopping up and down and clapping her hands. Eldress
Frieda was skipping around like Rachel when she was happy.
The short little brother she'd seen so often with Isaac was leaping up and grabbing at the air as though he thought he could
climb up into the sky. Lacey took a quick look around for Isaac
and felt a strange gladness that he wasn't taking part in the

wild dancing. That like her, he was standing and watching in amazement but staying separate from their frenzied worship.

Then Aurelia was beside her, grabbing her arm and pulling her toward the dance. "Come, Sister, it is a time for dancing."

"Nay, Sister Aurelia. I don't want to dance." Lacey tried to jerk away from Aurelia, but her fingers were like a vise on her arm. They stood there a moment with neither of them giving ground as Lacey stared into the eyes that she should have recognized at once as being so like Rachel's.

"Aurelia is not here. I am Esmolenda and you must dance. Dancing with the angels is a gift you cannot refuse."

"I see no angels. I see only Sister Aurelia who has been playing a game with me, pretending to be my friend while trying to steal my child's love." That was another thing Lacey should have known from the moment Rachel had talked about the angels saying Sister Rella loved her best. Sister Rella. Aurelia.

"Who stole the child first?"

"Not stolen. Given. The baby was given to Miss Mona. To me."

"Given. Gifts are given but we cannot always choose our gifts." Aurelia tightened her grip even more until she was bruising Lacey's arm.

"Turn loose of me, Aurelia. I will not pretend to see angels I do not see."

Aurelia's face changed, lost the fierceness that had been burning in her eyes. Her hand relaxed on Lacey's arm, but she still didn't turn her loose. "But don't you see, Lacey. Angels are all I have left to give you. Please come and dance with me." Her voice was pleading. "With Esmolenda."

What could she do but put her hand in Aurelia's and follow her as she twirled through the Shakers around the fountain that had no water? But then it wasn't much different from her spring dance to celebrate the return of dandelions. In fact, if she looked about, she could no doubt see a spot of yellow sunshine poking up out of the grass. But when she looked back over her shoulder, what she saw was Isaac, and she knew who she wanted to be dancing with as she followed Aurelia. Without a doubt, hysteria reigned.

31

Isaac watched Sister Aurelia pull Lacey down into the dancing Shakers. If what they were doing could be called dancing. Brother Asa had tried to describe what the Feast Day would be like, but some things defied description. Or understanding. Yet, now when Isaac caught sight of Asa among the dancers, he had a look of rapture on his face the likes of which Isaac never expected to know.

While Isaac had been feeling the timid desire to reach toward the Lord, doubts and fears kept pulling his hand back, but Brother Asa showed no sign of fear as he ran after the Lord with abandon. He believed. Isaac wanted to believe. He wanted to know Asa's kind of faith. His mother's kind of faith that was the bedrock of her life. Marian's kind of faith that lit up her face with joyful peace even now as she whirled around the fountain rock. She didn't look as if she'd ever had one doubt or one sin in need of forgiveness.

He had the urge to go down and put his hands on her shoulders to stop her spinning. To make her tell him how she got such faith. To show him how to lose his doubts and find forgiveness. But then she'd never done what he'd done. She'd lived in this tranquil place half her life and never been the reason for someone she loved to die. What did she know about the need for forgiveness?

The song they had practiced the night before came to mind. The Lord's Prayer. His mother had taught him the words even before he went to live with the McElroys, and Mrs. McElroy made him repeat the prayer at least once a week. *Forgive us our debts, as we forgive our debtors.* Debts. He had no debts and no one owed him the first thing. But Bible debts were different. Trespasses, transgressions, sins that could be held against him. Unless he forgave.

That was what Mrs. McElroy had told him. That to be forgiven he had to first forgive. He had stared the good woman in the eye and told her he didn't care about forgiving anybody. That wasn't going to bring his father back. His angry words had made her weep and pray over him, and when he was still unrepentant, she'd had Mr. McElroy take his belt to him. He'd taken the beating without protest. A just punishment for the unforgiven.

He didn't deserve forgiveness. Ella was dead because of him. Her parents bereft. The judge's wrath justified. It was only fitting that here in this place where he thought he could shut himself away from the world and live without feeling anything that he had fallen in love with a woman who could never be his. Another just punishment.

He was surprised when Lacey started dancing, but then he caught sight of her face. None of Brother Asa's rapture there. No hint of the ethereal joy that played across Sister Aurelia's face. She looked more like the awkward participant in a barn dance hoedown. A smile slipped back across his face. He didn't want her to be one of them. Even if she wasn't free to love him, he didn't want her to be closed off to the possibility of love. Love and forgiveness.

Forgive and be forgiven. The words echoed back in his

head. He could forgive the judge for trying to exact revenge on him. He could forgive the McElroys for not being kinder to a grieving child. He could forgive Brother Verne for his lack of brotherly love and for the way he looked at Lacey. He could forgive Lacey for being married to the preacher.

Then do it, a voice whispered in his head. He shut his eyes and once more reached for the Lord, this time with a steadier hand. "I forgive," he spoke aloud, but even the man standing right beside him couldn't have heard his words with the cacophony of songs and shouts rising all around them. "I forgive them all. Please. Grant me forgiveness in return."

He waited to feel something different. For a light to suddenly break over him. For one of the Shaker's angels to come down and touch his shoulder. Nothing happened. He wanted something to happen. Something he could feel. Maybe there were more people he needed to forgive. His father for dying and leaving him alone. Ella for calling out to her mother instead of to him as she was dying.

"I forgive them," he said.

A sudden silence surrounded him. He wasn't sure if it was only in his ears or all around him until he looked up and saw the dancing had stopped. Elder Joseph was calling forth some of the brethren to carry tubs to either side of the fountain. There were no tubs in sight, but several men stepped forward to pretend to pick up something and carry it to each side of the fountain rock.

The elder's voice rang out. "Come all who are free of sin to wash in the waters from the fountain and scrub yourselves clean. But be warned, those harboring sins unconfessed and unforgiven must not defile the fountain's waters."

Isaac had no thought of joining the line of brothers preparing for their scrubbing pantomime. Although it would surely feel good to be scrubbed clean and fresh. A kind of new beginning. Like the paralyzed man lowered down through the roof by his four friends. Jesus had forgiven his sins and the man had stood and rolled his bed up and walked home. A new beginning. Perhaps the Lord had put that story in his mind. Perhaps that was his shining light. His sign.

You are forgiven. Isaac didn't hear the words spoken aloud, but he heard them in his heart. He wished the Shakers were still dancing so that he could jump for joy. He wished Lacey was beside him so that he could swing her up in the air the way he had in the woods when the calf had raised his head and flapped his ears free of the birth sac.

He sought her among the Shaker sisters. Even with all their like dresses, he found her almost at once as though his eyes were drawn to her like iron filings to a magnet. She had pulled away from Sister Aurelia and was making her way back to the outer fringes. To those who merely watched. She looked his way but didn't allow her eyes to do more than touch on his face. She was right to do so. He was forgiven. It would be wrong to willfully jump back into sin.

A rumble of protest ran through the line of brethren waiting their turn to pretend to wash in the fountain as one of the brothers shoved through them. Some of the Shakers pushed their hands toward the ground and stomped as they began shouting, "Back from us old Ugly. Get away, Satan."

But Brother Elwood pushed on toward the fountain stone with no notice of the shouts or the hands that grabbed at him. He seemed to have the strength of five men as he moved forward with singular purpose.

"Nay, Brother Elwood. You must not defile the fountain." Elder Joseph's voice carried the sound of doom, but the man paid him no mind. His eyes were fixed on the stone.

Isaac looked back at Lacey. She had stopped in her tracks and was staring at her husband from the world. Isaac's heart squeezed together with sadness, but he made himself repeat the thought in his head. *Her husband.* She too looked suddenly very sad. Her shoulders drooped as she turned toward the fountain to go after Brother Elwood.

Lacey knew what she had to do as soon as she saw the preacher running toward the stone. It was time to pick up her cross and do the necessary thing. The poor man needed her. And he needed to be away from these people with their odd beliefs and weird ways of worship. She had danced with Aurelia, but she hadn't felt the first whisper of angel wings.

Whether it was all pretend with Aurelia, she had no way of knowing. Perhaps angels did come down and take over Aurelia's body. Perhaps Aurelia and Sister Lena and others did actually see angels, and it was more than some sort of strange hysteria leaping from one to another. She didn't know. What she did know was that Aurelia wanted to entertain angels. That it gave her a feeling of power. A way to shape her world here among the Shakers.

But Lacey had no desire to receive such gifts. All she wanted was Rachel. As soon as she thought it, she knew that wasn't true. Her eyes flicked back to Isaac, who was still watching her. She didn't let her gaze linger. He was not her husband. Preacher Palmer was her husband. And he needed her to take his hand and march him away from this place while he might yet retain a shred of sanity.

The preacher was up on the fence enclosing the fountain rock. He teetered there for a moment before booming out in his preacher's voice. "The spirits command me."

"Nay, it is the devil that leads you, Brother Elwood," the elder said. The other men, even Brother Forrest, must have believed the elder because they fell back as though afraid to draw too close to such evil.

"I will be forgiven," the preacher shouted toward the sky. Then he jumped into the enclosure and moved through the handful of brothers who had been pretending to scrub each other free of sin. He climbed up onto the fountain stone and raised his hands toward the sky.

A few woes began sounding around the enclosure and then other voices joined in until the sound hung over the place like a black cloud. Lacey ignored them all as she went through the gate into the Shakers' holy ground. The woes became like the sound of a gaggle of angry geese in the distance. She held her hand up toward the preacher.

"Come, Elwood. It's time for us to go home. The Lord called you to preach his Word. You have been neglecting your calling. That's all the balance you need. His Word in your mind and heart again."

He looked down at her, his face creased with lines of despair. In the weeks they had been with the Shakers he had aged ten years. "Lacey. Don't you understand? I have sinned."

"We have all sinned, Elwood. Every last one of us." She wasn't sure if the Shakers had softened the sound of their woes or if she was just so intent on the preacher that they no longer sounded as loud in her ears.

"But I must seek forgiveness."

"And it will be given to you."

"Do you forgive me?"

"I forgive you, Elwood." She reached her hand up a little higher. "Do you forgive me?"

"Blessed is the man unto whom the Lord imputeth not iniquity, and in whose spirit there is no guile."

"See. The Word of the Lord is coming to you. Blessed

are they who speak his Word." She didn't know if that was really in the Bible, but she thought it sounded like Scripture.

"Nay, you do not understand. 'In whose spirit there is no guile.'" His voice rose until he was shouting the last words.

She studied his face then and realized she did not know this man. She knew the man she thought he was. A man with faults and foibles like any other man but a man of God, nevertheless. But she had only carried her idea of who he was. They had never shared any moment of closeness in all the years she had lived in his house, first as a near child and then as a woman. She did not know him or the secret sins he carried in his heart that were spreading anguish across his face. But none of that changed the fact that he was her husband. She said a silent prayer for strength and did not let her resolve falter as she continued to reach toward him.

"Take my hand, Elwood. Whatever you've done that torments you can be forgiven. You can surrender your guile and repent of your wrongs. That is the balance you need." She made her voice strong and sure.

He stared at her for a long moment before he reached down and took her hand. Complete silence fell over the men and women around them as he stepped down off the Shaker's holy fountain to stand beside her. She saw the words engraved in the stone and tried to turn him away from them, but he stopped and ran his free hand over them.

"Anyone who defiles this stone while in sin be warned." He spoke the words slowly as though considering their meaning. He repeated the last two. "Be warned."

"You didn't try to bathe in the holy water," Lacey said softly as she put an arm around him to guide him away from the stone. "Come, Elwood. Away from this place. It is only holy to the Shakers. Not to us."

She kept her eyes straight in front of them as she led him

through the Shakers. She wanted to turn to them and tell them to go back to their shouting and jumping and dancing and pretend scrubbing away of sins, but she kept as silent as they were. A few scattered woes popped up again around them and then some began singing.

> Be joyful, be joyful, be joyful,
> Be joyful, For Old Ugly is going.
> Good riddance, good riddance, good riddance we say,
> And don't you never come here again.

"They're saying we're the devil." The preacher's voice was flat with no feeling.

"Pay them no mind," Lacey said as she squared her shoulders and kept walking.

She was as glad to be rid of them as they were to be rid of her. She wouldn't let their words bother her. Didn't she have enough things to grieve over already with thinking about being a proper wife to the preacher and never laying eyes on Isaac again? God's love. That's what she needed to dwell on. But she let her eyes stray over to where Isaac had been standing. He was gone.

She told herself that was good. It kept her from sinning in her heart, but she couldn't stop the wave of disappointment that surged through her. Still, she wouldn't let her eyes search through the brothers looking for him. It was pointless. He had been nothing but a dream of what might have been. Very few dreams came true. If she knew anything, she knew that.

But then he was standing directly by the path they were walking. Demanding her eyes meet his. He touched her arm. "You don't have to go with him. Don't go."

Those words echoed in her memory. The very words he'd spoken to her at the house before they'd come to the Shaker village. *Don't go.* But she had no way of listening to those words now any more than she had then.

"But I must. I am his wife."

Isaac held on to her arm another second. "I did love my wife very much."

"I know you did." She blinked her eyes to keep back the tears that wanted to spill out and smiled at him with lips that trembled.

He smiled back before he turned loose of her arm to let them pass. She would carry the treasure of that smile away with her in her heart.

The preacher didn't look up at Isaac or her while they talked. He kept his head down and muttered a word now and again that Lacey couldn't quite make out. She thought he might be quoting Scripture and hoped the words would calm his spirit.

It wasn't even noon yet. They could go find Rachel and walk away from this place. Back to Ebenezer. Even if the church had already found a new preacher, the people would help her. Help them both. And in time with prayer and the care of a dutiful wife, Preacher Palmer might find that balance he had lost here with these people. Or perhaps he had been drifting along in a sea of misery ever since Miss Mona passed on. They had been wrong to try to form a family without her.

What was it Sister Drayma had told her the Shakers believed about families? That the stress of worldly family relationships, husband and wife, parent and child, was the reason for much sin. Lacey had argued with Sister Drayma that God had planned for families from the Garden of Eden on.

"Yea, Sister Lacey," the woman had told her. "But that was only after Adam and Eve invited sin into the world. We as believers in the true way shut all reason for sin from our lives and seek our heaven on earth. We need no family but the family of God where all are brothers and sisters. And for that we are blessed."

Now Lacey wanted to run back down among the sisters and find Sister Drayma to tell her that she too was blessed. Blessed in her imperfection. Forgiven. Loved.

They were almost to the outer edge of the clearing when there was a sudden stir behind them. No cries of woe followed Aurelia as she ran after them, but there were many cries of concern that Aurelia might be tainted with their sin.

She stepped directly in front of them. Lacey had thought she might be running after her to share parting words, but she didn't even look at Lacey. Her eyes were on the preacher. "She may say she forgives you, Elwood Palmer, but only because the angels have not revealed to her the sin that torments you. She is too pure of heart to think on it. The angels have purified my heart too, but know that I have not forgiven you. I will never forgive you."

A tremble ran through the preacher's body. Lacey tightened her arm around his waist and stared at Aurelia. "Stop it, Aurelia. He has done no wrong to you."

Aurelia turned to look at Lacey. Her eyes so like Rachel's were wide and had an unnatural shine. "Are you sure of that, Sister Lacey? Ask him. He knows. Or ask the angels. If you dare. Angel tongues can speak nothing but truth."

Then Lacey knew without asking. She didn't know why she was surprised. She'd always known the preacher was a man like any other. A man who could fall into temptation. And obviously had. With Aurelia. Her arm stiffened around his waist.

Beside her, he looked up at the heavens and cried out, "Mine iniquities have taken hold of me. My sin cannot be hidden."

"Your sin was never hidden. Mona knew. I told her before I came here." Aurelia threw the words at him like stones.

"She forgave me. She told me she forgave me."

"But I do not." Aurelia suddenly spun away in a circle, her arms flinging wildly about. "Nor does the angel Esmolenda." She began singing sounds that had no meaning.

> O saniskan niskana, haw, haw, haw,
> Fannickana niskana, haw, haw, haw.

Hearing the strange words spilling out of Aurelia was eerie enough, but then the Shakers around them picked up the song and began singing with her like they were singing a well-known hymn.

While the words sounded like so much nonsense to Lacey, the preacher's face grew even more horrified as he clapped his hands over his ears. "Strike me down, Lord. End my misery." He jerked away from Lacey and took off running.

She might have caught him if she hadn't hesitated. And then when she did start after him, Aurelia moved deliberately in front of her. Her face was strange, unworldly. "You cannot help him. Only angels can help him now."

"Then send your angels to help him, Aurelia."

"Aurelia has no power over us. She is only our mouth and feet. Our God has the power."

"The Lord is merciful. He will forgive." Lacey pushed past her, lifted up her skirts and ran after the preacher. She looked back over her shoulder. "Please help me."

Isaac ran after her and then Brother Forrest and a couple of other brothers broke from the lines of Shakers to follow Lacey. They were not without compassion. Behind her the Shakers started singing again. Aurelia's voice rang out loudest of all.

Come down Shaker life. Come down holy.
Come let us all unite to chase away Old Ugly.

Preacher Palmer ran as if Aurelia's angels were chasing him. Lacey called out to him, but he gave no sign of hearing her and kept running.

32

When Isaac came around the Gathering Family House out onto the road that ran through the village, Brother Elwood was nowhere in sight. Isaac stopped and tried to catch his breath as he looked around. He'd run ahead of Lacey as fast as he could, but the man, old as he was, had been faster.

"He's gone," Isaac said when Lacey caught up with him.

Her cheeks were flushed from running and she was breathing hard. She didn't look at him but searched the road in front of them. "He has to be here somewhere."

"The Centre Family House," Brother Forrest said between panting breaths when he paused beside them.

They took off up the street, but when they got to the big stone house, both the men's and women's doors were locked. "Because all are away for Feast Day," Brother Forrest said. He looked around. "Think of another place of height. The pitiable man has seemed obsessed with high places."

"Maybe he stopped at the barn below the Gathering Family House. It has a loft," Isaac suggested.

They were turning to go back toward the barns when Lacey spotted the hat below an open window. Brother Forrest went over to pick it up.

"Yea, it looks to be his." He looked up at the window a

few feet over his head. "The window would not be in easy reach, but today he seems to have the strength of angels."

"I've heard enough talk of angels this day," Lacey said. "Lift me up and I'll go after him."

"Nay," Brother Forrest said. "Not you, Sister Lacey. Come, Brother Isaac. You are stronger and better suited for the task of helping our brother."

Brother Forrest and one of the other brothers laced their hands together to give Isaac a boost up to the window. Once inside he ran past the neatly made beds and hurried out into the hall and the stairway. Out of habit he ran to the brothers' stairs and climbed them two steps at a time all the way up to the attic. The air trapped under the roof was hot, but light spilled down from the cupola onto the rough roof beams. Still the preacher was nowhere in sight. Maybe he hadn't come this way at all. Maybe the hat had just blown over to land under the window.

Isaac climbed the steep stairs into the cupola. There was a door. A door that wasn't completely closed. Isaac stepped out on the roof that was thankfully flat in the middle with a low railing around it before it sloped steeply to the edge. Tall chimneys jutted up from each corner of the roof. A place for watching, Brother Verne had told him. Isaac could see both ends of the village and many of the back pathways. But he had no time to spy out the village. Brother Elwood was up on the railing beside one of the chimneys searching for handholds on the chimney brick to climb higher.

"Stay away!" Brother Elwood shouted when he saw him. He turned loose of the chimney with one of his hands and held it out toward Isaac to keep him back.

Isaac stopped a few feet away from him. "The roof is high, Brother Elwood. It would be best if you hold on as you climb down."

Brother Elwood looked down toward the ground below him. "I have no fear of falling. Not from this rooftop. A fall from grace is more to fear. 'Fear not them which kill the body, but are not able to kill the soul; but rather fear him which is able to destroy both soul and body in hell.'"

Isaac took slow steps closer to him. "The elders have said you must come down. They will pray with you."

"You're lying. The elders have nothing but scorn for me. They think I'm of the devil." Brother Elwood got a strange look on his face. "Perhaps I am."

"Nay, Brother. You are a man of God." Isaac edged a little closer. He was almost close enough to reach out and grab him.

"I was once a man of God. But no more. I was brought low by lust." He looked away from Isaac up toward the sky. "That is why I must seek a new balance. A new beginning."

"Lacey is waiting down on the ground for you to help you find that new beginning." Isaac knew at once from the man's face that he'd said the wrong thing.

"Lacey." Brother Elwood glanced down at the ground as his face changed from frantic to determined. "So many sins."

"Come down, Brother." Isaac kept his voice low and calm as he stepped up beside the man and reached for his hand.

"But the spirits say I must find balance."

"Balance can be found in less precarious places."

"The spirits led me here. I cannot let them think I am fearful." He let out a noise that might have been a laugh as he wildly threw up his hands. He wobbled on the railing before he began falling away from Isaac.

Isaac grabbed for him and caught the man's arm. The force of the man's fall pulled Isaac so hard against the railing that it cracked and gave way. They both fell down on the roof and began sliding toward the edge. Isaac grabbed with his other hand for something to stop them but found nothing to grasp as the shingles scrubbed the palm of his hand. He threw out his leg and caught his foot on the broken railing to halt their slide.

Brother Elwood stared up at Isaac. "Let me go."

"No." Isaac met the man's eyes. The fall seemed to have pulled him back to sanity.

"If you don't, we'll both die, but you may be able to climb back up if you turn me loose," the man said quietly.

He could. He didn't have to keep risking his life to help the man. The thought surfaced in his mind and settled there. The man's arm was already slipping through Isaac's hand. All Isaac had to do was relax his hold the barest bit and the man would slide on down the roof away from him and over the edge. Then Lacey would be free. Her screams were rising up to him. Screams for him. He'd seen the look in her eyes. He knew she cared for him. They could have the new beginning.

It seemed like an eternity passed as he stared down at the man before he tightened his grip on the man's arm. "Grab hold of my arm with your other hand, Brother Elwood. Help is coming."

"The Lord helps the weak and the weary."

For a second, Isaac thought Brother Elwood was reaching toward his arm. "That's right. Just grab hold. We can hang on until help comes." The railing popped ominously behind them and gave a few inches, but it held.

"'Surely thou didst set them in slippery places: thou castedst them down into destruction.' My sins have caused too much destruction already." He turned his eyes away from Isaac's face. "May the Lord have mercy on my soul."

He gave a sudden twist of his arm to break free of Isaac's hold. Isaac grabbed for him with his other hand, but he couldn't reach him. The man smiled up at him as he slid over the edge of the roof with no attempt to catch himself.

Isaac heard the man's body hit the ground. A sickening thud. And down below Lacey stopped screaming.

Brother Forrest drove them back to the Ebenezer church. The preacher's broken body lay in the bed of the wagon wrapped in a Shaker blanket. It was decided by everyone to be the best way.

Preacher Palmer hadn't been a true Shaker Believer. And there were those among the elders and eldresses who thought he had intended to fall from the roof, that it wasn't an accident brought about by his tormented mind. Such was a sin that could not be confessed and forgiven, so there was no way he could be laid in the sacred ground of the Shaker cemetery. As they spoke of what must be done, Lacey heard little sympathy in their voices. They had more sorrow in their voices when they talked of how their Feast Day had been spoiled.

Lacey had stood on the fringes and listened until she could bear no more. Wasn't it enough that the poor man lay battered and dead? And that his own wife had watched him sliding down the rooftop with more fear for the man trying to save him than for her husband?

Isaac had come down from the roof after Brother Forrest and one of the other brothers had climbed through the window and run up the stairs to pull him back to safety. They had led him away without letting him talk to her, but she had seen his eyes. As battered as the poor preacher's body.

And so she had gone right up to Eldress Frieda and told her what was going to happen. "I will take him back to Ebenezer where he can be buried beside his beloved wife."

"I thought you were his wife," Eldress Frieda said.

"Second wife, but never truly."

"And then what of you, Sister Lacey? Will you return to us to continue your journey to true salvation?"

"No."

"I thought not, but I mourn your return to the pits of sin." She appeared to be truly sorry as she looked at Lacey. "You showed promise of great gifts."

"I didn't ever see the first angel."

"My sister, there are many gifts of the spirit. The gift our mother honors most is the gift to be simple."

"The gift to be simple." Lacey repeated her words as she reached out and touched the woman's arm. "Do you think that's something like 'blessed are the meek'?"

The eldress tilted her head a little to the side as she considered Lacey's question. "The meek. Perhaps. Or the pure in heart for they know what things are to be treasured."

"Then that's what I'll carry away from here. The knowledge of what gifts to treasure in my heart. But I can never walk the Shaker way."

"Your words sadden me, but we make none stay against their will. I will send someone to fetch your daughter."

"Send Sister Aurelia." Lacey looked past the eldress to where Aurelia was surrounded by a bevy of sisters. Her face was pale and distraught.

"Nay, Sister Lacey," the eldress said as she looked over her shoulder at the sisters. "You can see for yourself her distress. She did not mean for this to happen. To ask her to go get Sister Rachel would be unkind."

"But necessary. She visited Rachel in the night and tried to turn her affections from me with stories that the angels say I don't want her anymore."

"Are you sure that you do?" Eldress Frieda studied Lacey's face. "After all, Sister Rachel is not your natural daughter, and if she has turned from you, then perhaps it would be best to leave the young sister with us. We have much to offer a child here. Much more than a lone woman going out into the world. If you truly love her, you will want what's best for her."

Lacey bit back the angry words that wanted to spill out and instead pulled in a slow breath. The simple gift of meekness, she reminded herself. The eldress wasn't intending to be heartless. She believed what she was saying. "Let me talk to Sister Aurelia and then I will let Rachel choose." Her heart went cold as her words echoed in her ears. How could she have said that? What if Rachel chose to stay?

"Very well. I will tell Sister Aurelia to come speak to you, but you must not torment her."

You mean the way she tormented the poor preacher. The words were in her head, but again she held them back as her eyes went to the man's body lying broken on the ground. Someone had mercifully spread a cover over him. A cover spotted now with drying blood.

The circle of sisters around Aurelia parted to allow Eldress Frieda to speak to her. Aurelia shook her head twice, but the eldress kept talking until Aurelia sent an agonized look toward Lacey and bowed her head in submission. She hesitantly walked toward Lacey, but stopped halfway. Lacey went to her. The other sisters didn't follow Aurelia, but they had their ears cocked their way to listen.

"I didn't think he would do this, Lacey. I didn't."

"What did you think, Aurelia?"

"He wouldn't help me. He said I was the one who had sinned and brought temptation to him. Me. Like none of it had to do with him." She looked at Lacey with beseeching eyes. "My father called me a Jezebel and made me get up out of my birthing bed and take the baby away. He hoped we would both die. He told me that."

"What of your mother?" Lacey hardened her heart. She didn't want to feel pity for her.

"She died when I was young. The same as your own. Elwood came to our church over in the next county to do a revival. My father has ever been cruel to me and Elwood was so kind, so thoughtful. He made me promises. Promises he later denied. I had no choice but to lay that precious child in a box on his porch. My tears fell on her tiny forehead while I asked the angels to watch over her."

Lacey shut her eyes for a moment and couldn't keep from imagining Aurelia's pain. "Then what did you do?"

"The angels led me here where I could be safe. I was sick for a long time, but my sisters healed me and they loved me and they forgave me."

"But you could never forgive him?"

"Nay." Aurelia sent a quick glance toward the preacher's body and shivered a little. "Could you have?"

"I don't know."

"No one can know who hasn't felt what I felt. But I was able to forget and find happiness here. I really do see the angels, Lacey. I really do." Her eyes appealed to Lacey. "I want you to believe that. It must have been the devil that brought him here to punish us both."

"And me? Did you want me to be punished?"

"Nay. I only wanted Rachel to love me. To know I loved her."

"Do you want to be her mother?" The words almost choked Lacey, but she said them.

Aurelia looked at Lacey for a long time without answering. "I cannot leave this place. I belong here. Evermore."

"You can be no more than a sister to Rachel here."

"I know that. Sometimes the things that are best to do hurt the most." Aurelia licked her lips. "I gave her to you once. I give her to you again."

Such a wave of relief swept through Lacey that she thought her knees might buckle, but she forced strength back through her. "First you must tell her the angels were wrong when they told her I gave her to the Shakers because I didn't want her."

"The angels are never wrong."

"But it wasn't the angels talking. It was you."

Aurelia stared at Lacey for a long moment before she squared her shoulders and said, "I will tell her. For you, Lacey, I will tell her. And then I will bring her to you."

While she was gone, Brother Forrest brought the wagon and the brothers picked up the preacher and laid him gently in the wagon bed as though even now he might feel pain. Then one of the sisters brought a clean blanket to spread atop the one that was stained with the preacher's blood. Eldress Frieda came back over to stand silently beside Lacey, whether to offer her support or to guard her, Lacey wasn't sure which.

"You can sit on the wagon if you wish," the eldress said after a long time.

"Nay, I am able to stand." She said the Shaker word purposely. A courtesy to the woman's kindness. She hesitated a long moment as the silence gathered around them again before she asked, "The other brother, Brother Isaac, was he all right?"

"They say he seemed so when he walked away, but if he has injuries, they will be tended to. You need have no worries in that regard."

"Thank you," Lacey said formally and let the silence gather again as the long minutes ticked by. A bell sounded to summon the Shakers back to their duties, and all but Eldress Frieda and Brother Forrest turned obediently for their houses. The day was passing. Not a day like any other, but come morning, they would once again go about their duties the same as yesterday and the day after tomorrow. Lacey had no idea what the days to come would hold for her. Or for Rachel.

"They come," the eldress said.

Lacey turned to watch Rachel and Aurelia walking slowly toward them. Aurelia held the child's hand. Rachel looked scared. Lacey had seen the same look on her face the day they'd buried Miss Mona. And the day Sister Janie had taken her hand to lead her away from Lacey here in the Shaker village.

"You must let her decide, as you promised," Eldress Frieda said.

Lacey didn't speak. She simply held her hand out to her child. Rachel looked up at Aurelia, who smiled down at her before she took Rachel's hand and put it into Lacey's hand. Her little hand felt so good that Lacey had to blink back tears.

"Do you want to go with her, Sister Rachel?" Eldress Frieda's voice was stern. "Or do you want to stay with your sisters?"

Rachel looked solemnly up at Lacey. "I want to go with Lacey. She loves me more than all the worms under the ground."

Lacey blinked hard and choked back a sob before she could say, "But not as much as Jesus."

"But plenty enough," Rachel said and grabbed Lacey around the waist.

The tears spilled out of Lacey's eyes and streamed down her cheeks. Aurelia reached over and gently wiped them away. "The pure in heart. Don't let her forget how much I loved her," she said softly before she turned to walk away with the eldress.

And now they were carrying the preacher back to his rightful burying spot beside Miss Mona. No one spoke the whole journey. Not Brother Forrest. Not Lacey. Not Rachel. But Rachel leaned her head against Lacey's breast and that was enough.

When Brother Forrest stopped the horses in front of the church, he stared down at his hands on the reins as he said, "What are you going to tell them when they ask how he died?"

He looked up at the church graveyard and she knew his thinking. Those who killed themselves were laid outside sanctified ground. Her voice carried not a whiff of doubt as she looked toward Miss Mona's headstone. "I'll tell them what happened. That he lost his balance and fell from a roof."

Brother Forrest was silent for a moment as he seemed to be considering her words. Then he nodded slightly. "Yea, you'll be speaking the truth."

33

The funeral was plain. The church was still without a pastor and nobody suggested bringing in a preacher from town for the services. This or that deacon had been filling the pulpit. What with it being planting season, none of them had the time to be out hunting preachers. Lacey was just as glad. It only seemed right to have one of the deacons stand up and read the Scripture and pray the prayers over the man who had been their leader for so many years.

Deacon Morrison spoke the words over the preacher's body. Normally Deacon Crutcher would have been the one chosen for such a job, but it had only been a week since he'd laid his youngest son in the ground. Nobody would have looked ill on him if he hadn't shown up at the church at all. But he had come, hammering and sawing with the rest to build the casket box while Reuben and some others dug a grave out next to Miss Mona.

Lacey had sat in the church the whole time. In the preacher's wife's pew. She hadn't been a proper wife to him in life, but she could do right by him in death. So she kept watch over the preacher in her Shaker dress. She stripped off the white collar and draped a black shawl over her shoulders that somebody brought her. She didn't remember who. The churchwomen had streamed to the church to offer kindness to her. And to Rachel. More than one of them offered to take Rachel home with them and give her a bed the night before. The women waited for Lacey to make the child go, but Rachel clung to Lacey.

So she had put her arm around Rachel and pulled her even closer while she told the well-meaning women no. "The last few weeks have been hard for Rachel. I'll let her do what she wants."

Rachel relaxed against her and Lacey was glad that she didn't have to stop touching her. Besides, the child needed to be there with her father. No one but Lacey and Aurelia knew that truth, but if someday Rachel asked about her father, Lacey could tell her that she'd kept the death watch over him. The churchwomen brought food and a quilt and a pillow for Rachel. Then after they prayed with Lacey and over the preacher, they'd all left except for two of the older women who had no young children at home.

Cassie and Jo Ann settled into the pew on either side of her and Rachel to sit through the night with them. They talked of grandchildren and crops and garden beans for a while, but eventually the talk turned to the trouble that had befallen the church. First little Jimmy's accident and now the preacher.

The older of the two, Jo Ann, clucked her tongue when she talked about how Sadie Rose had taken to her bed and turned her face to the wall. "Poor Deacon Crutcher is quite beside himself with grief not just for the boy but for Sadie Rose too. And the dear boys. Lost their little brother and now their mother can't pull herself together to give them any sort of comfort."

"Such a shame. She's always been so strong in the spirit." Cassie shook her head. She was a heavy woman who suffered in the heat, and now she plucked a cardboard fan from the pew behind them and began to wave it in front of her face. "She and Mona had a way of taking the Bible and walking a troubled soul through it until they found some peace. But they say the poor woman won't even put her hand on a Bible since little Jimmy passed on."

"It's only been a few days," Lacey murmured. "It can't be easy to lose a child." Her arm tightened around Rachel, dozing against her side.

"You don't have to tell me that. I've buried two," Cassie said, her voice solemn. "That was before you came to stay with Mona. One dear little baby girl never drew breath and the other, a boy, took a fever when he was two."

"We aren't promised a life without troubles. That's for sure," Jo Ann said as she reached across Lacey and Rachel to pat Cassie's hand. "But you carried on."

"What else can a body do?" Cassie sighed sadly. "The Bible promises the Lord won't heap more on us than we can bear up under, but there's been times when I've had to wonder." She gave Lacey a concerned look in the dim lamplight. "But I shouldn't be going on about my griefs. You've got enough troubles right now without me adding to your sorrow. If you want to try to doze a little, we'll keep the watch."

"No, I'll watch. I owe him that much. He tried to do right by me."

That was what she was prepared to tell his congregation if they asked her to say words, but they didn't. Deacon Morrison did the talking. For them all, he said. His voice shook as he told about building the church house and how young they'd all been then. Over thirty years before. Deacon Crutcher sat in his accustomed pew with his four remaining sons and listened. He looked pale and troubled and made no move to get up to add any words to Deacon Morrison's. He did add his strength to the other deacons and Reuben to carry the preacher out to the grave and carefully lower the coffin by ropes into the hole.

After Deacon Morrison solemnly spoke the dust-to-dust grave words, all but the deacons and Reuben turned back to the church house where the women had filled a wagon bed with covered dishes on the shady side of the church away from the graveyard. Lacey held Rachel's hand tight as they turned to follow the women, but Deacon Crutcher stepped in front of them.

"That's our boy's grave." He pointed toward a new mound of dirt in the far corner of the graveyard.

"Reuben told me. I'm sorry," Lacey said. "Both of us are." She held Rachel's hand even tighter.

"My Sadie Rose is taking it hard." The creases in his weather-beaten face got deeper.

"I guess that's no wonder." She wanted to say something to help him, but there were no words. "It's a grievous thing for the both of you."

"The Lord giveth and the Lord taketh away," he said quietly before he turned his eyes away from his child's grave back to her. "You planning on going back over there to that Shaker town?" He had his hat still in his hand from the funeral and he twisted the brim as he waited for her answer.

"No. They work hard and there is kindness among them. Some good men and women, but I couldn't wrap my mind around their peculiar way of worshiping. Or of dividing up families." Rachel eased a little closer to her and Lacey put her arm around the child and let the thankful prayer that she could do so rise up in her heart yet again.

"Then what are you thinking on doing?"

"I don't know." She hadn't really thought past the funeral. She looked over toward the preacher's house where she'd known so many happy days, but she couldn't expect them to let her stay there for long. They would need to move in a new preacher. "I don't know," she repeated.

"I'd count it a favor if you'd come stay with us a spell. You know, just till Sadie Rose finds her strength again. Me and the boys, we need to be out in the fields. But it's more than the chores. I'm thinking it might be good to have a woman in the house she could talk to."

"I have Rachel," Lacey said.

"I'm knowing that. I was meaning the both of you." His eyes touched on Rachel. He tried to smile, but his eyes stayed sad. "It will be good to have a little girl in the house."

So after the grave was filled in and they ate with the good sound of the church people's voices mixed with some laughter and a few tears, Lacey and Rachel climbed up on the seat of Deacon Crutcher's wagon beside him. The boys piled in the back with the oldest boy, Harry, carefully holding the heaped-up plate of food the churchwomen fixed for his mother.

"She won't eat it," Deacon Crutcher said with a nod back toward the boy. "She ain't hardly ate a bite since before."

Lacey was quiet for a while as they rode along. Finally she said, "I might not be able to help her."

For a minute she wasn't sure he'd heard her when he kept his eyes straight ahead on the road in front of them with his jaw clenched tight, but then he said, "That could be, but if it is, then at least we'll have helped you. And the little girl. The Lord will honor that."

At the house, Lacey made Rachel wait on the settee in the front room while she went in to talk to Sadie Rose. It was the first time she hadn't been touching the child since Aurelia put her hand in Lacey's the day before at the Shaker village. Rachel looked ready to cry until the second young-est boy, Richard, sat down beside her and began telling her about catching crawdads in the creek out behind the house.

Richard was like his mother. Or at least like his mother had been before. Lacey didn't know how she would be now.

She tapped lightly on the bedroom door and listened for a response but heard nothing. She hesitated a moment before she pushed open the door. The room was dark with heavy curtains pulled tight closed over the one window. Lacey stood still inside the door to let her eyes adjust to the dimness. "Miss Sadie Rose," she said softly. The woman was on the bed, covered with a quilt that had to be bringing out the sweat in the stuffy room. "You awake?"

Sadie Rose answered without lifting her head to look around. "I'm not up to talking to anybody today. The boys should have told you that."

Lacey ignored her words and walked over to the bed. She sat down right beside her. "It's me, Sadie Rose. I've come to stay with you a spell, seeing as how I don't have anywhere else to go. I hope you won't be upset with Deacon Crutcher for offering to take us in." She laid her hand on the woman's shoulder.

"Lacey, is that really you?" She shifted under the quilt and turned toward Lacey.

Lacey wished she'd gone over and pulled back the curtains so she could see the woman's face better. But maybe it wouldn't matter. Maybe the Lord would still put the right words in her mouth to offer the beginnings of comfort. "It's me. You knew the preacher died, didn't you?"

"Harold told me." The silence built in the room for a moment before she went on in a flat voice. "You heard about Jimmy."

"Reuben carried the news to me. I'm sorry."

"Sometimes I think my heart has withered up. I can't even cry anymore and he was my baby. A mother ought to cry for her baby, but I'm all dry ash inside. There's nothing left."

375

"No mother could love her baby any more than you loved Jimmy," Lacey said.

"Loving him didn't keep him from dying."

"I know. I'm sorry," Lacey said again. Useless words in the face of Sadie Rose's grief. If only she could call down Miss Mona to talk through her the way Aurelia said her angels spoke through her. But she couldn't. All she could do was keep her hand firm on Sadie Rose's shoulder and hurt with the woman.

Lacey had no idea how many minutes had ticked past when Sadie Rose said, "What about the Shaker village?" She turned her head to look at Lacey.

"It wasn't the right place for the preacher. Or for me."

"I should have gone. Me and Harold should have packed up and gone with Brother Palmer. We should have."

Lacey frowned. "Why would you think such a thing?"

"Don't you see? If I had gone with the preacher, Jimmy would still be alive. He wouldn't have got on that horse." Sadie Rose shifted uneasily in the bed and grabbed Lacey's hand. "Maybe that was how God punished my unbending spirit. I was too proud of what I believed and not willing to listen to what the Lord could have been telling me through the preacher."

"But the preacher died there when he might not have if he hadn't gone to the Shakers." Lacey squeezed her hand. "Bad things happen. Everywhere."

"That's what Harold tells me."

"But you don't believe it?"

Lacey thought Sadie Rose was going to turn her face back to the wall and not answer. In her mind Lacey whispered the silent prayer, *Blessed are those who mourn for they shall be comforted*. She wanted comfort for Sadie Rose. She wanted her to feel blessed even in the midst of sorrow. Blessed the way Lacey had told Aurelia she was. Even if Rachel had not come away from the Shaker village with her. Even if she never knew the kind of love that Isaac had known for his wife and that had seemed to be awakening between them. Even if she had to live dependent on others' charity forevermore, still she was blessed. Miss Mona had always told her that the Lord loved her. That he would put joy and belief in her heart if she would just let him. And now she'd let him.

"I've always believed," Sadie Rose finally whispered. "Always. Since before I can remember. But now I see nothing but darkness. I lay here and think about Mona and what she would say if she was here. She'd be ashamed of my weakness. I'm ashamed of my weakness."

"No, she'd grieve with you and maybe read the Bible to you. She'd show you where it says we are weak but he is strong."

"That's in Corinthians. I've shown that very verse to others in despair, never thinking I'd fall into the same despair myself some day." Sadie Rose clung to Lacey's hand as she raised her head up off the pillow. "What's another one she would tell me?"

Lacey shut her eyes and the verse came to her. From where she didn't know. "The Lord is nigh unto them that are of a broken heart."

"She'd tell me that. I can almost hear her voice right in here with us." She shoved the quilt back and pushed herself up to a sitting position against the headboard of the bed. "I'm glad you're here, Lacey. There's been times our spirits have been at odds, but could be the Lord set you down in this place for a reason. First Mona, then Rachel, and now me."

"I should have done more to help the preacher."

"What should you have done?"

"Loved him as a wife should."

"Love's not some kind of stew you can stir up on the stove anytime you want. It was wrong for Preacher Palmer to put you in the spot he put you in. Wrong of me and the other women too. But the good Lord knows we all fall short some of the time in doing what we ought." Sadie Rose clutched Lacey's hand. Then she looked toward the bedroom door. "Is Rachel with you? I want to see her."

"Are you sure?"

"I am."

"Then I'll have to open the curtains a little. The dark might frighten her."

"If you have to." She put her arm over her eyes as Lacey pulled back the curtains.

Rachel didn't seem frightened at all by Sadie Rose propped up in the bed. She ran straight to her and crawled up beside her. "Richard said Jimmy died. Like Papa died."

"He did."

"I wish he hadn't."

"I know." Sadie Rose put her arm around Rachel and the little girl snuggled down against her chest. "I know." Tears leaked out of Sadie Rose's eyes.

After a minute Rachel peeked up at Sadie Rose. "They took Maddie away from me. Do you think you could make another Maddie for me?"

"Rachel, now might not be—" Lacey started.

Sadie Rose stopped her. "Let me and Rachel work this out, Lacey." The woman actually smiled as she wiped the tears off her cheeks. "You know what, Rachel. I do think I can. I'll find me some material and go to work on it first thing in the morning."

Satisfied, Rachel put her head back down on Sadie Rose's chest. "I saw Jimmy's grave. It looked like Papa's. But Lacey says they'll both have dandelions on them just like Mama Mona's. And then we can do the dandelion dance again."

"The dandelion dance?" Sadie Rose looked down at the top of Rachel's head. "I don't think I know how to do that."

"Don't worry. I'll teach you," Rachel said. "Like Lacey taught me."

34

The sight of Brother Elwood jerking his arm free from Isaac's hand and sliding off the roof haunted Isaac. The image was burnt upon his mind.

Why couldn't he keep people from dying? His father. Ella. And now this man. He hadn't cared about this man. This Shaker brother. He'd barely known him. And yet the guilt was still there. Because of Lacey.

He hadn't turned him loose. It didn't matter that the thought of Lacey being free had swept through his mind while they were on the roof. He hadn't turned the man's arm loose. He hadn't. He told himself that a hundred times a day. At the same time he couldn't help wondering if maybe he could have held just a little tighter. Maybe he could have somehow made a better effort to grab the man with his other hand. And kept him from falling.

They hadn't let him talk to Lacey afterward. Brother Forrest and Brother William had pulled him back to safety. Barely catching Isaac's legs before the railing gave completely away. They had hustled him away from the brother's broken body and from Lacey.

A good ways down the road, a group of Shakers had been coming up from the Feast Day holy ground to deal with the tragedy. But there were no sisters yet there and Lacey had stood isolated and alone as she stared down at Brother Elwood's body. Then she stepped back and looked toward him. The cap kept her face shadowed so he couldn't tell what she was thinking. Sorrow or anger? Despair or relief?

Not relief. She was too decent to think that. Even if she hadn't loved the man. She had been prepared to lead him back to the world. To be his wife again. That's what Isaac needed to remember no matter how much he wanted to follow the wagon carrying her and her dead husband's body away from the Shaker village. He couldn't run after a man's wife when that man's body wasn't even cold to the touch. When that man might have lived if Isaac had only gripped his arm a little tighter.

In the days that followed, Brother Asa said it was good that Lacey was gone from the village. That it was the Lord removing a stumbling block from Isaac's path.

"By letting a man die?" Isaac asked.

"Nay. The Lord had naught to do with Brother Elwood's tormented mind." Brother Asa looked up at Isaac from the fence they were mending in the pasture field. "That had more to do with the devil."

"And was it the devil that kept me from being able to hold him?" Isaac held the plank in place and waited for Asa to hammer in the nails to secure it to the post.

But Asa straightened up to look Isaac in the face instead. "I sometimes fear that you are letting poor Brother Elwood's torment awaken in your mind, my brother. You have told me what happened. Brother Forrest and Brother William have told me of how near you came to following the man in death while you tried to pull him back from the edge. You did no wrong."

"I might have held tighter."

"And he might have not climbed to the roof to look for harmony with the spirits. A harmony he could have found in better ways. Such ways were freely available at the feast. Didn't you tell me you were feeling a peaceful forgiveness before Brother Elwood ruined the day?" Asa leaned down and hammered the nails with sure strokes to hold the plank in place. When he was finished, he stood up and lightly poked Isaac's chest with the hammer head. "Do not invite the devil to put doubts in your heart where belief is trying to grow."

Isaac looked off toward the woods where Lacey had led him to the cow. The calf was over behind him in the pasture, running and jumping. Alive because of Lacey. And what was he? Alive to the world or dead to the world?

"I want to go after her," he said. It was the time for truth between them.

"Nay," Brother Asa said, his voice distressed. "You want to jump too fast from one thing to another, my brother. It has only been a few weeks. Give yourself until the end of the hot weather."

"But what if she marries someone else?"

"Then you can rejoice in being saved from the sin of matrimony." He reached down to lift up the next fence plank and hammer it in place with firm strokes.

They didn't speak of it again. Isaac had not spoken any words of promise aloud, but somehow they both knew the pledge had been made. Till the end of the hot weather.

The first week in July a new preacher moved into the house by the church. Reverend Holman. Reverend Seth Holman. He wasn't married, which had made for questions in the church house and much talk out in the yard. Some thought a preacher needed to be married. Others said it didn't matter. Still others among the women eyed the new preacher and then let their eyes linger on Lacey. They felt it was somehow ordained. Not right away. Decency demanded a grieving period for Lacey even if she hadn't worn black but three Sundays before shedding the mourning garb.

Sadie Rose didn't care what she wore. She had gotten out of her bed and took up her sewing basket the first week Lacey and Rachel were there. After she made the Maddie doll, she stitched a mourning dress for Lacey to wear to church, but when Lacey told her she couldn't bear putting it on again, Sadie Rose hadn't said a word. She just found some rose-colored material and made a new dress for Lacey before the next Sunday.

As the weeks passed, Sadie Rose slowly picked up her load as mother and wife again, but she wasn't the same woman as before. That was how she and the Deacon Crutcher always spoke of little Jimmy's passing. What was before and what was after.

Before she'd had surety about what was right, she told Lacey. But now she couldn't say for sure about the right or wrong of what anybody did. She didn't entertain such questions, and if anybody from the church came carrying a bit of gossip or complaint, she'd just look off into the distance until the other woman's voice would sink to a whisper and then fade completely away. Then after a minute of uneasy silence on the part of the visitor, Sadie Rose would tell Lacey to go get them some tea.

The only time she smiled was when Rachel sat next to her and played with her Maddie doll, acting out the silly stories Lacey told her. And when the boys came in from the field and hugged her neck. Every time they came in the house, all four of those boys lined up to hug her neck. Even the gangly Harry who was going on seventeen. A good draught of medicine for the heart. The morning Lacey saw Sadie Rose reach for Deacon Crutcher's hand as they walked out of the church after a Sunday morning sermon, she knew Sadie Rose was back to coping with life.

The churchwomen must have been seeing the same thing, because they started fretting over Lacey and what was to become of her. Sadie Rose told her not to worry her head over it. That she had a home with them forever. But the churchwomen thought a few months might be forever enough. And when Reverend Holman moved in the preacher's house and didn't have the first person to take care of him, it wasn't two Sundays until the churchwomen had figured out the solution to both problems. Lacey needing a home and the reverend needing a housekeeper.

It didn't help that Reverend Holman had looked at Lacey wearing her new rose dress that first Sunday he stood in the pulpit and decided the very same thing. Or that Lacey had looked at the reverend and not thought about him one time the way the churchwomen were hoping. He wasn't a bad-looking man in spite of the fact that his nose was a little large for his face and his eyes had a droop that made him look sad even when he was smiling. He did have a booming preacher voice that filled up the church building when he was reading the Scripture, but he was a little man. Not an inch taller than Lacey. Not someone who could lift her up and swing her around no matter how joyful the moment might be.

She tried not to think about Isaac, but she might as well have tried not to breathe. She kept seeing him up on the roof hanging on to Preacher Palmer. Doing what he could to save him with little regard for his own safety. She kept seeing his face when he'd come down afterward. The sadness so plain there for a man he barely knew. Then to turn her thoughts away from that sorrow, Lacey would think about the little cow having the calf. And life.

More than once she considered asking Reuben to go back to the Shaker town to find out if Isaac was still there. But what good would that do her? She was a new widow. It couldn't be proper for new widows to go chasing after men who lived in villages with people who didn't believe in marriage. The whole idea was hopeless.

Reverend Holman didn't come courting until August. He sat on Sadie Rose's porch and pretended to be visiting the both of them the first time. The second time he asked Lacey to go for a walk with him. Lacey told him it was too hot for walking and she had supper to start. The third time he brought Rachel a peppermint candy stick and asked Rachel if she'd show him out to the field where the men were working. Like he wanted to visit with the deacon. Lacey didn't have any choice but to walk out to the field with them. Sadie Rose gave them a fresh jar of water from the well to take to the deacon and the boys.

The reverend carried the water and walked in almost a march as if everything was business to him. Lacey knew absolutely nothing to say to him, and she remembered how she'd felt the same with the preacher. He seemed at a loss for words too until Rachel ran ahead to chase after a yellow butterfly. Then he spilled out his speech in a rush. "Miss Martha and Miss Jo Ann have been telling me about you, Lacey. About how you and the preacher before me were married but that you didn't have what they would consider the conventional marriage."

"What is a conventional marriage?" Lacey asked.

"Well, it's, it's . . . " He sputtered for a minute, hunting the right words. "It's a joining of a man and woman in the sight of God. A holy union."

"Do they have to love one another? This man and woman when they marry?"

"At times. At other times love comes later as they settle into a good life together."

Lacey didn't say anything to that. She knew that years could pass and she wouldn't feel love for this man. But she couldn't very well tell him that.

He cleared his throat. "At any rate, it has come to my attention that you might be in need of a husband and I am already very aware of my need for a wife."

"A wife or a housekeeper?"

"I would hope both."

She kept her eyes on Rachel running back toward them as she picked her words carefully. "I couldn't possibly entertain thoughts of marriage. Not so soon after my husband's passing."

"Then you might think on it later on?"

There was hope in his voice. She should have smashed it and stomped on it the way the Shaker people stomped out the devil in their dances. But Rachel was showing her the dandelion flower she'd found. And she let his hope live on. His and the churchwomen's. And it grew every day until by the end of August he was coming by Sadie Rose's house nigh on every day. Even Lacey began to fear it was inevitable. Because the churchwomen were right. She and Rachel couldn't stay at Sadie Rose's forever. And hadn't she always done whatever had to be done?

July and August were hot. The first day in September the wind switched to the east and the day was unseasonably cool. It seemed a sign to Isaac. An answer to the prayers he'd silently offered in his awkward way as he knelt each morning and night by his Shaker bed. *You forgave me. Now help me know what to do next. If I'm supposed to forget Lacey, wipe her out of my head.* But the Lord hadn't made him forget. Instead Isaac thought of her more and more each day. And worried that the hot weather was lasting too long.

That night on the way to the bathhouse, Isaac told Brother Asa. "The hot weather is past."

"Nay, there will be many more hot days. This is only a brief respite from the heat." It was easy to tell Asa didn't want to hear what Isaac was ready to say.

"I'm going."

"Yea, I feared it so." Asa stopped walking and stared straight ahead for a moment before he turned to smile at Isaac. "Where will you go?"

"To find her." Isaac saw no reason to evade the truth.

"And if you don't find her?"

"I will."

Brother Asa reached over and touched Isaac's arm. "Perhaps you will. But if you don't, this door will stay open to you. You would make a good Shaker. If you could pick up your cross of living the celibate life."

"Do you truly believe marrying is a sin?" Isaac watched his face closely as he answered.

"For me, it is," Asa said. "I suppose you will have to depend on the Eternal Father to reveal what is sin for you."

"He forgave me my sins before."

"Then peace go with you, my brother. I will miss you." Brother Asa kept smiling but his face was sad.

"And I you. I owe you my life."

"Nay, only the good Lord gives and takes life. Owe him. Not me."

Isaac grabbed the man in a quick hug and then, without another look at his face, turned and walked down the middle of the road through the village and on. He had come to the Shaker village with nothing and he left with nothing. Then he knew that wasn't true. He'd come with a heart full of sorrow and was leaving with a heart lifted by forgiveness and love.

He caught a ride with a Dr. Wilson headed back to the nearby town. The doctor knew a farmer laid up with a broken leg who might have a horse he would trade for Isaac's labor. But the man knew nothing about anybody in the Ebenezer community.

"That's a good ways from here. I'm thinking Dr. Blacketer takes care of folks out there." The doctor peered over at Isaac in the dusky evening light. "You have kin out that way who might take you in?"

"I knew a woman from there. She lived at Harmony Hill a spell a few months back."

"But left." Dr. Wilson chuckled a little. "And now you're leaving. Guess I can make the right diagnosis on that one. It's ever been a wonderment to me that those Shaker folk expect young folks like you to be able to turn off the God-given inclination for marrying and such."

The farmer's wife fixed him a bunk on the back porch with quilts enough to keep him warm in the dead of winter. Then while he and the farmer agreed on a deal for the horse, she fried up some eggs for his supper. She had a baby in a sling under her breast and another toddling around underfoot.

When she saw Isaac watching the little boy, she grinned and said, "That's what you're needing. The Shaker people might not tell you that, but I'm telling you. Ain't that right, Jarvis?" She smiled at her husband.

"Just don't go falling out of a hayloft and breaking your leg if you do," he said with a laugh as he grabbed hold of his wife's hand and held it up against his cheek a moment after she set Isaac's plate of food in front of him.

It was two weeks before a rainy day gave Isaac the chance to get away from the farm and ride toward Ebenezer. It wasn't hard to find the house beside the church where they had loaded up Brother Elwood and Lacey's household things to take them to Harmony Hill. But when he knocked on the door, a short little man answered. Isaac didn't know what he was expecting. Maybe Lacey to be sitting there on the porch waiting for him like it had just been yesterday that she'd ridden away from the Shaker village with her husband a corpse behind her in the bed of the wagon.

The little man looked him over. "Is there some way I can help you?" His voice sounded like it belonged in a man twice his size.

"I was looking for somebody who used to live here. Lacey Palmer. She was married to the preacher."

"I'm the preacher now. Reverend Holman at your service." His voice boomed out his name as he stuck his hand out toward Isaac. "And what's your moniker?"

"Isaac Kingston." After he let the man pump his hand up and down vigorously a few times, Isaac asked, "Do you know where Lacey's living these days?"

"Lacey?" The man puckered up his mouth and frowned as he considered Isaac's question. "I've heard the church people speak some about her. But I haven't been here all that long. Seems like one of the women did tell me about this Lacey having family down in the western part of the state."

"You know what town?"

"Paducah, I'm thinking. Yes, I'm almost sure that's the town. Or maybe it was Owensboro. Either way a far piece from here, but not a bad trip on the river. I hear there's a landing over at a Shaker village near here where you can get passage on a steamboat." He spoke the words fast and then stepped out on the porch to peer at the sky. "Looks to be some weather coming up. Could be you should be moving on."

Isaac stepped to the edge of the porch to look up. The sky was gray but he didn't see any thunderclouds. Behind him the door snapped shut, and when he looked around the little man had disappeared back into the house.

"Not a very friendly preacher," Isaac muttered as he went down the steps off the porch and then led his horse over toward the church. He wondered if they'd buried Brother Elwood in the graveyard. If so, that would prove Lacey had been back here at least long enough to do the burying and somebody might know for sure where she'd gone. He'd follow her. As soon as he found a way to make money to buy his passage on the steamboat.

It wasn't hard to find the new graves. Grass hadn't grown on them in the heat of the summer, and they were covered with weeds. Mostly dandelions. There were two. One a little grave at the back of the cemetery, but it was for a boy of six. JAMES CRUTCHER. BELOVED SON OF HAROLD AND SADIE CRUTCHER. According to the date chiseled there, the boy had died just days before Brother Elwood. The graves all had fine markers with the names plain to read. Brother Elwood's name was on the same stone as his first wife's. REV. ELWOOD PALMER. A MAN OF GOD. Isaac ran his fingers over the words, feeling the rough surface of the stone.

"Did you know the preacher?" A man came out from behind the church and lifted himself up over the wooden fence at the back of the graveyard. He was a heavyset man. Not fat, just thick through the middle. Like a barrel. He was smiling like a man welcoming somebody into their house. A better welcome than Isaac had gotten from the preacher next door for sure.

"Not well, but I knew him." The image of the man's desperate face came to him, but he pushed it away with the same prayer Brother Elwood had said before he fell. "May the Lord have mercy on his soul."

"Amen," the man beside him said. He talked slow as though measuring each word before speaking it. "He was my preacher here at Ebenezer since I can remember. And now I take care of his grave." He waved his hand around. "I take care of all the graves."

"I'm sure the church people appreciate it."

"They do." The man leaned over and yanked up a hogweed from close to the tombstone. When he stood up he said, "My name's Reuben."

"I'm Isaac." First names seemed enough with Reuben.

Reuben gave him a long look. "You one of them Shaker men? You ain't wearing the clothes, but you remind me some of the men I saw over there. The way your hair's cut and all."

Isaac ran his hand through the hair lapping his collar. He should have borrowed the farmer's wife's scissors. "I used to be," he told Reuben. "Not anymore."

"Neither is the preacher." He stared down at the grave at their feet. "Not anymore."

Isaac wasn't sure what to say to that, so he just kept quiet and waited for Reuben to be ready to talk again. They both looked up when they heard a horse galloping away from the house next door. "Wonder where's he going in such a hurry?" Isaac said more to himself than to Reuben.

But Reuben smiled a little. "Courting, I expect. He's been real sweet on Miss Lacey ever since the church called him to preach. Guess he thinks she knows how to be a preacher's wife since she's already had practice."

"Lacey?" Isaac stared at Reuben. "I thought she'd gone off to Paducah or somewhere."

"Paducah? That ain't anywhere near here, is it?" He didn't wait for Isaac to answer him. "Miss Lacey ain't off nowhere. She's right down the road a ways with Miss Sadie Rose. But she walks up here some to help me keep the weeds down around the stones. But she don't want me to pull the dandelion weeds off'n Preacher Palmer's grave so the grass can come on. I ain't exactly figured out why, but she and little Rachel seem to favor those little yellow flowers."

Isaac only half listened to him going on about the dandelions as he looked off down the road where the unfriendly preacher's horse had disappeared. He interrupted Reuben talking about how he thought Lacey brought dandelion puffs to blow over the grave.

"I'd count it a favor if you could tell me how to get to Miss Sadie Rose's house, Reuben."

35

Lacey was surprised to look up from hanging clothes out on the line to see the Reverend Holman riding up all in a lather like the church house was on fire. He'd been showing up more and more, but he generally waited till the afternoon when she could set aside her chores for a spell. Rachel, who had been handing her the clothespins, eased around behind Lacey when she saw who was coming. Even his peppermint sticks hadn't been enough to make her warm up to him. She would lick the peppermint but keep a wary eye on the little man all the time he was around. Something of the same kind of inner wary eye Lacey kept pinning on him.

Without Lacey saying the first favorable word, half the people at church thought it was a given that she would marry the little man as soon as a decent mourning period passed. Lacey was thinking she might mourn poor Preacher Palmer a few years at the least. But then she'd see how it was crowding Sadie Rose for her and Rachel to keep living there. The boys were taking turns sleeping on the back porch now and it wasn't going to be many weeks until winter was going to push them back indoors. There might be worse things than stepping back into her place as the wife of the Ebenezer church's pastor. There might be.

She pulled in a deep breath and pushed a smile across her face as the little preacher slid off his horse and hustled over toward her.

"Morning, Reverend Holman. I hope nothing's wrong." He'd asked her a dozen times to call him Seth, but so far the word hadn't crossed her lips. Just like with Preacher Palmer. She hadn't ever been able to use his given name. Not with any kind of ease.

"Not at all. Not at all." He sounded out of breath as he looked around and asked, "Where's Miss Sadie Rose?"

"She's in the kitchen. I can send Rachel to fetch her if you have need to talk to her."

"No, no. It's you I came to see, but I would be beholden for a drink of water if your little girl can bring me one. Fresh water out of the well. It'll be cooler that way."

Lacey sent Rachel off for the water and waited uneasily for the little man to speak his mind.

He took hold of Lacey's arm. "Why don't we go sit on the front porch? Out of the sun."

Lacey looked at the basket of clothes on the ground and hesitated.

"I won't keep you from your chores long." He tightened his hold on her arm and turned her toward the house. "I've got something to ask you. Something important."

What could she do but go with him?

She sat in one of the straight chairs Sadie Rose had on the porch. She wasn't about to sit on the swing where he could settle down beside her. "Is there something at the church that needs doing?" she asked.

"There is," he said solemnly. But he didn't go on and say what. Instead he pulled one of the other chairs over to face hers. After he settled down in it, he leaned toward her until there wasn't much more than a few inches between them. "You're a woman of honor, Lacey, aren't you?"

She hesitated, wondering where he was headed with his talk. "I try to do what's right."

He reached over and took one of her hands and rushed out his next words. "And if you made me a promise, you'd keep it, wouldn't you? It wouldn't be right to break a solemn vow."

"I can't recall promising you anything, Reverend Holman." She eased back in her chair away from him.

"Not in so many words, but you've let me come courting. God called me to the ministry and to this church. His hand is in this. You're being called to be my wife." He leaned toward her until she could feel his breath on her face.

"Are you asking or telling?" Lacey slid her eyes to the side as though looking for a way out of a trap.

"There's no escaping what the good Lord in his wisdom has ordained for us."

"I don't think I heard that calling," Lacey said. "Not even the first time I was a preacher's wife."

"I'm a man of God. I have heard the calling." His preaching voice boomed out. "For both of us. But if you want a proper proposal I'll supply you one." He slid off the chair, brushing against her lap as he knelt in front of her. "Lacey Palmer, will you marry me?"

She stared at him while her heart sank down in her stomach. It was amazing how quickly a person's life could be thrown into a tangle. *Dear Father in heaven*. The words slipped through her mind, but then she couldn't think of a single thing else to pray. She opened her mouth, but before she could speak, he jumped in front of her words.

"Don't you want to be married, Lacey? To have a good

father for little Rachel? To be loved?" He took hold of both of her hands.

She did want all those things. But not to this man any more than she'd sought them with Preacher Palmer. Words seemed to have deserted her mouth and her mind. She could only reach for the promise of the Scripture that said the Holy Spirit sent up prayers in groans and mumblings for her when she couldn't grab hold of proper prayer words. Blessed. She was blessed. But that didn't mean she would never have to do any hard thing again. She shut her eyes, unable to bear looking into the man's face so full of determination to make her answer as he wished. As he claimed the Lord demanded. After all, he was a man of God.

Isaac's face floated in front of her closed eyes.

Reverend Holman grasped her hands tighter and gave them both a shake as if waking her not very gently from a sleep. "You have to answer me, Lacey Palmer. If you don't agree to marry me today, I may never ask you again."

"I can't marry yet. Not for at least a year."

"You married Reverend Palmer before his wife was dead a year." He pushed the words at her.

"But that didn't make it right. A person can learn from past wrongs."

"All right. Then make me a sacred promise that you will marry me next May."

She didn't want to open her eyes and look at him. She didn't want to answer him. *Dear Father in heaven, help me.* She was so intent on her prayer she didn't hear Rachel come out on the porch followed by Sadie Rose. She didn't even hear the horse riding straight off the road across the yard to the porch. She did want to be loved. But not by the man holding her hands.

Rachel eased over beside her and laid her head on Lacey's

shoulder. Perhaps that was the Lord's answer. Rachel. His blessing to her. Perhaps being the preacher's wife was her payment in return. Miss Mona's words echoed in her mind from some lesson learned long ago in the past. *My dear child, there is no payment great enough to buy us the Lord's blessings. His grace is a free gift if we only reach for it. Remember your Scripture. "Now we have received, not the spirit of the world, but the spirit which is of God; that we might know the things that are freely given to us of God."*

She was opening her eyes to refuse the man in the gentlest way possible when she heard her name. "Lacey."

She knew the voice at once, but even after her eyes flew open and she was staring at him still astride his horse she wasn't sure he was really there. An answer to those prayers she'd been unable to voice.

Isaac's heart jumped up in his throat when he saw the little man kneeling so close in front of Lacey on the porch. He was afraid he was too late. Afraid she had already given her heart to another. Another preacher.

He almost rode past without stopping. There was no need upsetting her world or opening his heart to more pain than was already there, but then he remembered how the preacher had lied to him about knowing Lacey. With intent to send him on a fool's errand. He turned his horse's head into the yard.

Her eyes were closed tight as she listened to the man but nothing about her face or her rigid posture suggested happiness. The child came over to lean against Lacey and still she kept her eyes closed. Another woman, older than Lacey, came out the door and watched him ride his horse right up to her porch but without any indication of surprise. Instead it was as if she'd been expecting him and now was glad to see him there.

When Isaac spoke Lacey's name, the little preacher spun around on his knees to glare at him.

Isaac kept his eyes on Lacey's face. "You don't have to promise him anything."

Lacey gently pulled her hands away from the preacher and eased to the side away from him to stand up and look back at Isaac. "And I have not," she said clearly. "It is good to see you, Isaac."

"And you still here in Ebenezer instead of Paducah." He shot a look over at the preacher.

"Paducah?" She sounded puzzled.

"Reverend Holman told me that was where you might be."

The little man clambered to his feet and said stoutly, "I never said she was. I said she had family there. Not once did I lie. Not once."

"There are many ways to lie," she said softly. "To ourselves may be the worst way of all."

"I've never done that either," the preacher said.

She looked away from Isaac, then to the other man. "You did if you thought I could ever love you. It wasn't a lie I was prepared to live. Not again."

"Well." The man sounded irate over her words. "You won't find me on my knees asking you again. I'll leave you to your just deserts."

Lacey hardly seemed to notice the man's jabbering as he picked up his hat and stomped down the steps off the porch.

The woman at the door called out to him. "Good day, Reverend. You come back now, you hear. Harold will be glad to see you anytime."

Nobody spoke again until the man was out of sight on his horse. There was a feeling of communication on the porch

398

that didn't seem to need words. Isaac got down off his horse and tied the reins to the porch post. Then he climbed up to stand beside Lacey. She reached out and took his hand as if it were the most natural thing in the world.

"Sadie Rose, this is Isaac," she said as she glanced over at the other woman. "Isaac Kingston. He tried to keep Preacher Palmer from falling off the Shaker house, but he couldn't." She looked back at Isaac.

"May the Lord have mercy on his soul," Isaac said. "That's the last thing he said. Right before he jerked his arm away from me. He feared he was going to make me fall too. I didn't turn him loose."

"I know you didn't," Lacey said. "It wasn't you or me. He had torments we knew nothing about." She put her arm around Rachel and pulled her close for a moment.

The woman she'd called Sadie Rose stepped across the porch to take Rachel's hand and lead her back in the house. "Let's go find your Maddie doll. I think she may need a new dress."

The little girl started away and then turned back to grab Isaac's waist in a quick hug. "Thank you for trying to save my papa."

Lacey watched her follow the woman into the house. "I've never seen her do anything like that before." She turned her eyes back to Isaac. "But it is thanks I give you as well."

"I saw his grave. Reuben says you sow dandelion seeds on it of a purpose."

Lacey laughed. A good sound that was better than the Shakers' voices when they said the angels were singing through them. "It's a bother to him, but he's patient with me," she said. "We could sit on the porch, but that wouldn't get the basket of clothes I deserted out back on the line. If you want, we can talk while I work."

He followed her around the house. "It looks some like rain."

"But look there." She pointed up toward the sky. "There's a bit of blue. The sunshine may sneak through it. Or if it rains, the clothes will get another rinsing."

She picked up a boy's shirt and a couple of clothespins.

"Brother Asa told me the Shakers came up with those." Isaac pointed at the clothespin. "He said they're always inventing something to make work easier."

She looked at the clothespin a minute and then pushed it down over the shirt and the line. "So have you left them?"

"Two weeks ago. I promised Brother Asa I'd stay through the hot weather."

"Why?"

"I don't know. It seemed the right thing to do at the time."

She picked up another shirt and Isaac reached down to hand her a clothespin.

"But what I really wanted to do was come after you."

"Why?" She kept her eyes fastened on the shirt she was pinning to the line. "You hardly know me."

"I know you here." He put one hand over his heart and reached with his other hand to wrap his fingers around her wrist. "Where it matters."

"What about your first wife?" She let him turn her to look at him.

"I loved her, Lacey. But now I'm ready to love another. You." He watched her face. "Do you think you might someday love me back? When you get to know me better."

"I know you already, Isaac." Her voice was barely above a whisper. She put her free hand over her heart. "I know you here."

He gently tugged her closer to him and put his finger under her chin to lift her face up toward him. "I want to kiss you, Lacey. I want to kiss you so much."

In answer she moved her face closer to his. He dropped his head down to cover her lips with his. The joy in that kiss tingled down to his very toes. Then at the very moment he pulled away to gaze down into her beautiful brown eyes, the sun broke through the clouds and bathed them in light like a blessing from above. He raised his face toward the sunlight and laughed. Then he picked her up and swung her around the way he had in the woods after the calf was born.

"Will you marry me, Lacey Palmer?" he asked.

She laughed too and then said, "I will, Isaac Kingston."

"When? Today?"

"No, not today. But when the first dandelions bloom in the spring and it's time to do the dandelion dance."

He looked at her, a little puzzled. "Is that a dance the Shakers taught you?"

"Not at all. It's a family thing passed from mother to child."

"Will you teach me?"

"I don't have to. You already know it. I think we just did it. A dance of joy."

"I love you, Lacey Palmer."

She smiled at him. "Then dance with me again."

And he did.

Acknowledgments

I've been writing down stories nearly all my life. Some of those stories spew up out of that mysterious well of imagination in a great rush, while others have to be dipped out one cup of words at a time. Lacey's story was some of both. I met Lacey while writing my last Shaker book, *The Seeker*. I had planned to make her a colorful side character to add to Charlotte's story, but Lacey stared me right in the face and said, "But what about my story?" So with encouragement from my editor, Lonnie Hull DuPont, I decided to write down Lacey's story.

I'm forever grateful to Lonnie for her support and help. I thank the whole team at Revell and Baker who play a part in making each of my books the best it can be, from the eye-catching covers to inviting back copy and everything in between. But they don't stop there. They keep working to get my story in front of you, the reader.

I thank my agent, Wendy Lawton for her business savvy and friendship as well as the way she's always ready to help me look to the future and imagine the stories I have yet to tell.

I can never thank my family enough for their love and support. And for understanding that when a deadline is looming, a writer can go a little bonkers. And of course, I'm forever grateful to the Lord for putting this will to write inside me and for giving me stories to tell.

Last but never least, I thank each and every one of you who picks up one of my books to read. We have a partnership—you and I. The story that springs up out of my imagination never comes truly to life until you invite my characters into your hearts and minds. Thank you for reading Lacey's story.

Song Credits

Page 215—"Come Mother's Sons and Daughters" (Song recorded by Henry DeWitt, 1837, *Manuscript Hymnals*)

Page 215—"Holy Order" (Manuscript Hymnals, 1839)

Page 216—"Sweep, Sweep and Cleanse Your Floor" (*New Lebanon Hymnal*, 1839)

Page 224—Untitled Song (Watervliet, prior to 1838)

Page 226—"Shake off the Flesh" (*Manuscript Hymnals*, 1808–1858; source and exact date unknown)

Page 340—"Vision Song" (Henry DeWitt's *New Lebanon Hymnal*, 1837)

Page 354—"Dismission of the Devil" ("Warring" song; *Manuscript Hymnals*)

Page 357—"O San-nisk-a-na" (Vision Song; New Lebanon, 1838; Henry DeWitt manuscript)

Ann H. Gabhart and her husband live on a farm just over the hill from where she grew up in central Kentucky. She's active in her country church, and her husband sings bass in a Southern Gospel quartet. Ann is the author of over twenty novels for adults and young adults. Her first inspirational novel, *The Scent of Lilacs*, was one of Booklist's top ten inspirational novels of 2006. Her novel *The Outsider* was a finalist for the 2009 Christian Book Awards in the fiction category.

Visit Ann's website at www.annhgabhart.com.

Meet ANN H. GABHART at
WWW.ANNHGABHART.COM

Learn about New Books, Read Her Blog,
and Sign Up for Her Newsletter

CONNECT WITH ANN AT
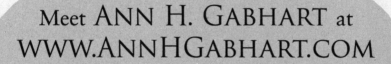 Ann H Gabhart
AnnHGabhart

THEY LIVE IN A COMMUNITY WHERE LOVE IS FORBIDDEN,

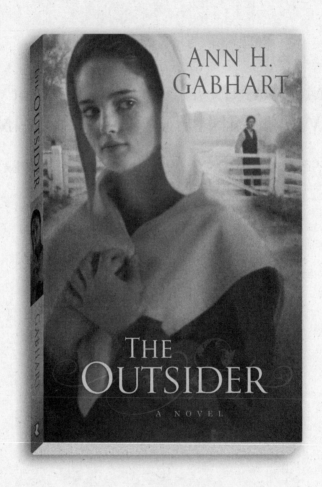

Gabrielle thought she was content—until a love from the outside world turned her world upside down.

Revell
a division of Baker Publishing Group
www.RevellBooks.com

BUT WILL THAT QUENCH THE PASSION IN THEIR HEARTS?

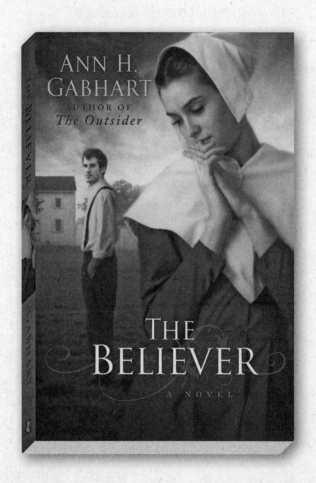

Elizabeth only wanted a home for her brother and sister.
Will her forbidden love separate her from her family?
Or will Ethan's love for her change their lives forever?

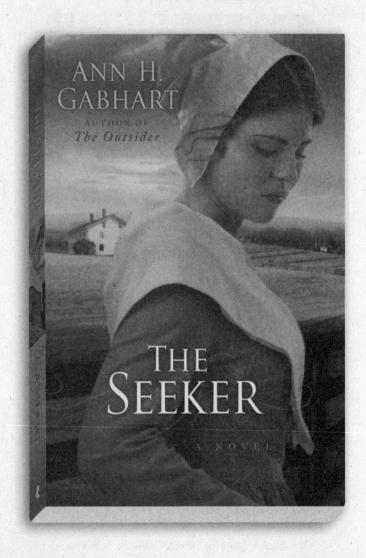

A New Novel by Bestselling Author
ANN H. GABHART
Will Capture Your Heart

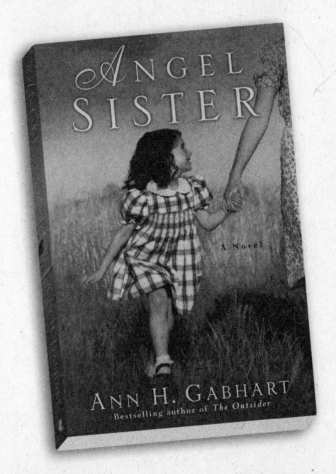

In this richly textured novel, award-winning author Ann H. Gabhart reveals the power of true love, the freedom of forgiveness, and the strength to persevere through troubled times.

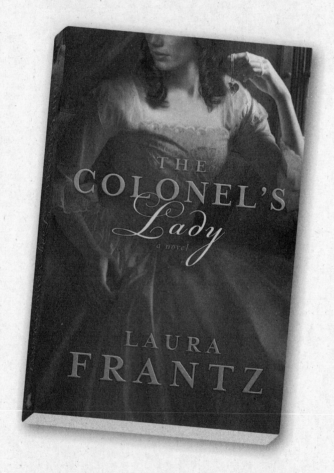

"*You'll disappear into another place and time and be both encouraged and enriched for having taken the journey.*"

—Jane Kirkpatrick, bestselling author

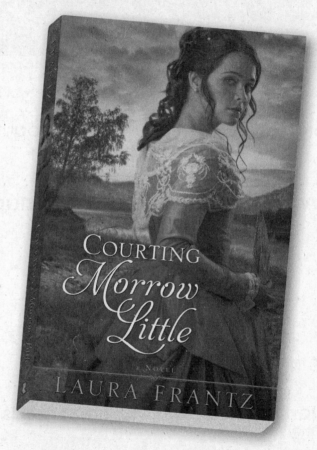

This sweeping tale of romance and forgiveness will
envelop readers as it takes them from a Kentucky
fort through the vast wilderness to the West.

R Revell
a division of Baker Publishing Group
www.RevellBooks.com

Available wherever books are sold.